"The artwork is beautiful . . . It really is stunning."

—TODAY

"I was immediately impressed with the interactive nature of the book. Although not all books lend themselves to this style, books that include elements of interactivity help resonate with kids more so when there's a lesson to be learned. Some books ask questions of kids, and some books, like this one, encourage kids to touch the picture, lean into the story, and really feel like they're in the book."

—Motherhood Moment

"A very timely book. . . . A children's book, if done well, and this one is, lives on and on."

—Al Roker

"A passion project that comes from the heart, this stunningly illustrated book is inspired by the white feather he was given by his father when he was young."

—Mom and More

THE MORNING TRIBE

THE MORNING TRIBE

JULIAN LENNON WITH BART DAVIS
ILLUSTRATED BY ALEJANDRA GREEN AND FANNY RODRIGUEZ
FOREWORD BY UNCLE BUNNA LAWRIE, MIRNING SENIOR ELDER

Sky Pony Press
New York

Sky Pony Press books may be purchased in bulk at special discounts for sales promotion, corporate gifts, fund-raising, or educational purposes. Special editions can also be created to specifications. For details, contact the Special Sales Department, Sky Pony Press, 307 West 36th Street, 11th Floor, New York, NY 10018 or info@skyhorsepublishing.com.

Sky Pony® is a registered trademark of Skyhorse Publishing, Inc.®, a Delaware corporation.

Visit our website at www.skyponypress.com.

10 9 8 7 6 5 4 3 2 1

Library of Congress Cataloging-in-Publication Data is available on file.

Cover design by Brian Peterson
Cover illustrations by Alejandra Green and Fanny Rodriguez

Print ISBN: 978-1-5107-6619-8
Ebook ISBN: 978-1-5107-6620-4

Printed in China

JL—

For my brother Sean: There is no end to Love. . . .
Keep fighting the Good fight! Love always & forever.

BD—

To Sharon, from the very beginning, always believing.

A Personal Message from Julian Lennon

THE
WHITE FEATHER
FOUNDATION

"It is my great hope that this, and all my books, promote a dialogue between children and their parents about what we can do to help solve the problems of our planet, and to empower children to believe they can make a real difference. We've been overwhelmed by the wonderful response. More than ever, I know if we all pitch in, all work together, we can achieve as a group what none of us can accomplish alone.

The history of the White Feather symbolized in the story began when my dad told me that should he pass away, if there was some way of letting me know he was okay—that we were all going to be okay—the message would come to me in the form of a White Feather. Then, whilst on tour in Australia, I was presented with a White Feather by an Aboriginal tribal elder of the Mirning people seeking help for her tribe. Having the White Feather bestowed upon me, I knew this endeavor was to be part of my destiny from then on. It led me to create The White Feather Foundation to give a voice and support to those who have not been able to be heard. One thing for sure is that the White Feather has always represented peace to me, and the love that it brings.

Let's continue to teach the children of the world to love and understand the planet so they will naturally want to take care of it. And let's all follow the White Feather Flier to touch, heal, and love the earth. I believe together we can, and will, make the Earth better for everyone."

~Julian Lennon

To learn more about us, please visit
The White Feather Foundation at:
www.whitefeatherfoundation.com/

FOREWORD

I am Uncle Bunna Lawrie, Senior Elder and Whale Songman of The Mirning Whale Tribe. Many years ago, Julian Lennon came to Australia and heard how we were the whale keepers and protectors; custodians of nature. I sang a Mirning welcome song in our language to welcome him into our Elders' gathering. There was much connection and friendship made as we talked and shared stories of the ancient Mirning People and the necessity to help the children's future. We asked Julian to add his voice to our struggle of traditional custodianship to protect our country. In our Mirning way, we are not separate from country; the land and sea live within us.

Some moments hold magic. No one knew how powerful the magic would be when one of our Mirning Tribe Elders, Iris Burgoyne, came forward to present young Julian with a white feather to symbolize the peace between us. No one knew what the White Feather meant to Julian, or the message from his father it represented, or that it would not only change his path in life forever, but those surrounding him, too. We are proud to see how Julian has turned that moment into The White Feather Foundation.

In this book, Julian continues to help the children's future and helps them see this world, planet Earth, in a healthy and peaceful way. We, Mirning Elders, are proud of Julian for what he does. We wish that many children and adults enjoy and learn much from this book.

Together with Julian, we created the documentary Whaledreamers to share our voice with the world. Now we share with you what it means to be Mirning—to listen, learn, understand, observe, and then you will receive wisdom and knowledge.

Uncle Bunna Lawrie,
Mirning Senior Elder and Whale Songman

CHAPTER 1

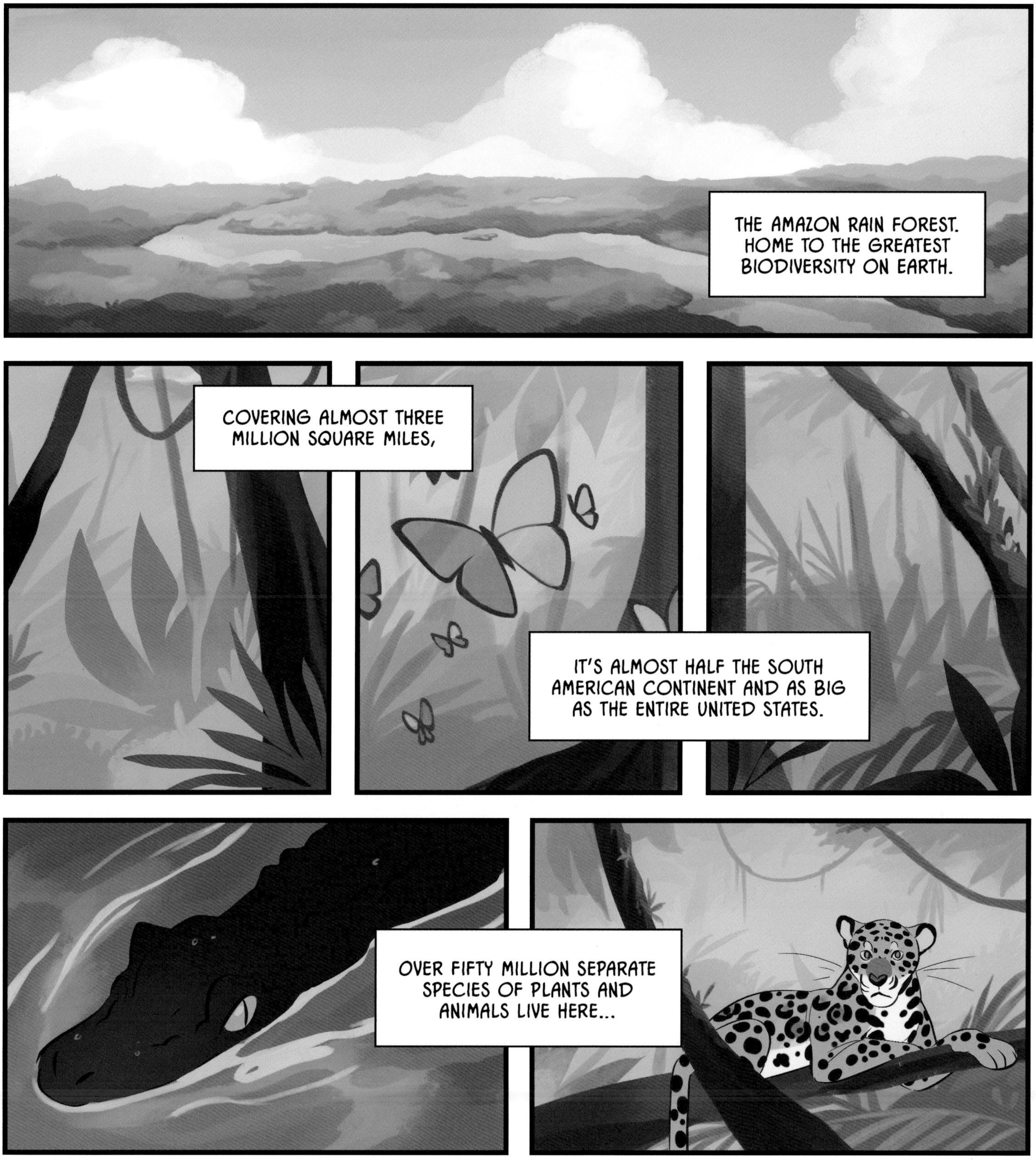
THE AMAZON RAIN FOREST. HOME TO THE GREATEST BIODIVERSITY ON EARTH.
COVERING ALMOST THREE MILLION SQUARE MILES,
IT'S ALMOST HALF THE SOUTH AMERICAN CONTINENT AND AS BIG AS THE ENTIRE UNITED STATES.
OVER FIFTY MILLION SEPARATE SPECIES OF PLANTS AND ANIMALS LIVE HERE...

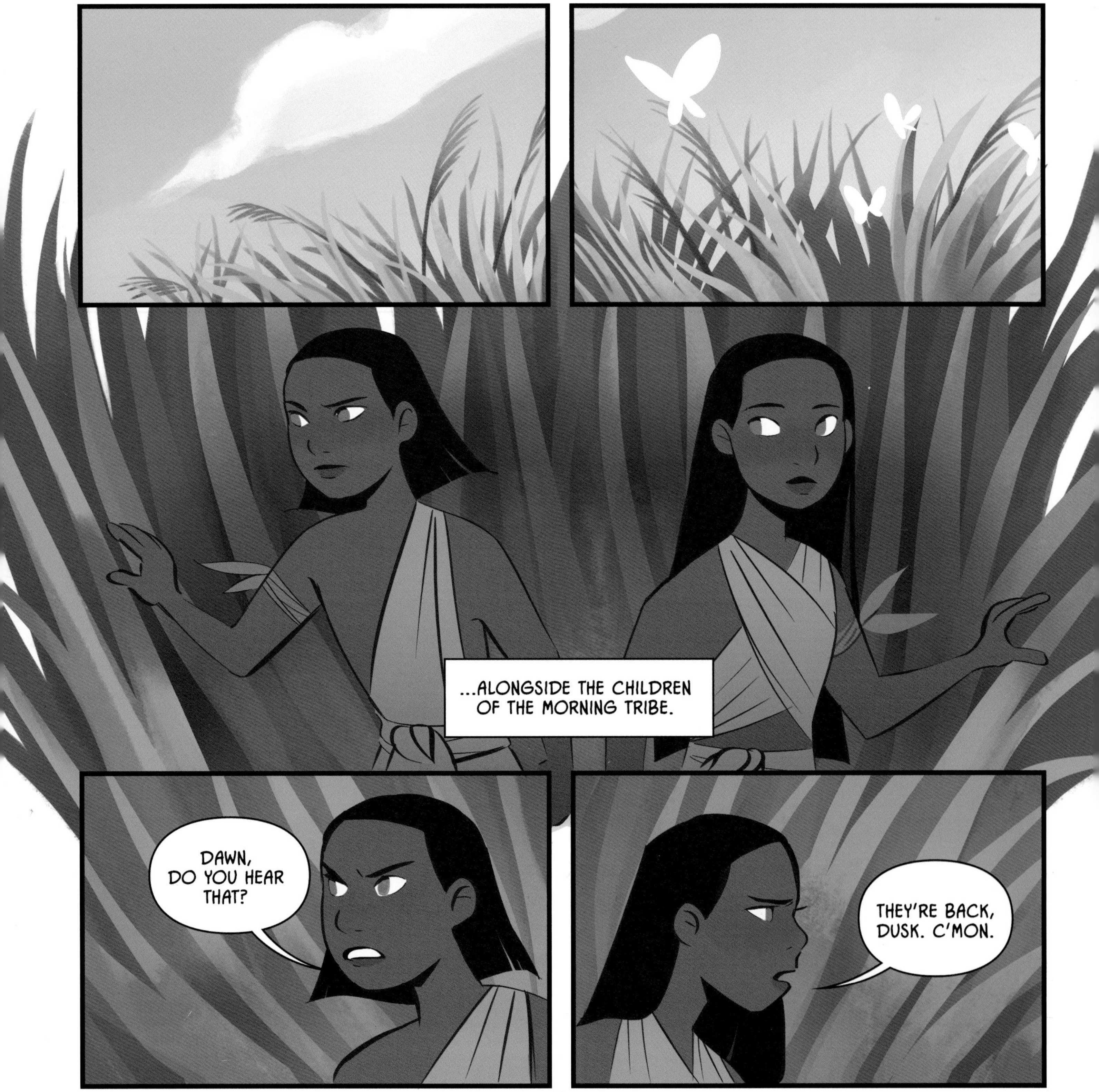
...ALONGSIDE THE CHILDREN OF THE MORNING TRIBE.
DAWN, DO YOU HEAR THAT?
THEY'RE BACK, DUSK. C'MON.

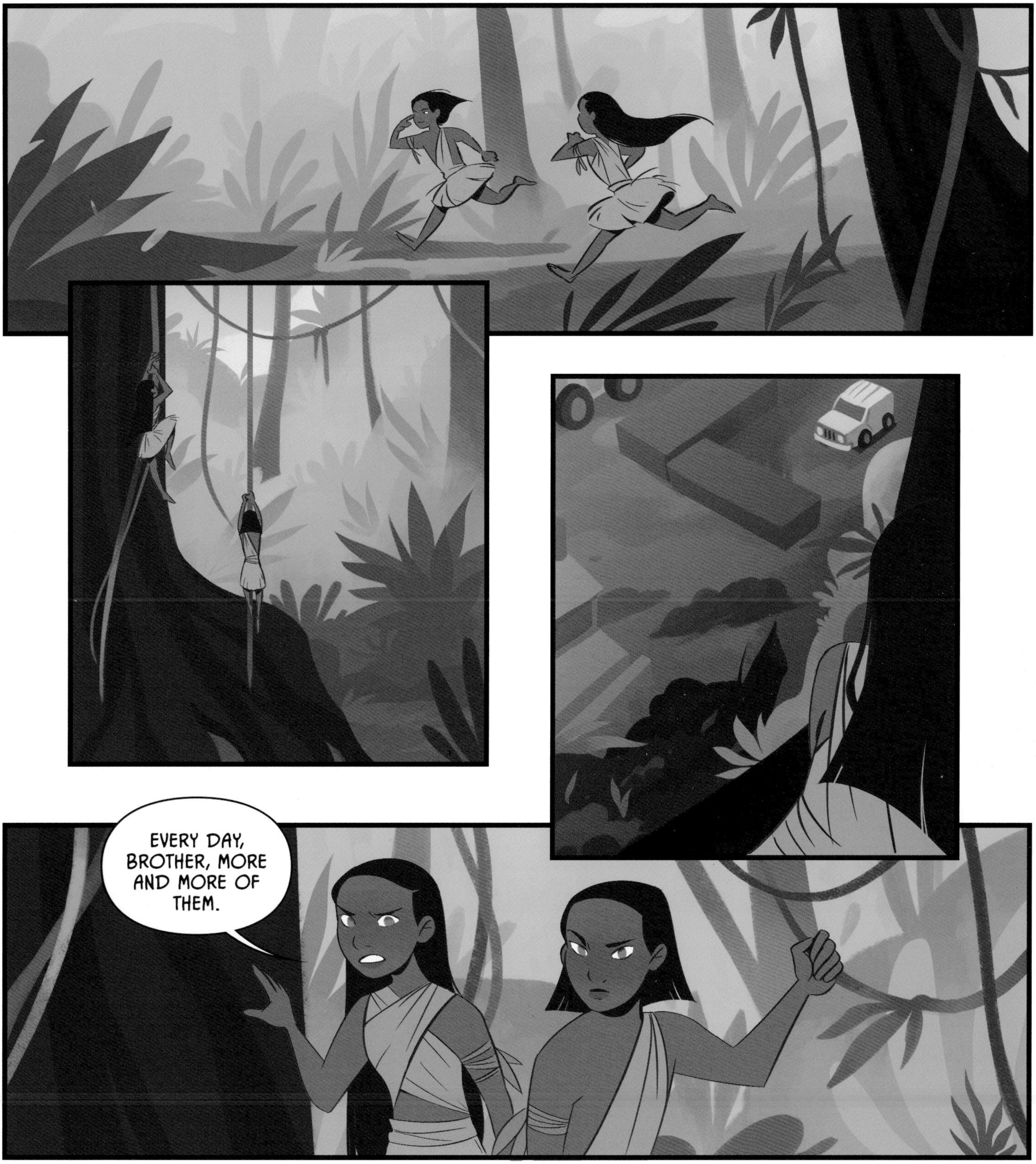
EVERY DAY, BROTHER, MORE AND MORE OF THEM.

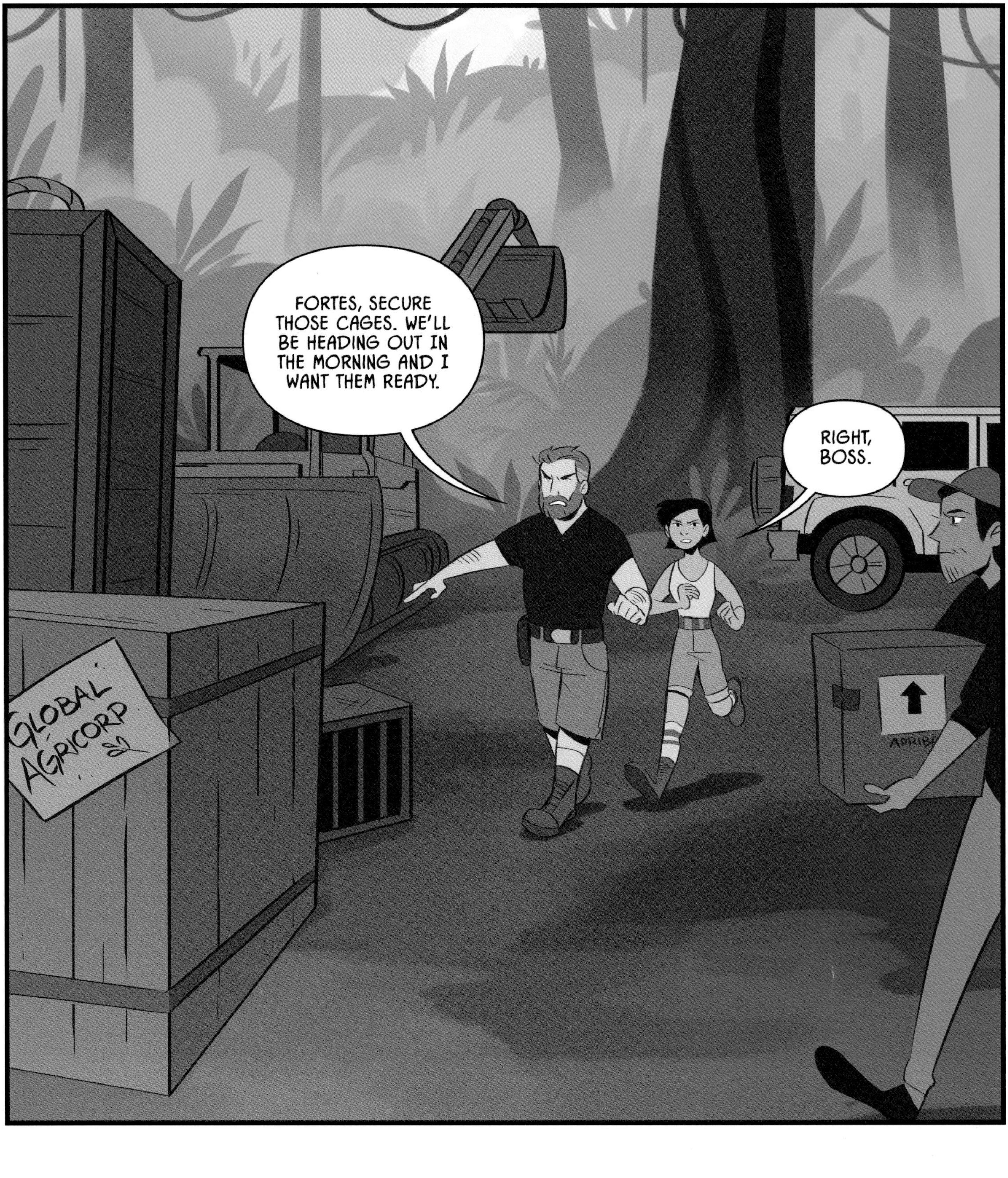
FORTES, SECURE THOSE CAGES. WE'LL BE HEADING OUT IN THE MORNING AND I WANT THEM READY.
RIGHT, BOSS.
GLOBAL AGRICORP
ARRIBA

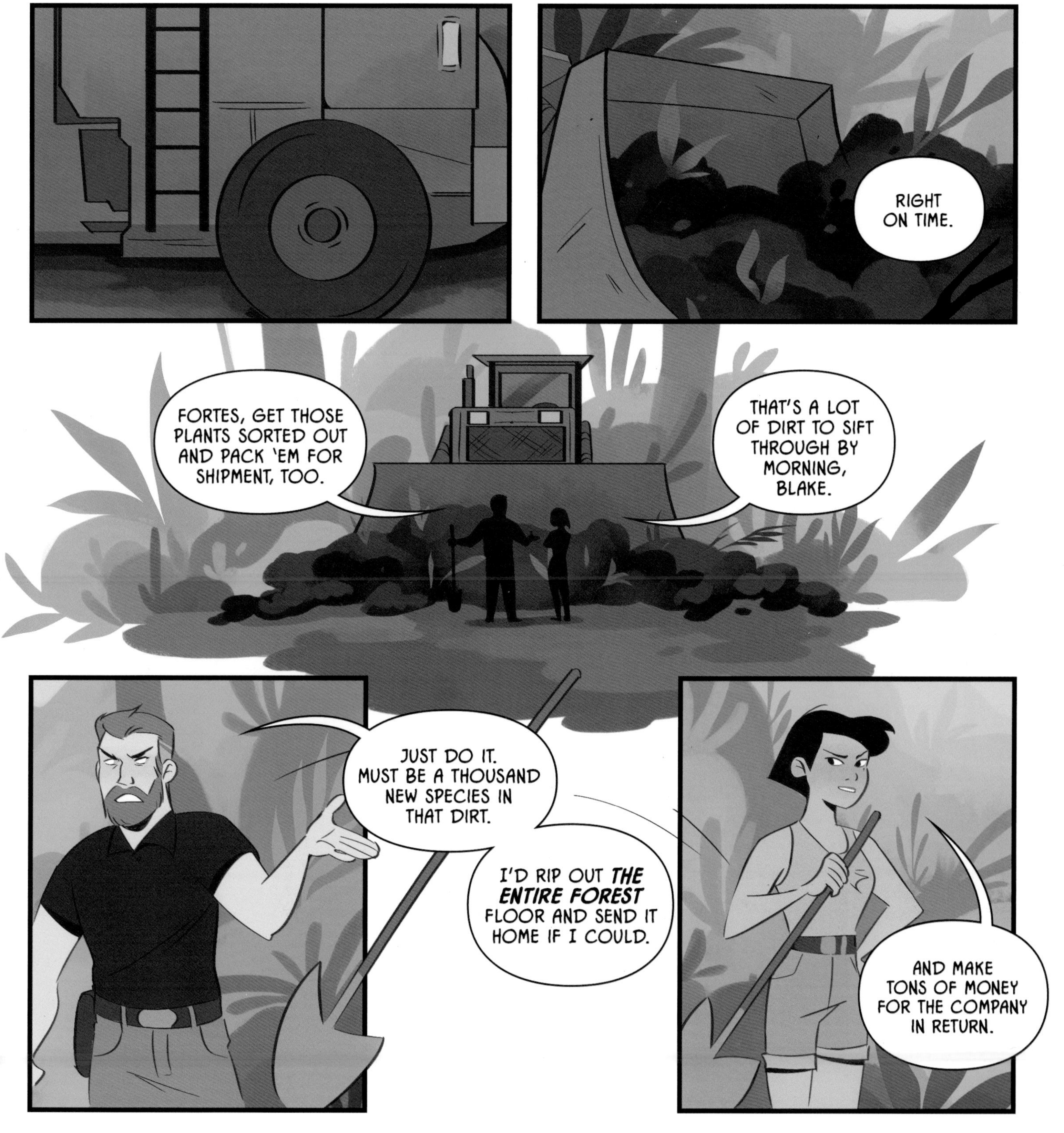
RIGHT ON TIME.
FORTES, GET THOSE PLANTS SORTED OUT AND PACK 'EM FOR SHIPMENT, TOO.
THAT'S A LOT OF DIRT TO SIFT THROUGH BY MORNING, BLAKE.
JUST DO IT. MUST BE A THOUSAND NEW SPECIES IN THAT DIRT.
I'D RIP OUT THE ENTIRE FOREST FLOOR AND SEND IT HOME IF I COULD.
AND MAKE TONS OF MONEY FOR THE COMPANY IN RETURN.

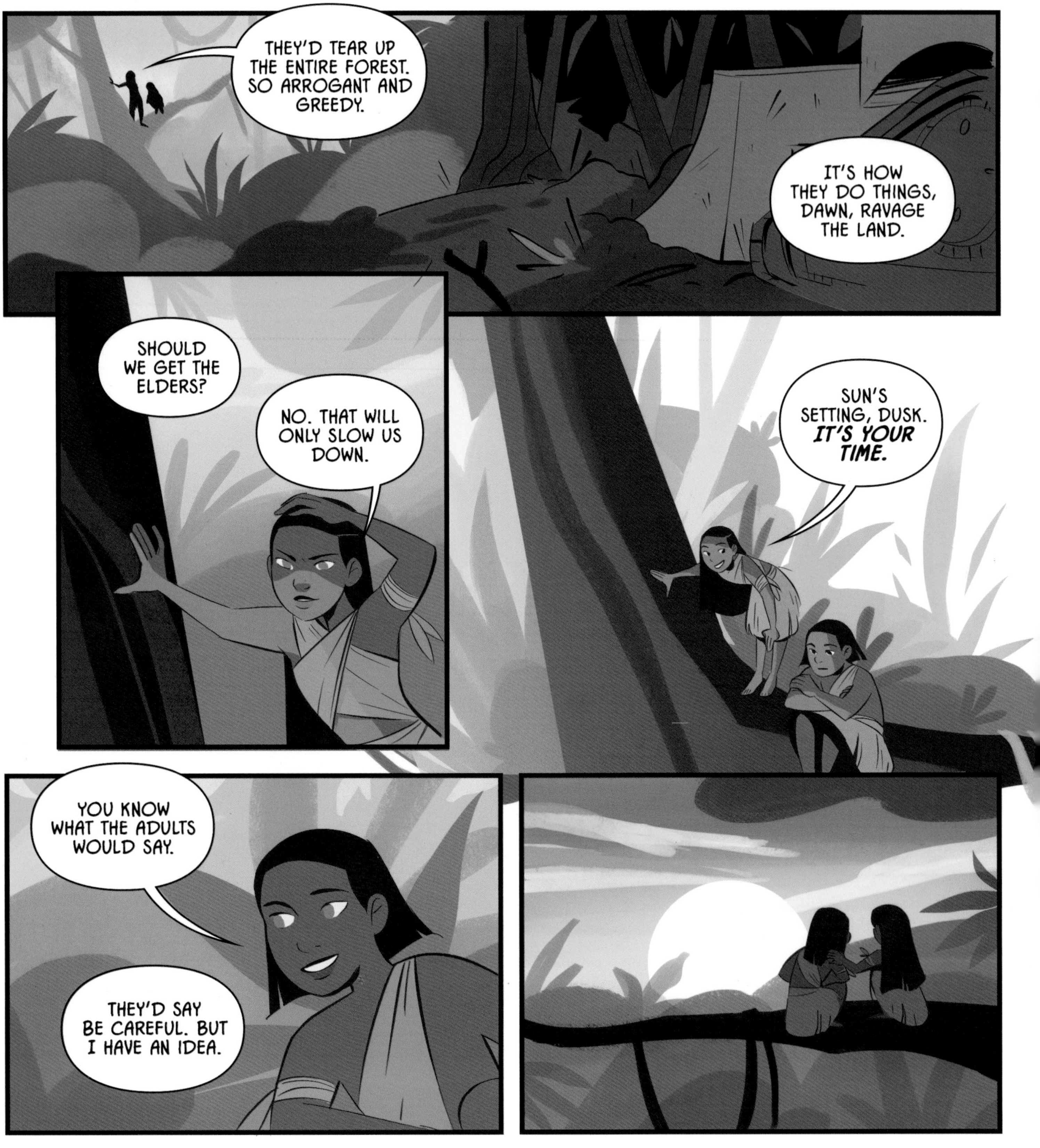
THEY'D TEAR UP THE ENTIRE FOREST. SO ARROGANT AND GREEDY.
IT'S HOW THEY DO THINGS, DAWN, RAVAGE THE LAND.
SHOULD WE GET THE ELDERS?
NO. THAT WILL ONLY SLOW US DOWN.
SUN'S SETTING, DUSK. *IT'S YOUR TIME.*
YOU KNOW WHAT THE ADULTS WOULD SAY.
THEY'D SAY BE CAREFUL. BUT I HAVE AN IDEA.

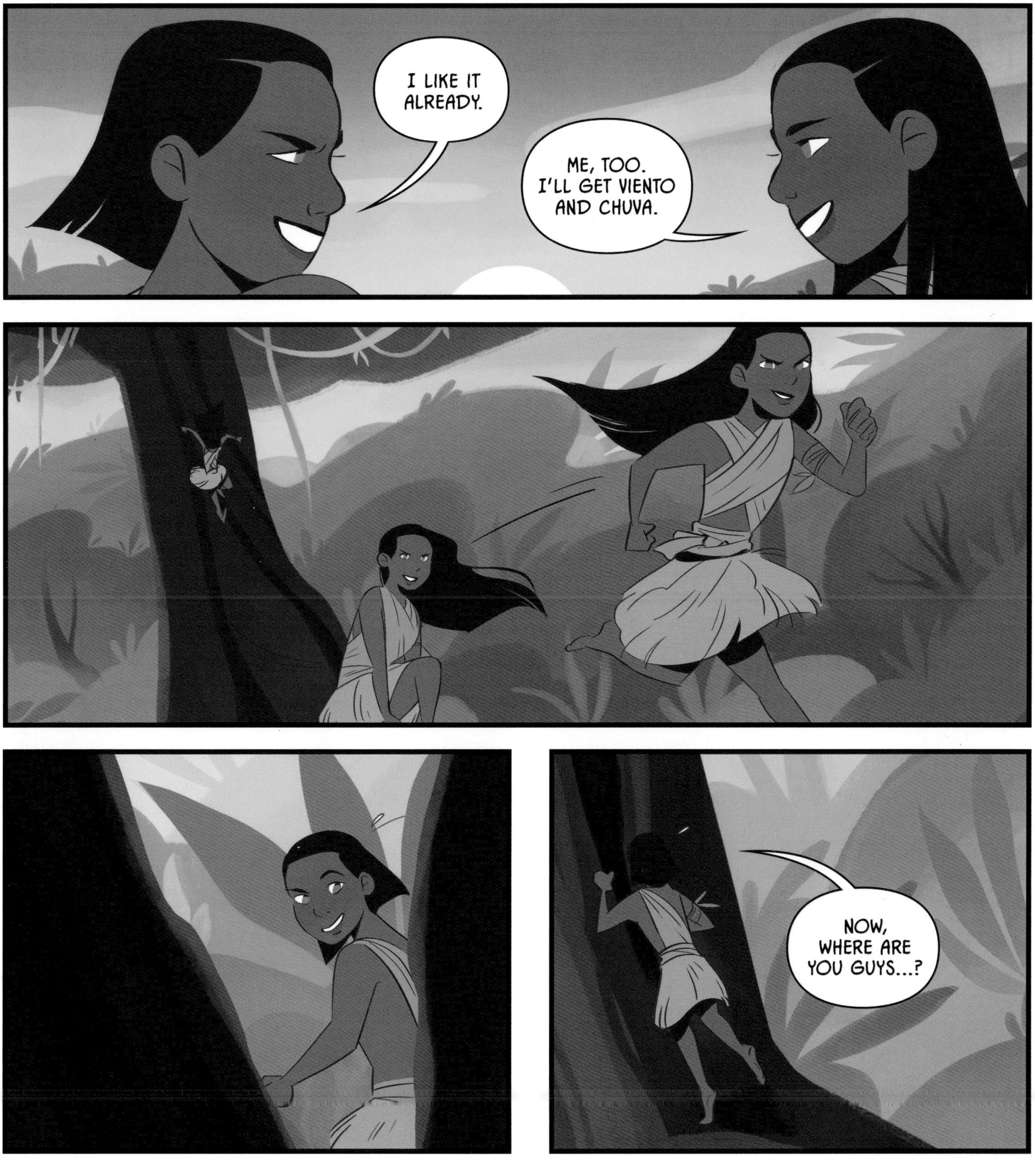
I LIKE IT ALREADY.
ME, TOO. I'LL GET VIENTO AND CHUVA.
NOW, WHERE ARE YOU GUYS...?

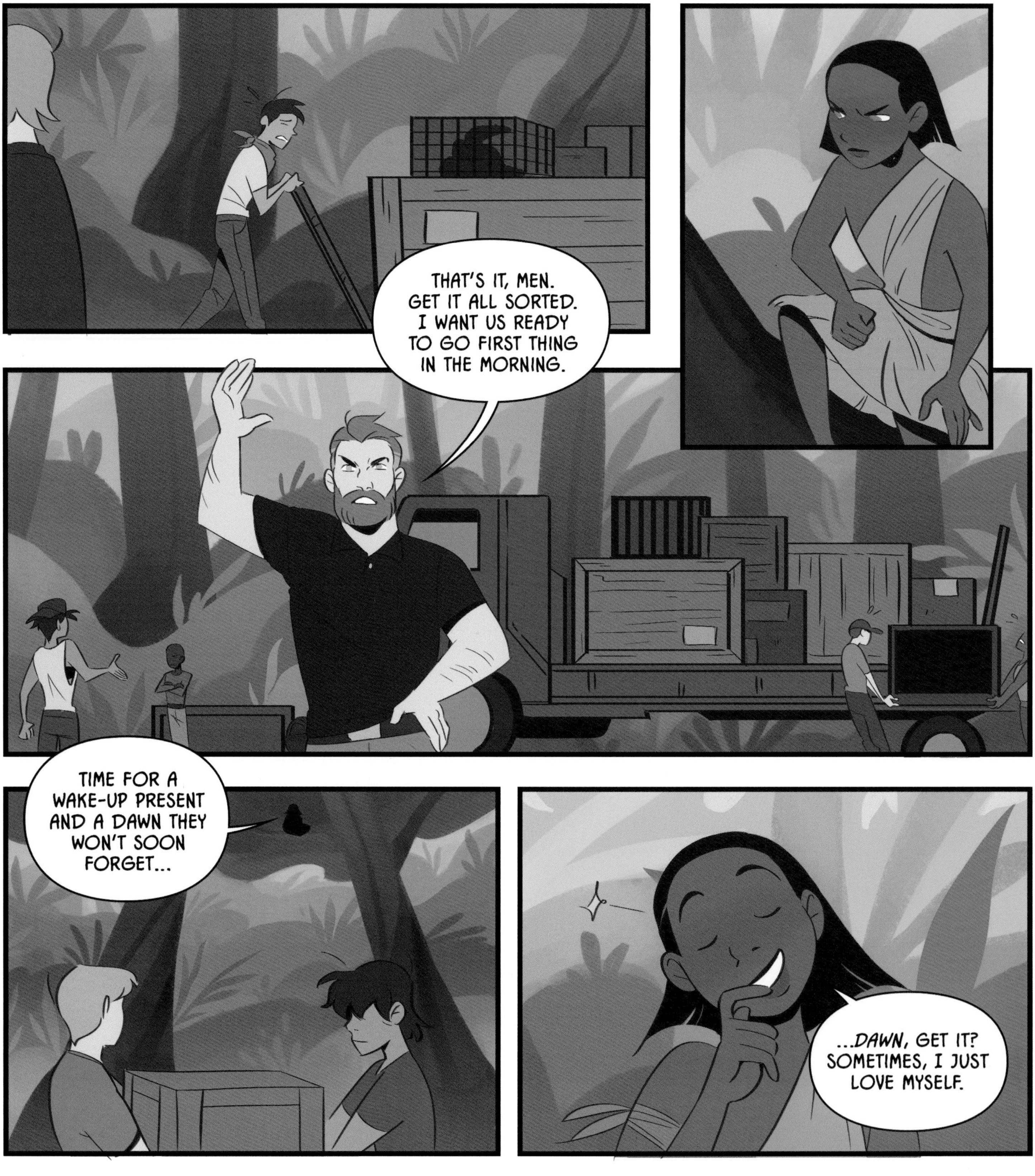
THAT'S IT, MEN. GET IT ALL SORTED. I WANT US READY TO GO FIRST THING IN THE MORNING.
TIME FOR A WAKE-UP PRESENT AND A DAWN THEY WON'T SOON FORGET...
...DAWN, GET IT? SOMETIMES, I JUST LOVE MYSELF.

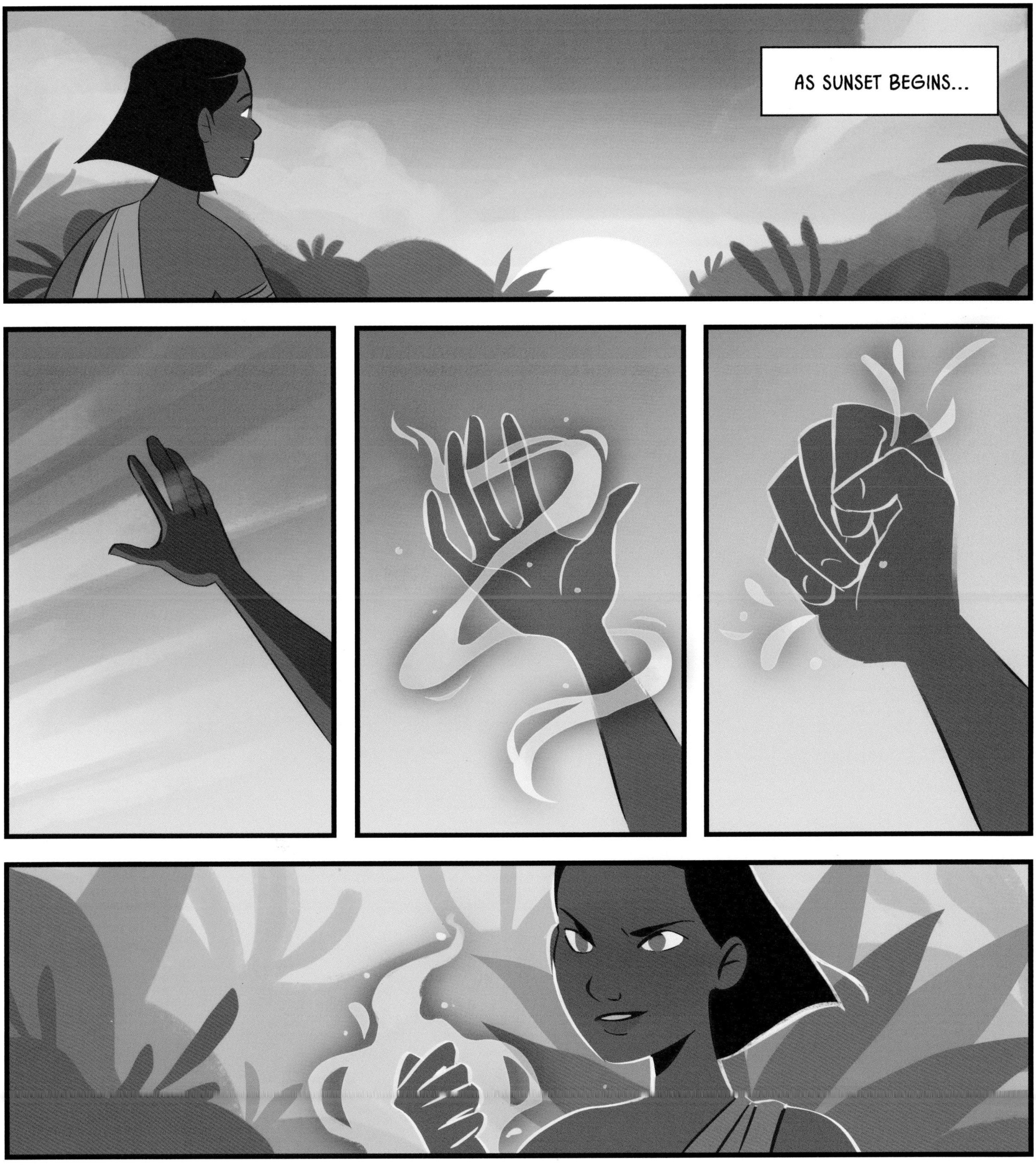
AS SUNSET BEGINS...

CHAPTER 2

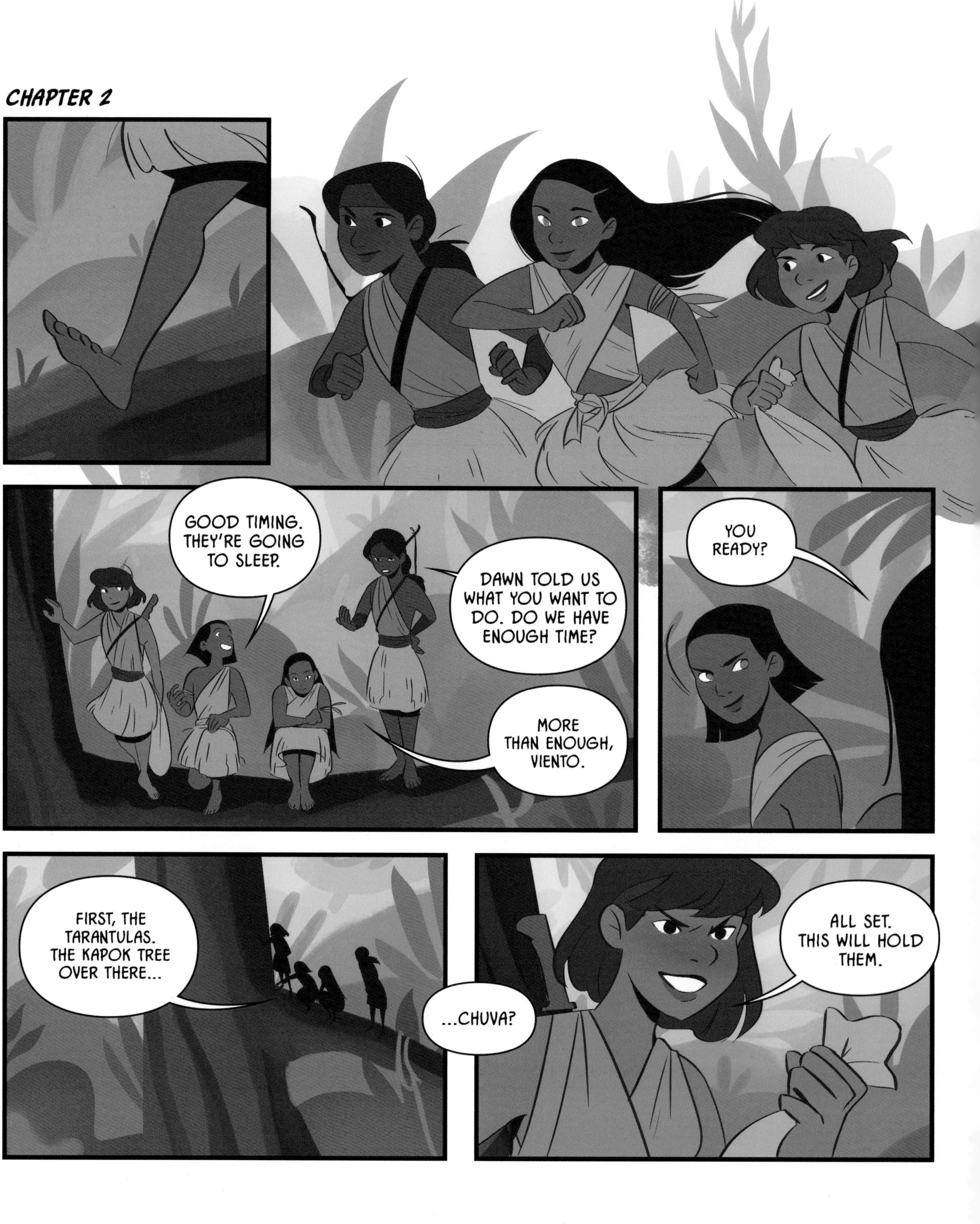
GOOD TIMING. THEY'RE GOING TO SLEEP.
DAWN TOLD US WHAT YOU WANT TO DO. DO WE HAVE ENOUGH TIME?
MORE THAN ENOUGH, VIENTO.
YOU READY?
FIRST, THE TARANTULAS. THE KAPOK TREE OVER THERE...
...CHUVA?
ALL SET. THIS WILL HOLD THEM.

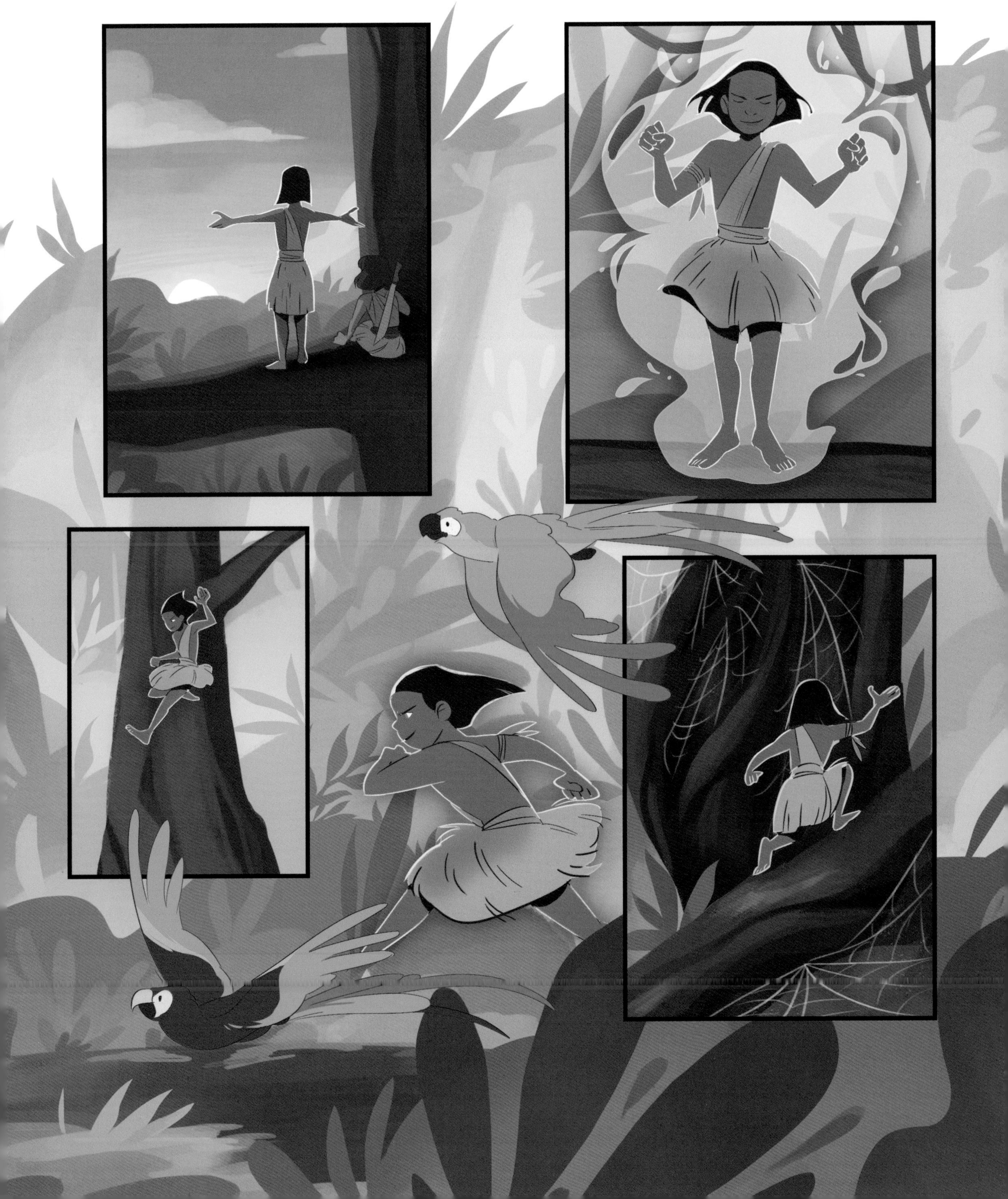

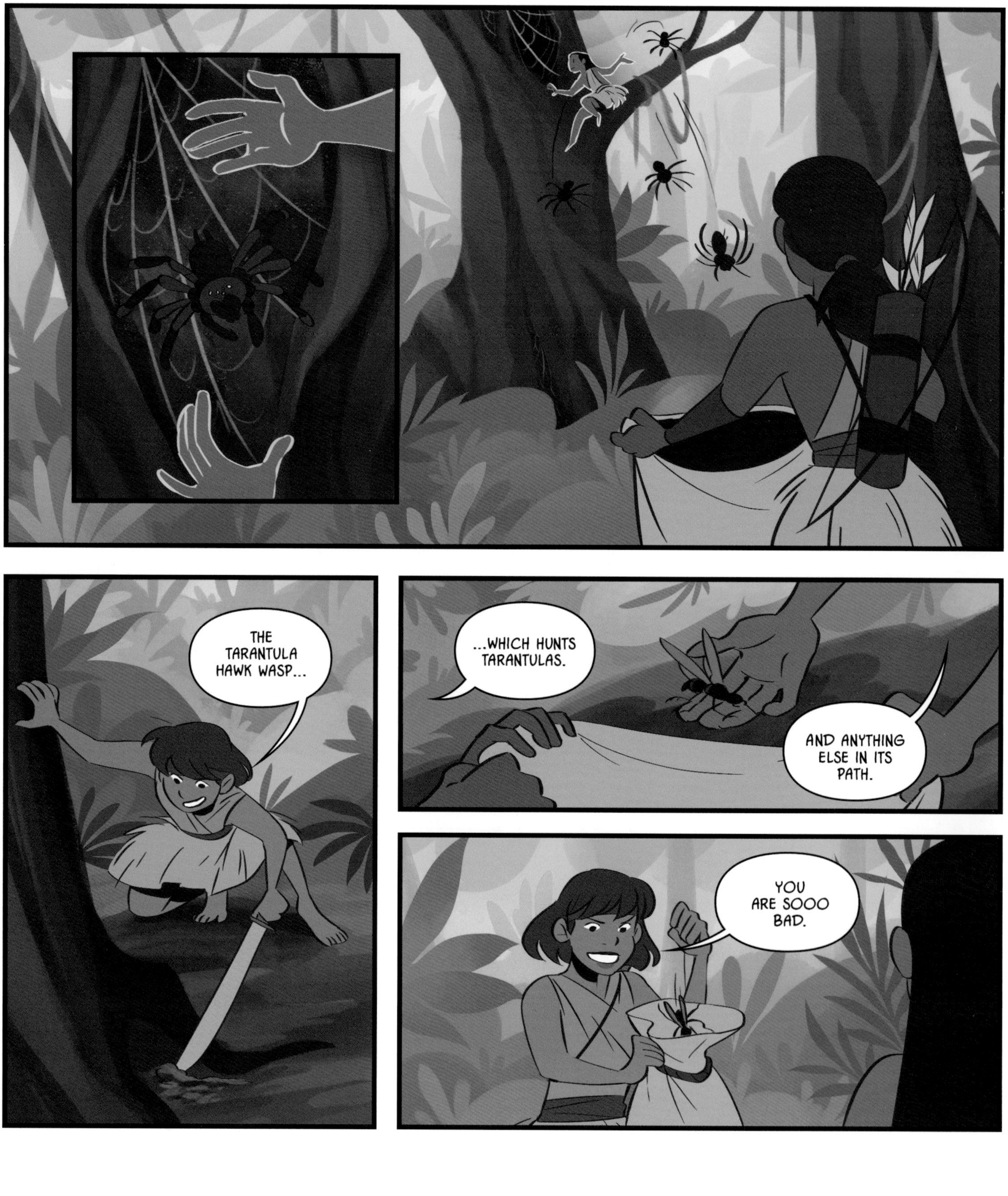
THE TARANTULA HAWK WASP...
...WHICH HUNTS TARANTULAS.
AND ANYTHING ELSE IN ITS PATH.
YOU ARE SOOO BAD.

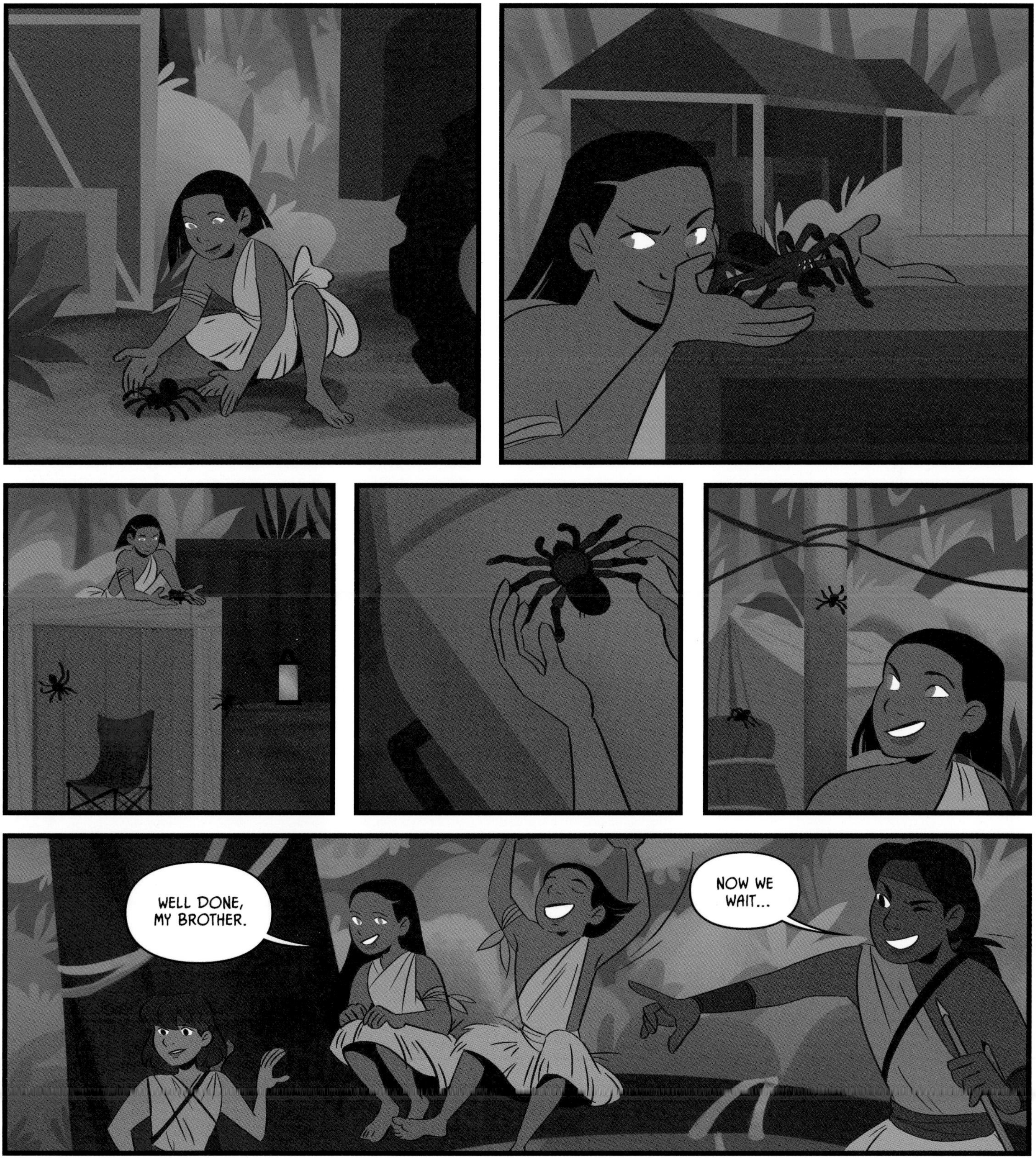
WELL DONE, MY BROTHER.
NOW WE WAIT...

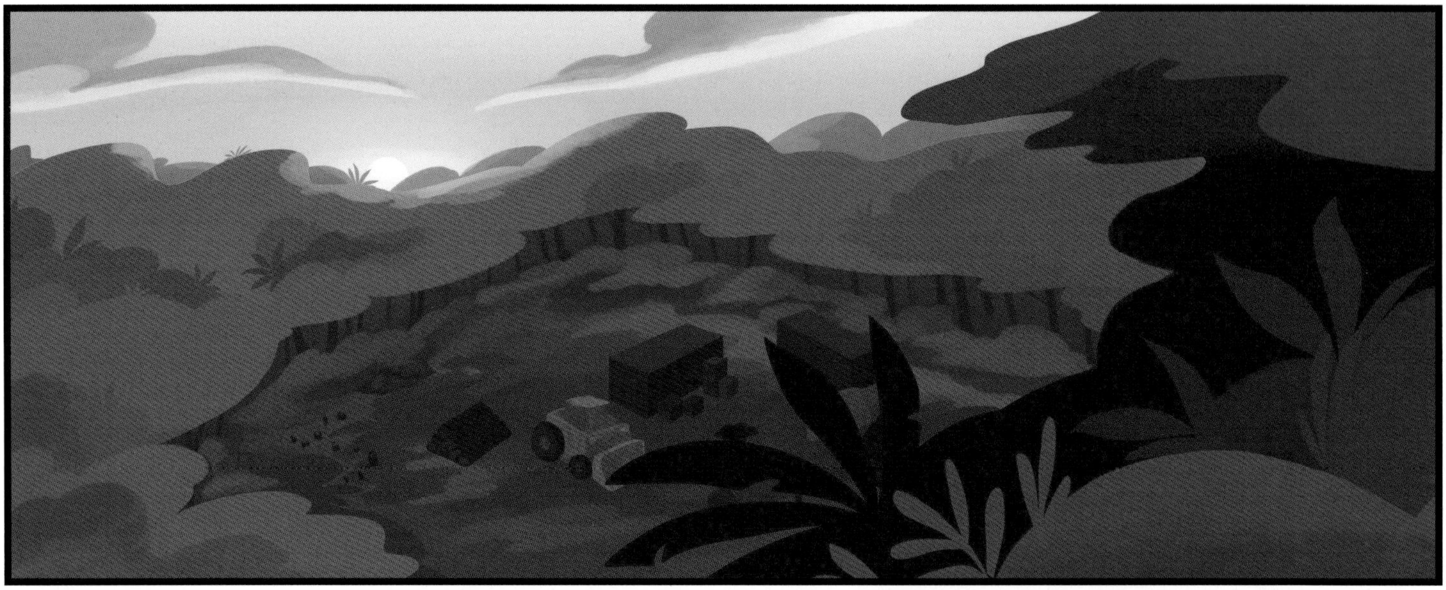

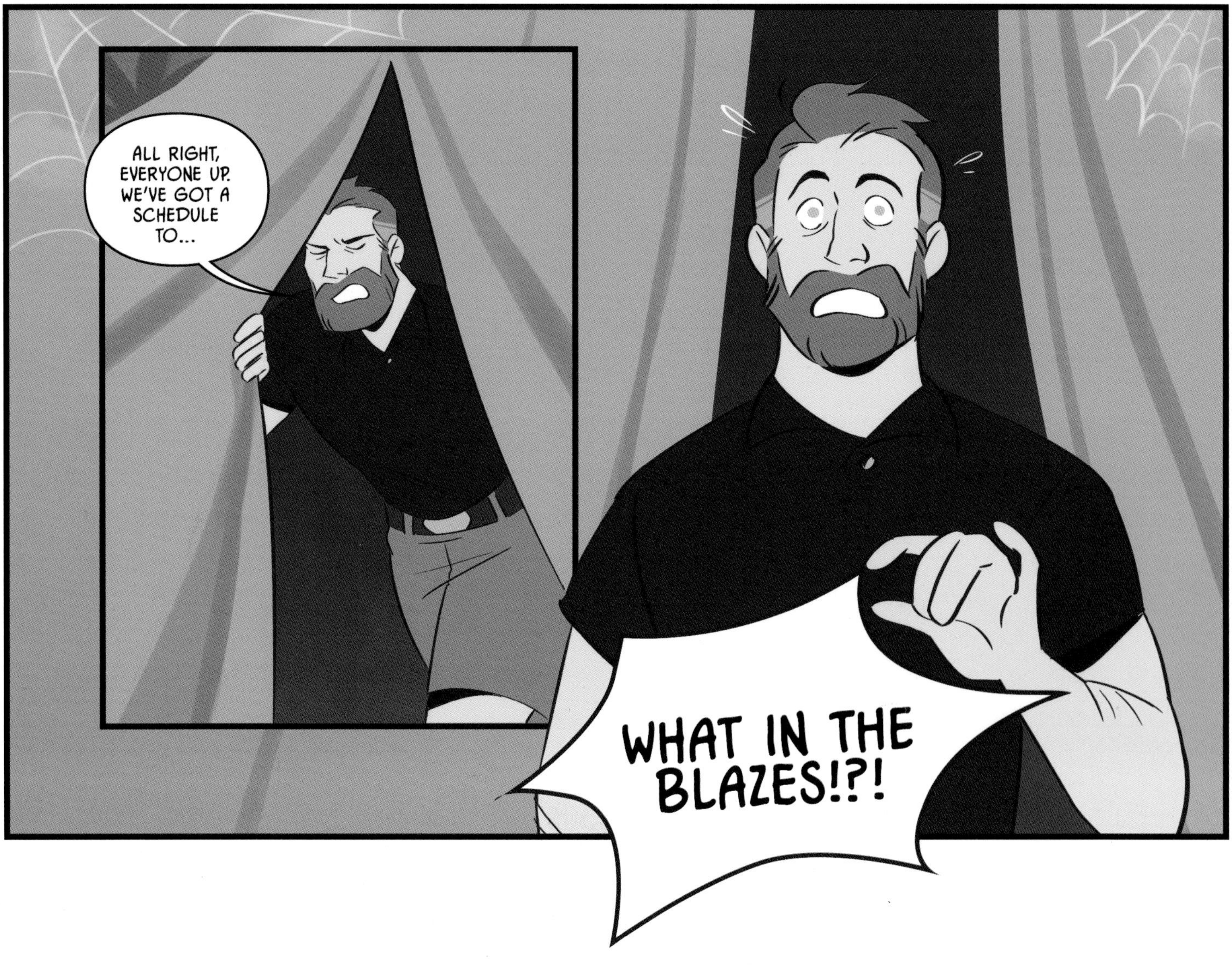
ALL RIGHT, EVERYONE UP. WE'VE GOT A SCHEDULE TO...
WHAT IN THE BLAZES!?!

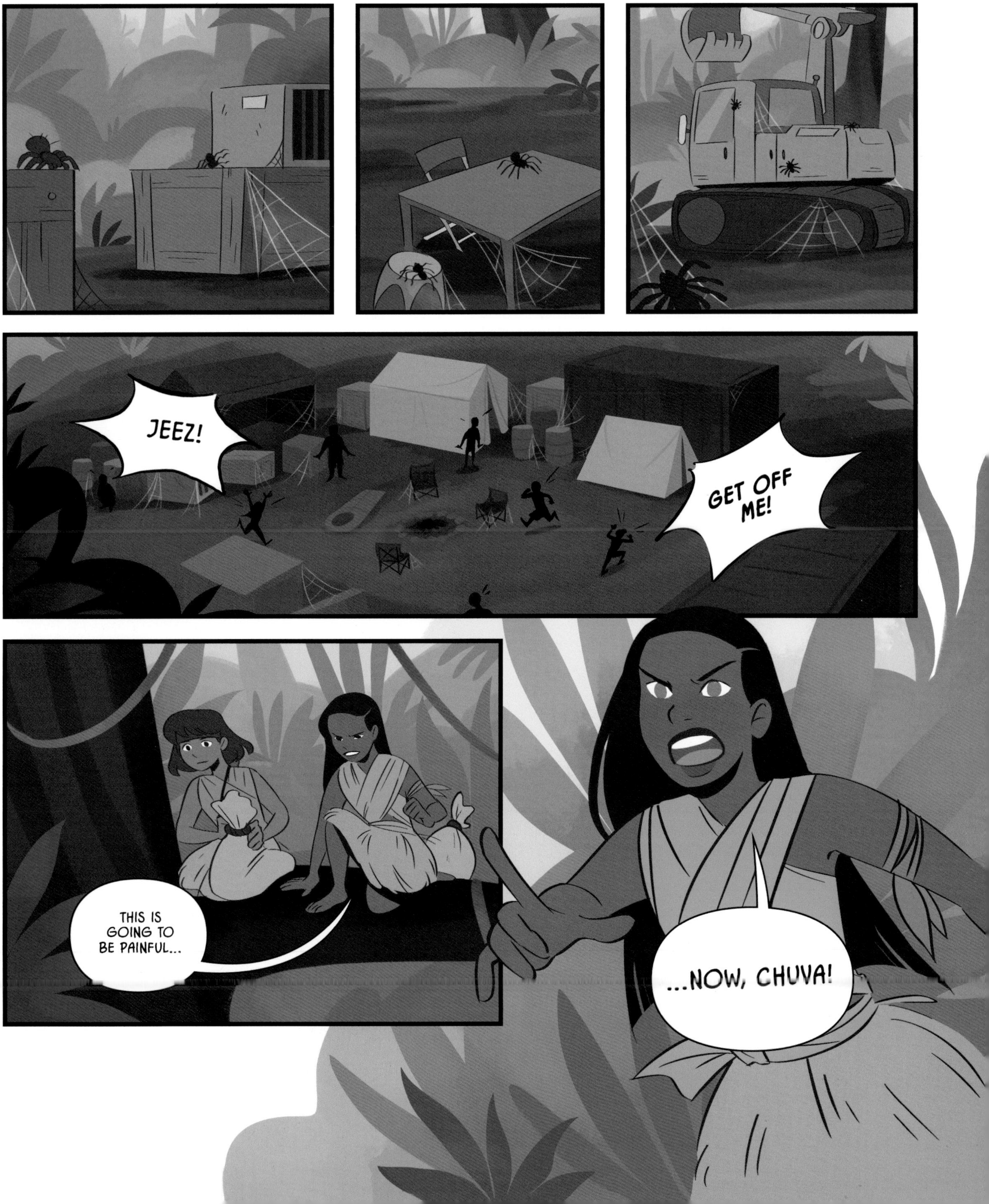
JEEZ!
GET OFF ME!
THIS IS GOING TO BE PAINFUL...
...NOW, CHUVA!

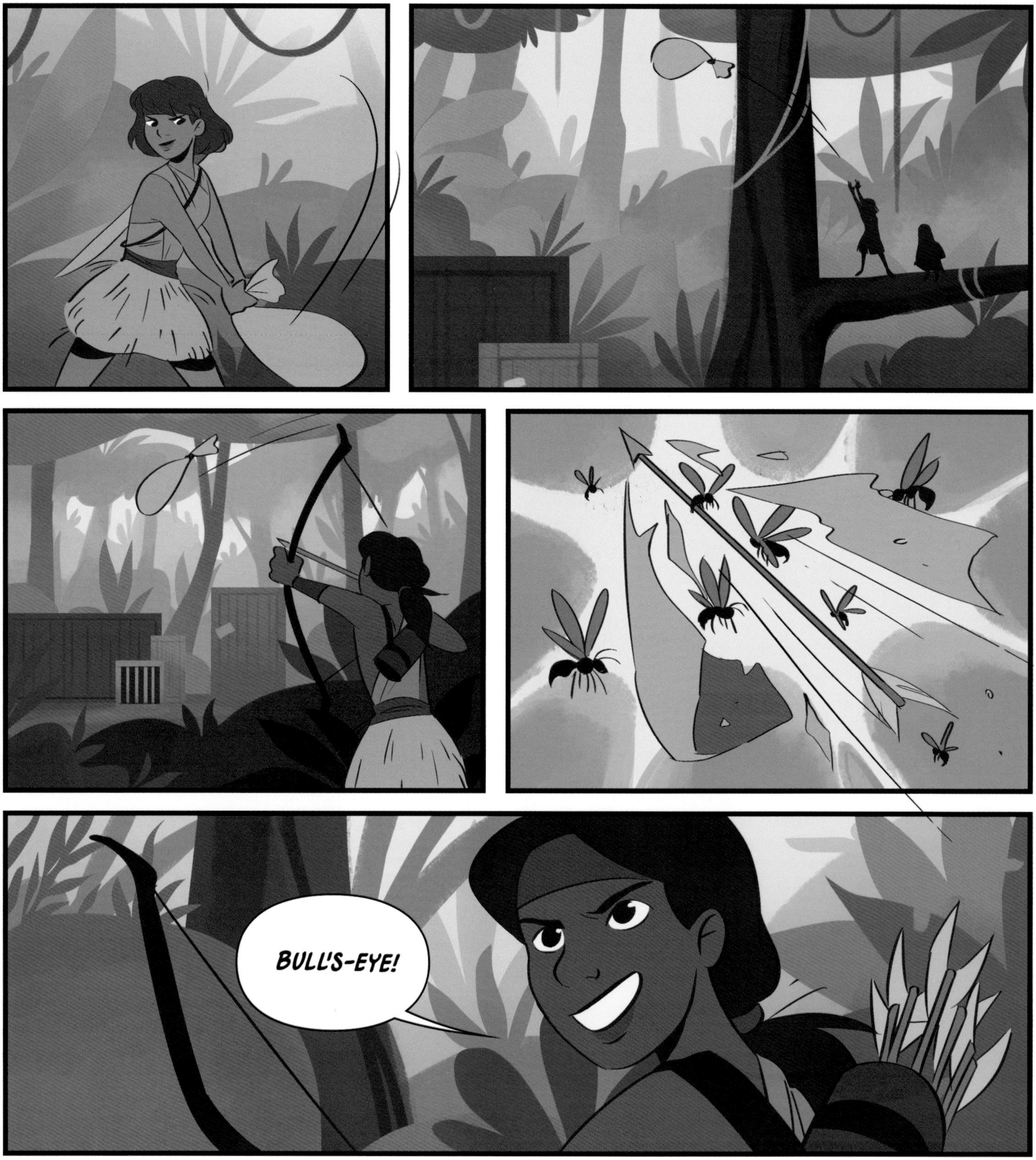
BULL'S-EYE!

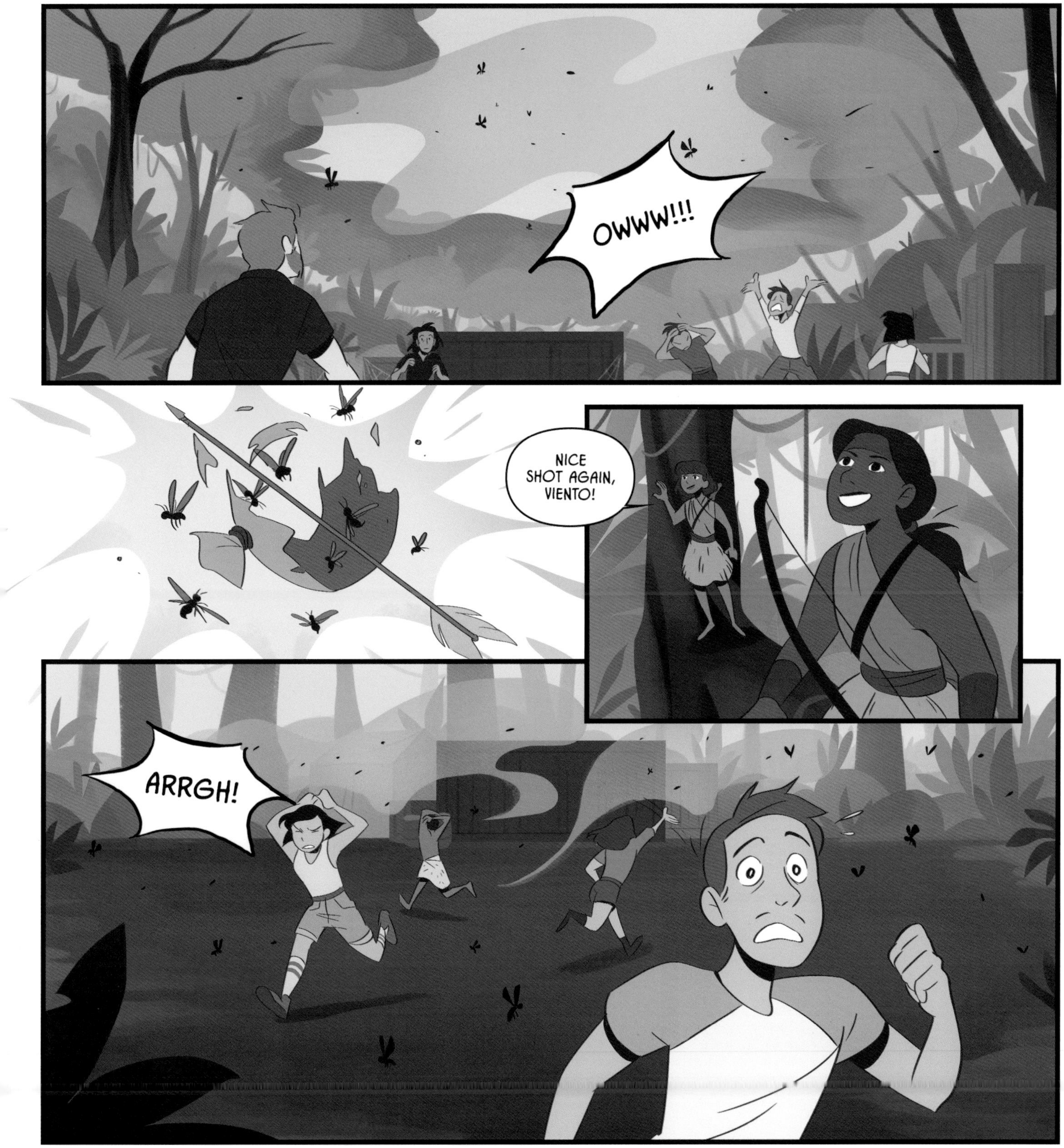
OWWW!!!
NICE SHOT AGAIN, VIENTO!
ARRGH!

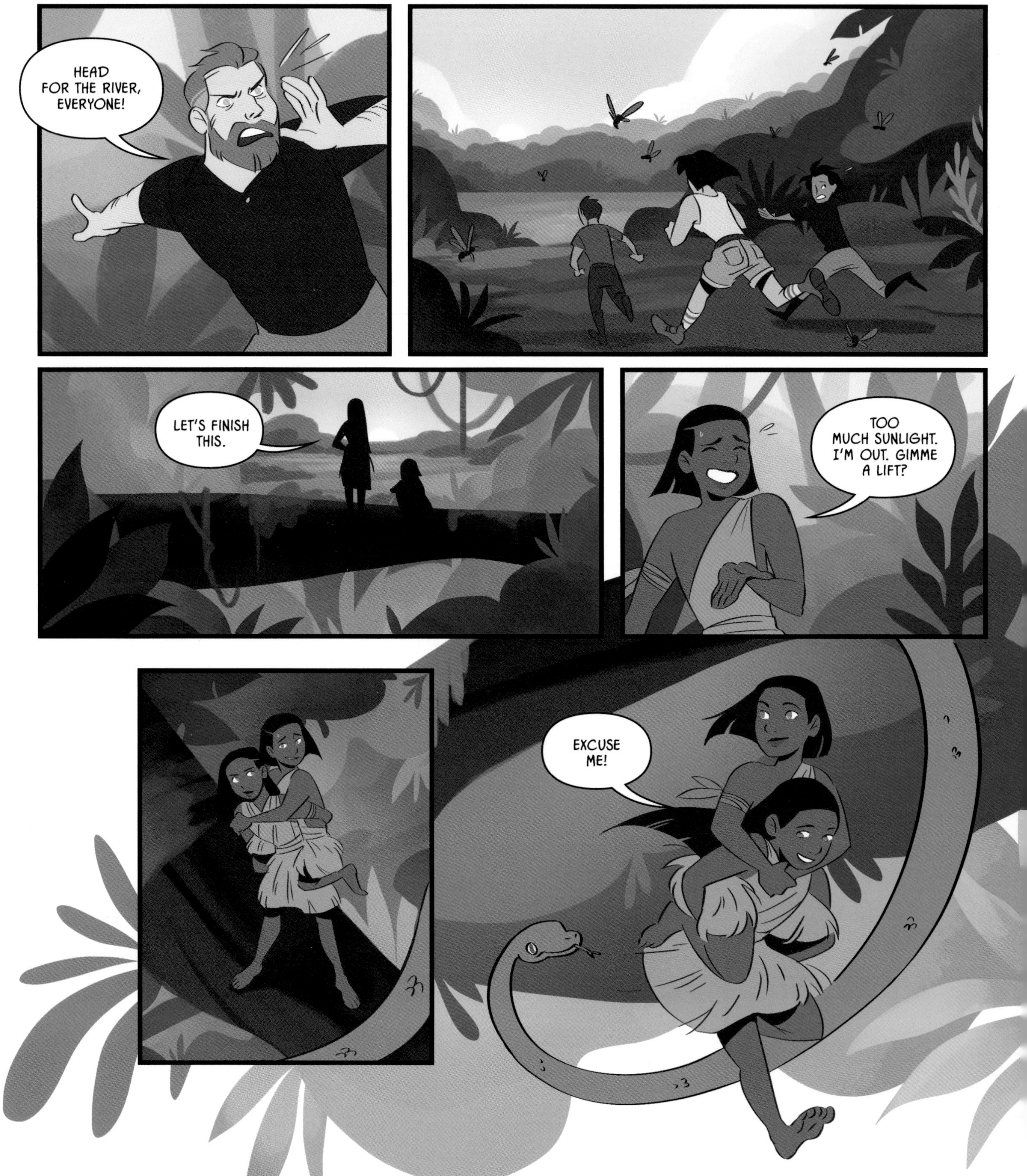
HEAD FOR THE RIVER, EVERYONE!
LET'S FINISH THIS.
TOO MUCH SUNLIGHT. I'M OUT. GIMME A LIFT?
EXCUSE ME!

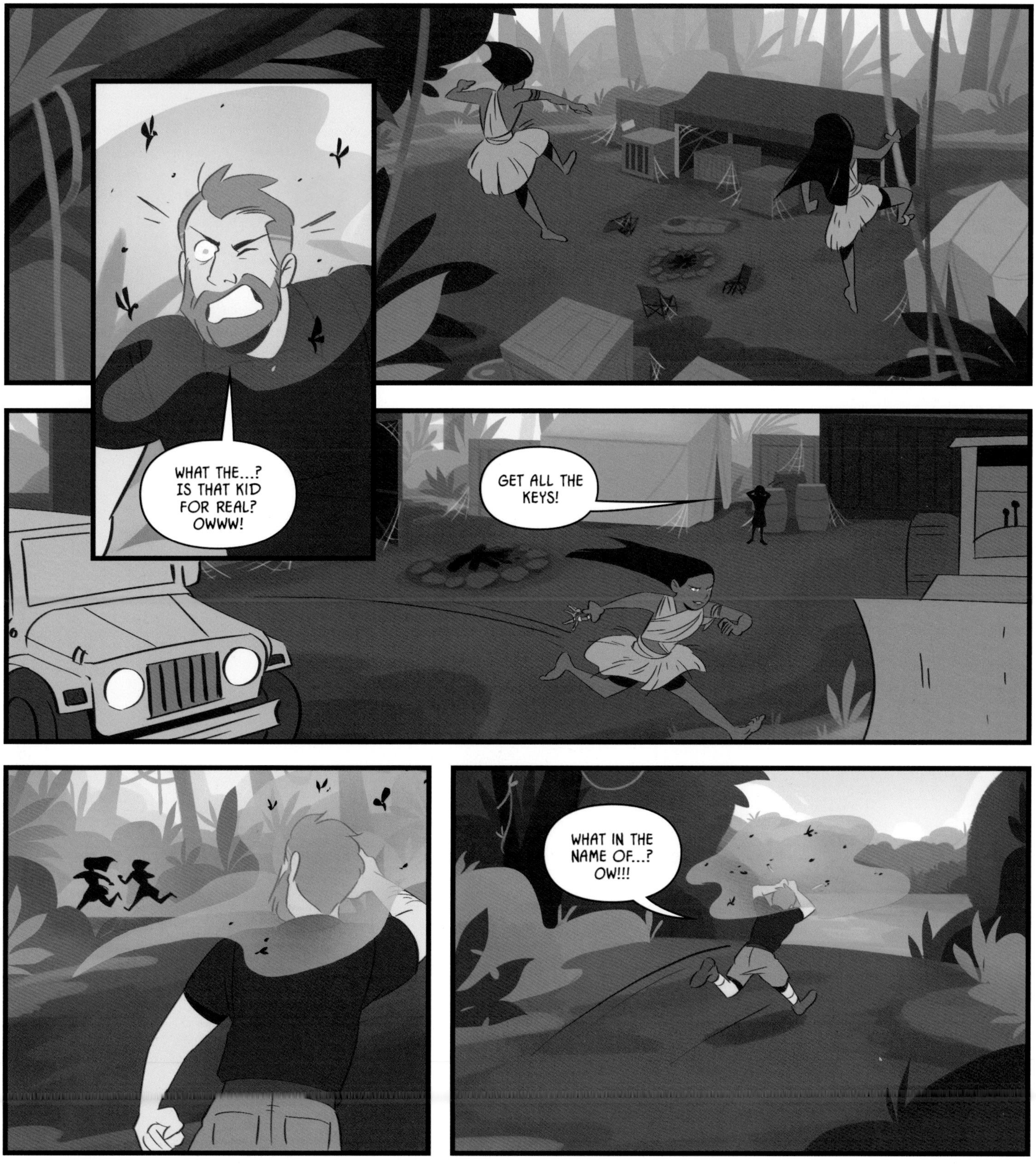
WHAT THE...? IS THAT KID FOR REAL? OWWW!
GET ALL THE KEYS!
WHAT IN THE NAME OF...? OW!!!

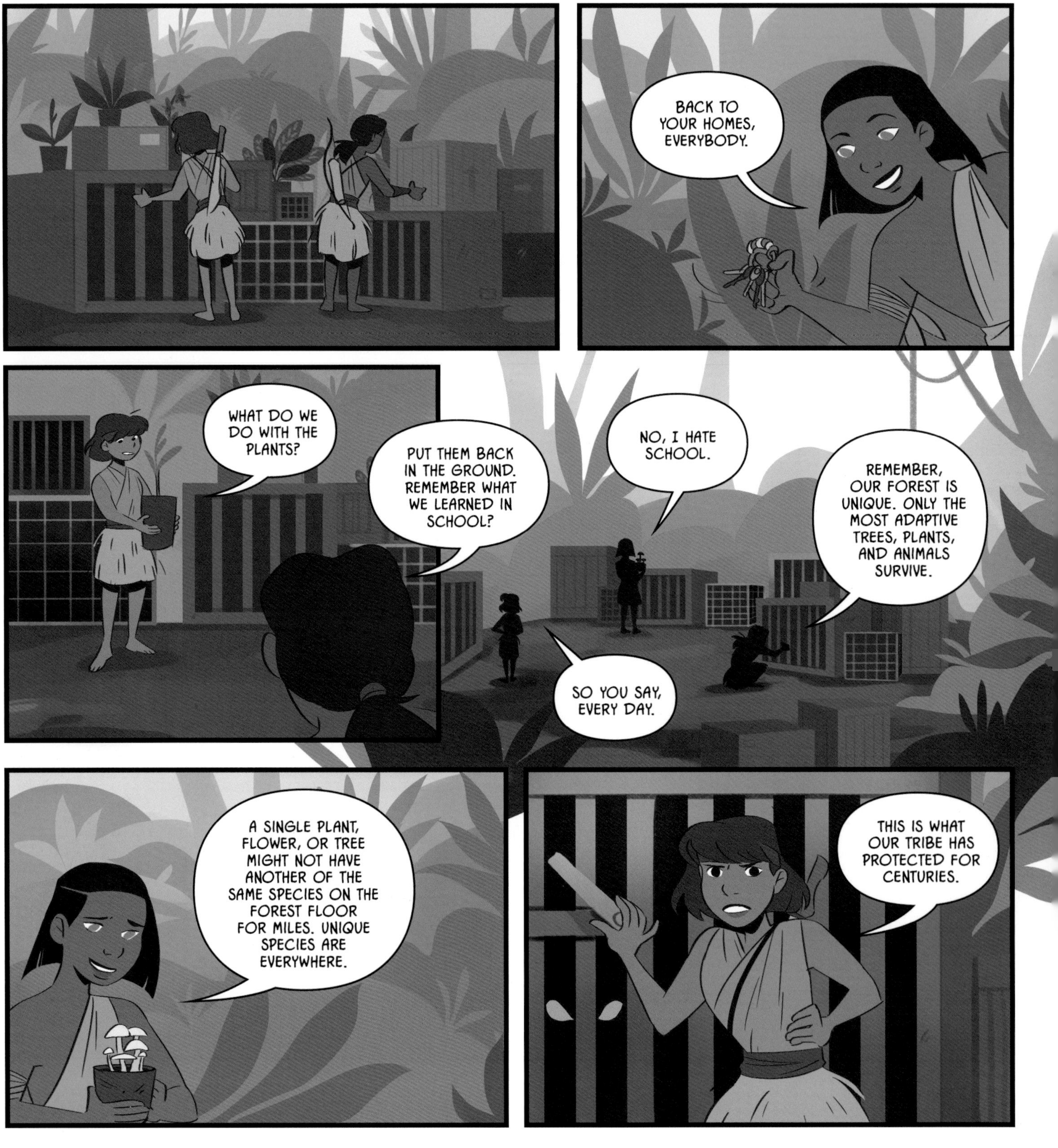
BACK TO YOUR HOMES, EVERYBODY.
WHAT DO WE DO WITH THE PLANTS?
PUT THEM BACK IN THE GROUND. REMEMBER WHAT WE LEARNED IN SCHOOL?
NO, I HATE SCHOOL.
REMEMBER, OUR FOREST IS UNIQUE. ONLY THE MOST ADAPTIVE TREES, PLANTS, AND ANIMALS SURVIVE.
SO YOU SAY, EVERY DAY.
A SINGLE PLANT, FLOWER, OR TREE MIGHT NOT HAVE ANOTHER OF THE SAME SPECIES ON THE FOREST FLOOR FOR MILES. UNIQUE SPECIES ARE EVERYWHERE.
THIS IS WHAT OUR TRIBE HAS PROTECTED FOR CENTURIES.

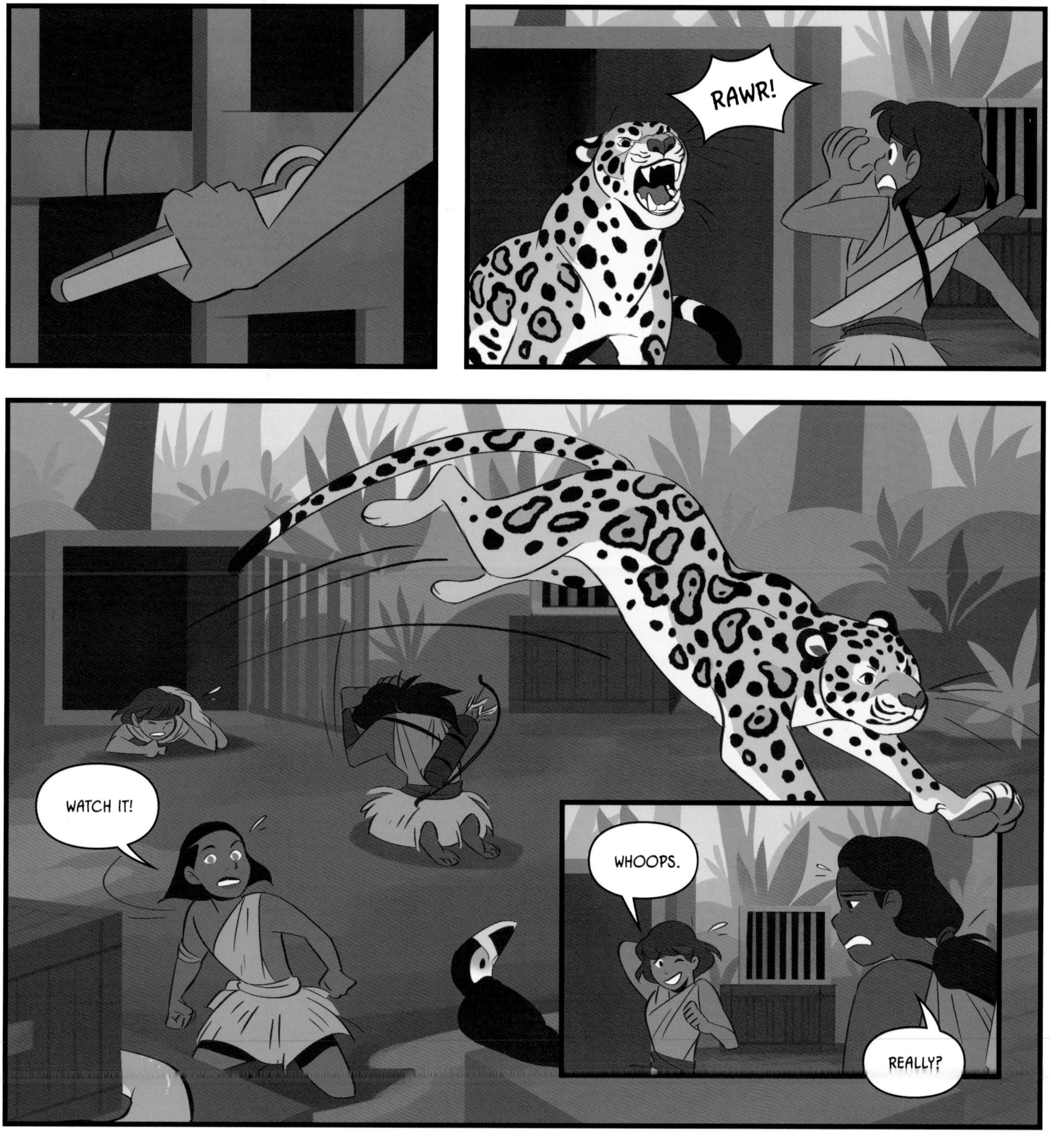
RAWR!
WATCH IT!
WHOOPS.
REALLY?

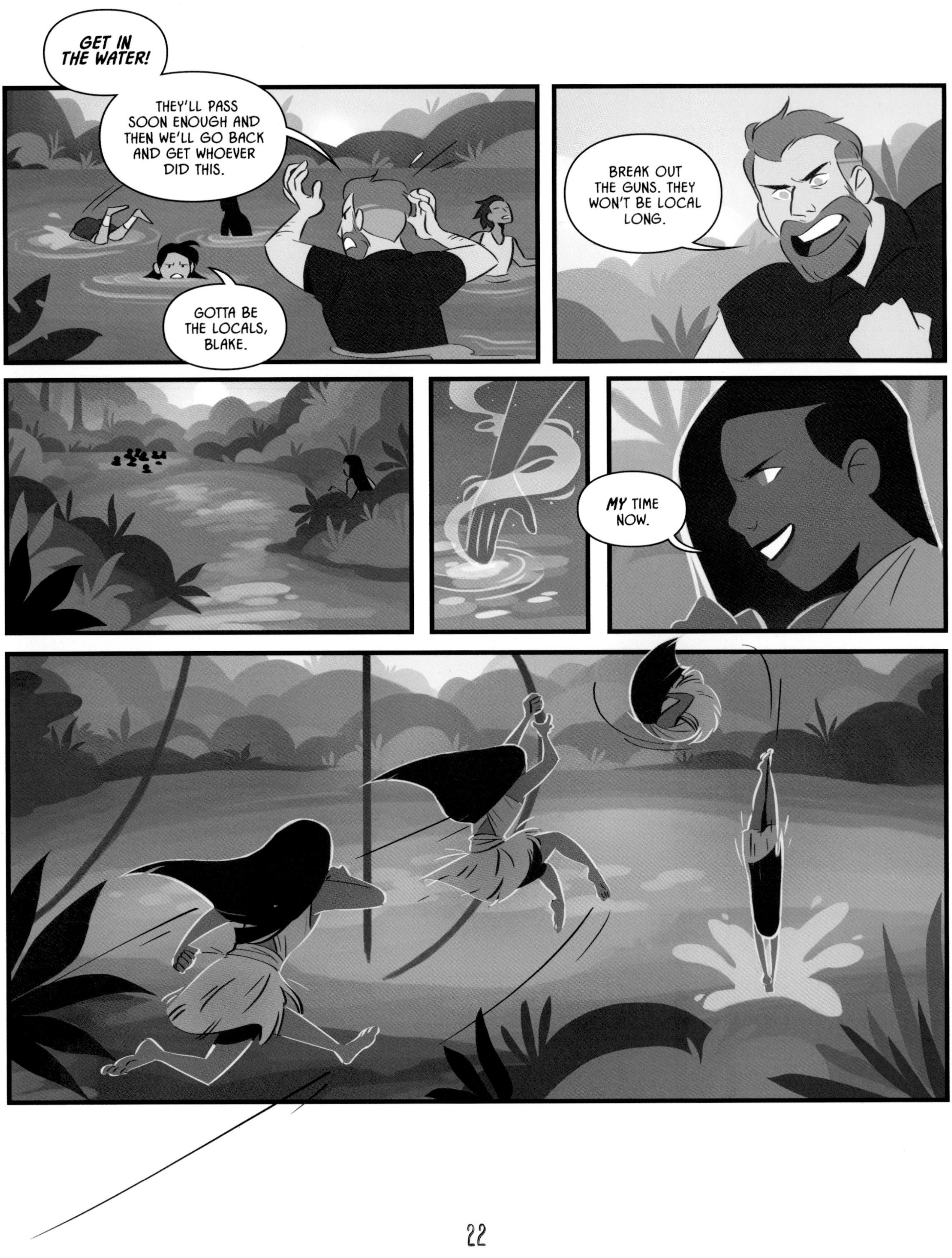

GET IN THE WATER!
THEY'LL PASS SOON ENOUGH AND THEN WE'LL GO BACK AND GET WHOEVER DID THIS.
GOTTA BE THE LOCALS, BLAKE.
BREAK OUT THE GUNS. THEY WON'T BE LOCAL LONG.
MY TIME NOW.

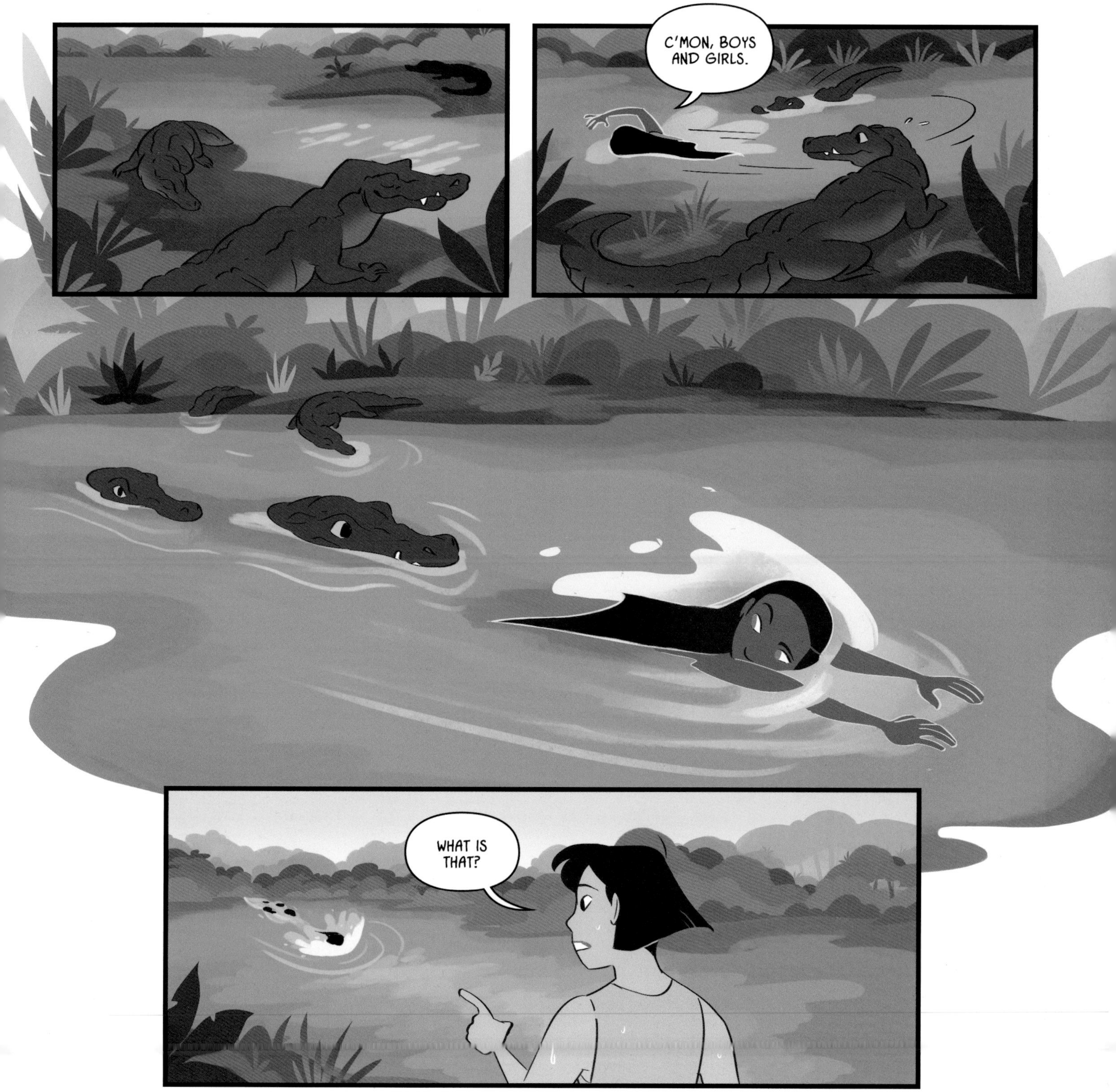
C'MON, BOYS AND GIRLS.
WHAT IS THAT?

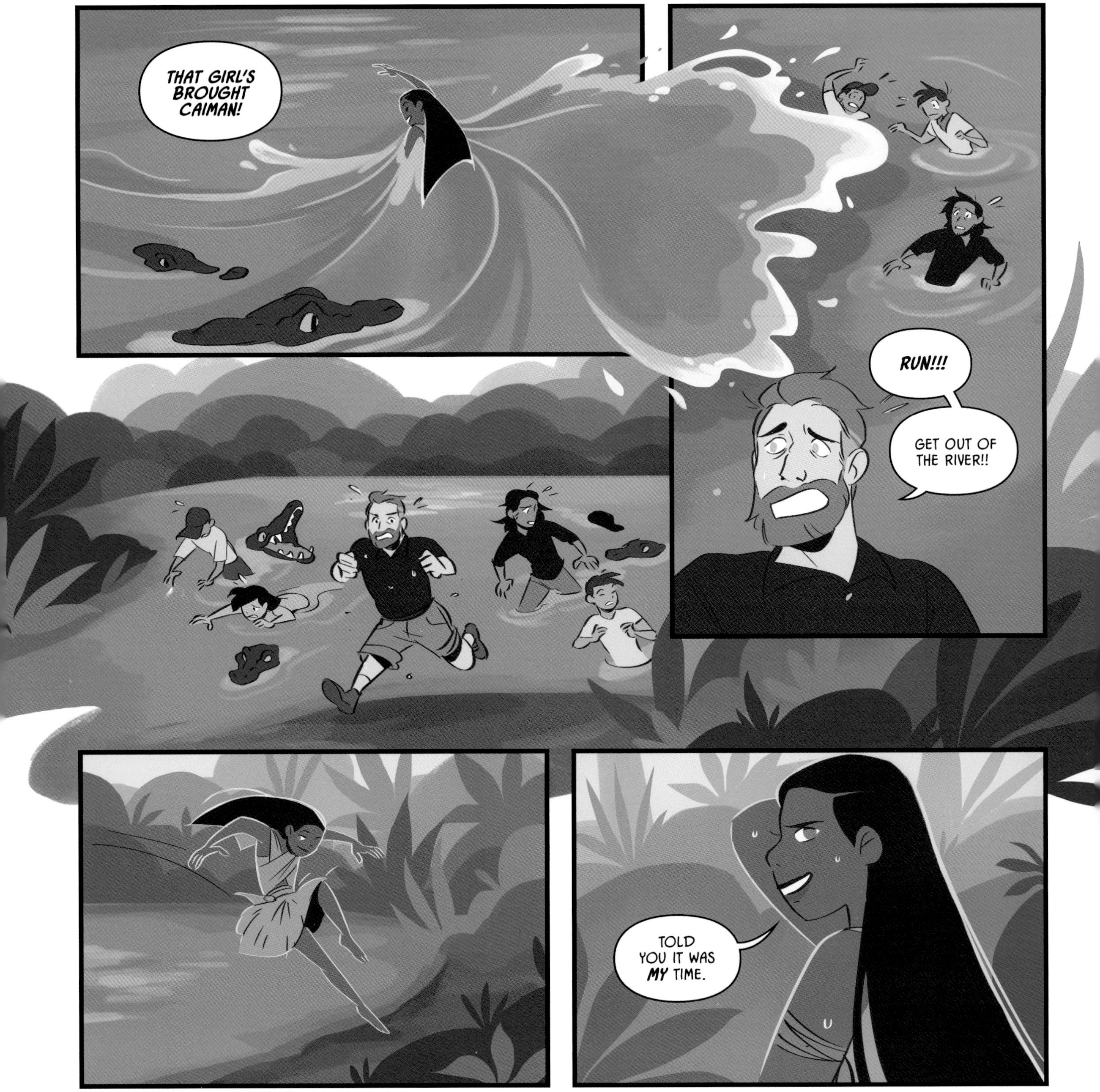
THAT GIRL'S BROUGHT CAIMAN!
RUN!!!
GET OUT OF THE RIVER!!
TOLD YOU IT WAS MY TIME.

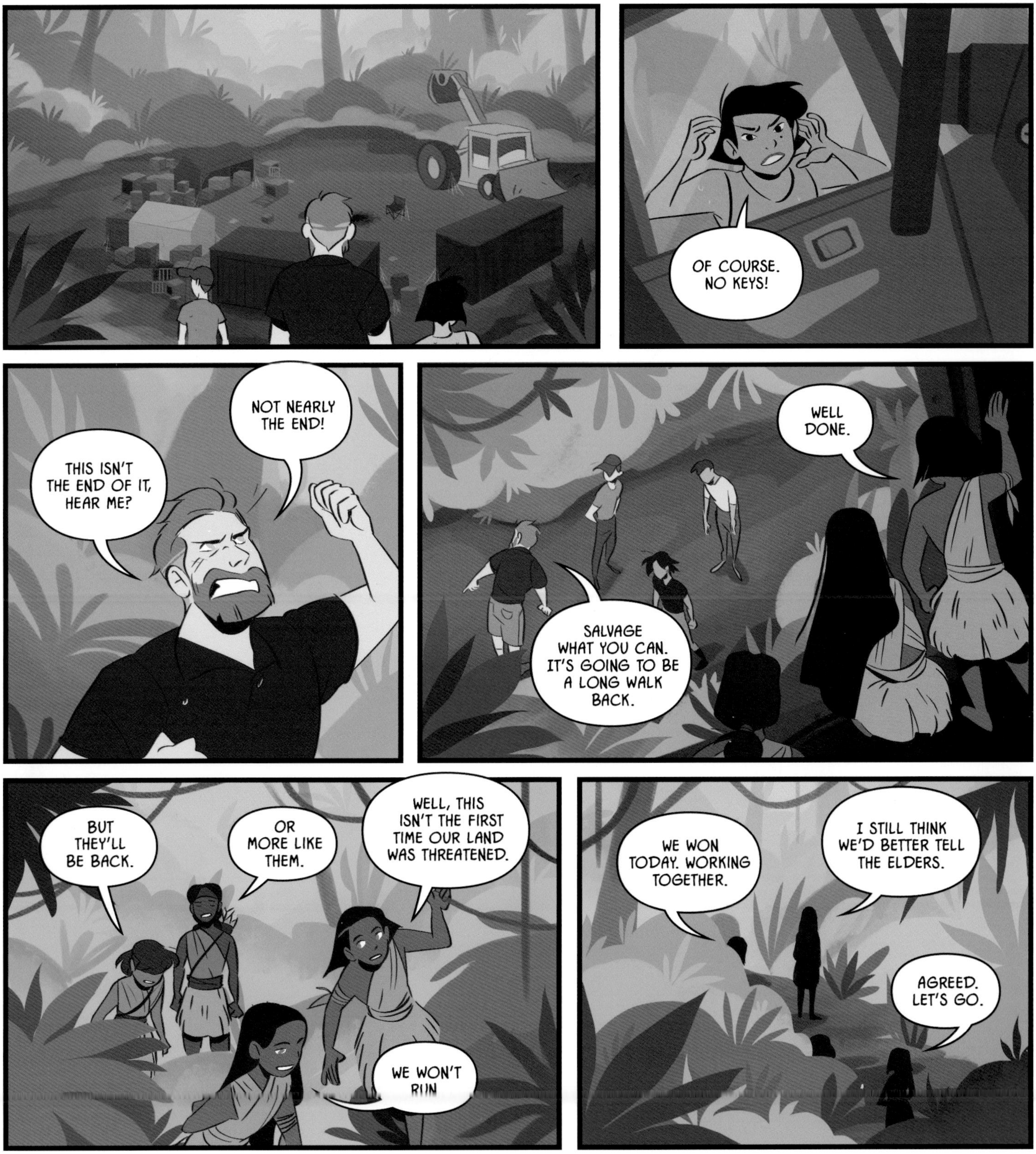
OF COURSE. NO KEYS!
THIS ISN'T THE END OF IT, HEAR ME?
NOT NEARLY THE END!
WELL DONE.
SALVAGE WHAT YOU CAN. IT'S GOING TO BE A LONG WALK BACK.
BUT THEY'LL BE BACK.
OR MORE LIKE THEM.
WELL, THIS ISN'T THE FIRST TIME OUR LAND WAS THREATENED.
WE WON'T RUN
WE WON TODAY. WORKING TOGETHER.
I STILL THINK WE'D BETTER TELL THE ELDERS.
AGREED. LET'S GO.

CHAPTER 3

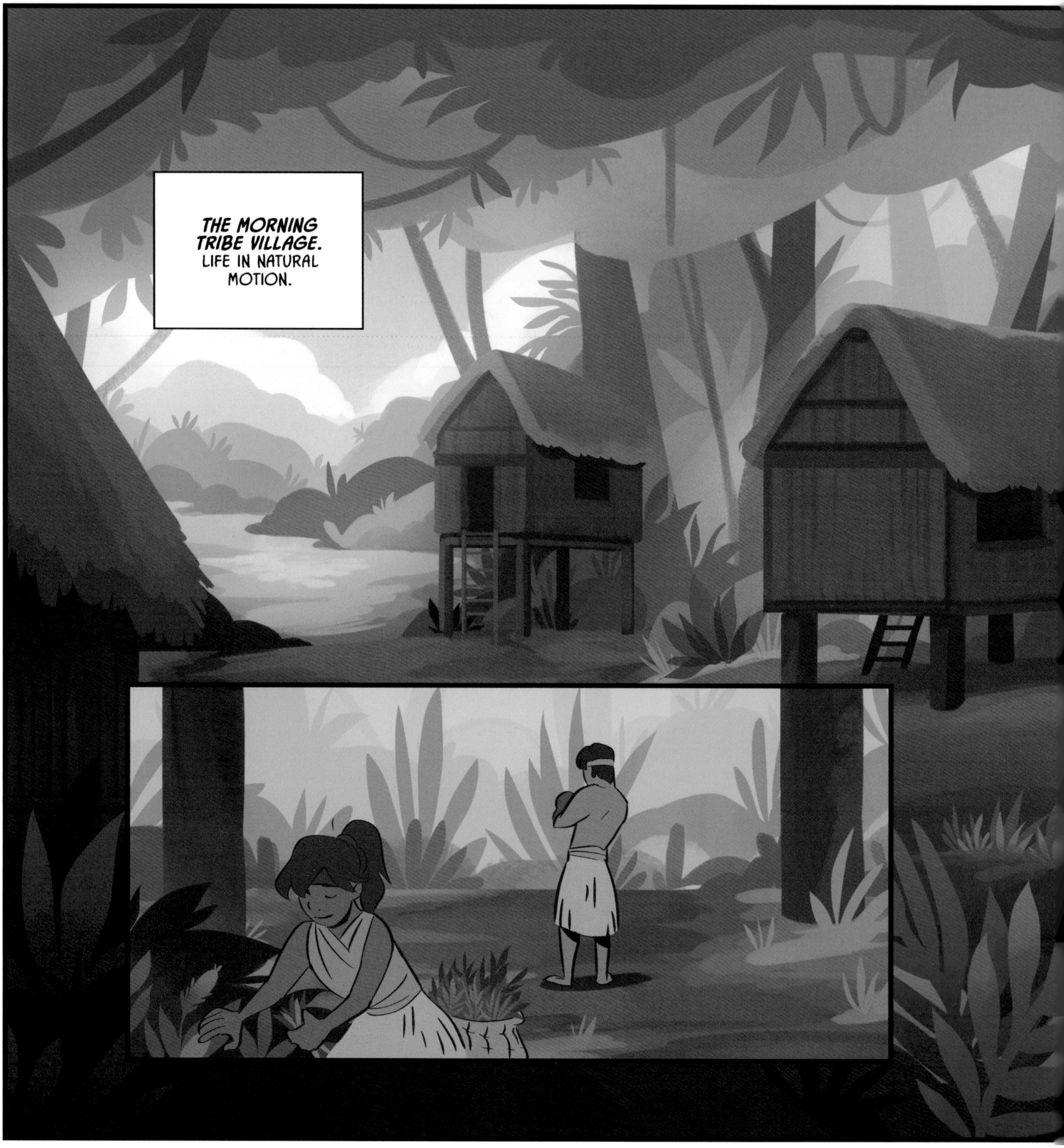
THE MORNING TRIBE VILLAGE. LIFE IN NATURAL MOTION.

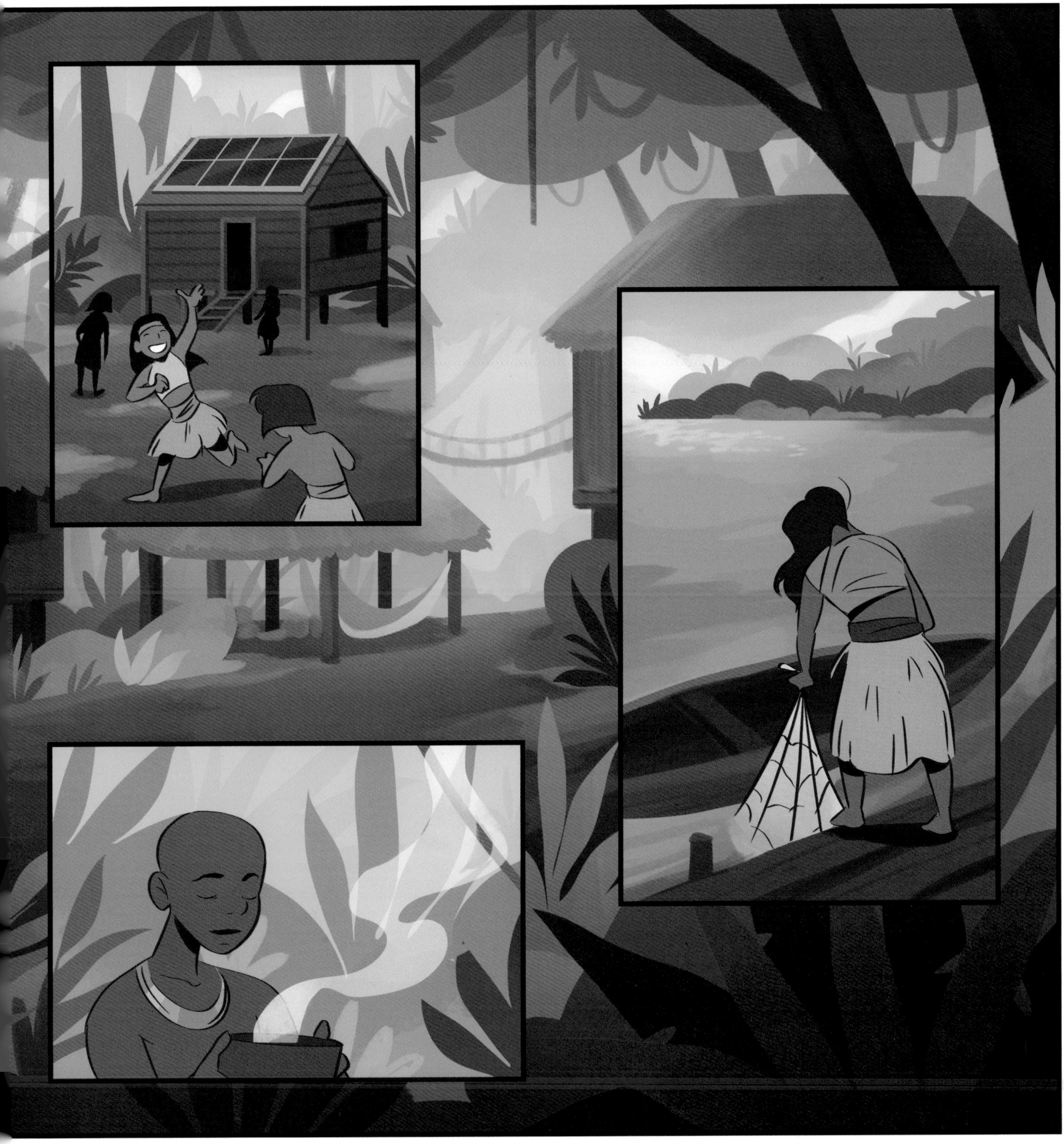

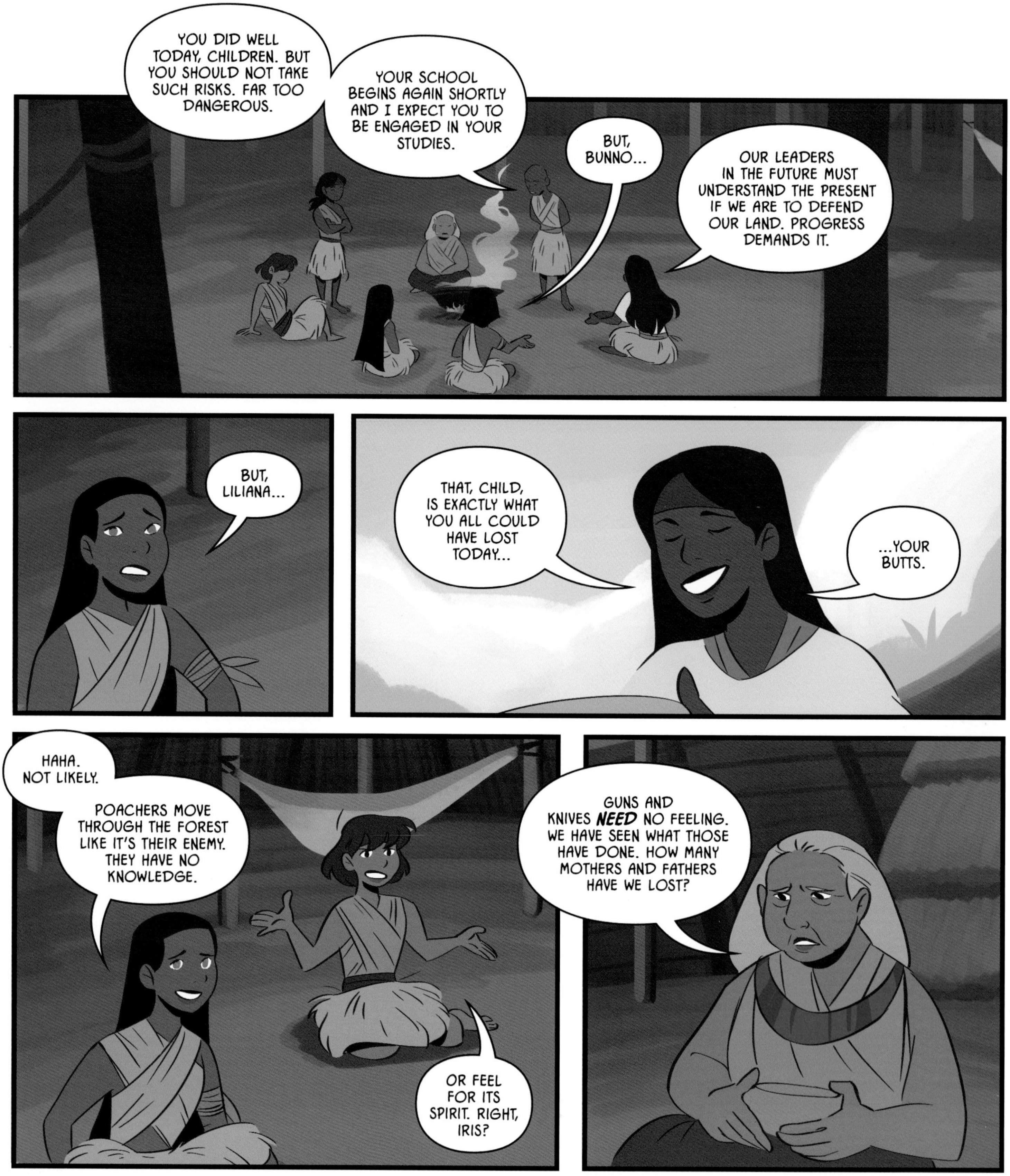
YOU DID WELL TODAY, CHILDREN. BUT YOU SHOULD NOT TAKE SUCH RISKS. FAR TOO DANGEROUS.
YOUR SCHOOL BEGINS AGAIN SHORTLY AND I EXPECT YOU TO BE ENGAGED IN YOUR STUDIES.
BUT, BUNNO...
OUR LEADERS IN THE FUTURE MUST UNDERSTAND THE PRESENT IF WE ARE TO DEFEND OUR LAND. PROGRESS DEMANDS IT.
BUT, LILIANA...
THAT, CHILD, IS EXACTLY WHAT YOU ALL COULD HAVE LOST TODAY...
...YOUR BUTTS.
HAHA. NOT LIKELY.
POACHERS MOVE THROUGH THE FOREST LIKE IT'S THEIR ENEMY. THEY HAVE NO KNOWLEDGE.
OR FEEL FOR ITS SPIRIT. RIGHT, IRIS?
GUNS AND KNIVES ***NEED*** NO FEELING. WE HAVE SEEN WHAT THOSE HAVE DONE. HOW MANY MOTHERS AND FATHERS HAVE WE LOST?

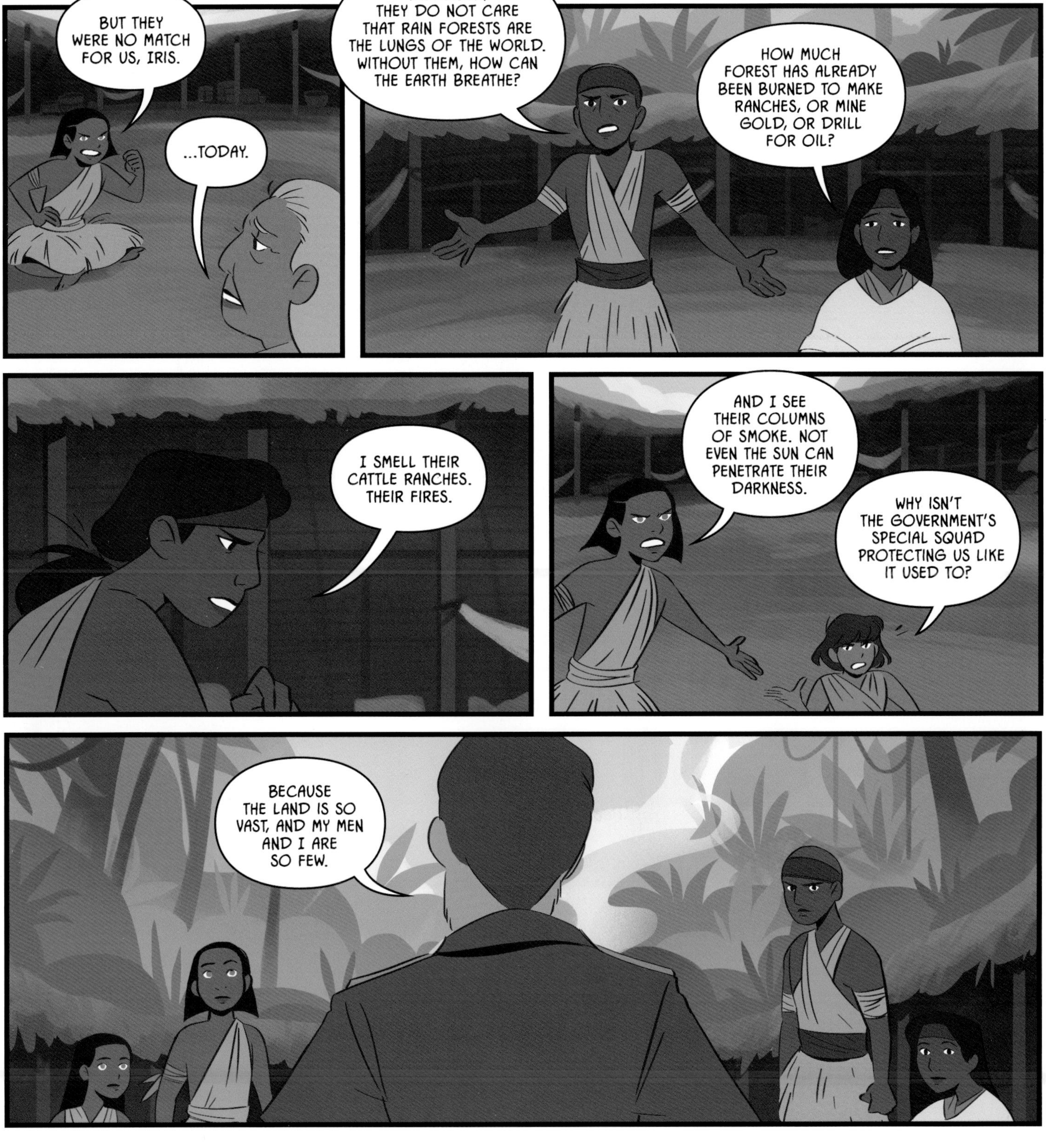
BUT THEY WERE NO MATCH FOR US, IRIS.
...TODAY.
REMEMBER, THEY DO NOT CARE THAT RAIN FORESTS ARE THE LUNGS OF THE WORLD. WITHOUT THEM, HOW CAN THE EARTH BREATHE?
HOW MUCH FOREST HAS ALREADY BEEN BURNED TO MAKE RANCHES, OR MINE GOLD, OR DRILL FOR OIL?
I SMELL THEIR CATTLE RANCHES. THEIR FIRES.
AND I SEE THEIR COLUMNS OF SMOKE. NOT EVEN THE SUN CAN PENETRATE THEIR DARKNESS.
WHY ISN'T THE GOVERNMENT'S SPECIAL SQUAD PROTECTING US LIKE IT USED TO?
BECAUSE THE LAND IS SO VAST, AND MY MEN AND I ARE SO FEW.

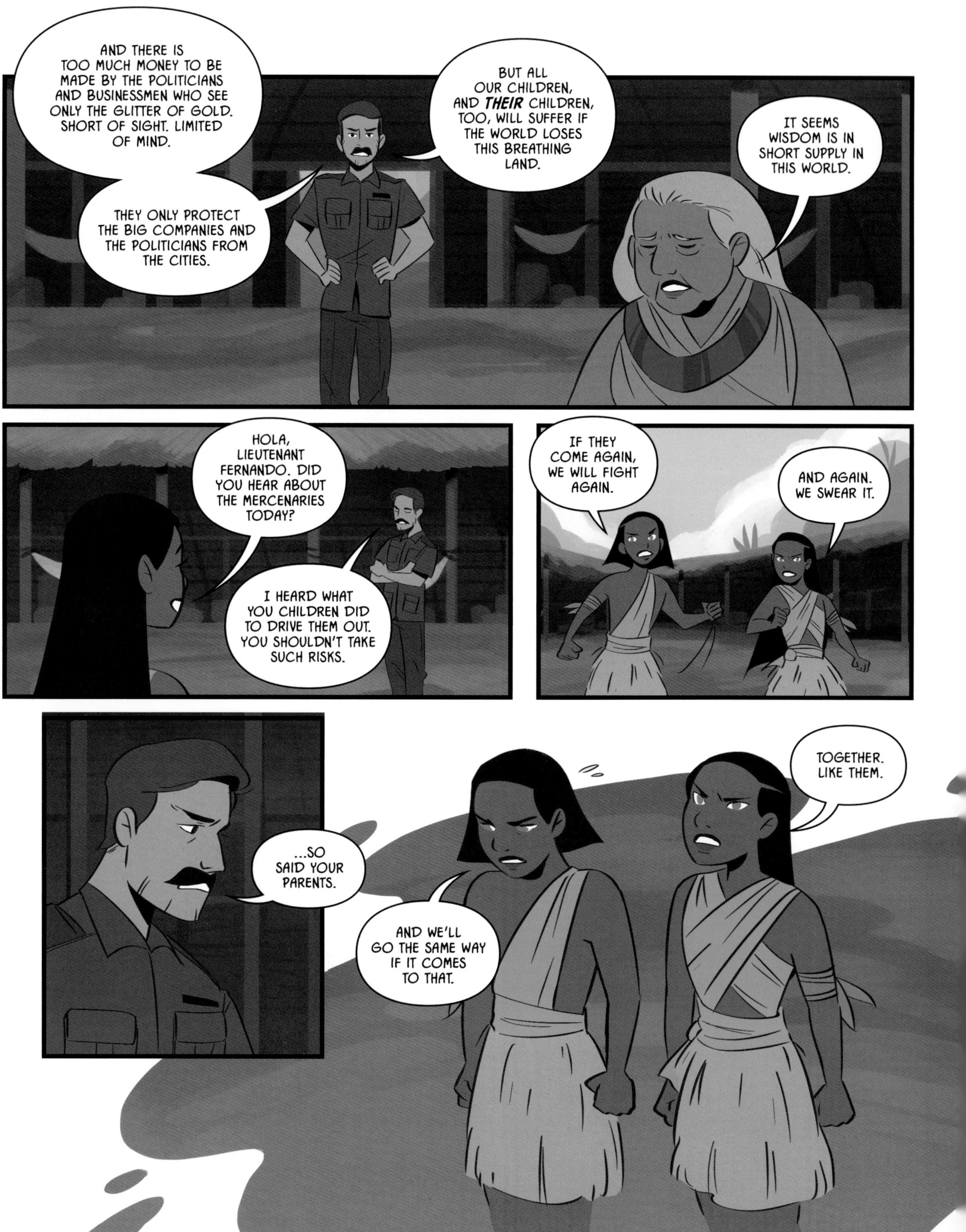
AND THERE IS TOO MUCH MONEY TO BE MADE BY THE POLITICIANS AND BUSINESSMEN WHO SEE ONLY THE GLITTER OF GOLD. SHORT OF SIGHT. LIMITED OF MIND.
THEY ONLY PROTECT THE BIG COMPANIES AND THE POLITICIANS FROM THE CITIES.
BUT ALL OUR CHILDREN, AND *THEIR* CHILDREN, TOO, WILL SUFFER IF THE WORLD LOSES THIS BREATHING LAND.
IT SEEMS WISDOM IS IN SHORT SUPPLY IN THIS WORLD.
HOLA, LIEUTENANT FERNANDO. DID YOU HEAR ABOUT THE MERCENARIES TODAY?
I HEARD WHAT YOU CHILDREN DID TO DRIVE THEM OUT. YOU SHOULDN'T TAKE SUCH RISKS.
IF THEY COME AGAIN, WE WILL FIGHT AGAIN.
AND AGAIN. WE SWEAR IT.
...SO SAID YOUR PARENTS.
AND WE'LL GO THE SAME WAY IF IT COMES TO THAT.
TOGETHER. LIKE THEM.

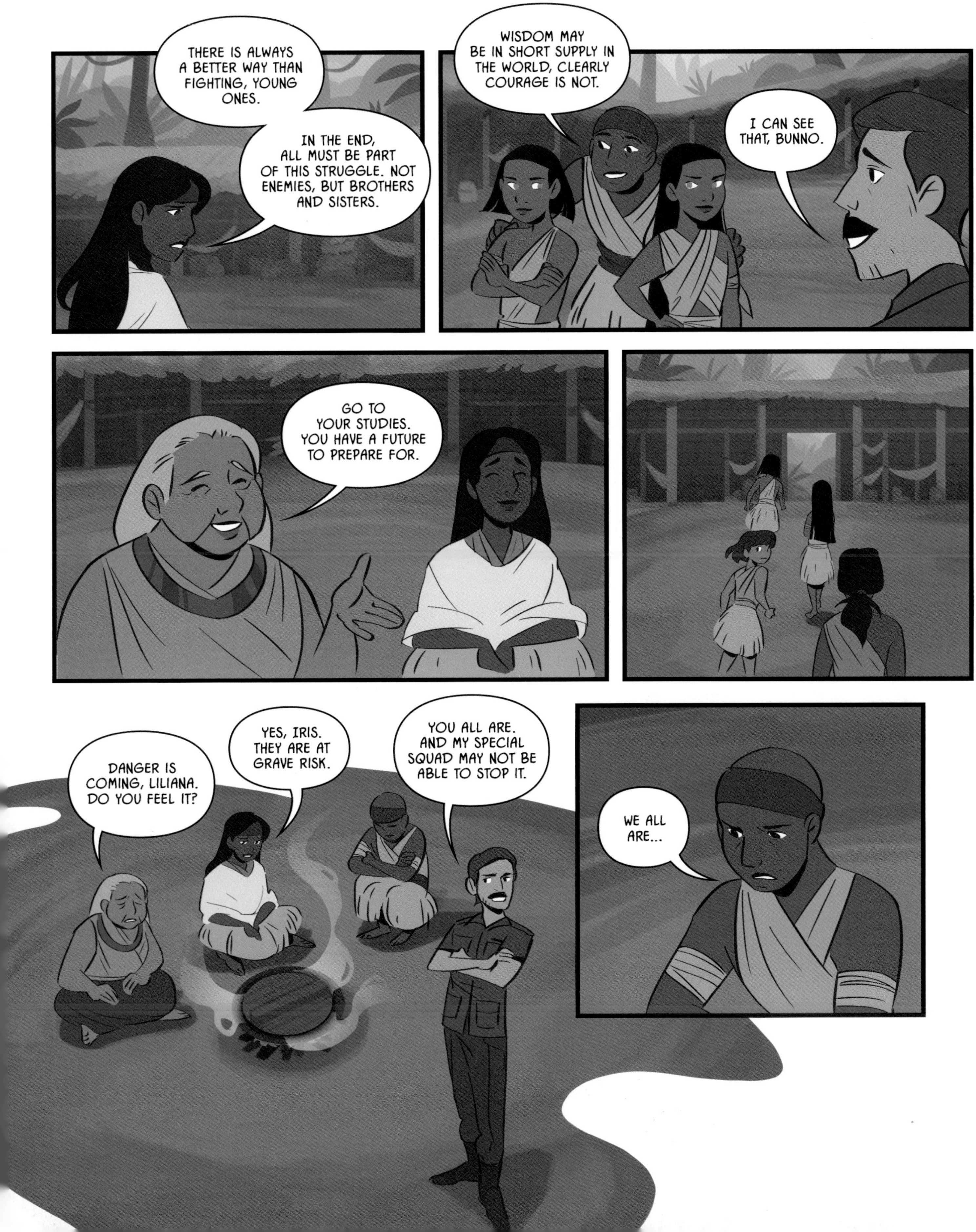
THERE IS ALWAYS A BETTER WAY THAN FIGHTING, YOUNG ONES.
IN THE END, ALL MUST BE PART OF THIS STRUGGLE. NOT ENEMIES, BUT BROTHERS AND SISTERS.
WISDOM MAY BE IN SHORT SUPPLY IN THE WORLD, CLEARLY COURAGE IS NOT.
I CAN SEE THAT, BUNNO.
GO TO YOUR STUDIES. YOU HAVE A FUTURE TO PREPARE FOR.
DANGER IS COMING, LILIANA. DO YOU FEEL IT?
YES, IRIS. THEY ARE AT GRAVE RISK.
YOU ALL ARE. AND MY SPECIAL SQUAD MAY NOT BE ABLE TO STOP IT.
WE ALL ARE...

CHAPTER 4

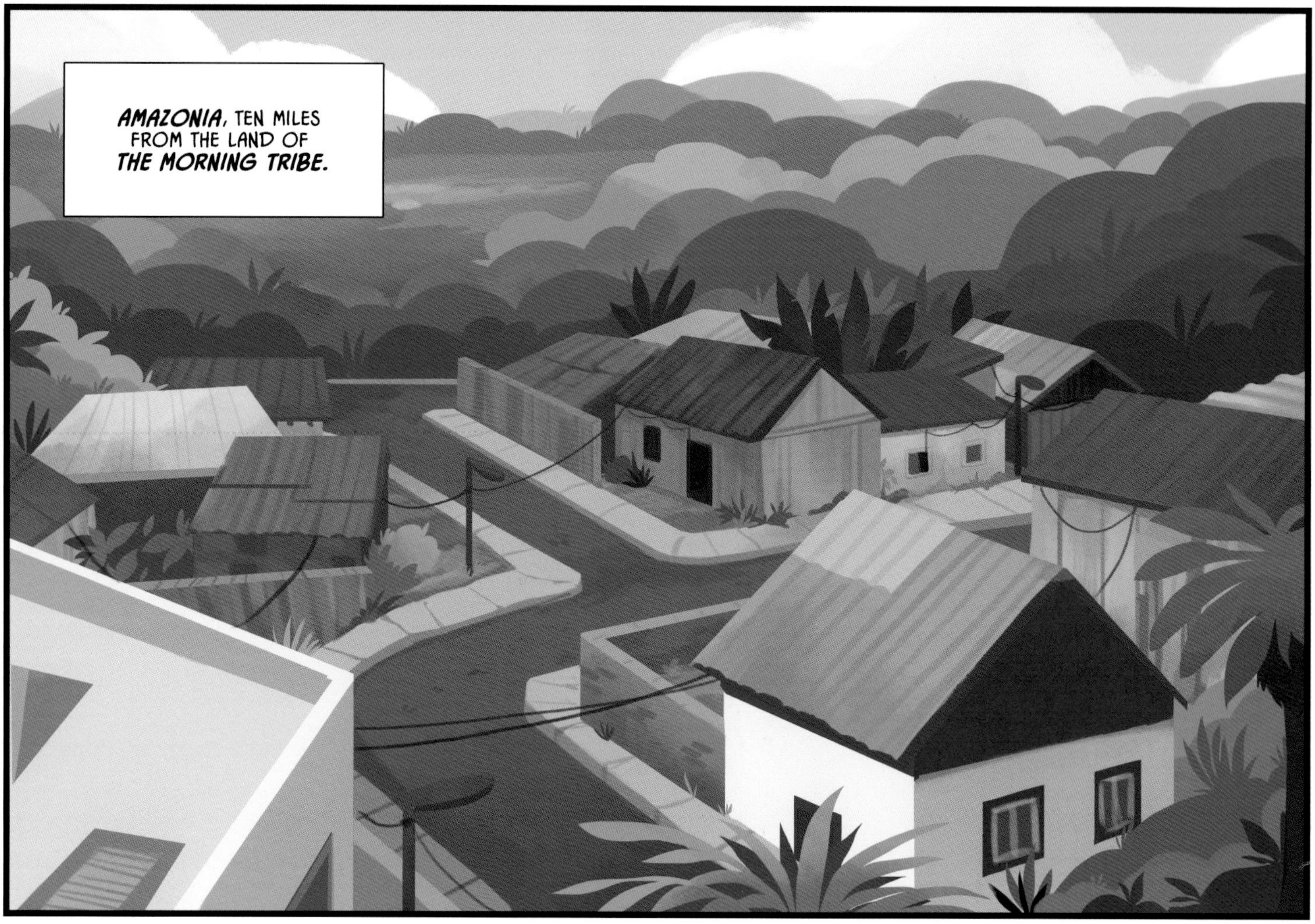
AMAZONIA, TEN MILES FROM THE LAND OF THE MORNING TRIBE.

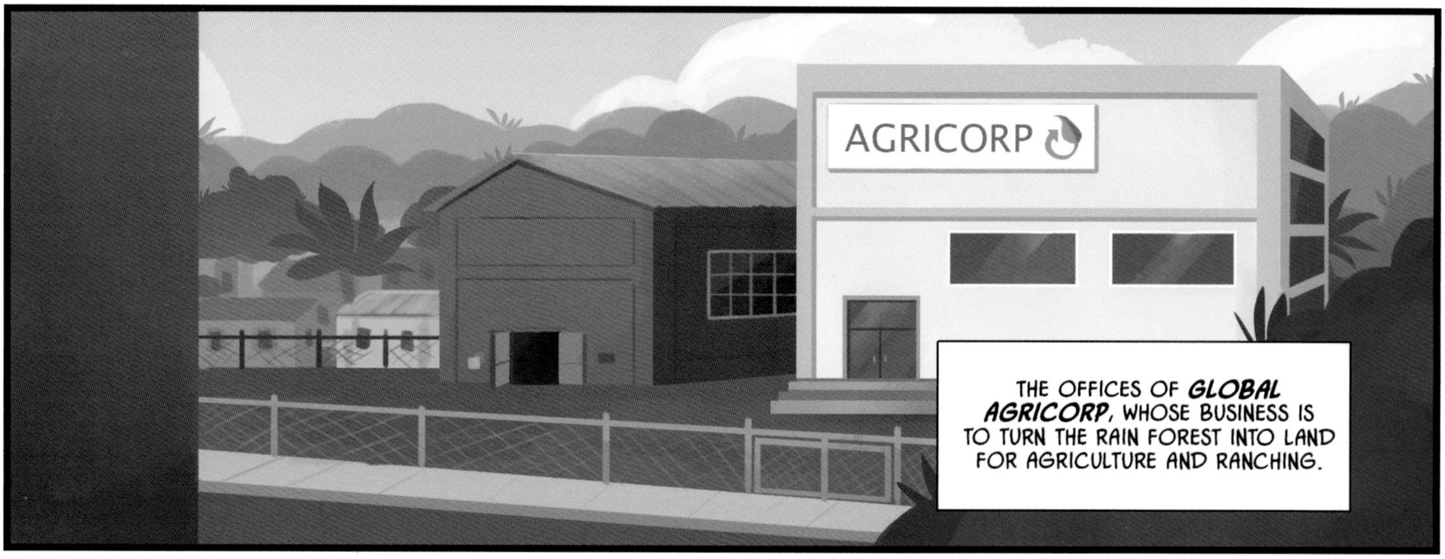
AGRICORP
THE OFFICES OF GLOBAL AGRICORP, WHOSE BUSINESS IS TO TURN THE RAIN FOREST INTO LAND FOR AGRICULTURE AND RANCHING.

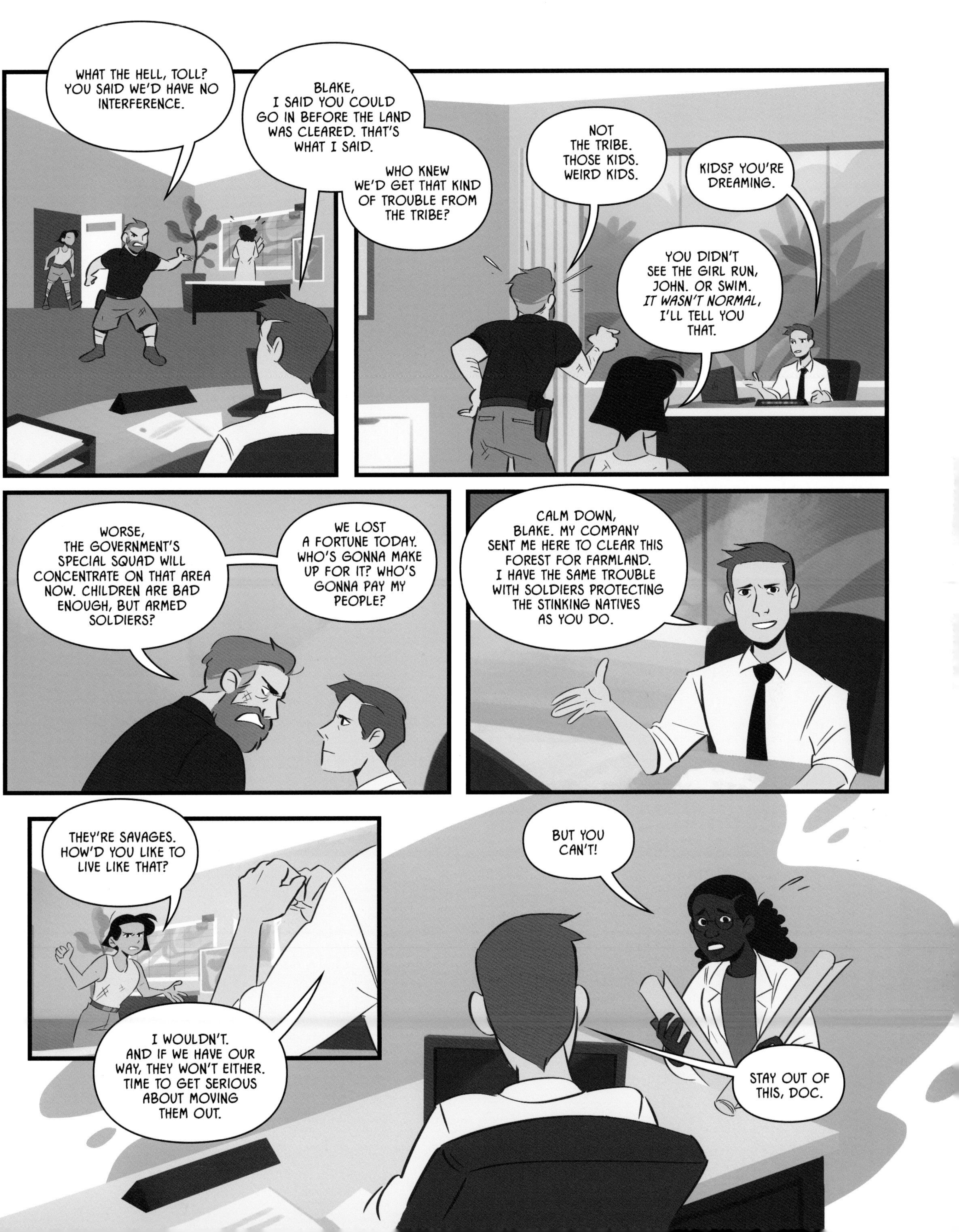
WHAT THE HELL, TOLL? YOU SAID WE'D HAVE NO INTERFERENCE.
BLAKE, I SAID YOU COULD GO IN BEFORE THE LAND WAS CLEARED. THAT'S WHAT I SAID.
WHO KNEW WE'D GET THAT KIND OF TROUBLE FROM THE TRIBE?
NOT THE TRIBE. THOSE KIDS. WEIRD KIDS.
KIDS? YOU'RE DREAMING.
YOU DIDN'T SEE THE GIRL RUN, JOHN. OR SWIM. *IT WASN'T NORMAL*, I'LL TELL YOU THAT.
WORSE, THE GOVERNMENT'S SPECIAL SQUAD WILL CONCENTRATE ON THAT AREA NOW. CHILDREN ARE BAD ENOUGH, BUT ARMED SOLDIERS?
WE LOST A FORTUNE TODAY. WHO'S GONNA MAKE UP FOR IT? WHO'S GONNA PAY MY PEOPLE?
CALM DOWN, BLAKE. MY COMPANY SENT ME HERE TO CLEAR THIS FOREST FOR FARMLAND. I HAVE THE SAME TROUBLE WITH SOLDIERS PROTECTING THE STINKING NATIVES AS YOU DO.
THEY'RE SAVAGES. HOW'D YOU LIKE TO LIVE LIKE THAT?
I WOULDN'T. AND IF WE HAVE OUR WAY, THEY WON'T EITHER. TIME TO GET SERIOUS ABOUT MOVING THEM OUT.
BUT YOU CAN'T!
STAY OUT OF THIS, DOC.

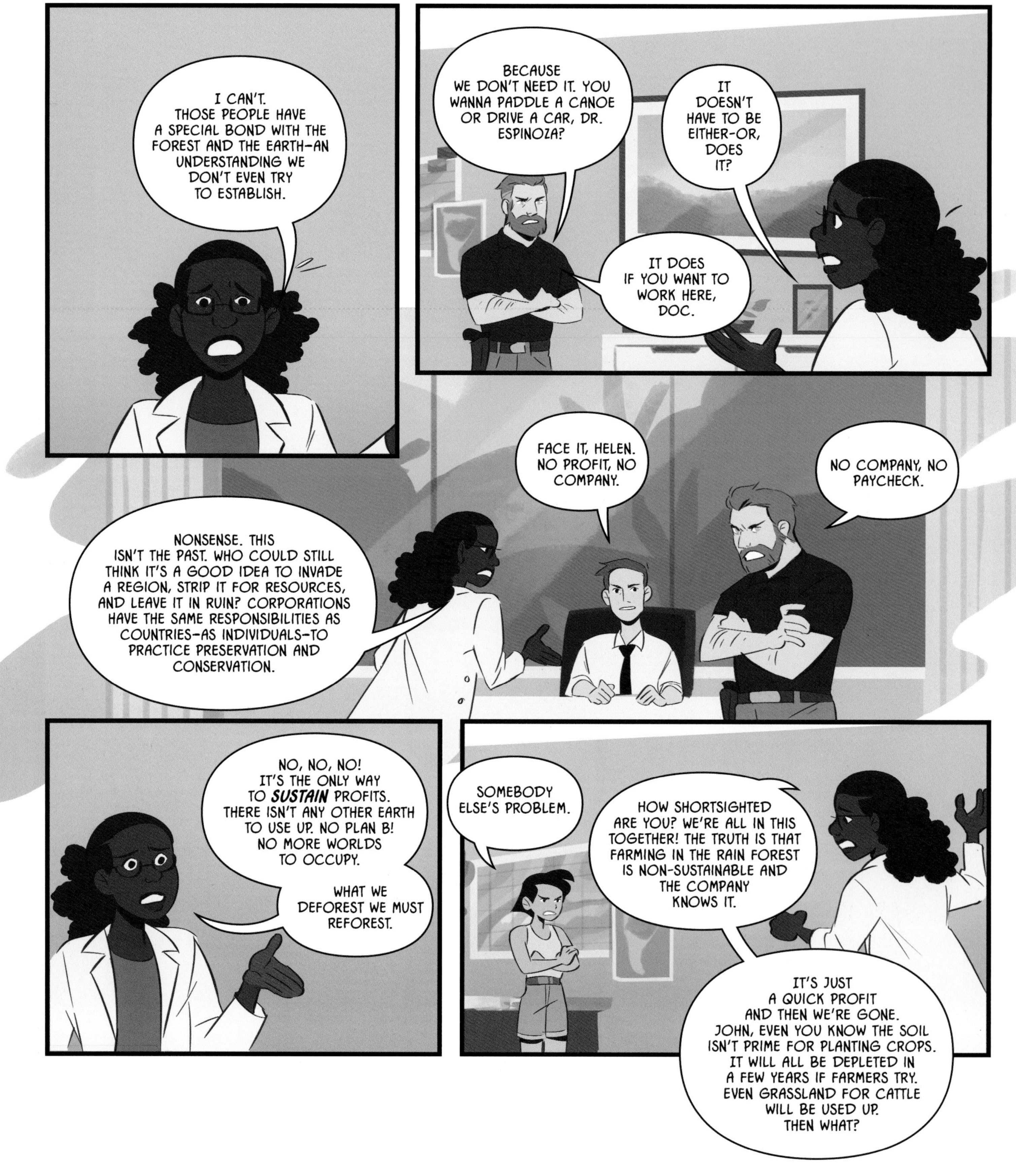
I CAN'T. THOSE PEOPLE HAVE A SPECIAL BOND WITH THE FOREST AND THE EARTH—AN UNDERSTANDING WE DON'T EVEN TRY TO ESTABLISH.
BECAUSE WE DON'T NEED IT. YOU WANNA PADDLE A CANOE OR DRIVE A CAR, DR. ESPINOZA?
IT DOESN'T HAVE TO BE EITHER-OR, DOES IT?
IT DOES IF YOU WANT TO WORK HERE, DOC.
NONSENSE. THIS ISN'T THE PAST. WHO COULD STILL THINK IT'S A GOOD IDEA TO INVADE A REGION, STRIP IT FOR RESOURCES, AND LEAVE IT IN RUIN? CORPORATIONS HAVE THE SAME RESPONSIBILITIES AS COUNTRIES—AS INDIVIDUALS—TO PRACTICE PRESERVATION AND CONSERVATION.
FACE IT, HELEN. NO PROFIT, NO COMPANY.
NO COMPANY, NO PAYCHECK.
NO, NO, NO! IT'S THE ONLY WAY TO **SUSTAIN** PROFITS. THERE ISN'T ANY OTHER EARTH TO USE UP. NO PLAN B! NO MORE WORLDS TO OCCUPY.
WHAT WE DEFOREST WE MUST REFOREST.
SOMEBODY ELSE'S PROBLEM.
HOW SHORTSIGHTED ARE YOU? WE'RE ALL IN THIS TOGETHER! THE TRUTH IS THAT FARMING IN THE RAIN FOREST IS NON-SUSTAINABLE AND THE COMPANY KNOWS IT.
IT'S JUST A QUICK PROFIT AND THEN WE'RE GONE. JOHN, EVEN YOU KNOW THE SOIL ISN'T PRIME FOR PLANTING CROPS. IT WILL ALL BE DEPLETED IN A FEW YEARS IF FARMERS TRY. EVEN GRASSLAND FOR CATTLE WILL BE USED UP. THEN WHAT?

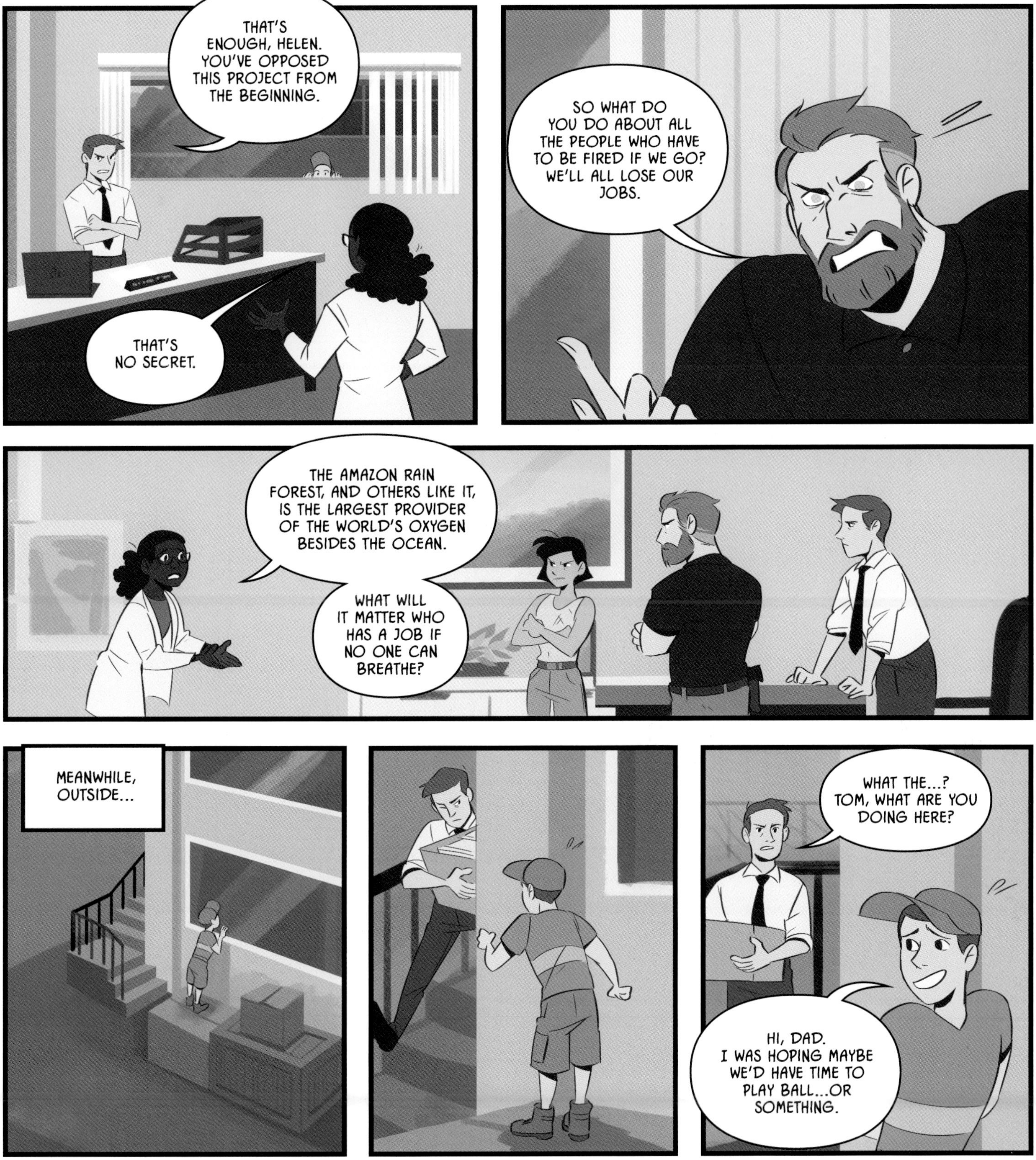
THAT'S ENOUGH, HELEN. YOU'VE OPPOSED THIS PROJECT FROM THE BEGINNING.
THAT'S NO SECRET.
SO WHAT DO YOU DO ABOUT ALL THE PEOPLE WHO HAVE TO BE FIRED IF WE GO? WE'LL ALL LOSE OUR JOBS.
THE AMAZON RAIN FOREST, AND OTHERS LIKE IT, IS THE LARGEST PROVIDER OF THE WORLD'S OXYGEN BESIDES THE OCEAN.
WHAT WILL IT MATTER WHO HAS A JOB IF NO ONE CAN BREATHE?
MEANWHILE, OUTSIDE...
WHAT THE...? TOM, WHAT ARE YOU DOING HERE?
HI, DAD. I WAS HOPING MAYBE WE'D HAVE TIME TO PLAY BALL...OR SOMETHING.

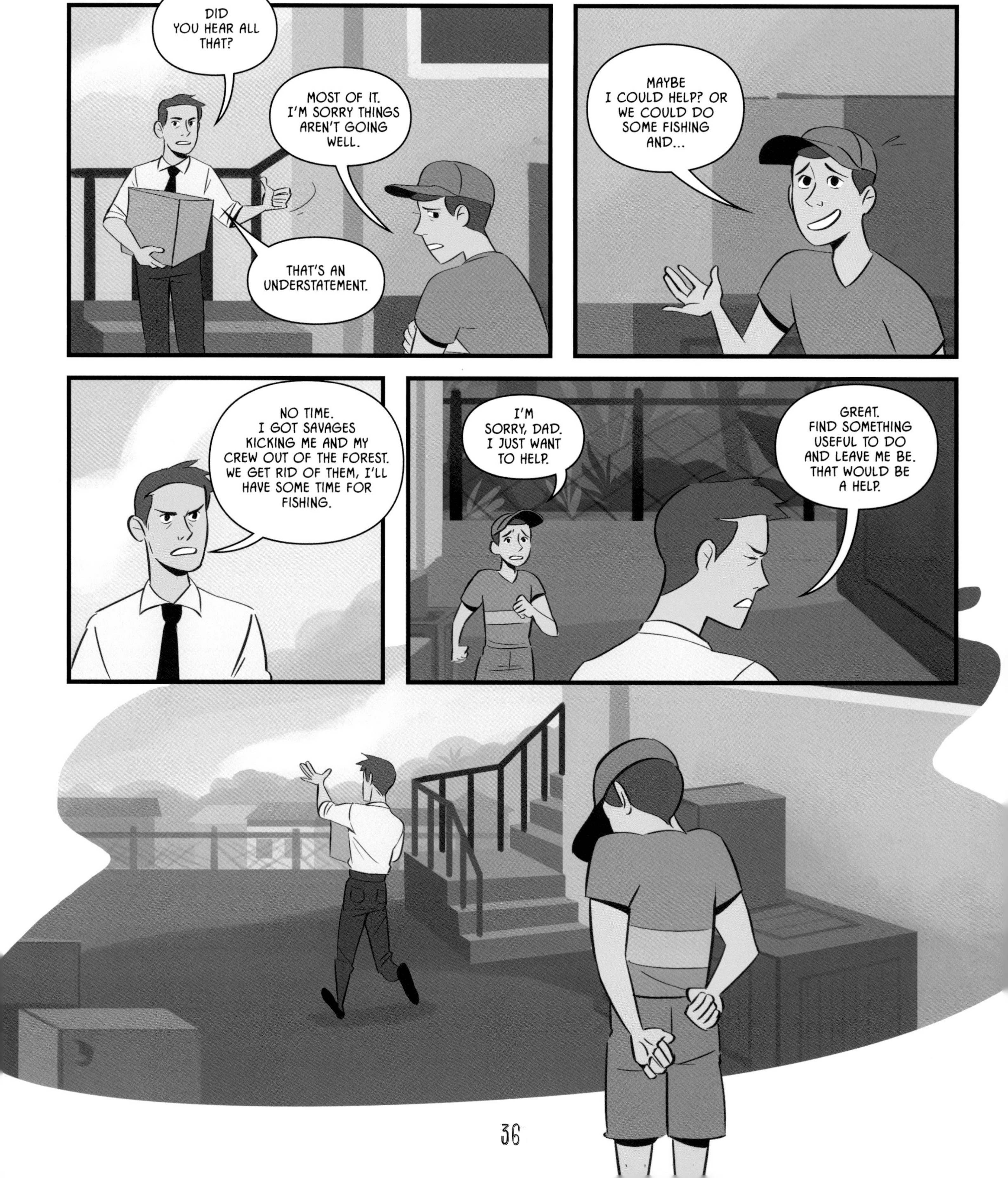
DID YOU HEAR ALL THAT?
MOST OF IT. I'M SORRY THINGS AREN'T GOING WELL.
THAT'S AN UNDERSTATEMENT.
MAYBE I COULD HELP? OR WE COULD DO SOME FISHING AND...
NO TIME. I GOT SAVAGES KICKING ME AND MY CREW OUT OF THE FOREST. WE GET RID OF THEM, I'LL HAVE SOME TIME FOR FISHING.
I'M SORRY, DAD. I JUST WANT TO HELP.
GREAT. FIND SOMETHING USEFUL TO DO AND LEAVE ME BE. THAT WOULD BE A HELP.

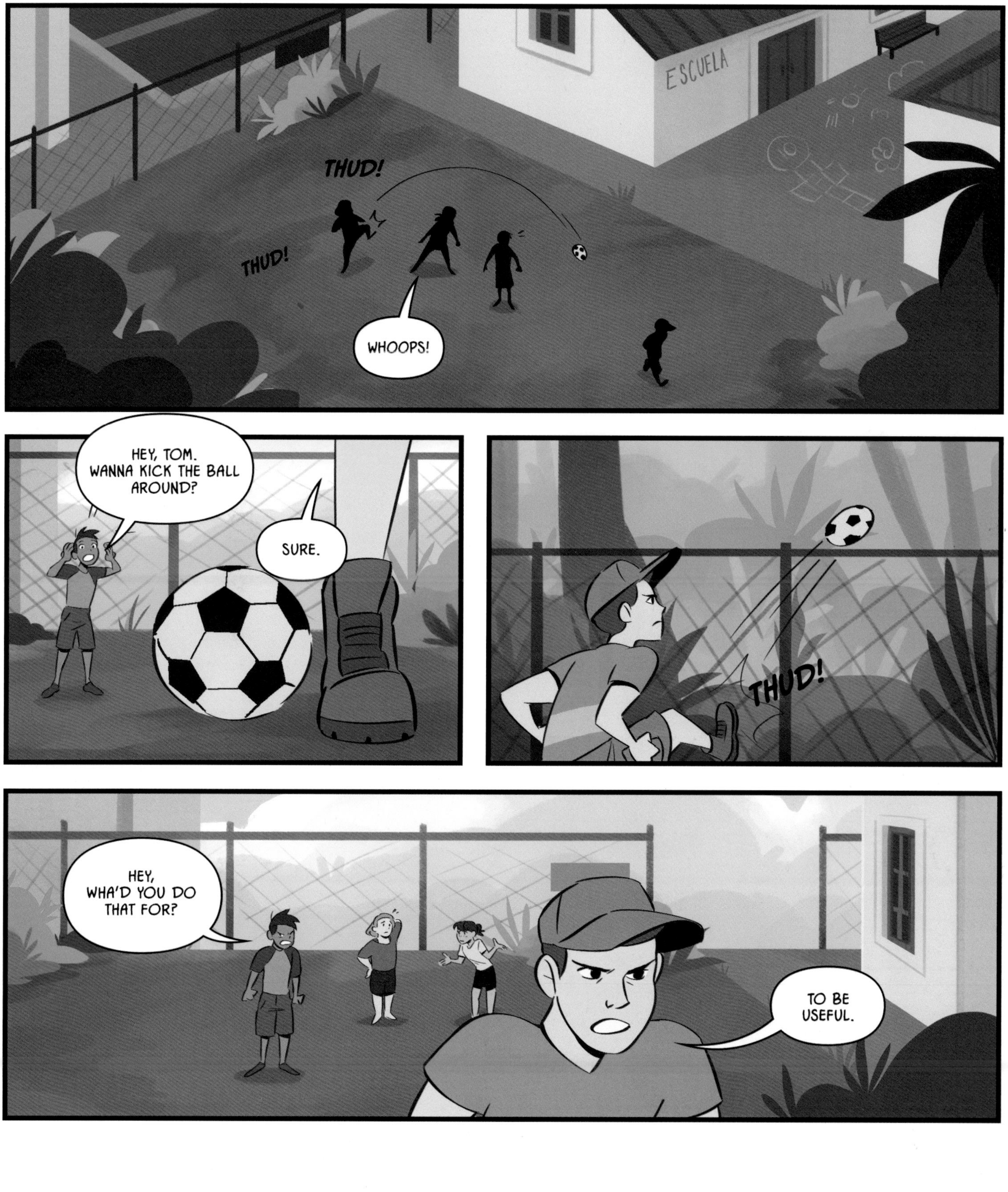
ESCUELA
THUD!
THUD!
WHOOPS!
HEY, TOM. WANNA KICK THE BALL AROUND?
SURE.
THUD!
HEY, WHA'D YOU DO THAT FOR?
TO BE USEFUL.

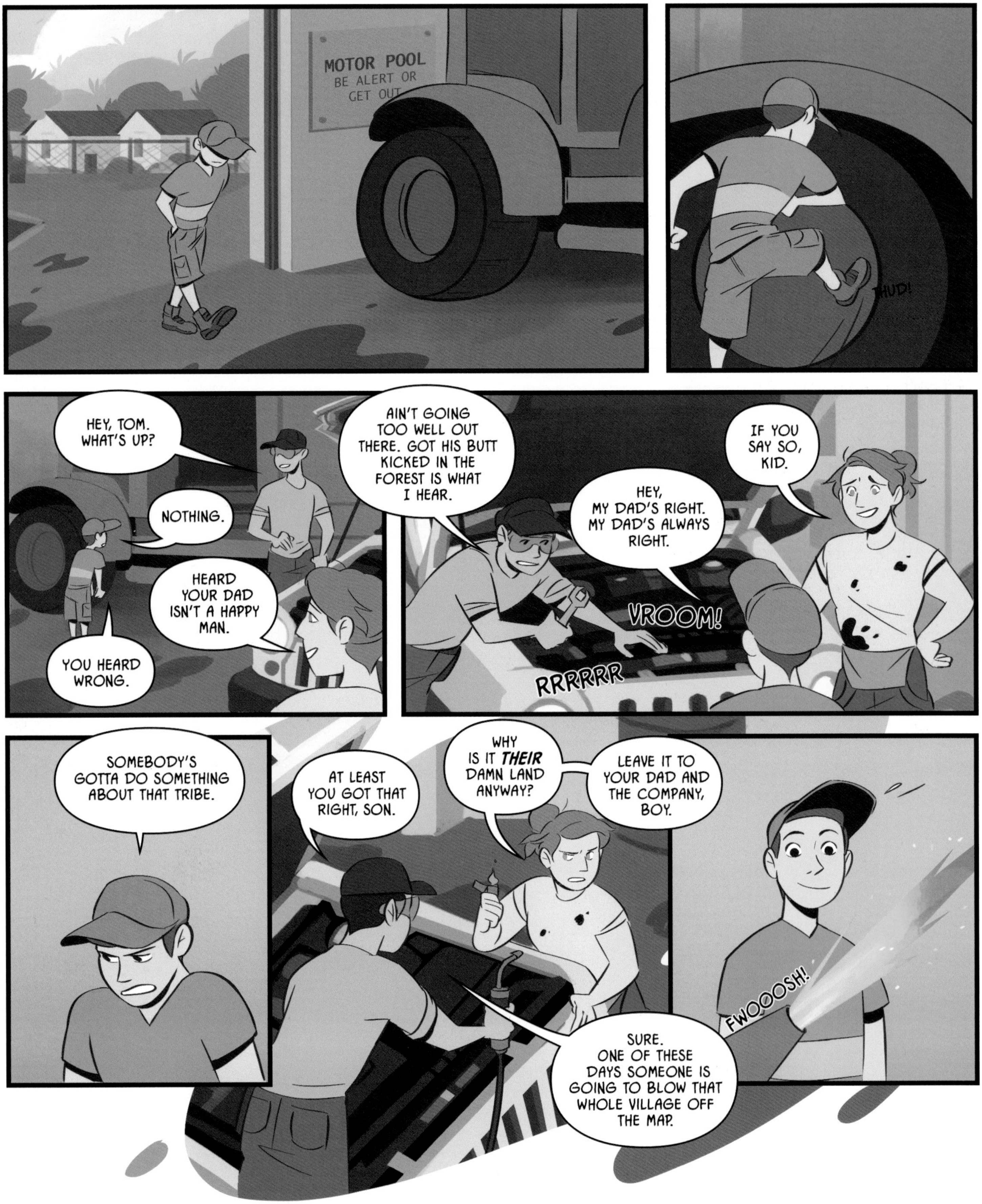
MOTOR POOL
BE ALERT OR GET OUT
THUD!
HEY, TOM. WHAT'S UP?
NOTHING.
HEARD YOUR DAD ISN'T A HAPPY MAN.
YOU HEARD WRONG.
AIN'T GOING TOO WELL OUT THERE. GOT HIS BUTT KICKED IN THE FOREST IS WHAT I HEAR.
HEY, MY DAD'S RIGHT. MY DAD'S ALWAYS RIGHT.
IF YOU SAY SO, KID.
VROOM!
RRRRRR
SOMEBODY'S GOTTA DO SOMETHING ABOUT THAT TRIBE.
AT LEAST YOU GOT THAT RIGHT, SON.
WHY IS IT *THEIR* DAMN LAND ANYWAY?
LEAVE IT TO YOUR DAD AND THE COMPANY, BOY.
FWOOOSH!
SURE. ONE OF THESE DAYS SOMEONE IS GOING TO BLOW THAT WHOLE VILLAGE OFF THE MAP.

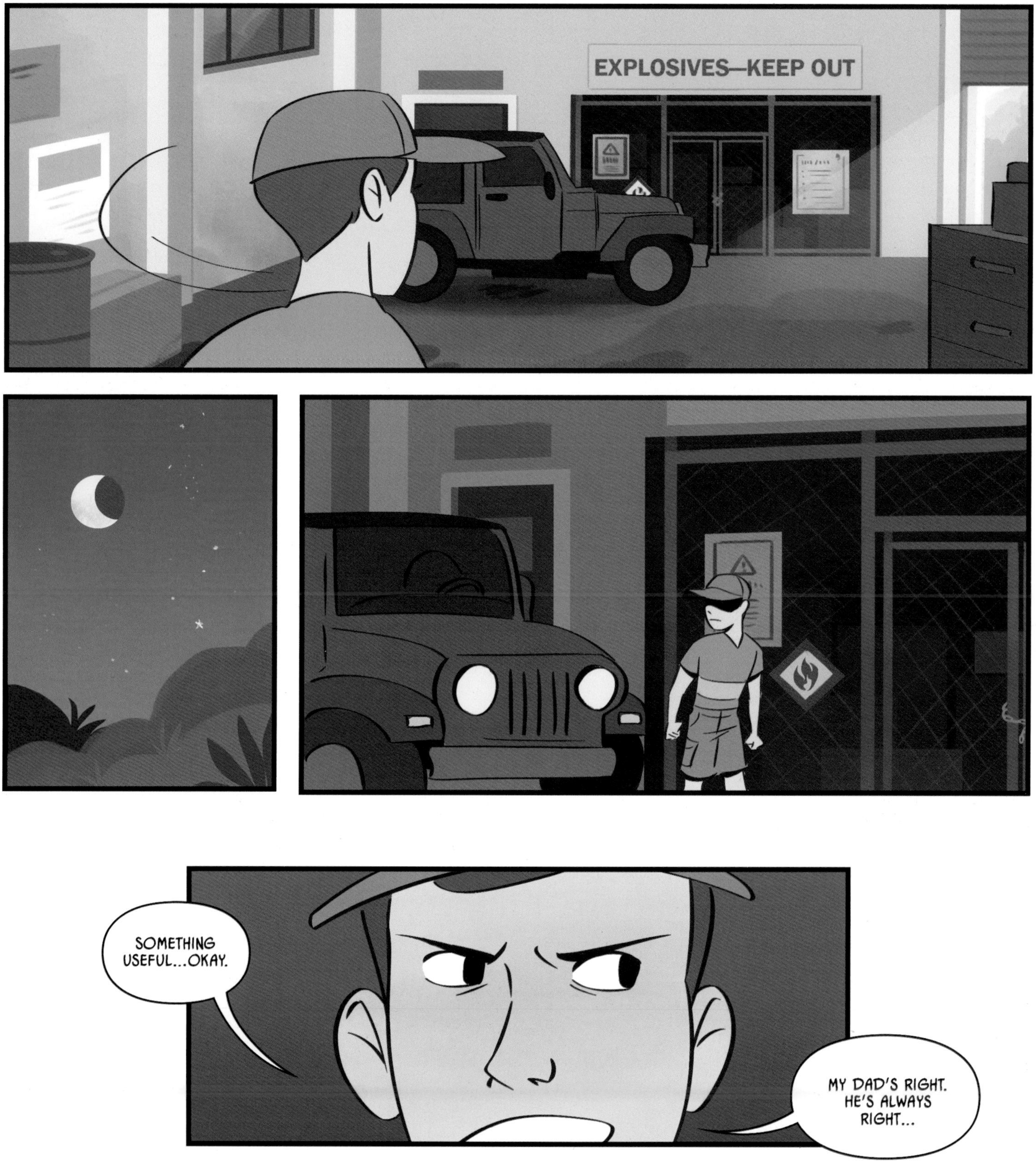
EXPLOSIVES—KEEP OUT
SOMETHING USEFUL...OKAY.
MY DAD'S RIGHT. HE'S ALWAYS RIGHT...

CHAPTER 5

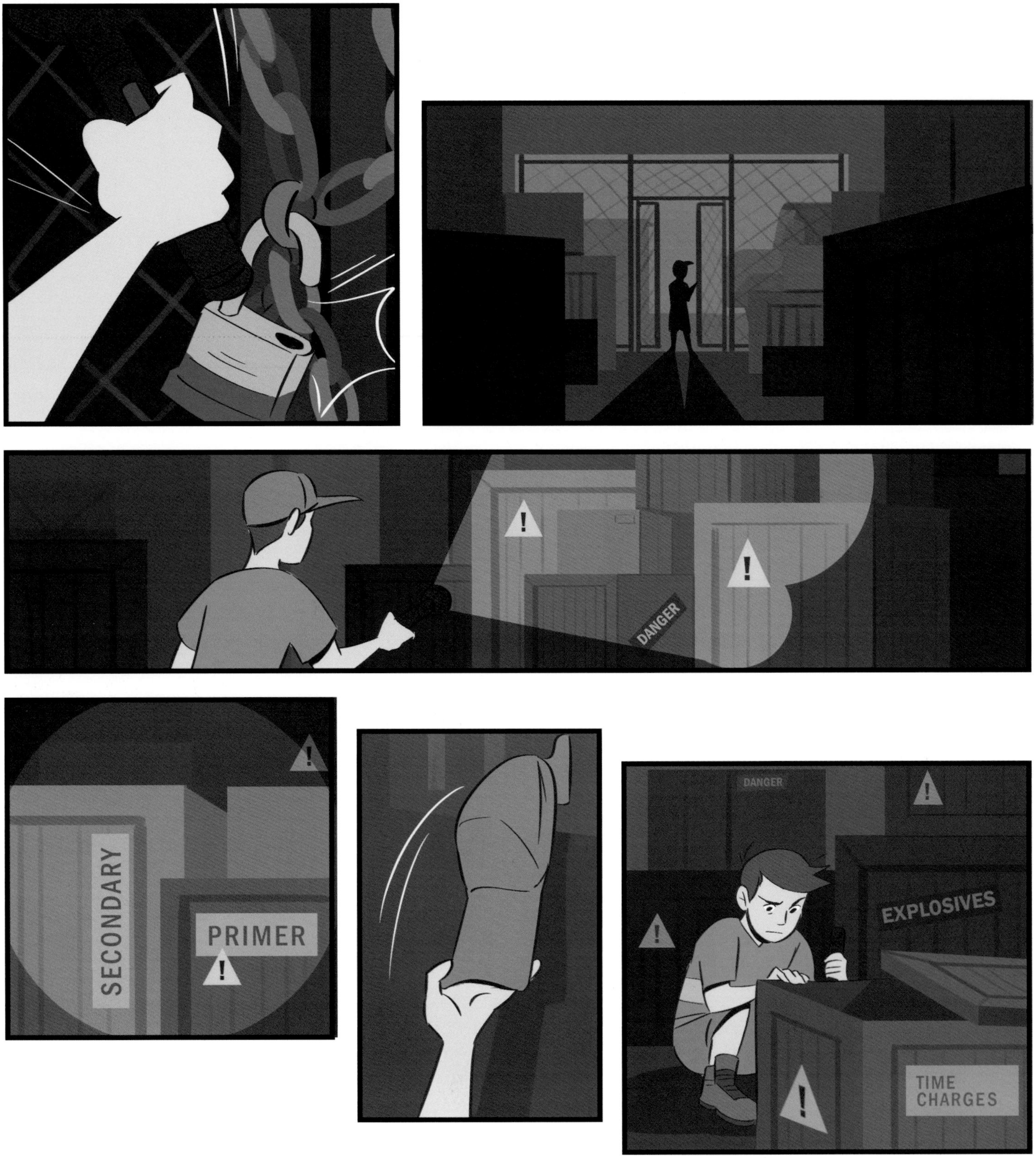
DANGER
SECONDARY
PRIMER
DANGER
EXPLOSIVES
TIME CHARGES

THEY'RE SET FOR 15 SECONDS. THAT OUGHT TO DO IT.

YOU WAIT RIGHT THERE.

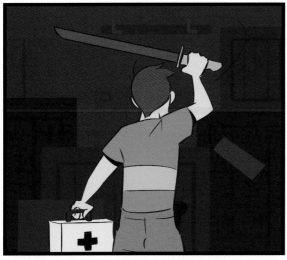

HERE COMES TOM TOLL!

GET READY FOR JOHN TOLL'S KID, SAVAGES.

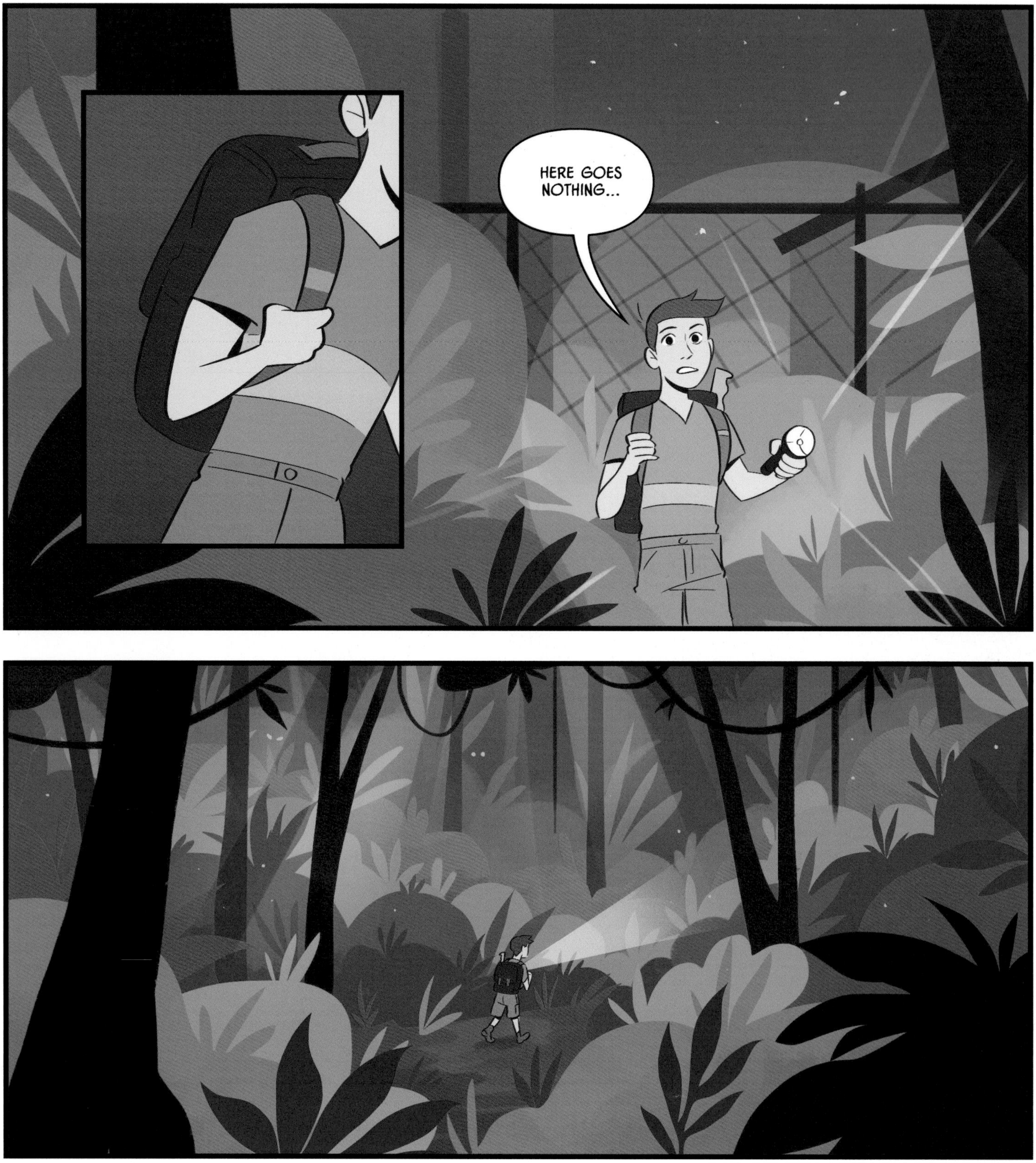
HERE GOES NOTHING...

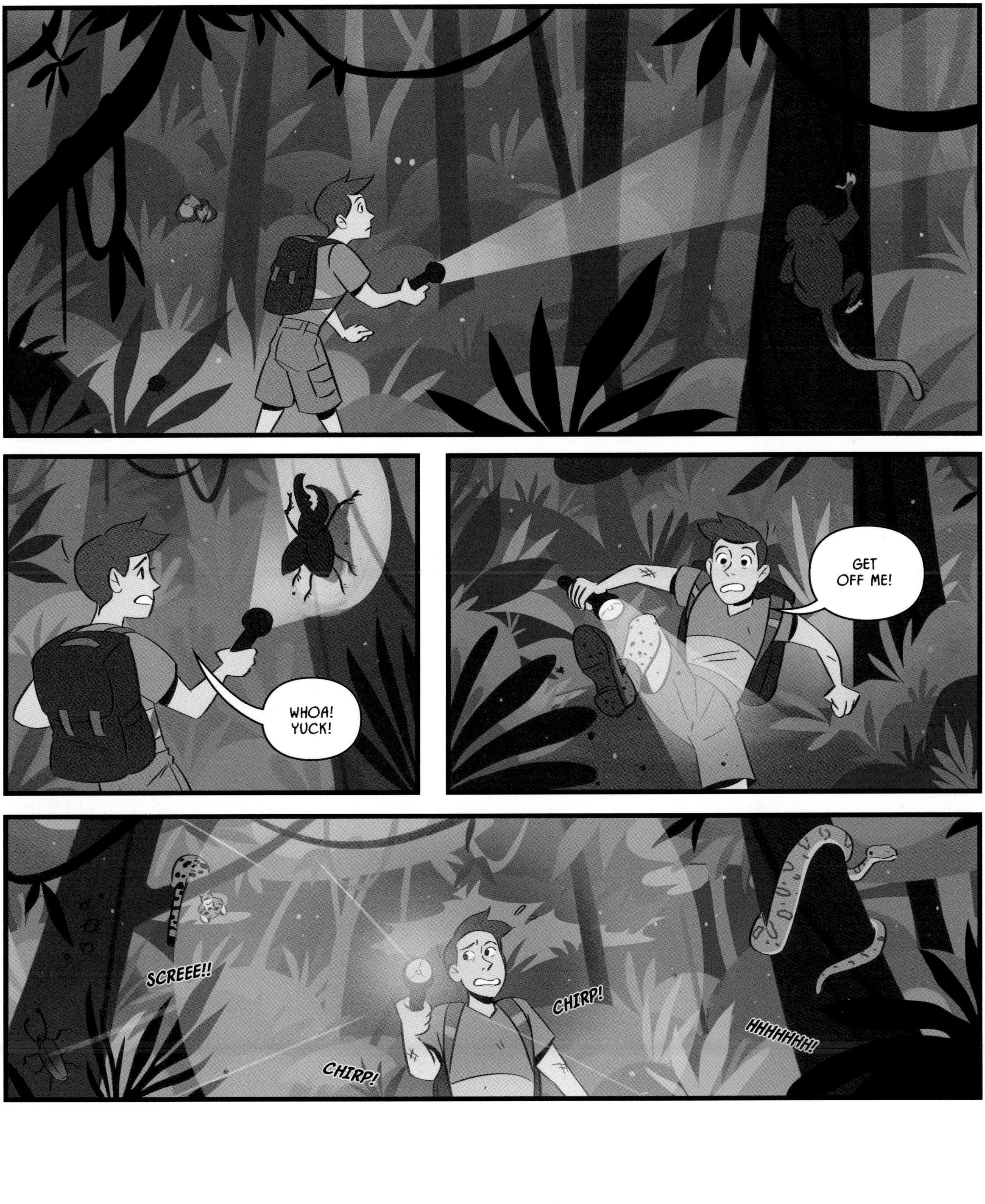
WHOA! YUCK!
GET OFF ME!
SCREEE!!
CHIRP!
CHIRP!
HHHHHHH!

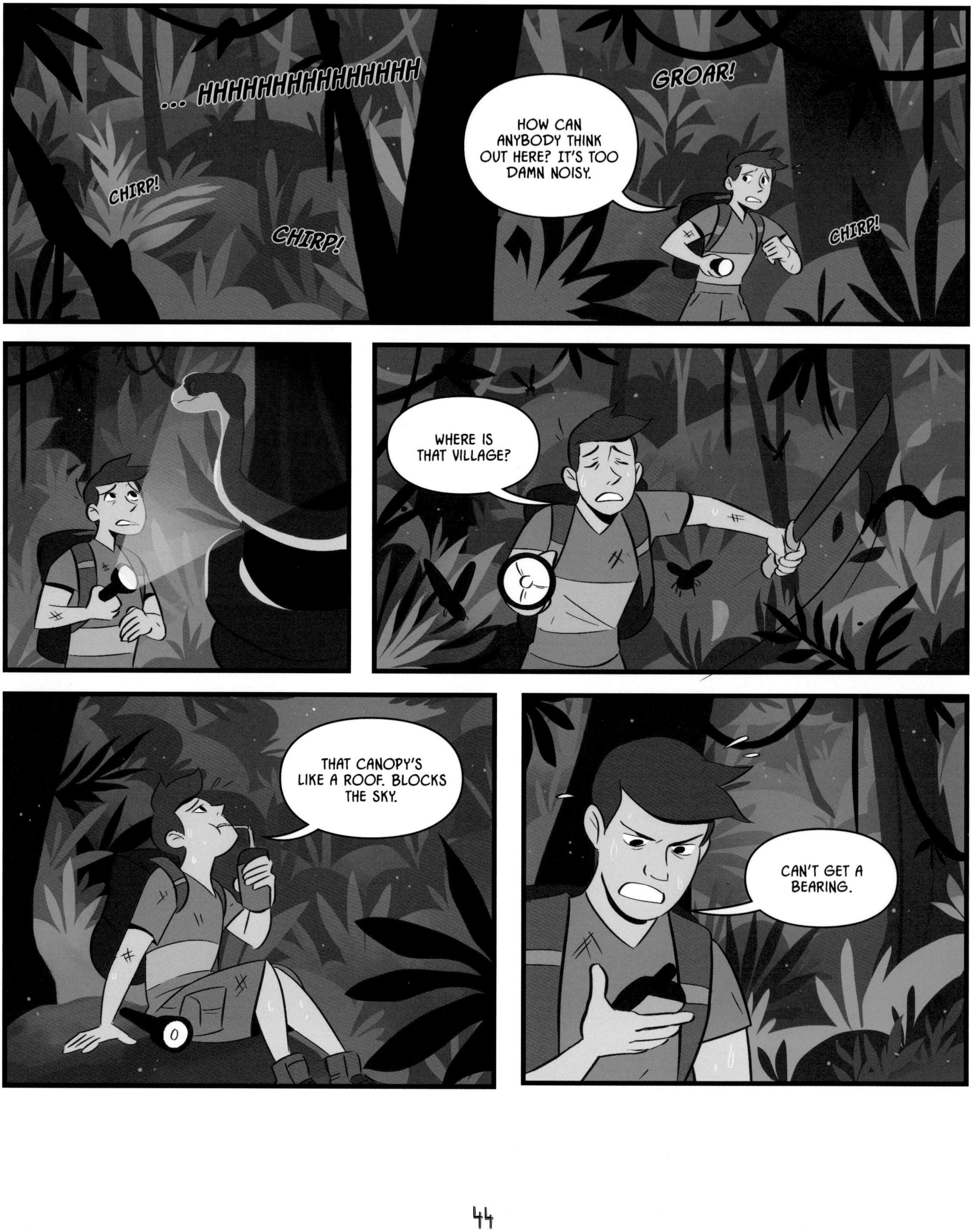
... HHHHHHHHHHHHHHH
CHIRP!
CHIRP!
HOW CAN ANYBODY THINK OUT HERE? IT'S TOO DAMN NOISY.
GROAR!
CHIRP!
WHERE IS THAT VILLAGE?
THAT CANOPY'S LIKE A ROOF. BLOCKS THE SKY.
CAN'T GET A BEARING.

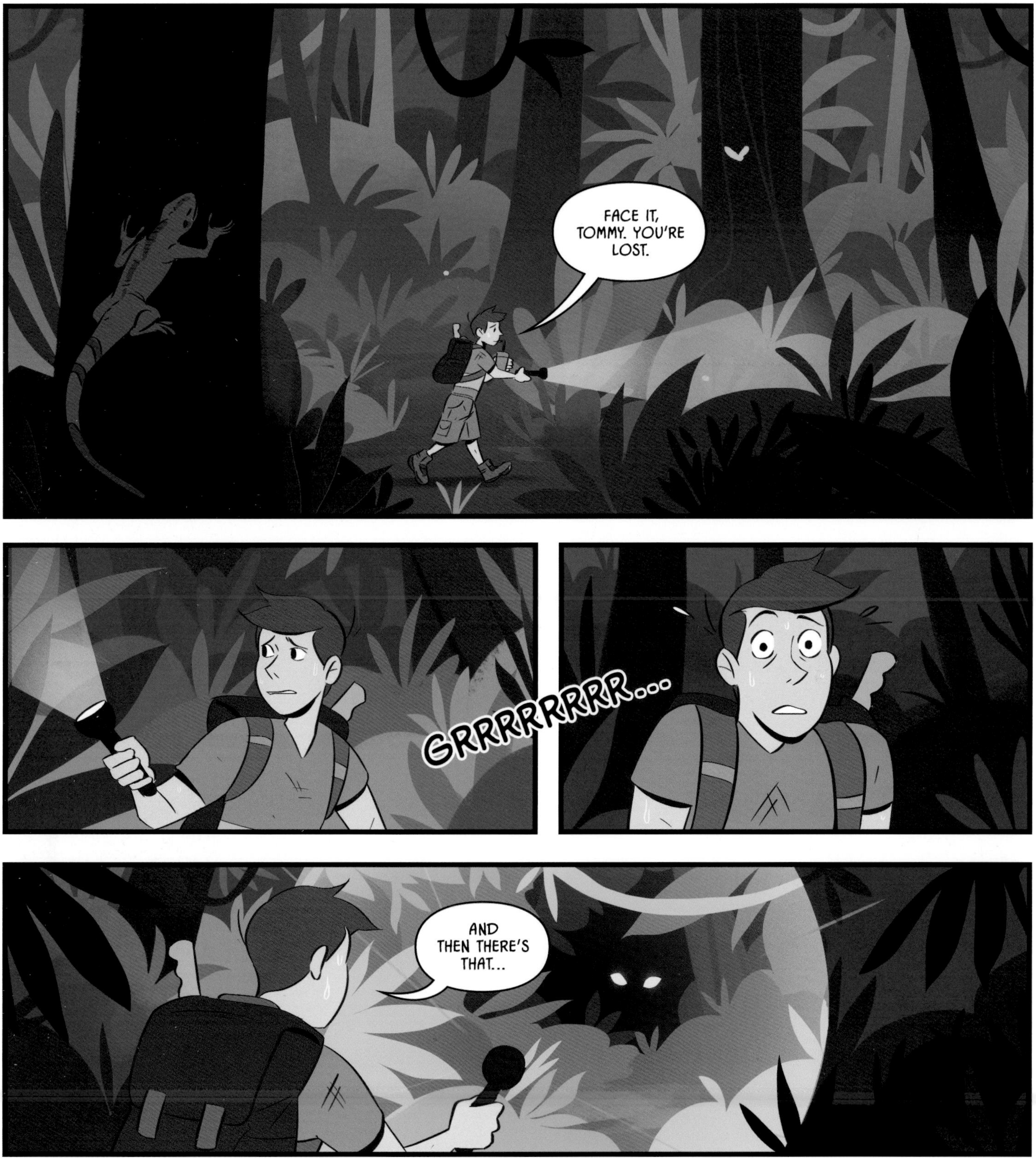
FACE IT, TOMMY. YOU'RE LOST.
GRRRRRRRR...
AND THEN THERE'S THAT...

CHAPTER 6

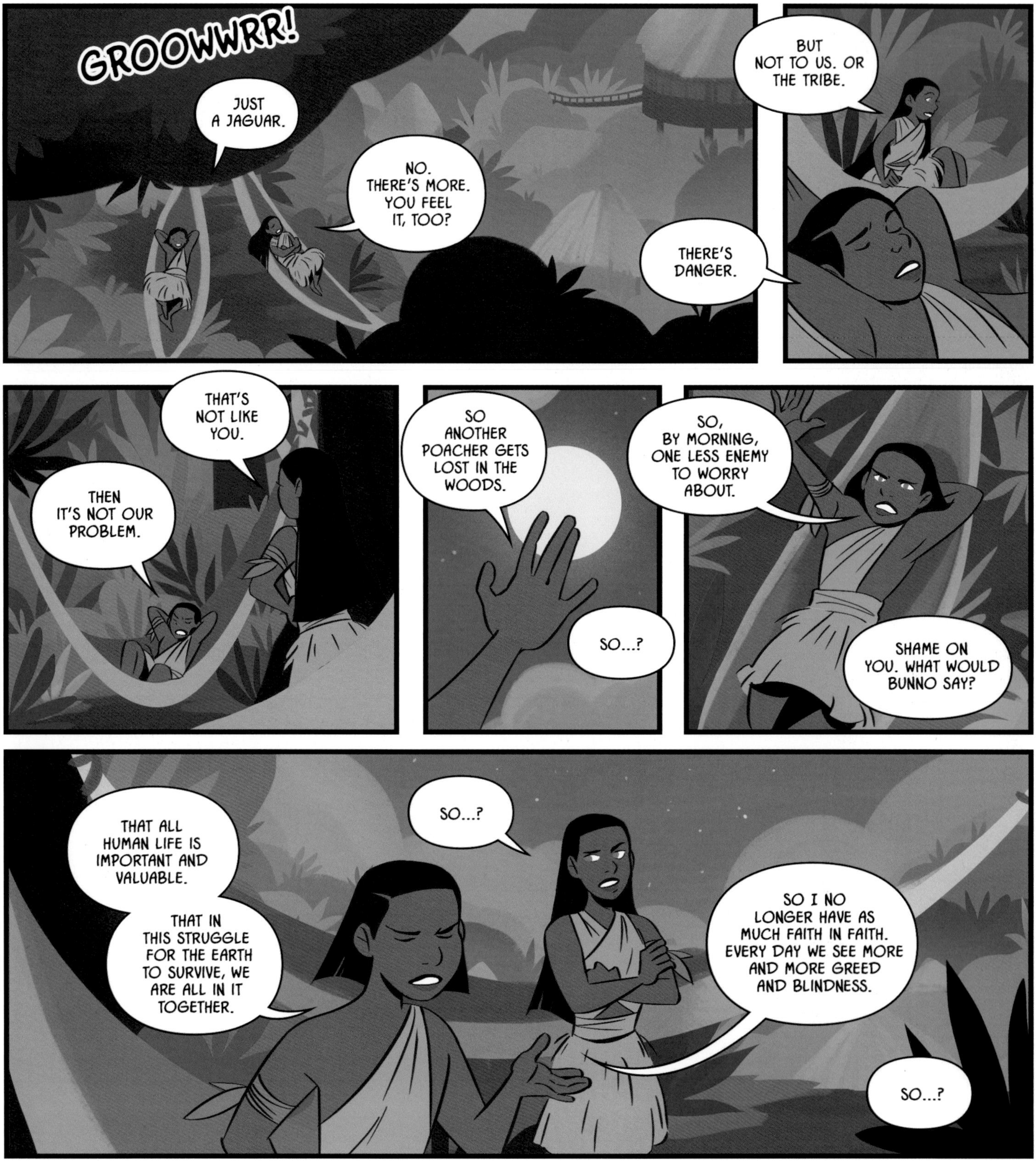
GROOWWRR!
JUST A JAGUAR.
NO. THERE'S MORE. YOU FEEL IT, TOO?
BUT NOT TO US. OR THE TRIBE.
THERE'S DANGER.
THAT'S NOT LIKE YOU.
THEN IT'S NOT OUR PROBLEM.
SO ANOTHER POACHER GETS LOST IN THE WOODS.
SO...?
SO, BY MORNING, ONE LESS ENEMY TO WORRY ABOUT.
SHAME ON YOU. WHAT WOULD BUNNO SAY?
THAT ALL HUMAN LIFE IS IMPORTANT AND VALUABLE.
SO...?
THAT IN THIS STRUGGLE FOR THE EARTH TO SURVIVE, WE ARE ALL IN IT TOGETHER.
SO I NO LONGER HAVE AS MUCH FAITH IN FAITH. EVERY DAY WE SEE MORE AND MORE GREED AND BLINDNESS.
SO...?

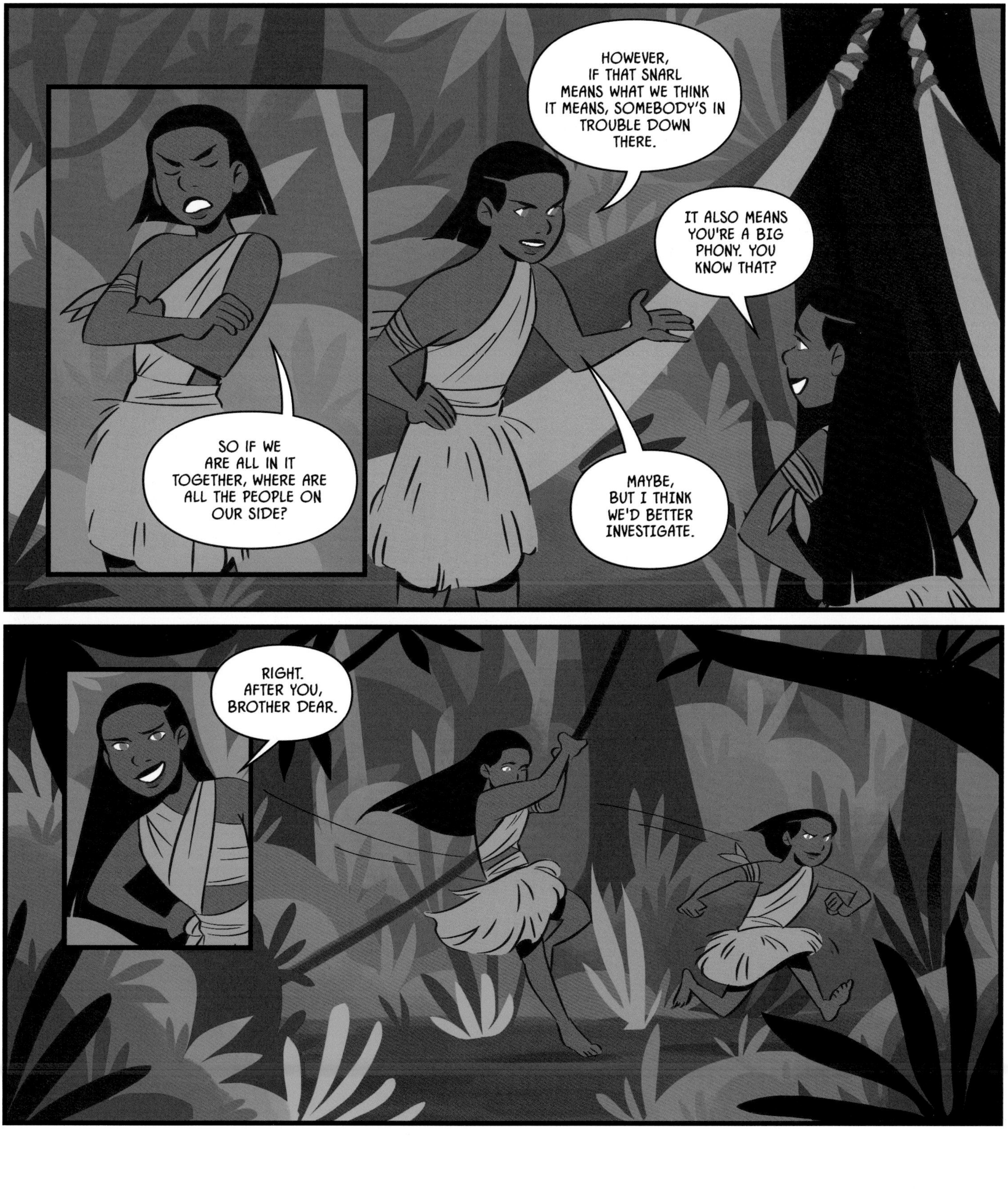
SO IF WE ARE ALL IN IT TOGETHER, WHERE ARE ALL THE PEOPLE ON OUR SIDE?
HOWEVER, IF THAT SNARL MEANS WHAT WE THINK IT MEANS, SOMEBODY'S IN TROUBLE DOWN THERE.
IT ALSO MEANS YOU'RE A BIG PHONY. YOU KNOW THAT?
MAYBE, BUT I THINK WE'D BETTER INVESTIGATE.
RIGHT. AFTER YOU, BROTHER DEAR.

CHAPTER 7

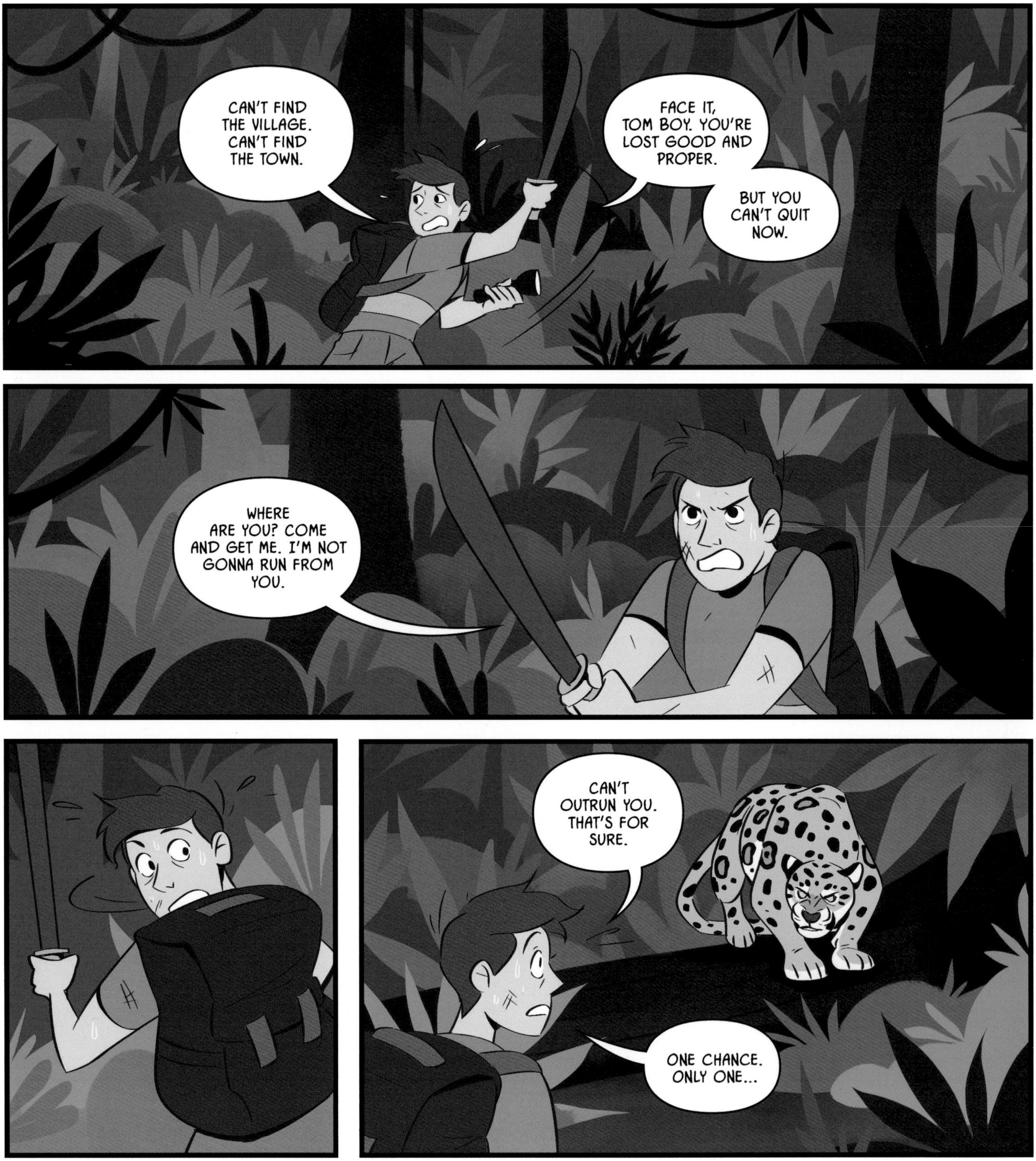
CAN'T FIND THE VILLAGE. CAN'T FIND THE TOWN.
FACE IT, TOM BOY. YOU'RE LOST GOOD AND PROPER.
BUT YOU CAN'T QUIT NOW.
WHERE ARE YOU? COME AND GET ME. I'M NOT GONNA RUN FROM YOU.
CAN'T OUTRUN YOU. THAT'S FOR SURE.
ONE CHANCE. ONLY ONE...

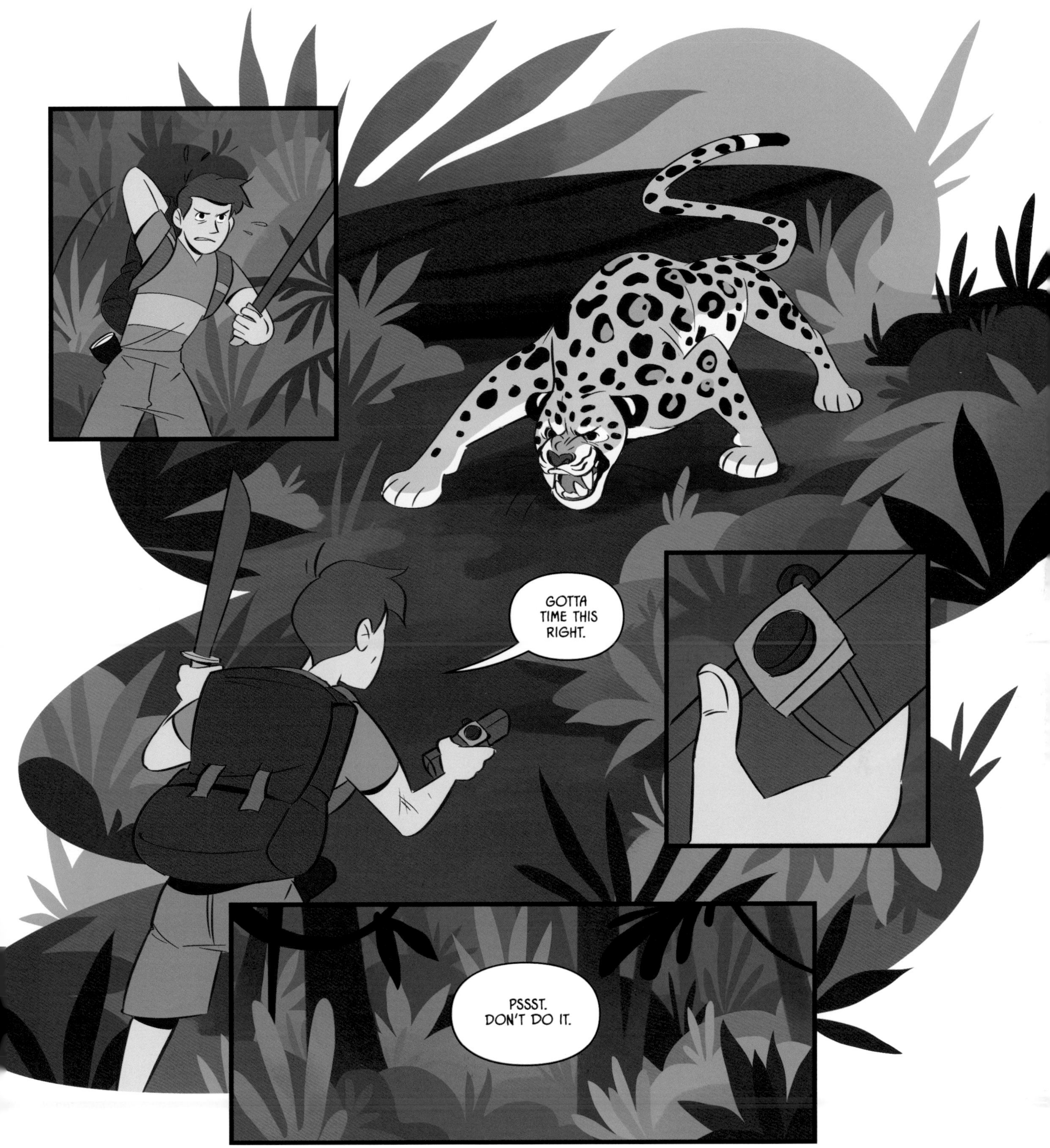
GOTTA TIME THIS RIGHT.
PSSST. DON'T DO IT.

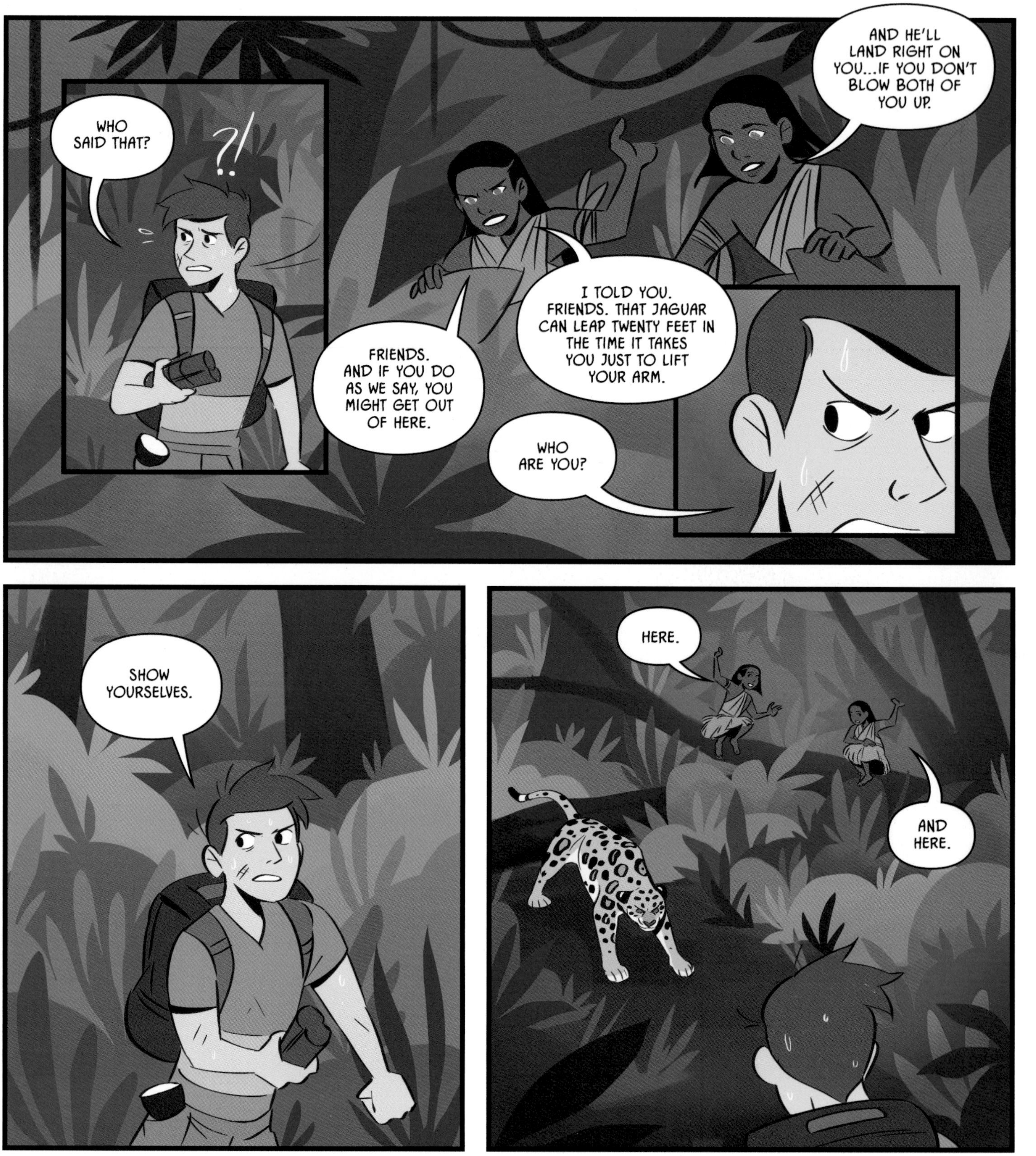
WHO SAID THAT?
?!
AND HE'LL LAND RIGHT ON YOU...IF YOU DON'T BLOW BOTH OF YOU UP.
FRIENDS. AND IF YOU DO AS WE SAY, YOU MIGHT GET OUT OF HERE.
I TOLD YOU. FRIENDS. THAT JAGUAR CAN LEAP TWENTY FEET IN THE TIME IT TAKES YOU JUST TO LIFT YOUR ARM.
WHO ARE YOU?
SHOW YOURSELVES.
HERE.
AND HERE.

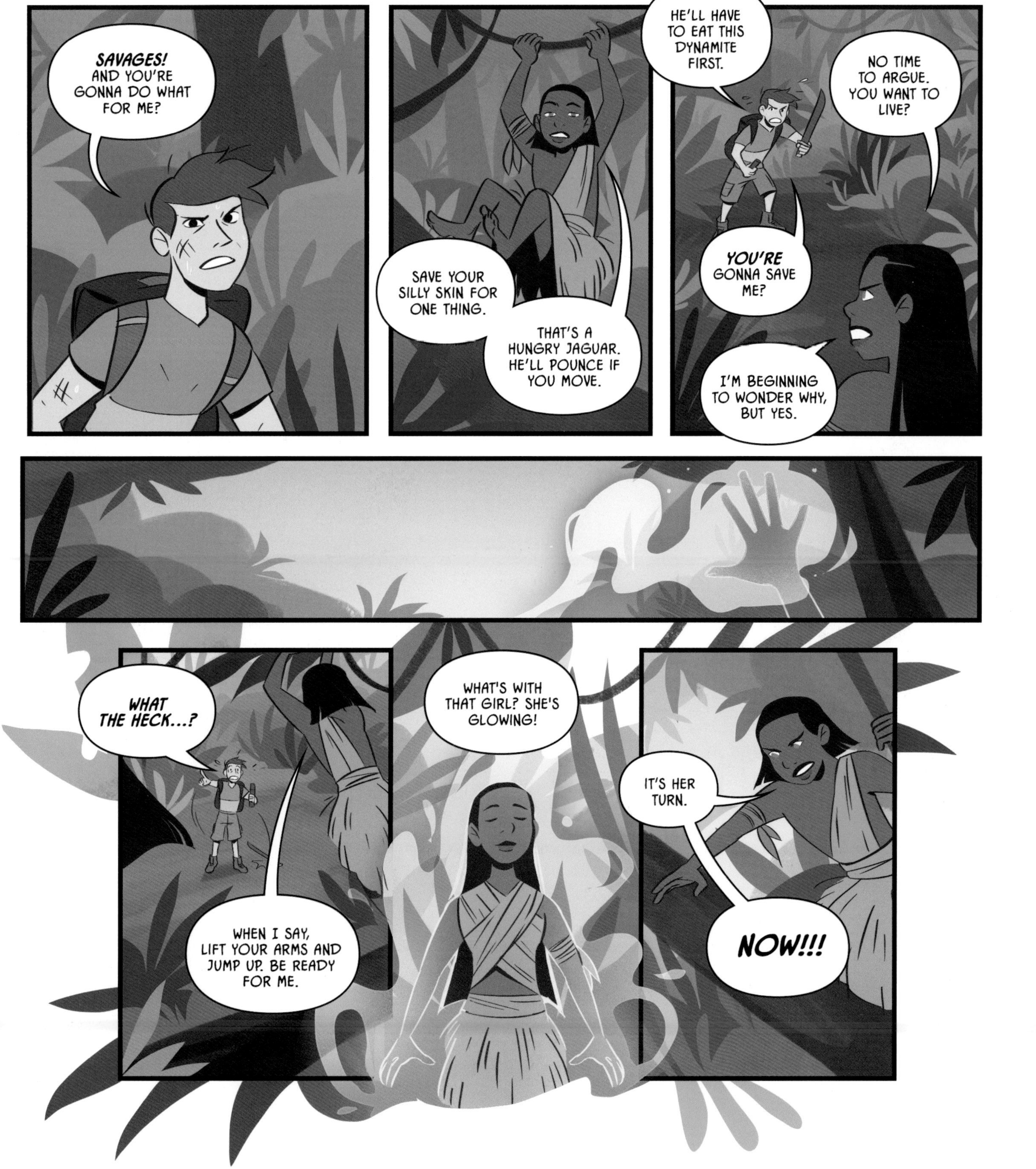
SAVAGES! AND YOU'RE GONNA DO WHAT FOR ME?
SAVE YOUR SILLY SKIN FOR ONE THING.
THAT'S A HUNGRY JAGUAR. HE'LL POUNCE IF YOU MOVE.
HE'LL HAVE TO EAT THIS DYNAMITE FIRST.
NO TIME TO ARGUE. YOU WANT TO LIVE?
YOU'RE GONNA SAVE ME?
I'M BEGINNING TO WONDER WHY, BUT YES.
WHAT THE HECK...?
WHEN I SAY, LIFT YOUR ARMS AND JUMP UP. BE READY FOR ME.
WHAT'S WITH THAT GIRL? SHE'S GLOWING!
IT'S HER TURN.
NOW!!!

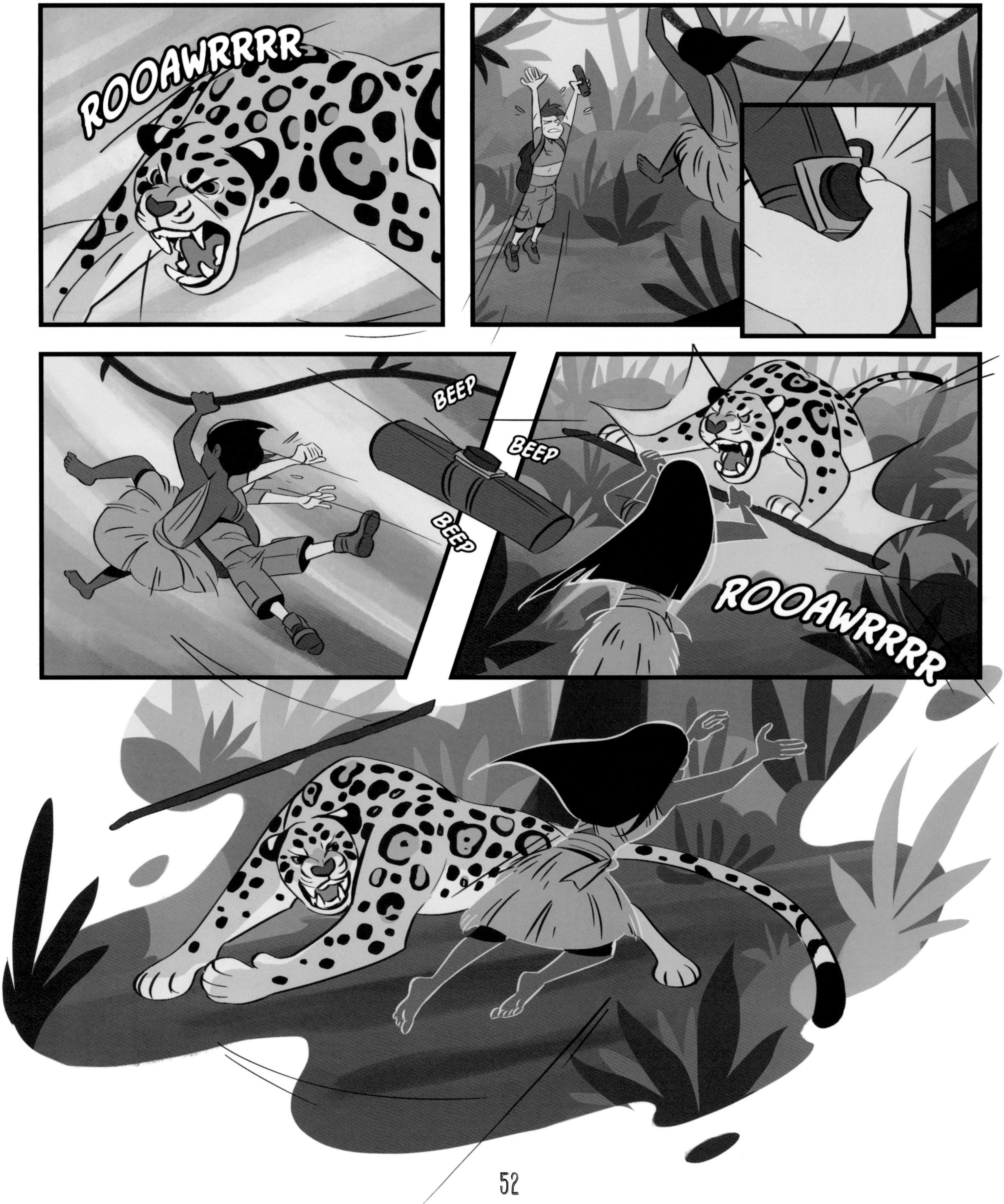
ROOAWRRRR
BEEP
BEEP
BEEP
ROOAWRRRR

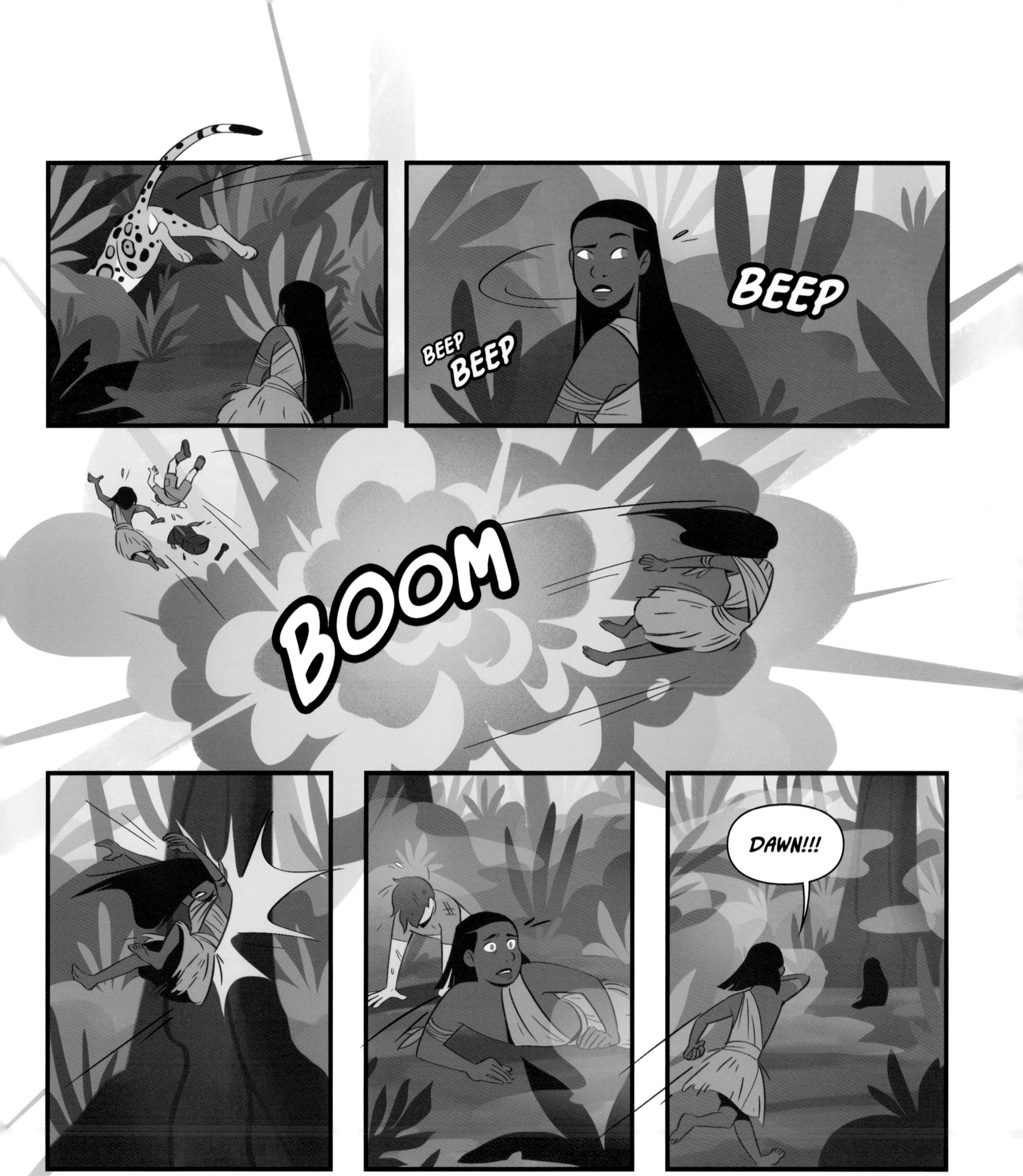
BEEP
BEEP
BEEP
BOOM
DAWN!!!

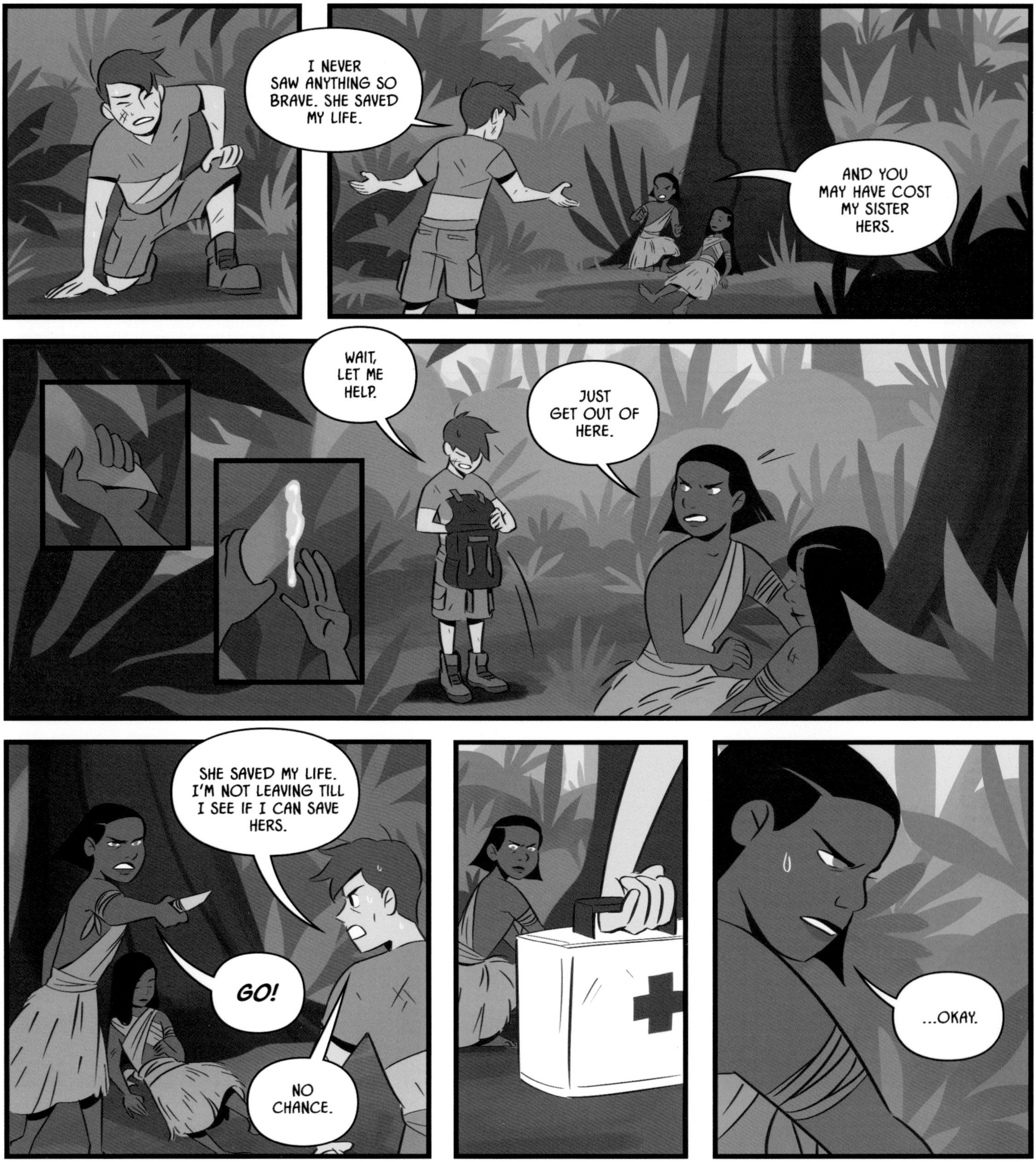
I NEVER SAW ANYTHING SO BRAVE. SHE SAVED MY LIFE.
AND YOU MAY HAVE COST MY SISTER HERS.
WAIT, LET ME HELP.
JUST GET OUT OF HERE.
SHE SAVED MY LIFE. I'M NOT LEAVING TILL I SEE IF I CAN SAVE HERS.
GO!
NO CHANCE.
...OKAY.

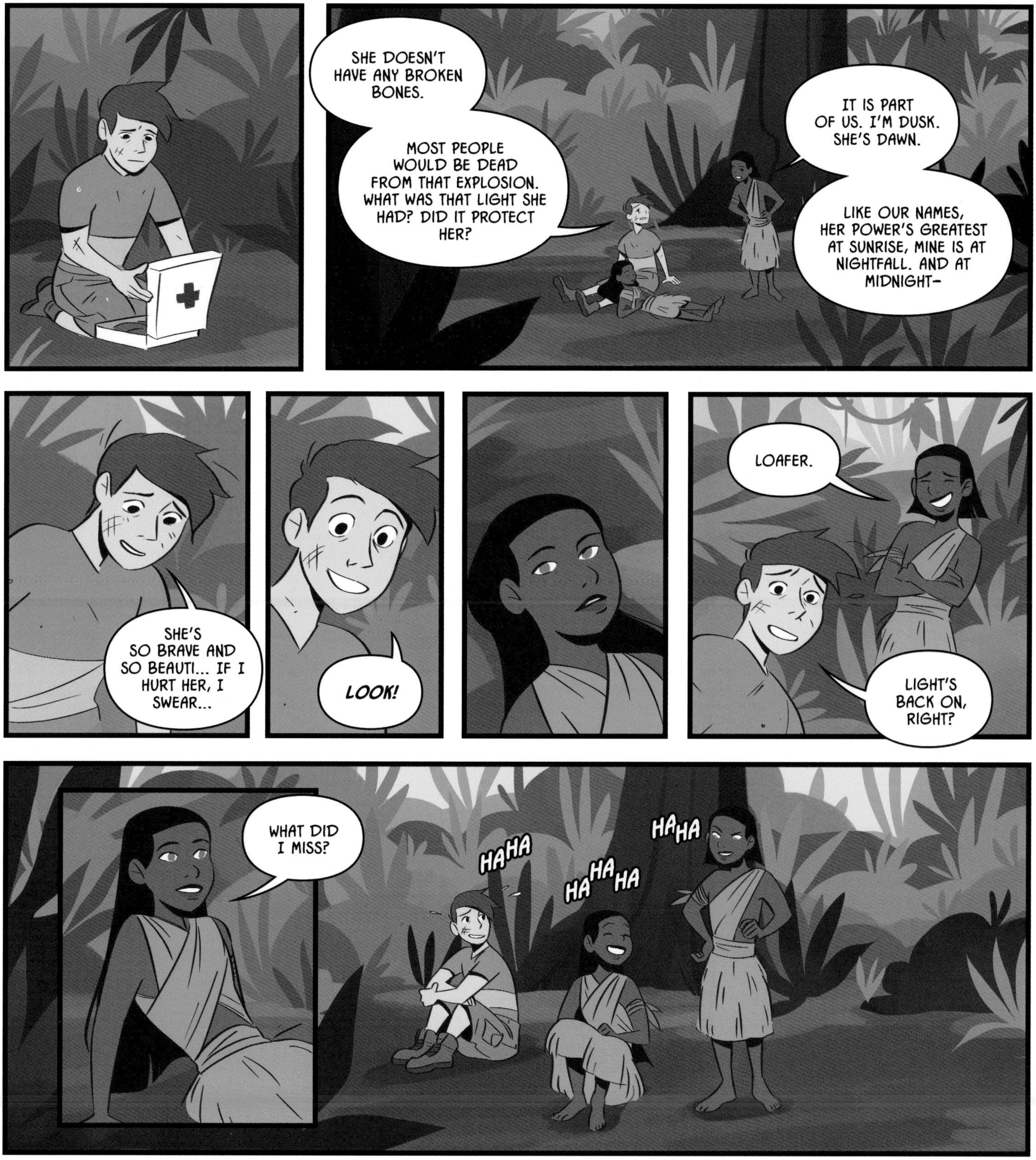

SHE DOESN'T HAVE ANY BROKEN BONES.
MOST PEOPLE WOULD BE DEAD FROM THAT EXPLOSION. WHAT WAS THAT LIGHT SHE HAD? DID IT PROTECT HER?
IT IS PART OF US. I'M DUSK. SHE'S DAWN.
LIKE OUR NAMES, HER POWER'S GREATEST AT SUNRISE, MINE IS AT NIGHTFALL. AND AT MIDNIGHT–
SHE'S SO BRAVE AND SO BEAUTI... IF I HURT HER, I SWEAR...
LOOK!
LOAFER.
LIGHT'S BACK ON, RIGHT?
WHAT DID I MISS?
HAHA
HAHA
HAHAHA

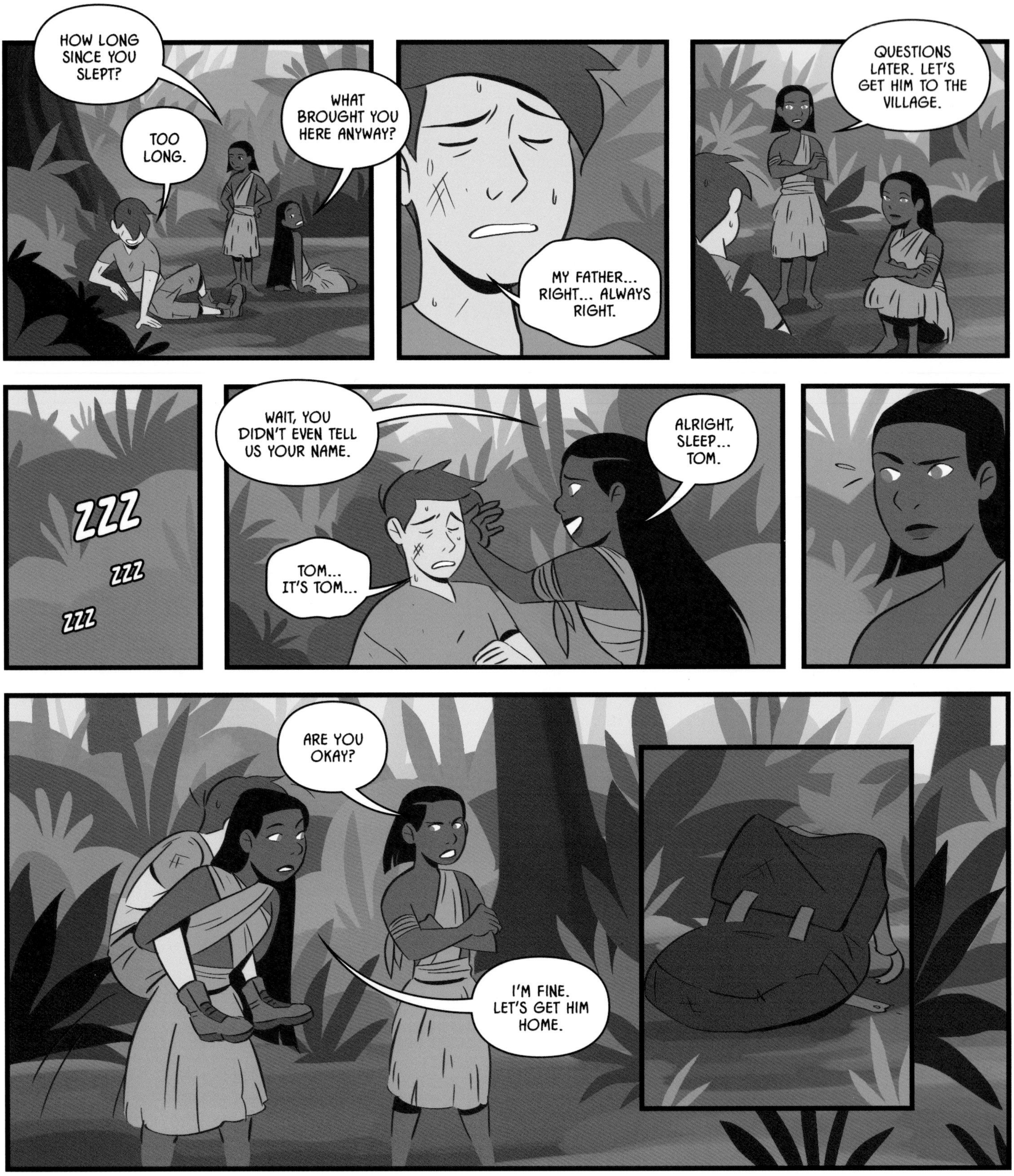
HOW LONG SINCE YOU SLEPT?
TOO LONG.
WHAT BROUGHT YOU HERE ANYWAY?
MY FATHER... RIGHT... ALWAYS RIGHT.
QUESTIONS LATER. LET'S GET HIM TO THE VILLAGE.
ZZZ
ZZZ
ZZZ
WAIT, YOU DIDN'T EVEN TELL US YOUR NAME.
TOM... IT'S TOM...
ALRIGHT, SLEEP... TOM.
ARE YOU OKAY?
I'M FINE. LET'S GET HIM HOME.

CHAPTER 8

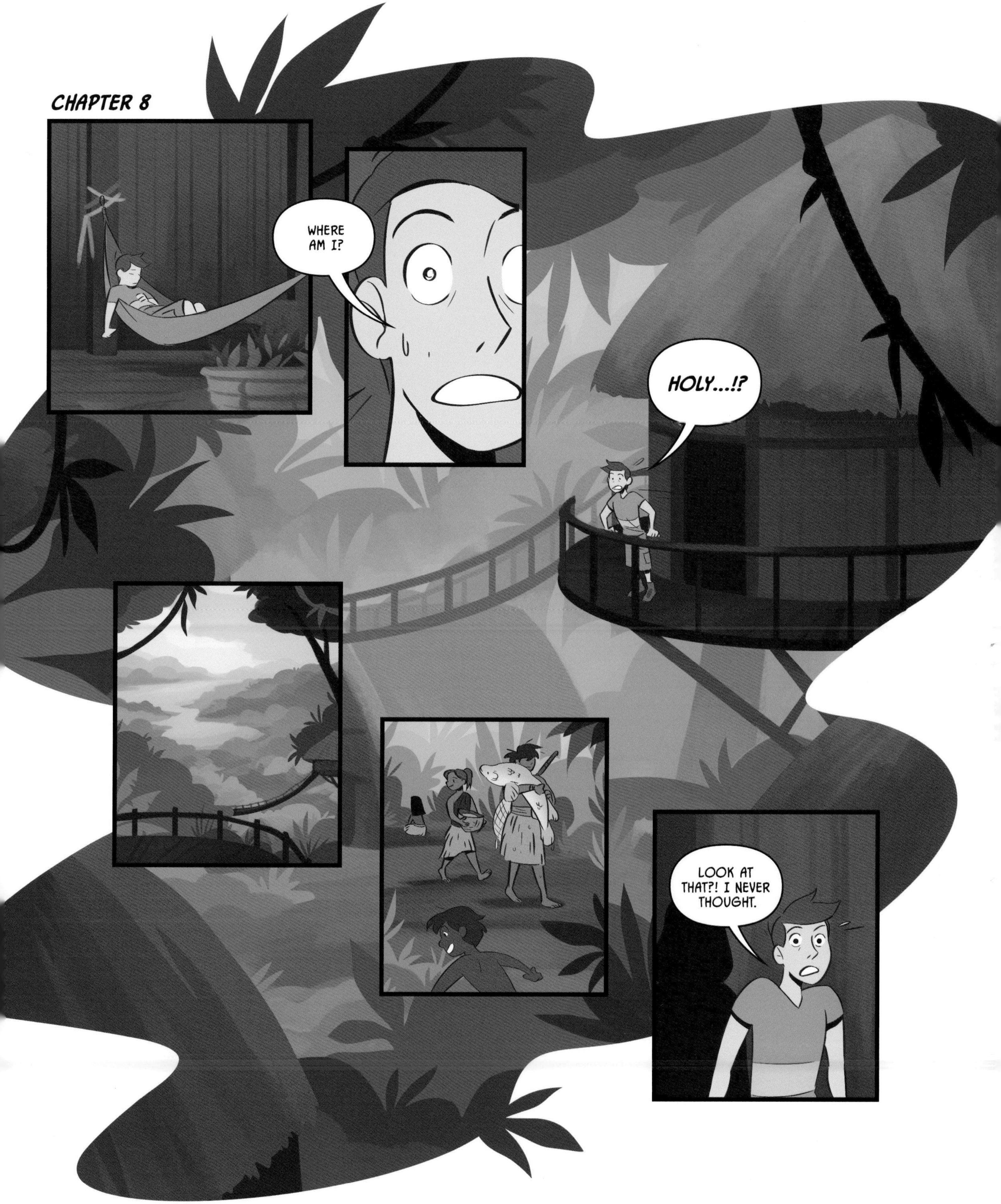
WHERE AM I?
HOLY...!?
LOOK AT THAT?! I NEVER THOUGHT.

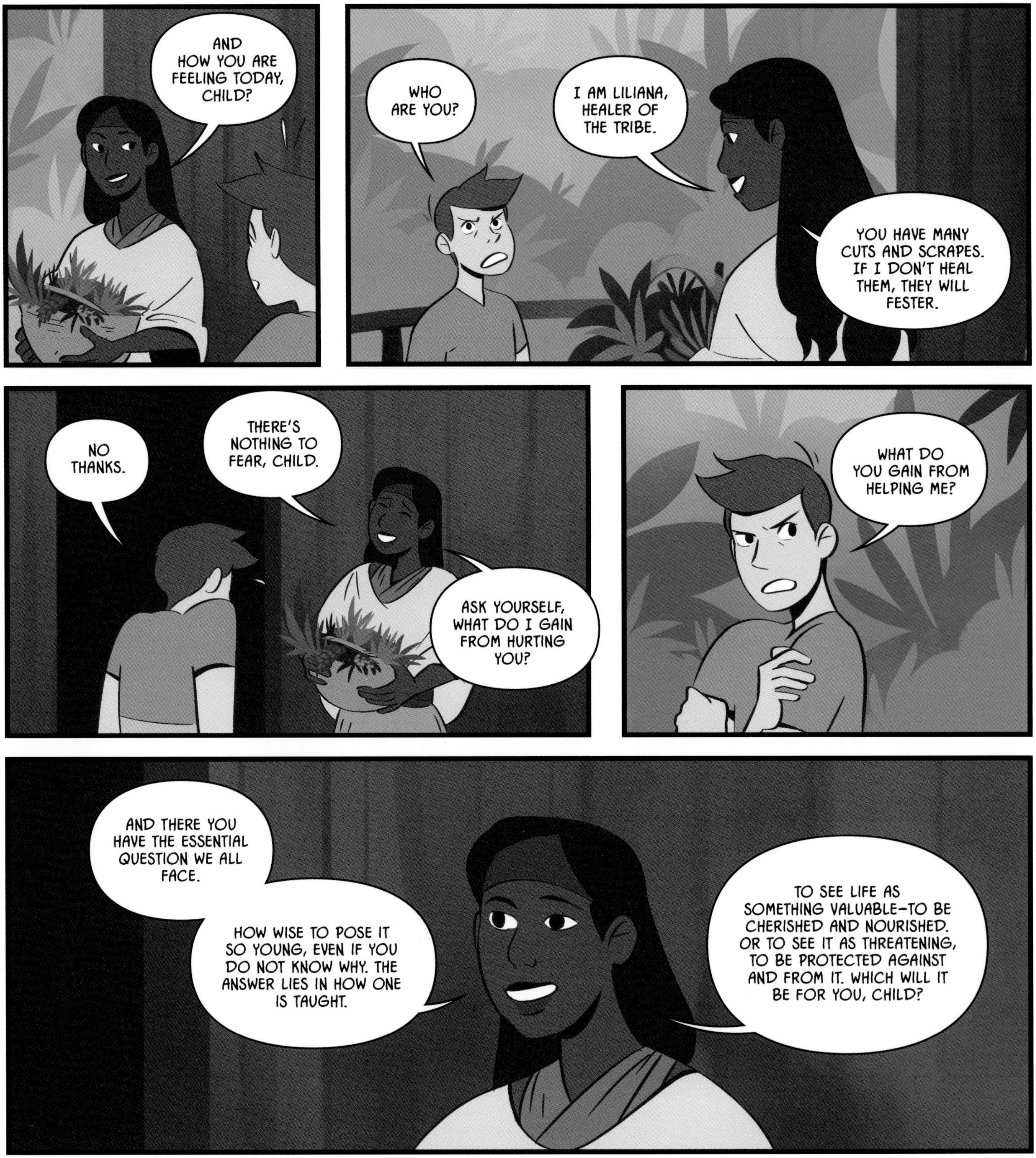
AND HOW YOU ARE FEELING TODAY, CHILD?
WHO ARE YOU?
I AM LILIANA, HEALER OF THE TRIBE.
YOU HAVE MANY CUTS AND SCRAPES. IF I DON'T HEAL THEM, THEY WILL FESTER.
NO THANKS.
THERE'S NOTHING TO FEAR, CHILD.
ASK YOURSELF, WHAT DO I GAIN FROM HURTING YOU?
WHAT DO YOU GAIN FROM HELPING ME?
AND THERE YOU HAVE THE ESSENTIAL QUESTION WE ALL FACE.
HOW WISE TO POSE IT SO YOUNG, EVEN IF YOU DO NOT KNOW WHY. THE ANSWER LIES IN HOW ONE IS TAUGHT.
TO SEE LIFE AS SOMETHING VALUABLE—TO BE CHERISHED AND NOURISHED. OR TO SEE IT AS THREATENING, TO BE PROTECTED AGAINST AND FROM IT. WHICH WILL IT BE FOR YOU, CHILD?

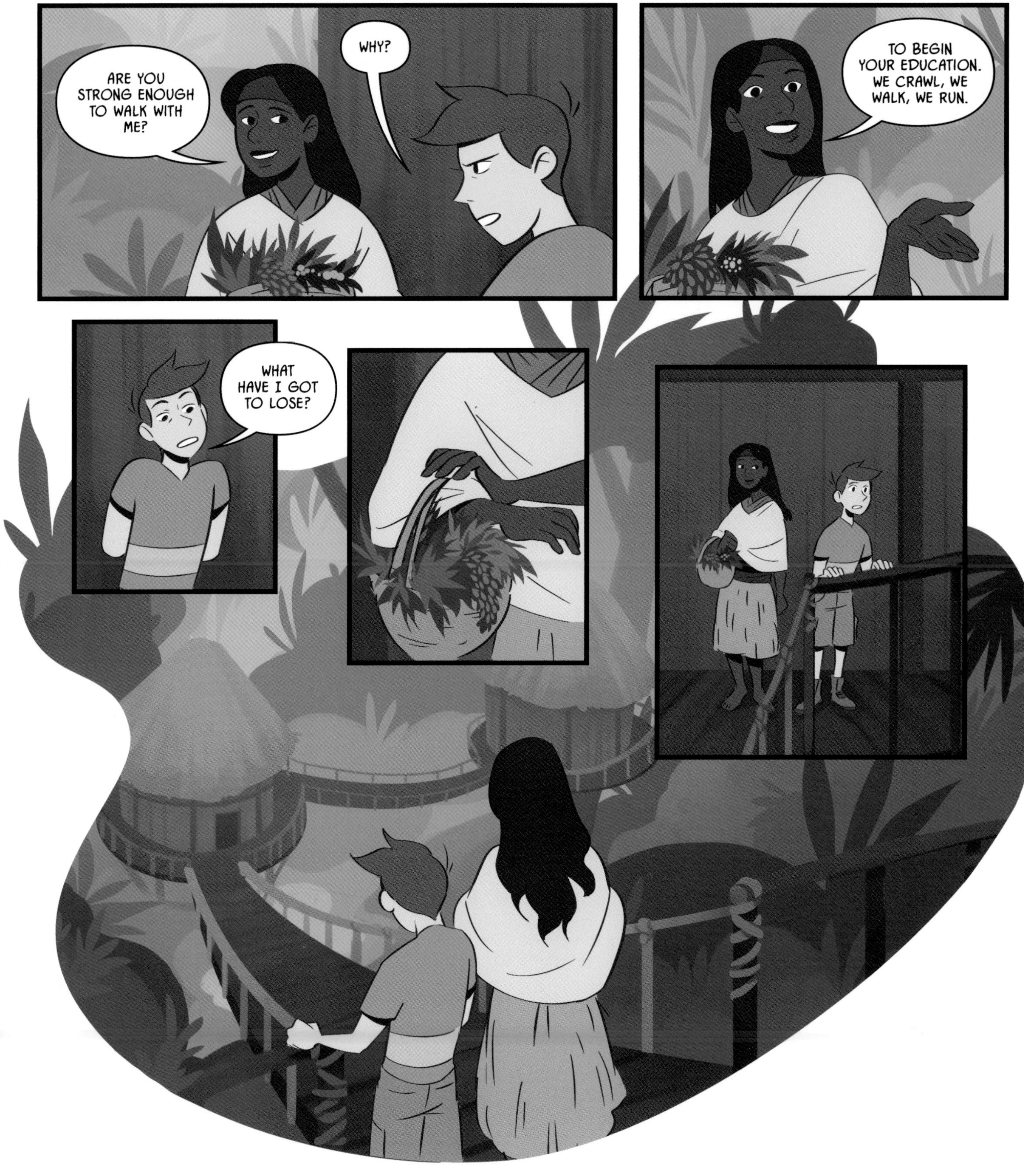
ARE YOU STRONG ENOUGH TO WALK WITH ME?
WHY?
TO BEGIN YOUR EDUCATION. WE CRAWL, WE WALK, WE RUN.
WHAT HAVE I GOT TO LOSE?

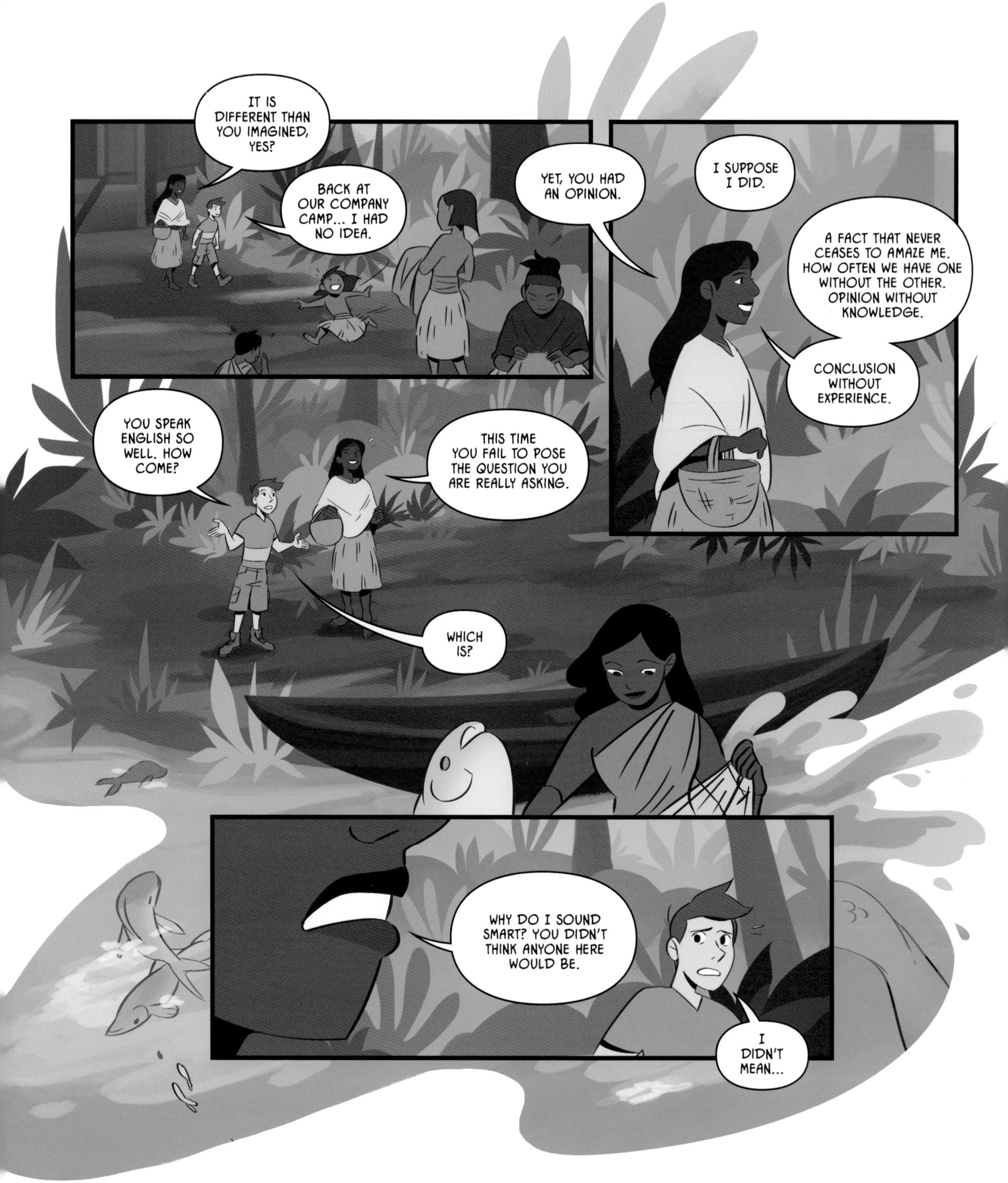
IT IS DIFFERENT THAN YOU IMAGINED, YES?
BACK AT OUR COMPANY CAMP... I HAD NO IDEA.
YET, YOU HAD AN OPINION.
I SUPPOSE I DID.
A FACT THAT NEVER CEASES TO AMAZE ME. HOW OFTEN WE HAVE ONE WITHOUT THE OTHER. OPINION WITHOUT KNOWLEDGE.
CONCLUSION WITHOUT EXPERIENCE.
YOU SPEAK ENGLISH SO WELL. HOW COME?
THIS TIME YOU FAIL TO POSE THE QUESTION YOU ARE REALLY ASKING.
WHICH IS?
WHY DO I SOUND SMART? YOU DIDN'T THINK ANYONE HERE WOULD BE.
I DIDN'T MEAN...

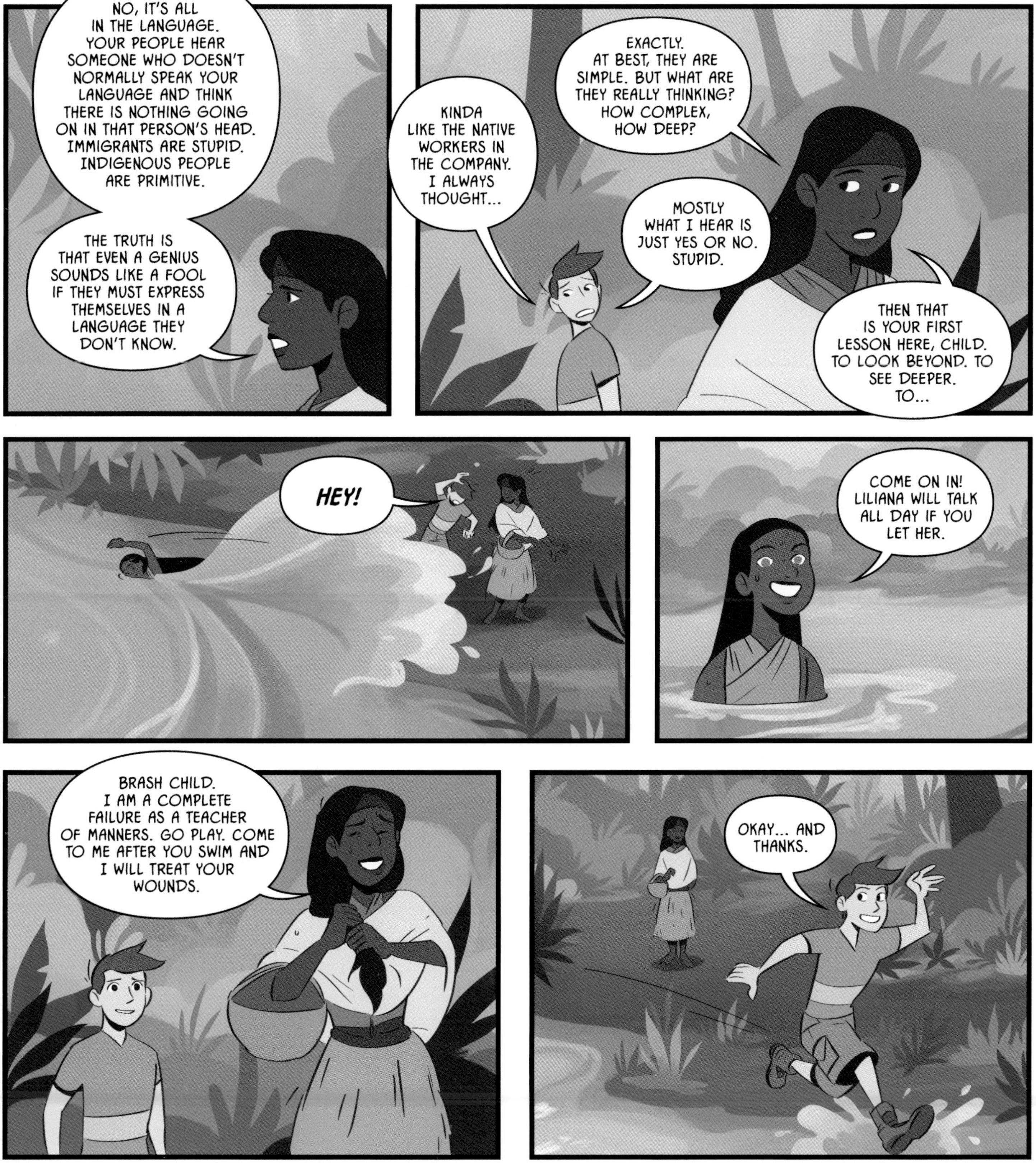

NO, IT'S ALL IN THE LANGUAGE. YOUR PEOPLE HEAR SOMEONE WHO DOESN'T NORMALLY SPEAK YOUR LANGUAGE AND THINK THERE IS NOTHING GOING ON IN THAT PERSON'S HEAD. IMMIGRANTS ARE STUPID. INDIGENOUS PEOPLE ARE PRIMITIVE.
THE TRUTH IS THAT EVEN A GENIUS SOUNDS LIKE A FOOL IF THEY MUST EXPRESS THEMSELVES IN A LANGUAGE THEY DON'T KNOW.
KINDA LIKE THE NATIVE WORKERS IN THE COMPANY. I ALWAYS THOUGHT...
EXACTLY. AT BEST, THEY ARE SIMPLE. BUT WHAT ARE THEY REALLY THINKING? HOW COMPLEX, HOW DEEP?
MOSTLY WHAT I HEAR IS JUST YES OR NO. STUPID.
THEN THAT IS YOUR FIRST LESSON HERE, CHILD. TO LOOK BEYOND. TO SEE DEEPER. TO...
HEY!
COME ON IN! LILIANA WILL TALK ALL DAY IF YOU LET HER.
BRASH CHILD. I AM A COMPLETE FAILURE AS A TEACHER OF MANNERS. GO PLAY. COME TO ME AFTER YOU SWIM AND I WILL TREAT YOUR WOUNDS.
OKAY... AND THANKS.

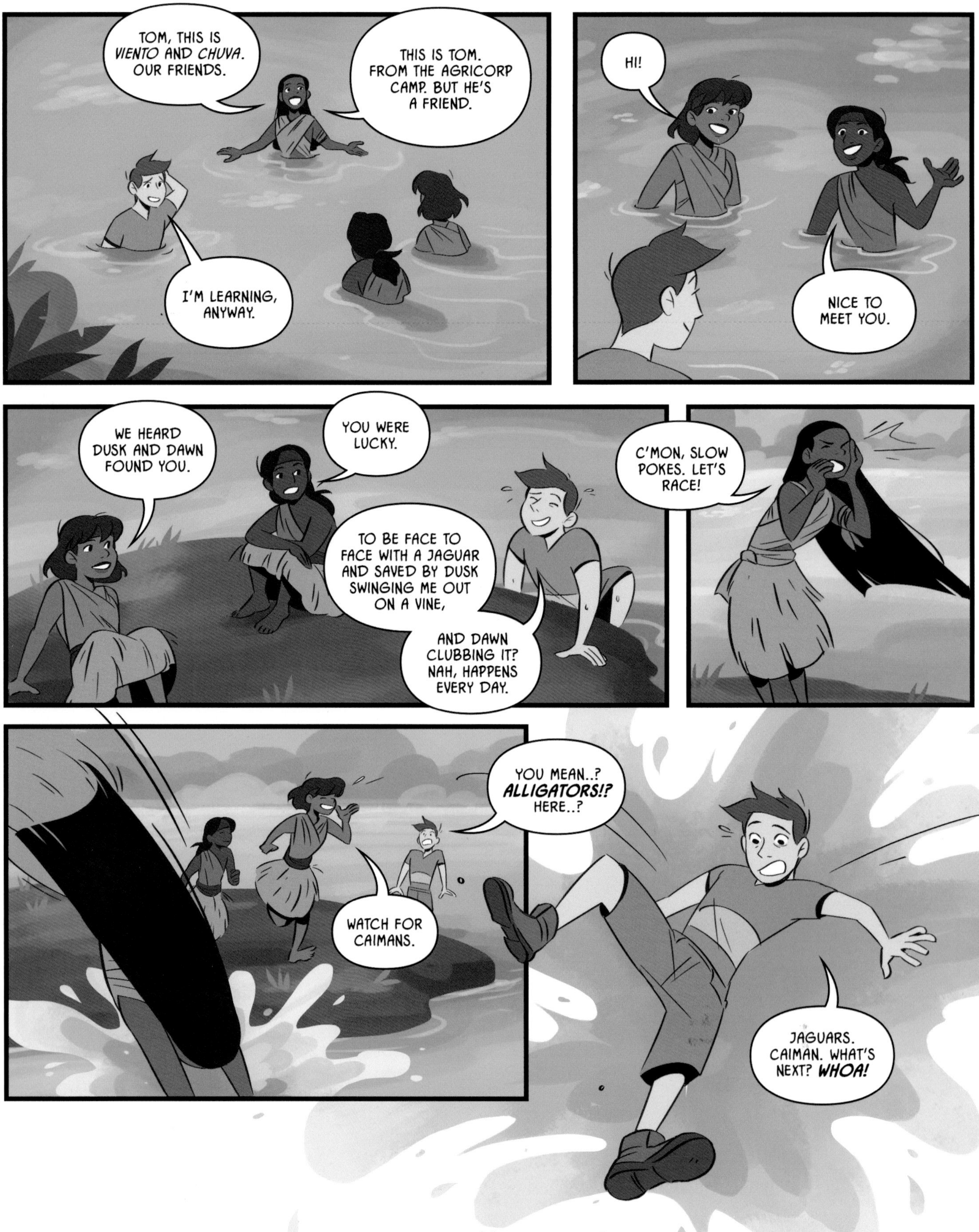
TOM, THIS IS *VIENTO* AND *CHUVA*. OUR FRIENDS.
THIS IS TOM. FROM THE AGRICORP CAMP. BUT HE'S A FRIEND.
I'M LEARNING, ANYWAY.
HI!
NICE TO MEET YOU.
WE HEARD DUSK AND DAWN FOUND YOU.
YOU WERE LUCKY.
TO BE FACE TO FACE WITH A JAGUAR AND SAVED BY DUSK SWINGING ME OUT ON A VINE,
AND DAWN CLUBBING IT? NAH, HAPPENS EVERY DAY.
C'MON, SLOW POKES. LET'S RACE!
WATCH FOR CAIMANS.
YOU MEAN..? ***ALLIGATORS!?*** HERE..?
JAGUARS. CAIMAN. WHAT'S NEXT? ***WHOA!***

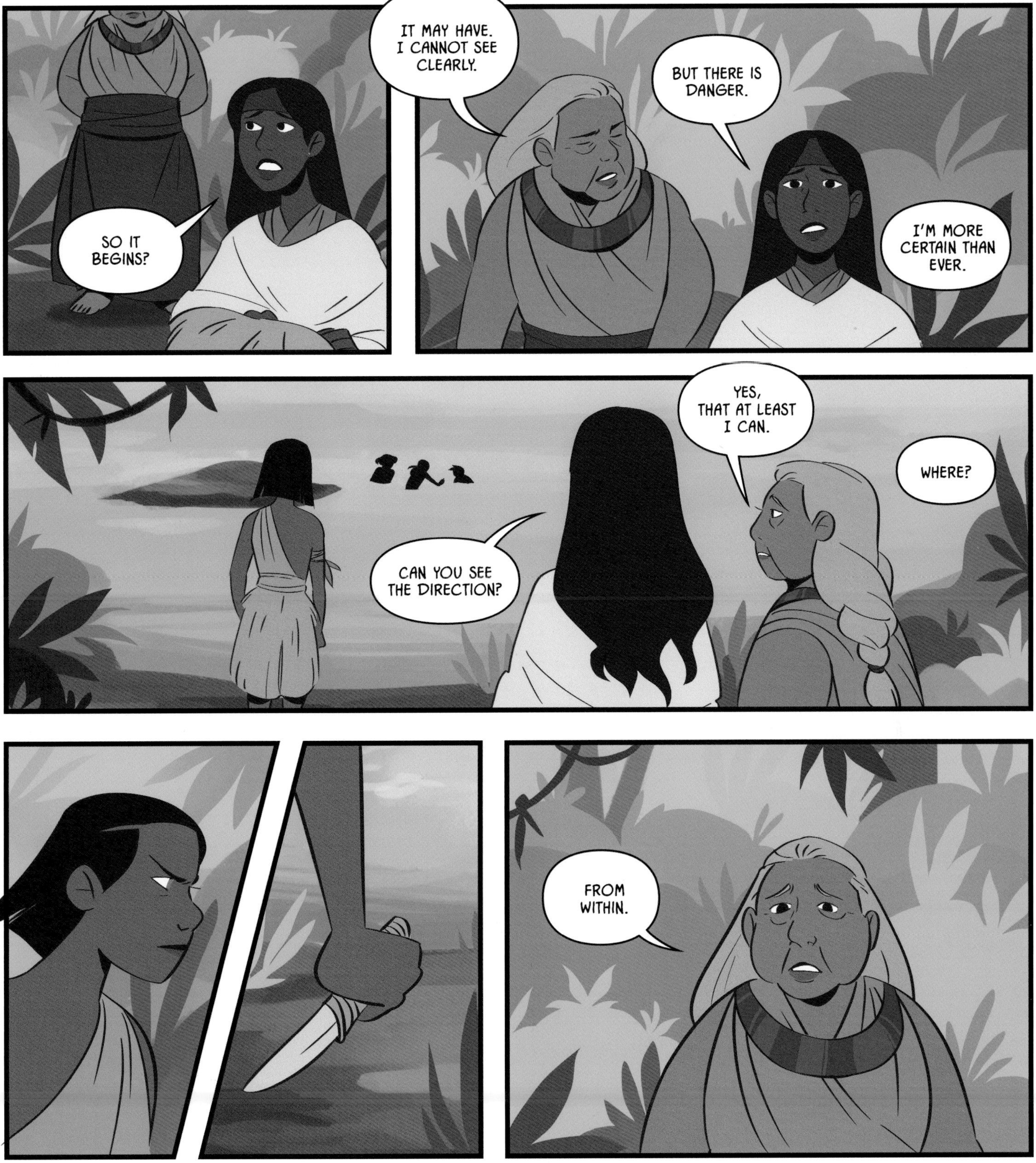
SO IT BEGINS?
IT MAY HAVE. I CANNOT SEE CLEARLY.
BUT THERE IS DANGER.
I'M MORE CERTAIN THAN EVER.
CAN YOU SEE THE DIRECTION?
YES, THAT AT LEAST I CAN.
WHERE?
FROM WITHIN.

CHAPTER 9

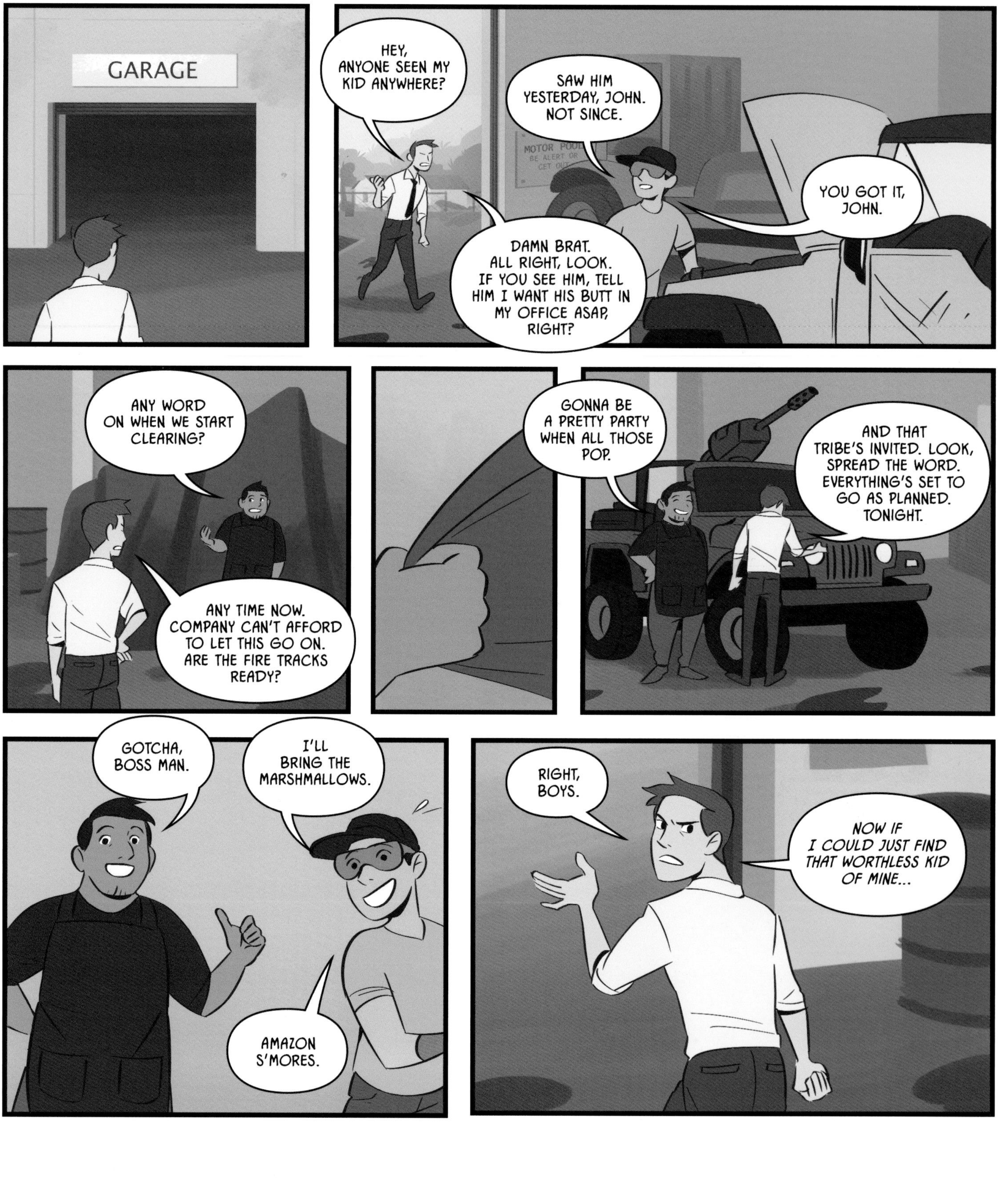
GARAGE
HEY, ANYONE SEEN MY KID ANYWHERE?
SAW HIM YESTERDAY, JOHN. NOT SINCE.
DAMN BRAT. ALL RIGHT, LOOK. IF YOU SEE HIM, TELL HIM I WANT HIS BUTT IN MY OFFICE ASAP, RIGHT?
YOU GOT IT, JOHN.
ANY WORD ON WHEN WE START CLEARING?
ANY TIME NOW. COMPANY CAN'T AFFORD TO LET THIS GO ON. ARE THE FIRE TRACKS READY?
GONNA BE A PRETTY PARTY WHEN ALL THOSE POP.
AND THAT TRIBE'S INVITED. LOOK, SPREAD THE WORD. EVERYTHING'S SET TO GO AS PLANNED. TONIGHT.
GOTCHA, BOSS MAN.
I'LL BRING THE MARSHMALLOWS.
AMAZON S'MORES.
RIGHT, BOYS.
NOW IF I COULD JUST FIND THAT WORTHLESS KID OF MINE...

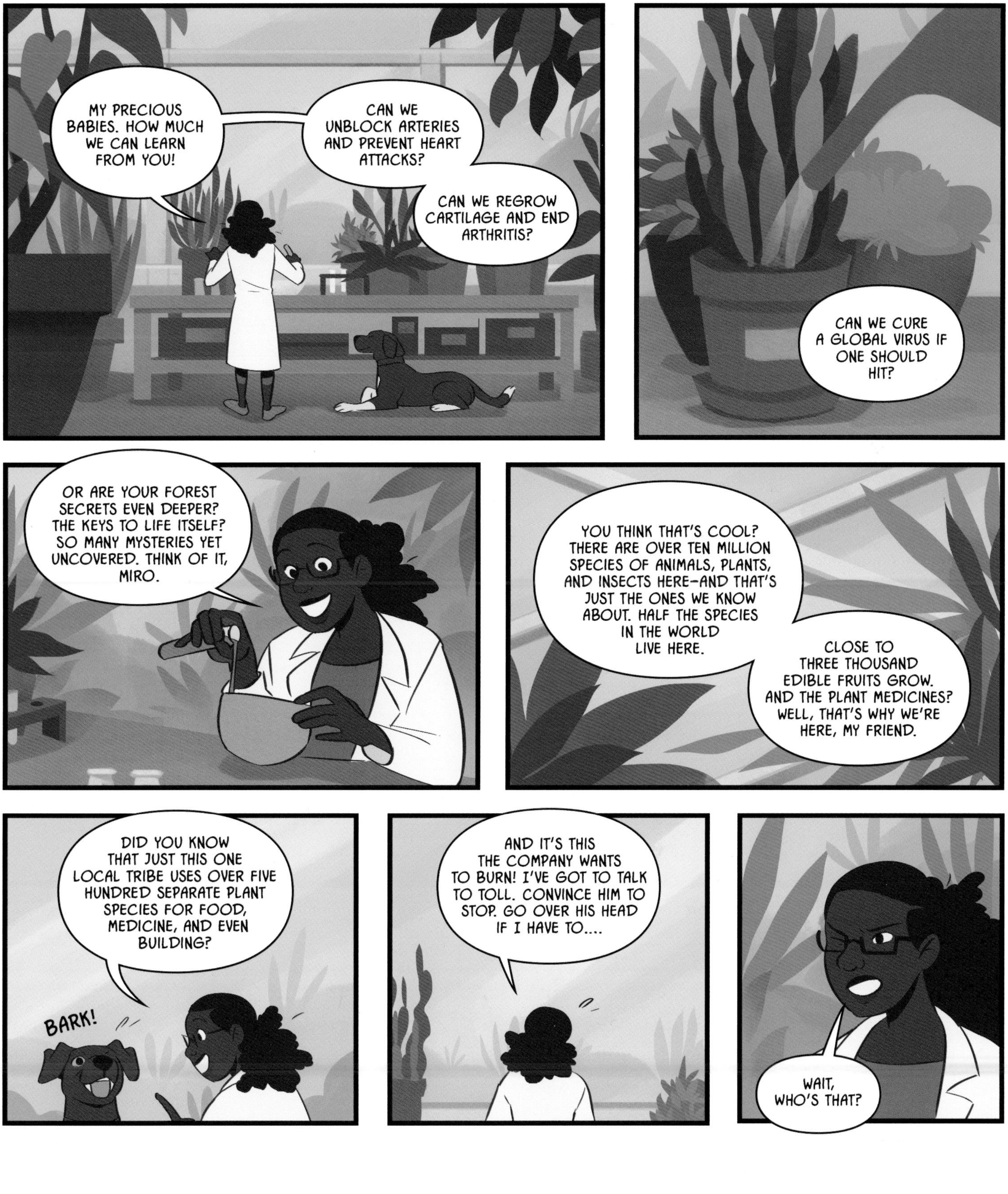
MY PRECIOUS BABIES. HOW MUCH WE CAN LEARN FROM YOU!
CAN WE UNBLOCK ARTERIES AND PREVENT HEART ATTACKS?
CAN WE REGROW CARTILAGE AND END ARTHRITIS?
CAN WE CURE A GLOBAL VIRUS IF ONE SHOULD HIT?
OR ARE YOUR FOREST SECRETS EVEN DEEPER? THE KEYS TO LIFE ITSELF? SO MANY MYSTERIES YET UNCOVERED. THINK OF IT, MIRO.
YOU THINK THAT'S COOL? THERE ARE OVER TEN MILLION SPECIES OF ANIMALS, PLANTS, AND INSECTS HERE—AND THAT'S JUST THE ONES WE KNOW ABOUT. HALF THE SPECIES IN THE WORLD LIVE HERE.
CLOSE TO THREE THOUSAND EDIBLE FRUITS GROW. AND THE PLANT MEDICINES? WELL, THAT'S WHY WE'RE HERE, MY FRIEND.
DID YOU KNOW THAT JUST THIS ONE LOCAL TRIBE USES OVER FIVE HUNDRED SEPARATE PLANT SPECIES FOR FOOD, MEDICINE, AND EVEN BUILDING?
BARK!
AND IT'S THIS THE COMPANY WANTS TO BURN! I'VE GOT TO TALK TO TOLL. CONVINCE HIM TO STOP. GO OVER HIS HEAD IF I HAVE TO....
WAIT, WHO'S THAT?

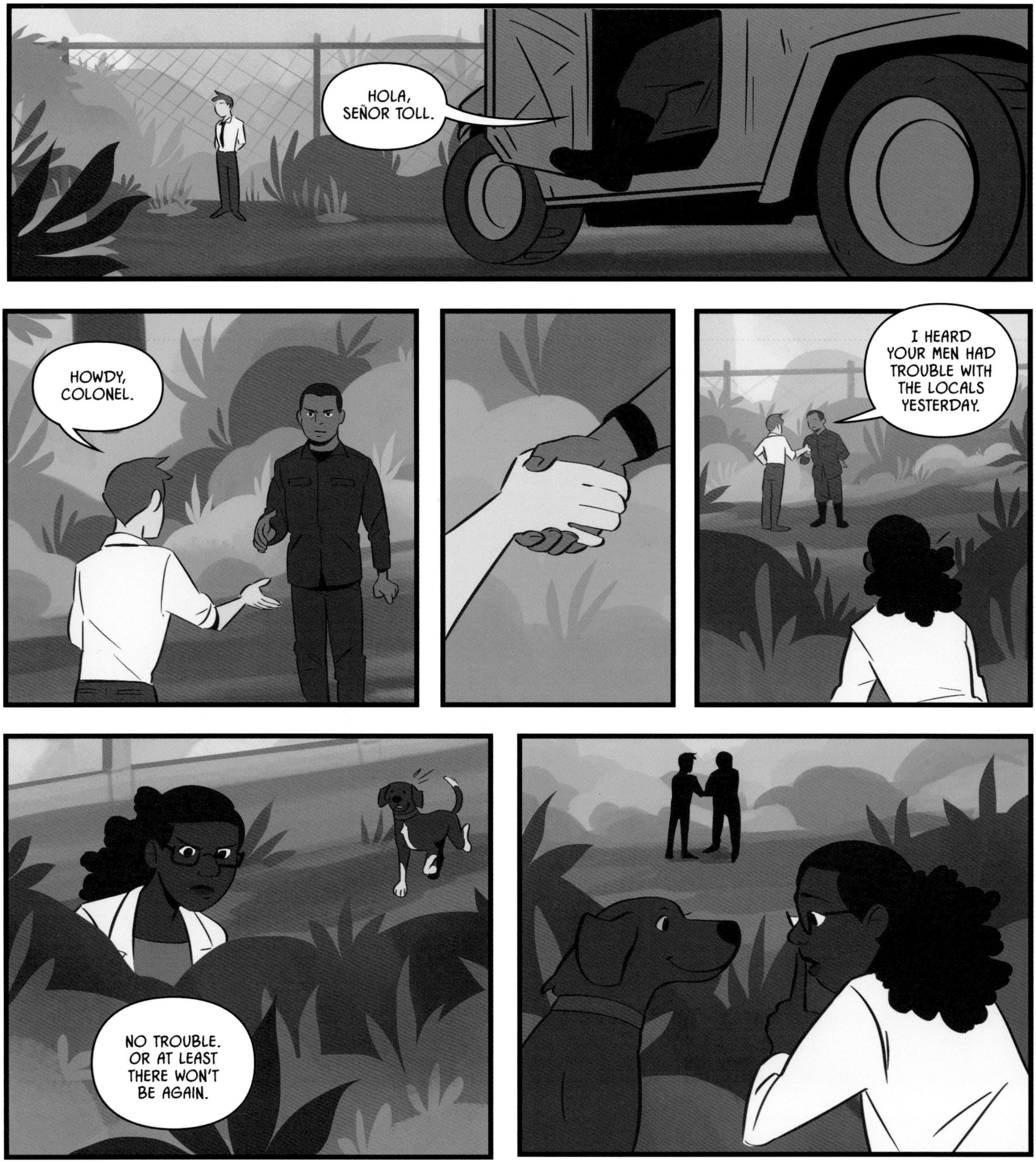
HOLA, SEÑOR TOLL.
HOWDY, COLONEL.
I HEARD YOUR MEN HAD TROUBLE WITH THE LOCALS YESTERDAY.
NO TROUBLE. OR AT LEAST THERE WON'T BE AGAIN.

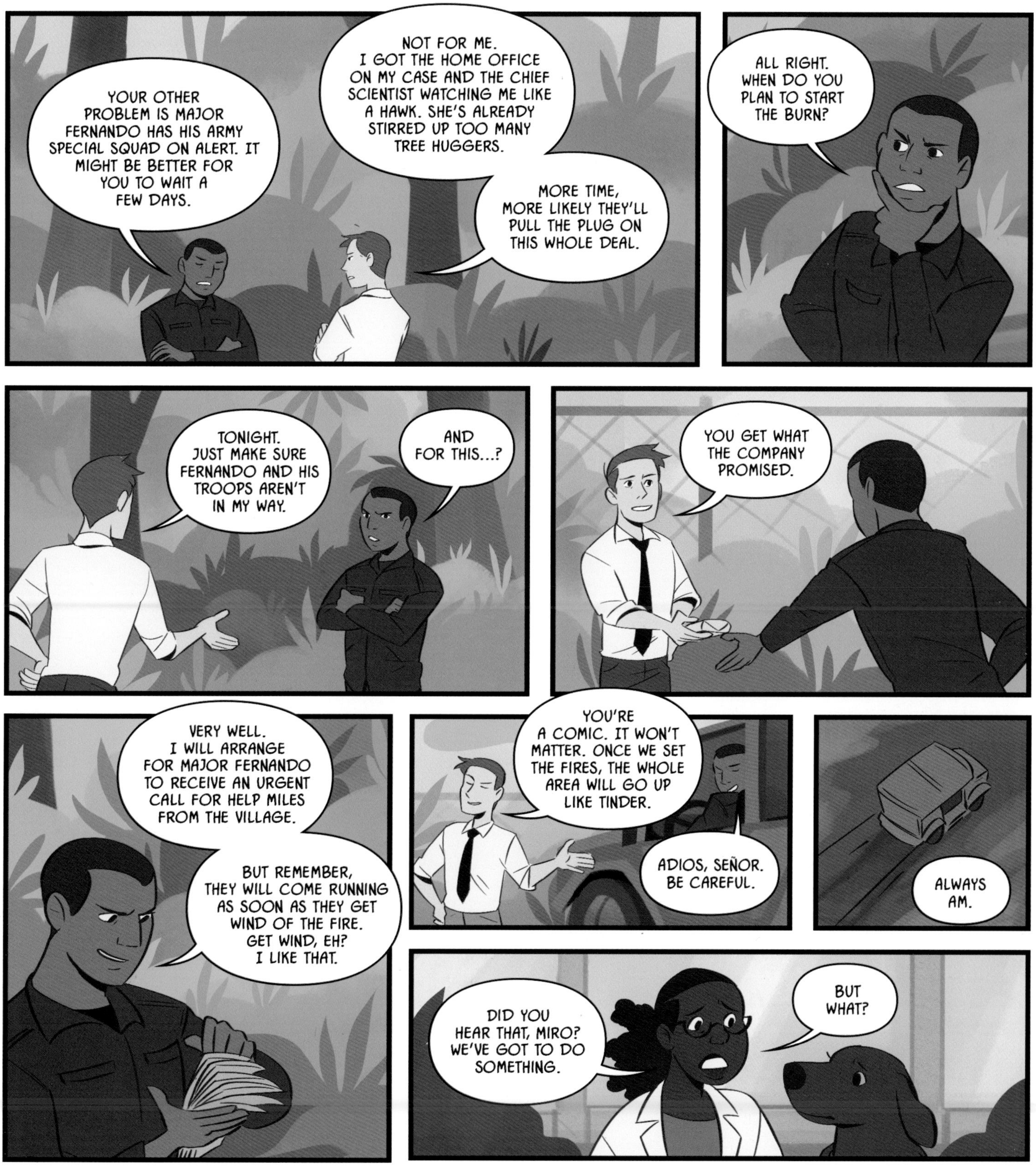
YOUR OTHER PROBLEM IS MAJOR FERNANDO HAS HIS ARMY SPECIAL SQUAD ON ALERT. IT MIGHT BE BETTER FOR YOU TO WAIT A FEW DAYS.
NOT FOR ME. I GOT THE HOME OFFICE ON MY CASE AND THE CHIEF SCIENTIST WATCHING ME LIKE A HAWK. SHE'S ALREADY STIRRED UP TOO MANY TREE HUGGERS.
MORE TIME, MORE LIKELY THEY'LL PULL THE PLUG ON THIS WHOLE DEAL.
ALL RIGHT. WHEN DO YOU PLAN TO START THE BURN?
TONIGHT. JUST MAKE SURE FERNANDO AND HIS TROOPS AREN'T IN MY WAY.
AND FOR THIS...?
YOU GET WHAT THE COMPANY PROMISED.
VERY WELL. I WILL ARRANGE FOR MAJOR FERNANDO TO RECEIVE AN URGENT CALL FOR HELP MILES FROM THE VILLAGE.
BUT REMEMBER, THEY WILL COME RUNNING AS SOON AS THEY GET WIND OF THE FIRE. GET WIND, EH? I LIKE THAT.
YOU'RE A COMIC. IT WON'T MATTER. ONCE WE SET THE FIRES, THE WHOLE AREA WILL GO UP LIKE TINDER.
ADIOS, SEÑOR. BE CAREFUL.
ALWAYS AM.
DID YOU HEAR THAT, MIRO? WE'VE GOT TO DO SOMETHING.
BUT WHAT?

CHAPTER 10

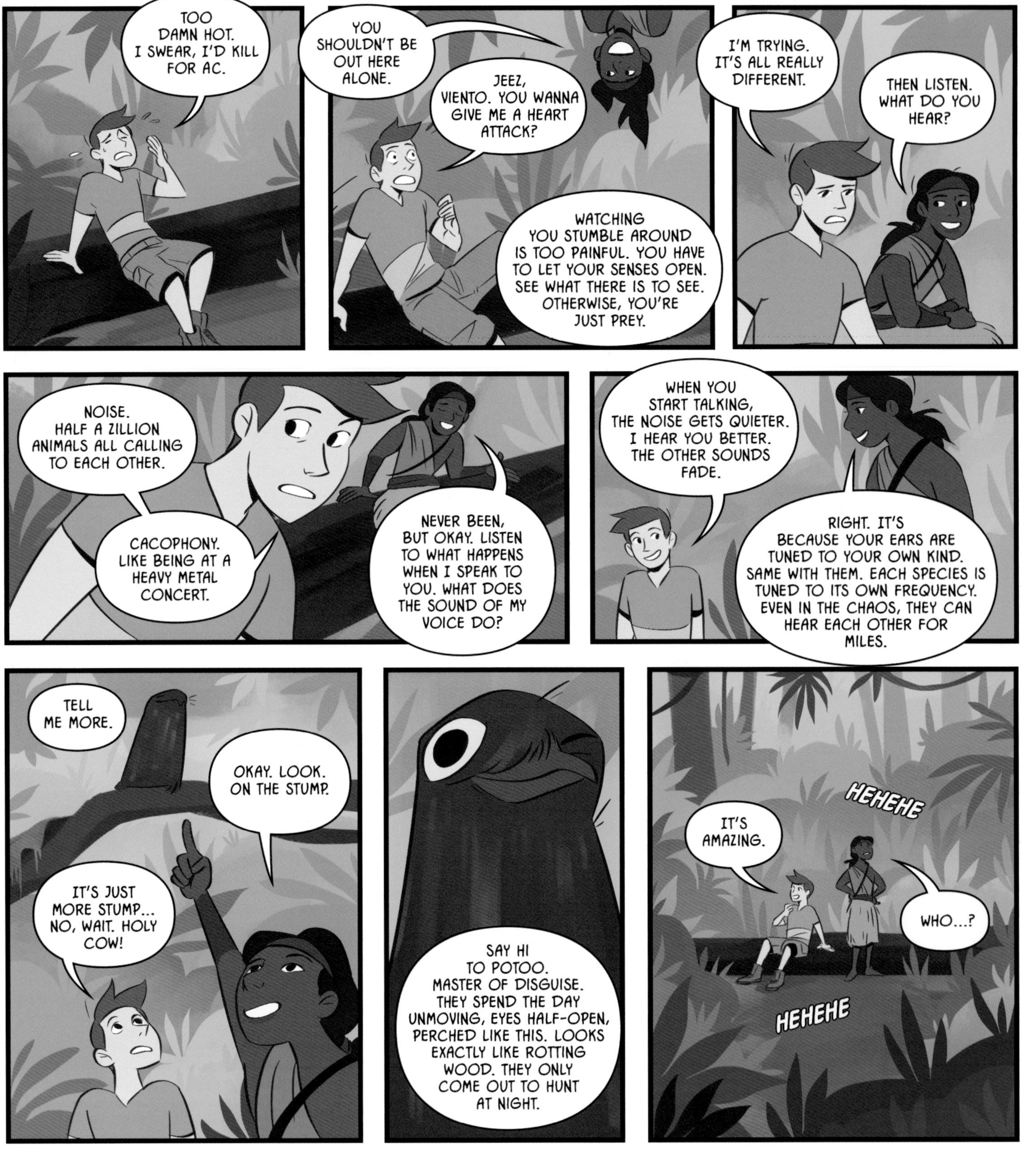
TOO DAMN HOT. I SWEAR, I'D KILL FOR AC.
YOU SHOULDN'T BE OUT HERE ALONE.
JEEZ, VIENTO. YOU WANNA GIVE ME A HEART ATTACK?
WATCHING YOU STUMBLE AROUND IS TOO PAINFUL. YOU HAVE TO LET YOUR SENSES OPEN. SEE WHAT THERE IS TO SEE. OTHERWISE, YOU'RE JUST PREY.
I'M TRYING. IT'S ALL REALLY DIFFERENT.
THEN LISTEN. WHAT DO YOU HEAR?
NOISE. HALF A ZILLION ANIMALS ALL CALLING TO EACH OTHER.
CACOPHONY. LIKE BEING AT A HEAVY METAL CONCERT.
NEVER BEEN, BUT OKAY. LISTEN TO WHAT HAPPENS WHEN I SPEAK TO YOU. WHAT DOES THE SOUND OF MY VOICE DO?
WHEN YOU START TALKING, THE NOISE GETS QUIETER. I HEAR YOU BETTER. THE OTHER SOUNDS FADE.
RIGHT. IT'S BECAUSE YOUR EARS ARE TUNED TO YOUR OWN KIND. SAME WITH THEM. EACH SPECIES IS TUNED TO ITS OWN FREQUENCY. EVEN IN THE CHAOS, THEY CAN HEAR EACH OTHER FOR MILES.
TELL ME MORE.
OKAY. LOOK. ON THE STUMP.
IT'S JUST MORE STUMP... NO, WAIT. HOLY COW!
SAY HI TO POTOO. MASTER OF DISGUISE. THEY SPEND THE DAY UNMOVING, EYES HALF-OPEN, PERCHED LIKE THIS. LOOKS EXACTLY LIKE ROTTING WOOD. THEY ONLY COME OUT TO HUNT AT NIGHT.
HEHEHE
IT'S AMAZING.
WHO...?
HEHEHE

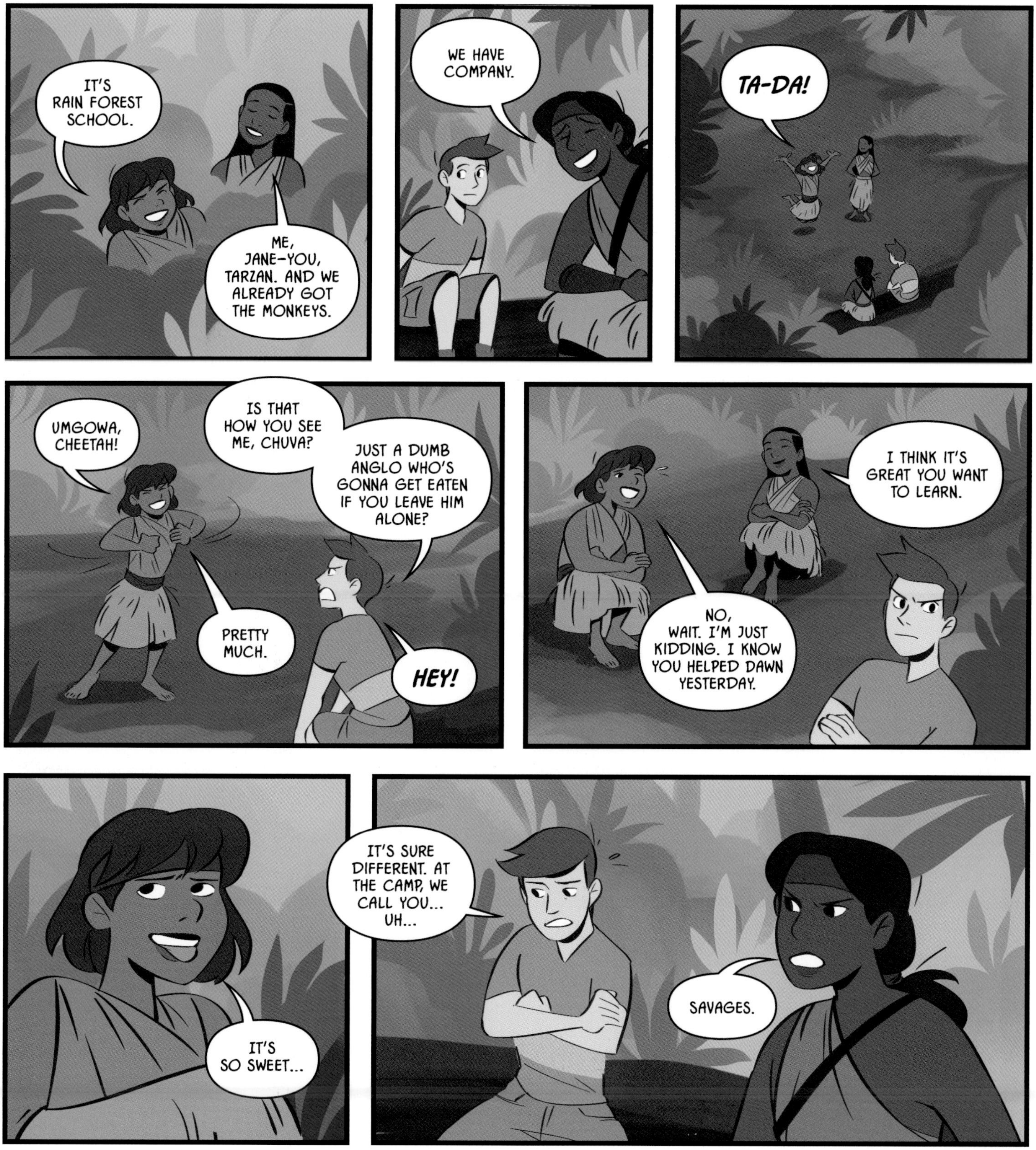
IT'S RAIN FOREST SCHOOL.
ME, JANE—YOU, TARZAN. AND WE ALREADY GOT THE MONKEYS.
WE HAVE COMPANY.
TA-DA!
UMGOWA, CHEETAH!
IS THAT HOW YOU SEE ME, CHUVA?
JUST A DUMB ANGLO WHO'S GONNA GET EATEN IF YOU LEAVE HIM ALONE?
PRETTY MUCH.
HEY!
I THINK IT'S GREAT YOU WANT TO LEARN.
NO, WAIT. I'M JUST KIDDING. I KNOW YOU HELPED DAWN YESTERDAY.
IT'S SO SWEET...
IT'S SURE DIFFERENT. AT THE CAMP, WE CALL YOU... UH...
SAVAGES.

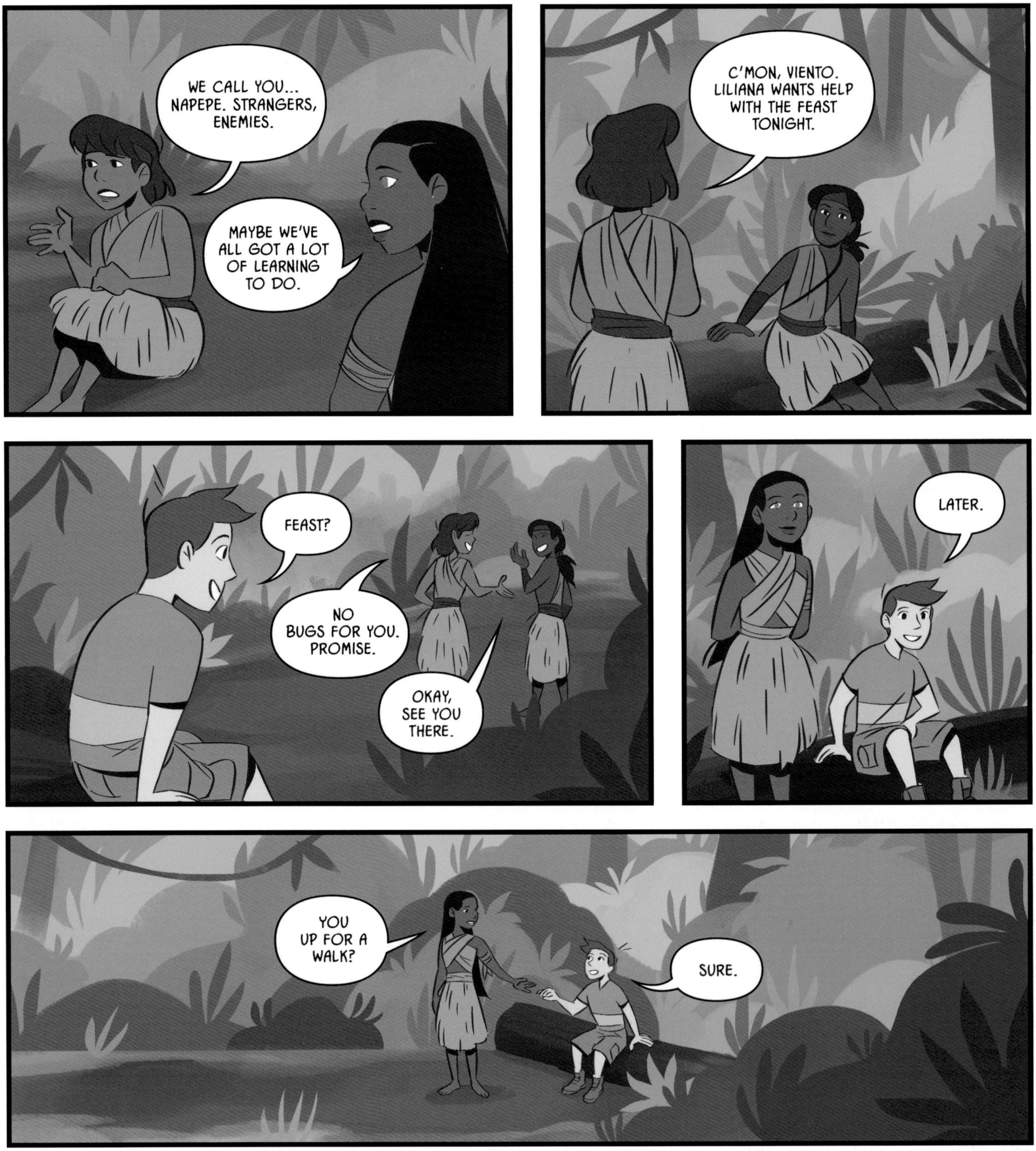
WE CALL YOU... NAPEPE. STRANGERS, ENEMIES.
MAYBE WE'VE ALL GOT A LOT OF LEARNING TO DO.
C'MON, VIENTO. LILIANA WANTS HELP WITH THE FEAST TONIGHT.
FEAST?
NO BUGS FOR YOU. PROMISE.
OKAY, SEE YOU THERE.
LATER.
YOU UP FOR A WALK?
SURE.

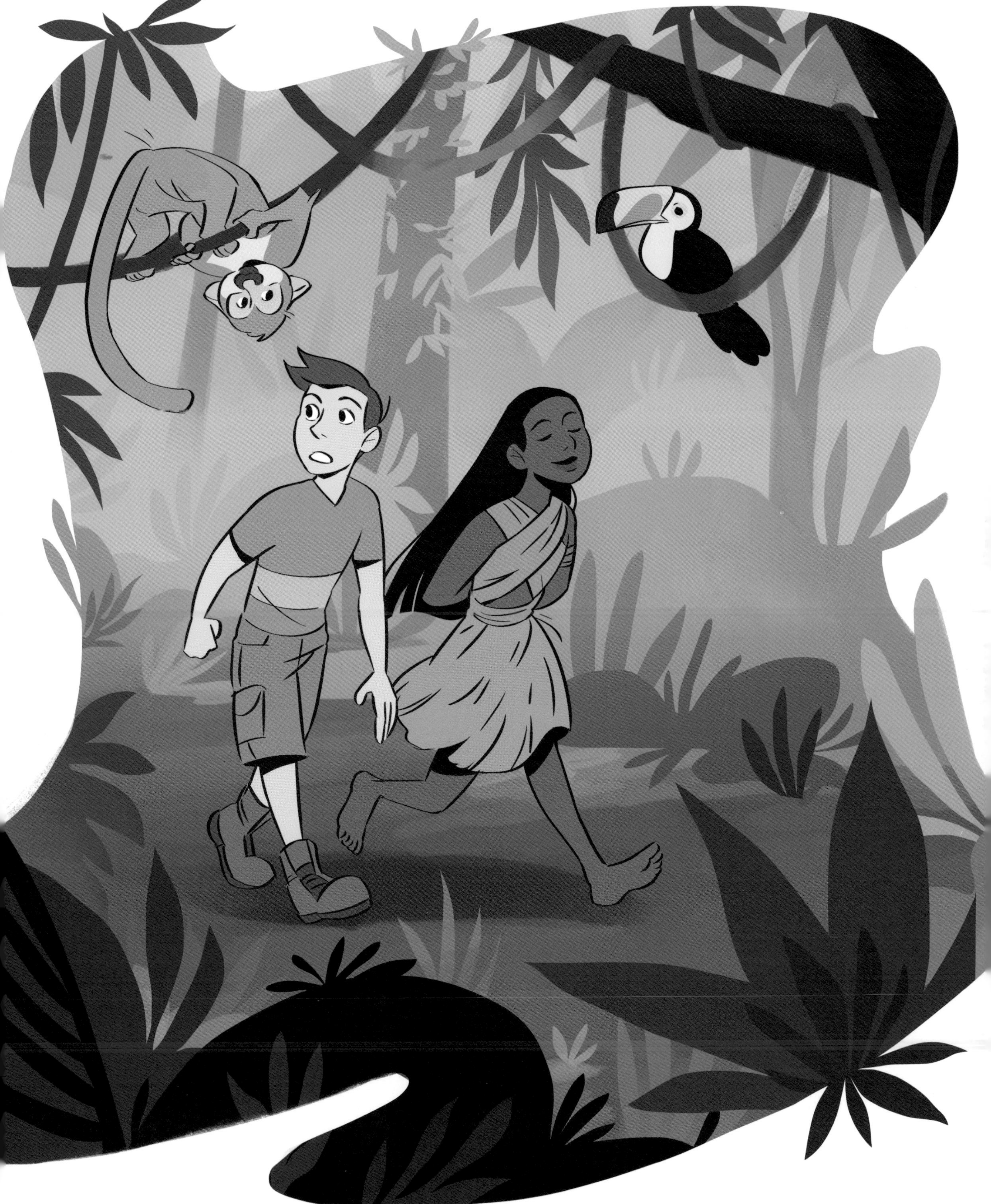

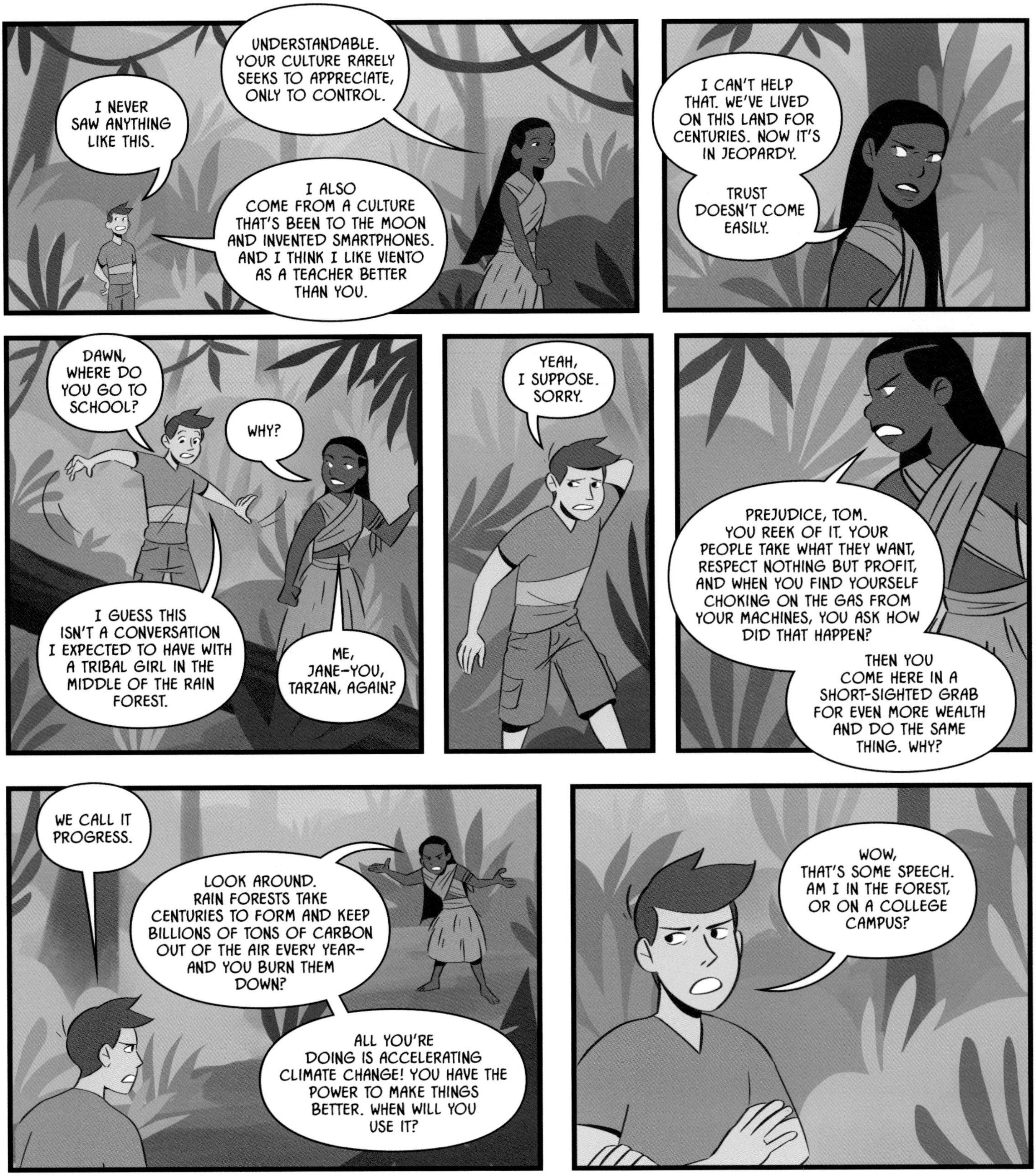
I NEVER SAW ANYTHING LIKE THIS.
UNDERSTANDABLE. YOUR CULTURE RARELY SEEKS TO APPRECIATE, ONLY TO CONTROL.
I ALSO COME FROM A CULTURE THAT'S BEEN TO THE MOON AND INVENTED SMARTPHONES. AND I THINK I LIKE VIENTO AS A TEACHER BETTER THAN YOU.
I CAN'T HELP THAT. WE'VE LIVED ON THIS LAND FOR CENTURIES. NOW IT'S IN JEOPARDY.
TRUST DOESN'T COME EASILY.
DAWN, WHERE DO YOU GO TO SCHOOL?
WHY?
I GUESS THIS ISN'T A CONVERSATION I EXPECTED TO HAVE WITH A TRIBAL GIRL IN THE MIDDLE OF THE RAIN FOREST.
ME, JANE—YOU, TARZAN, AGAIN?
YEAH, I SUPPOSE. SORRY.
PREJUDICE, TOM. YOU REEK OF IT. YOUR PEOPLE TAKE WHAT THEY WANT, RESPECT NOTHING BUT PROFIT, AND WHEN YOU FIND YOURSELF CHOKING ON THE GAS FROM YOUR MACHINES, YOU ASK HOW DID THAT HAPPEN?
THEN YOU COME HERE IN A SHORT-SIGHTED GRAB FOR EVEN MORE WEALTH AND DO THE SAME THING. WHY?
WE CALL IT PROGRESS.
LOOK AROUND. RAIN FORESTS TAKE CENTURIES TO FORM AND KEEP BILLIONS OF TONS OF CARBON OUT OF THE AIR EVERY YEAR—AND YOU BURN THEM DOWN?
ALL YOU'RE DOING IS ACCELERATING CLIMATE CHANGE! YOU HAVE THE POWER TO MAKE THINGS BETTER. WHEN WILL YOU USE IT?
WOW, THAT'S SOME SPEECH. AM I IN THE FOREST, OR ON A COLLEGE CAMPUS?

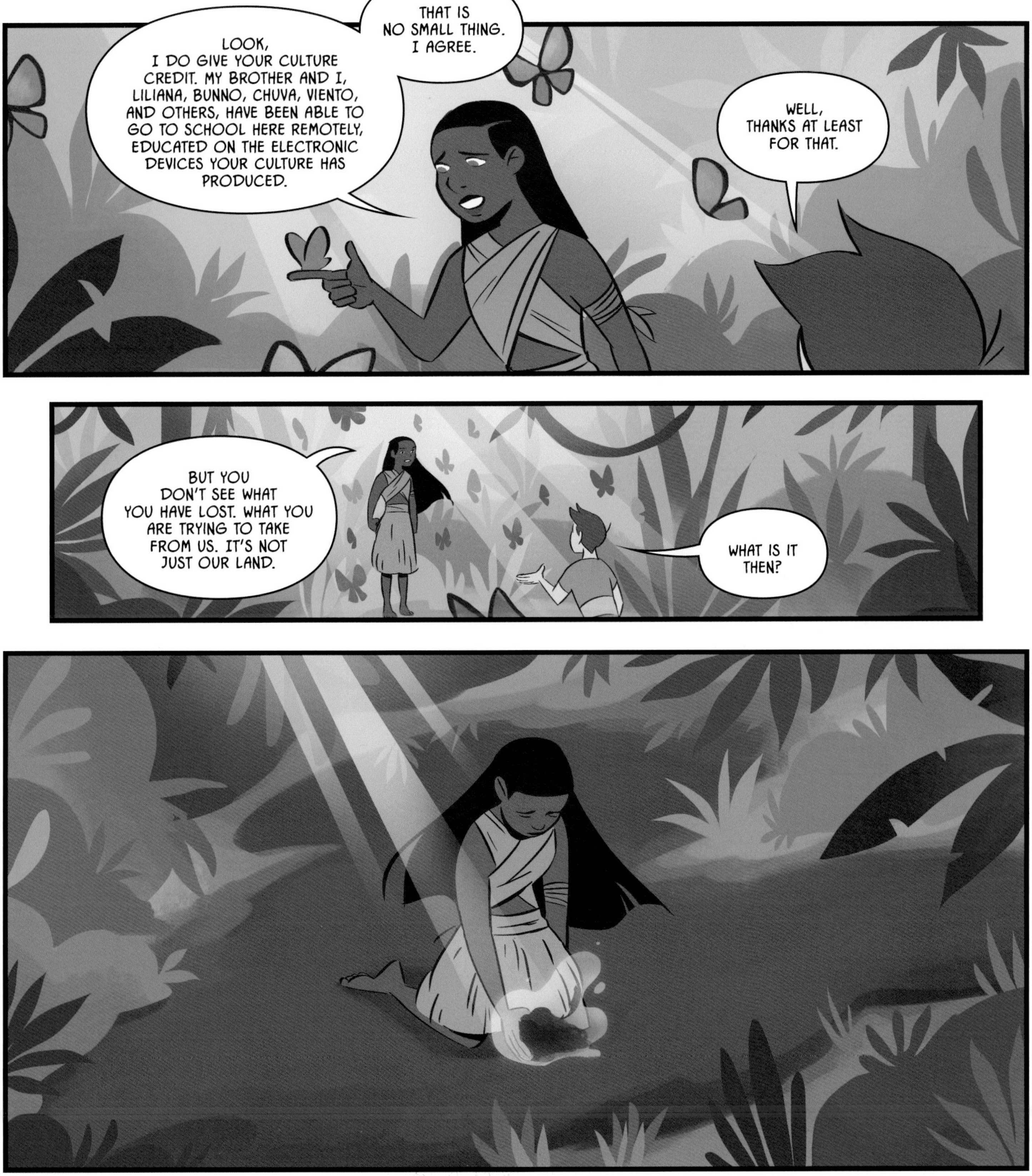
LOOK, I DO GIVE YOUR CULTURE CREDIT. MY BROTHER AND I, LILIANA, BUNNO, CHUVA, VIENTO, AND OTHERS, HAVE BEEN ABLE TO GO TO SCHOOL HERE REMOTELY, EDUCATED ON THE ELECTRONIC DEVICES YOUR CULTURE HAS PRODUCED.
THAT IS NO SMALL THING. I AGREE.
WELL, THANKS AT LEAST FOR THAT.
BUT YOU DON'T SEE WHAT YOU HAVE LOST. WHAT YOU ARE TRYING TO TAKE FROM US. IT'S NOT JUST OUR LAND.
WHAT IS IT THEN?

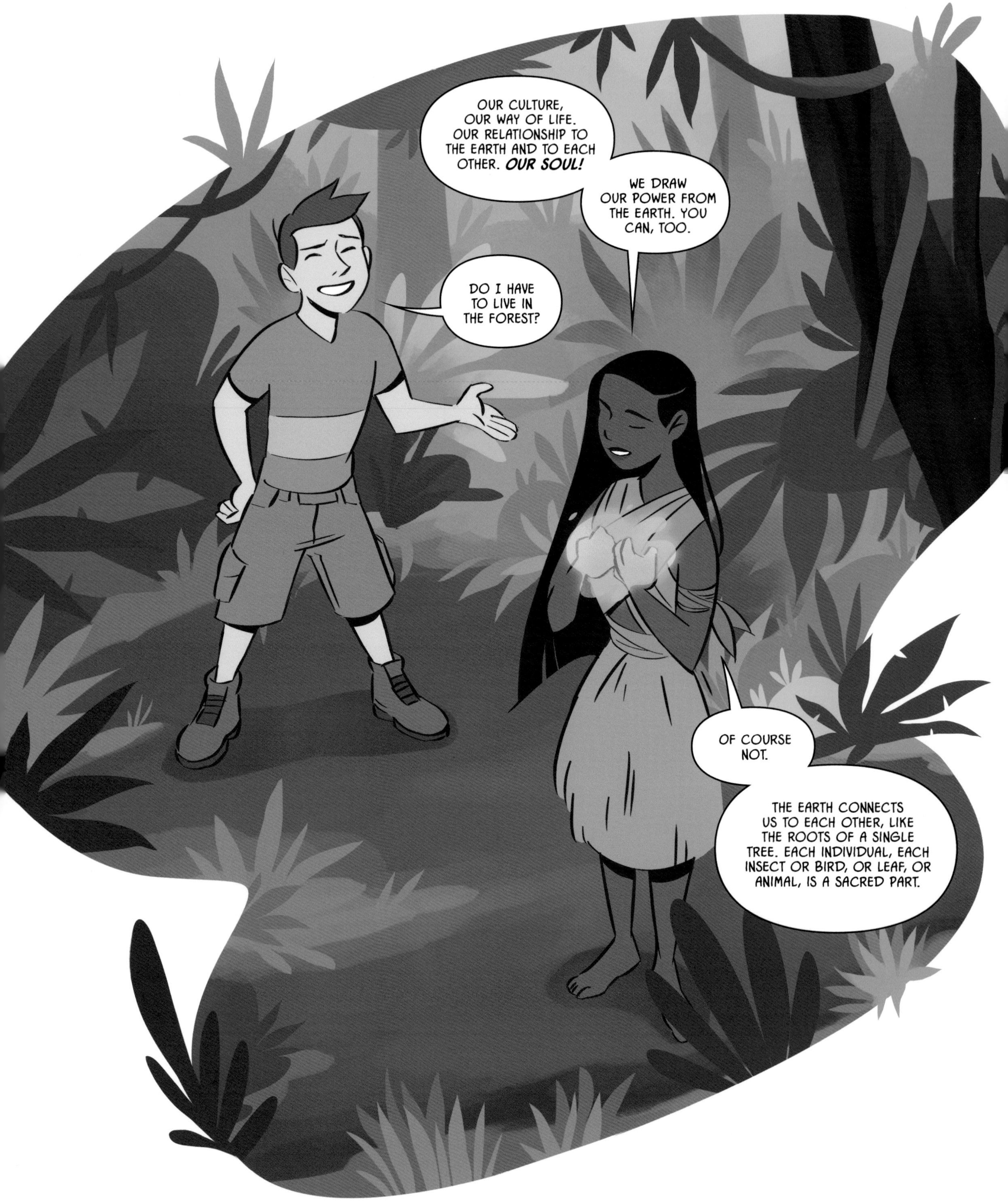
OUR CULTURE, OUR WAY OF LIFE. OUR RELATIONSHIP TO THE EARTH AND TO EACH OTHER. ***OUR SOUL!***
WE DRAW OUR POWER FROM THE EARTH. YOU CAN, TOO.
DO I HAVE TO LIVE IN THE FOREST?
OF COURSE NOT.
THE EARTH CONNECTS US TO EACH OTHER, LIKE THE ROOTS OF A SINGLE TREE. EACH INDIVIDUAL, EACH INSECT OR BIRD, OR LEAF, OR ANIMAL, IS A SACRED PART.

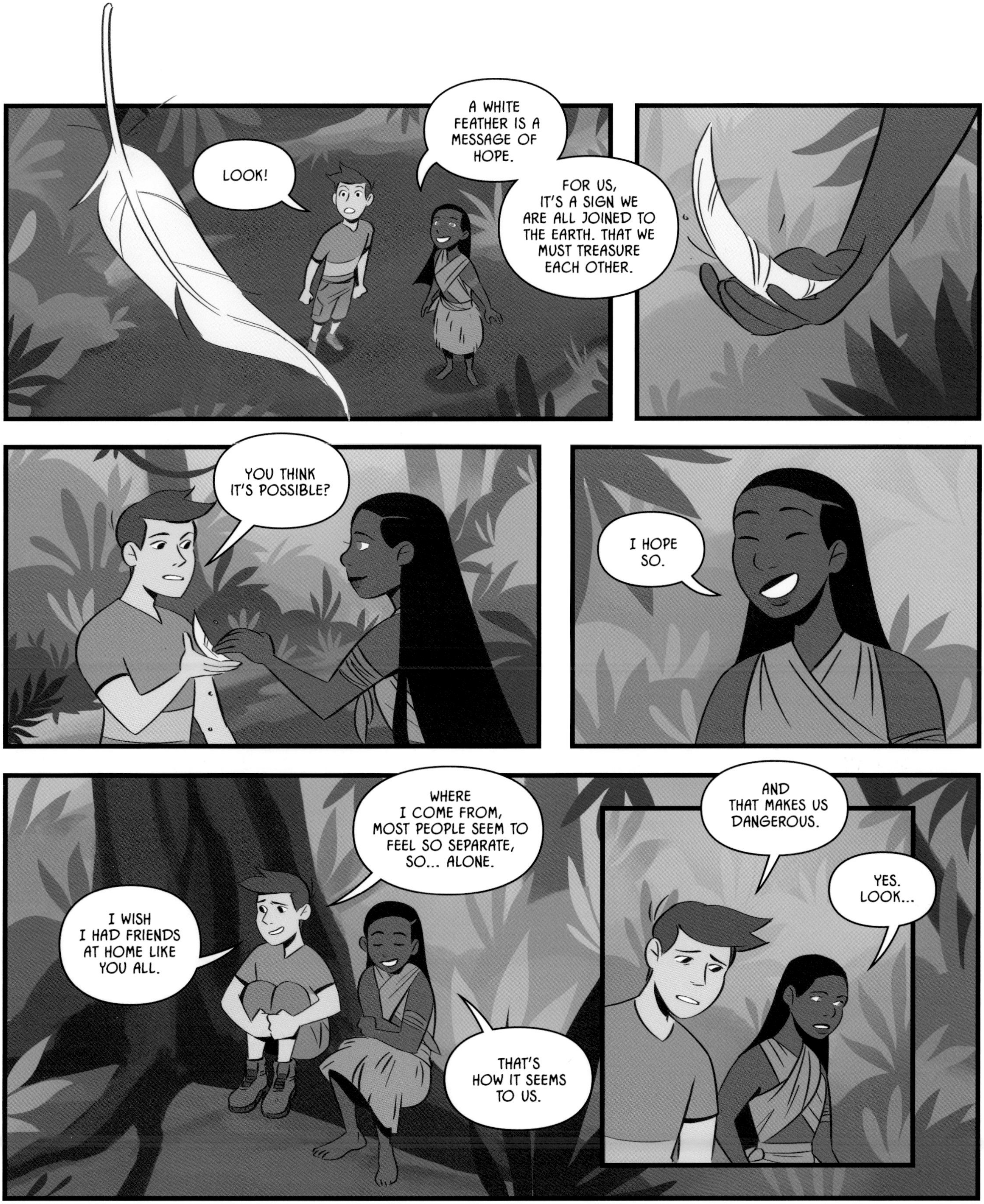
LOOK!
A WHITE FEATHER IS A MESSAGE OF HOPE.
FOR US, IT'S A SIGN WE ARE ALL JOINED TO THE EARTH. THAT WE MUST TREASURE EACH OTHER.
YOU THINK IT'S POSSIBLE?
I HOPE SO.
I WISH I HAD FRIENDS AT HOME LIKE YOU ALL.
WHERE I COME FROM, MOST PEOPLE SEEM TO FEEL SO SEPARATE, SO... ALONE.
THAT'S HOW IT SEEMS TO US.
AND THAT MAKES US DANGEROUS.
YES. LOOK...

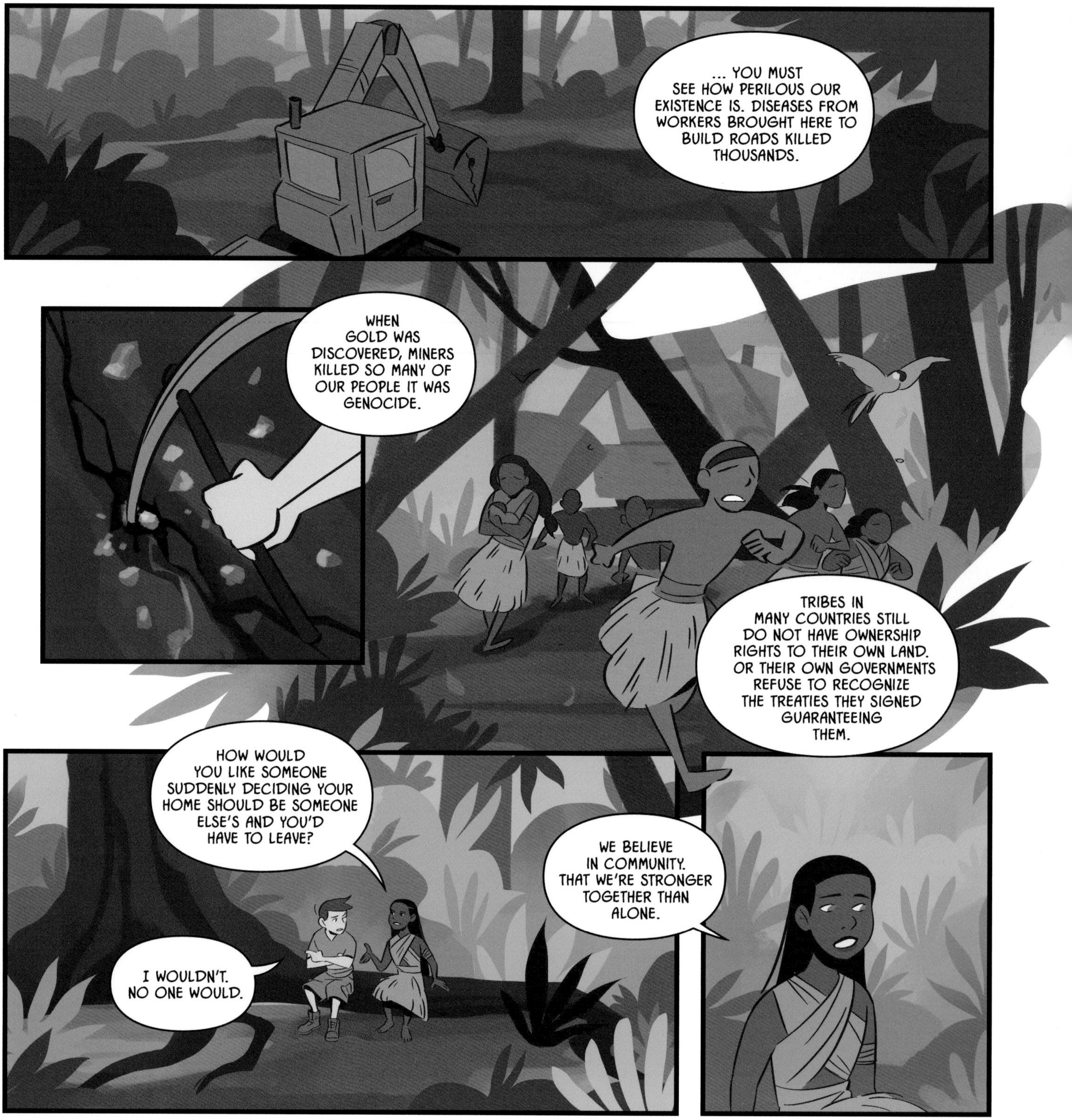

... YOU MUST SEE HOW PERILOUS OUR EXISTENCE IS. DISEASES FROM WORKERS BROUGHT HERE TO BUILD ROADS KILLED THOUSANDS.
WHEN GOLD WAS DISCOVERED, MINERS KILLED SO MANY OF OUR PEOPLE IT WAS GENOCIDE.
TRIBES IN MANY COUNTRIES STILL DO NOT HAVE OWNERSHIP RIGHTS TO THEIR OWN LAND. OR THEIR OWN GOVERNMENTS REFUSE TO RECOGNIZE THE TREATIES THEY SIGNED GUARANTEEING THEM.
HOW WOULD YOU LIKE SOMEONE SUDDENLY DECIDING YOUR HOME SHOULD BE SOMEONE ELSE'S AND YOU'D HAVE TO LEAVE?
I WOULDN'T. NO ONE WOULD.
WE BELIEVE IN COMMUNITY. THAT WE'RE STRONGER TOGETHER THAN ALONE.

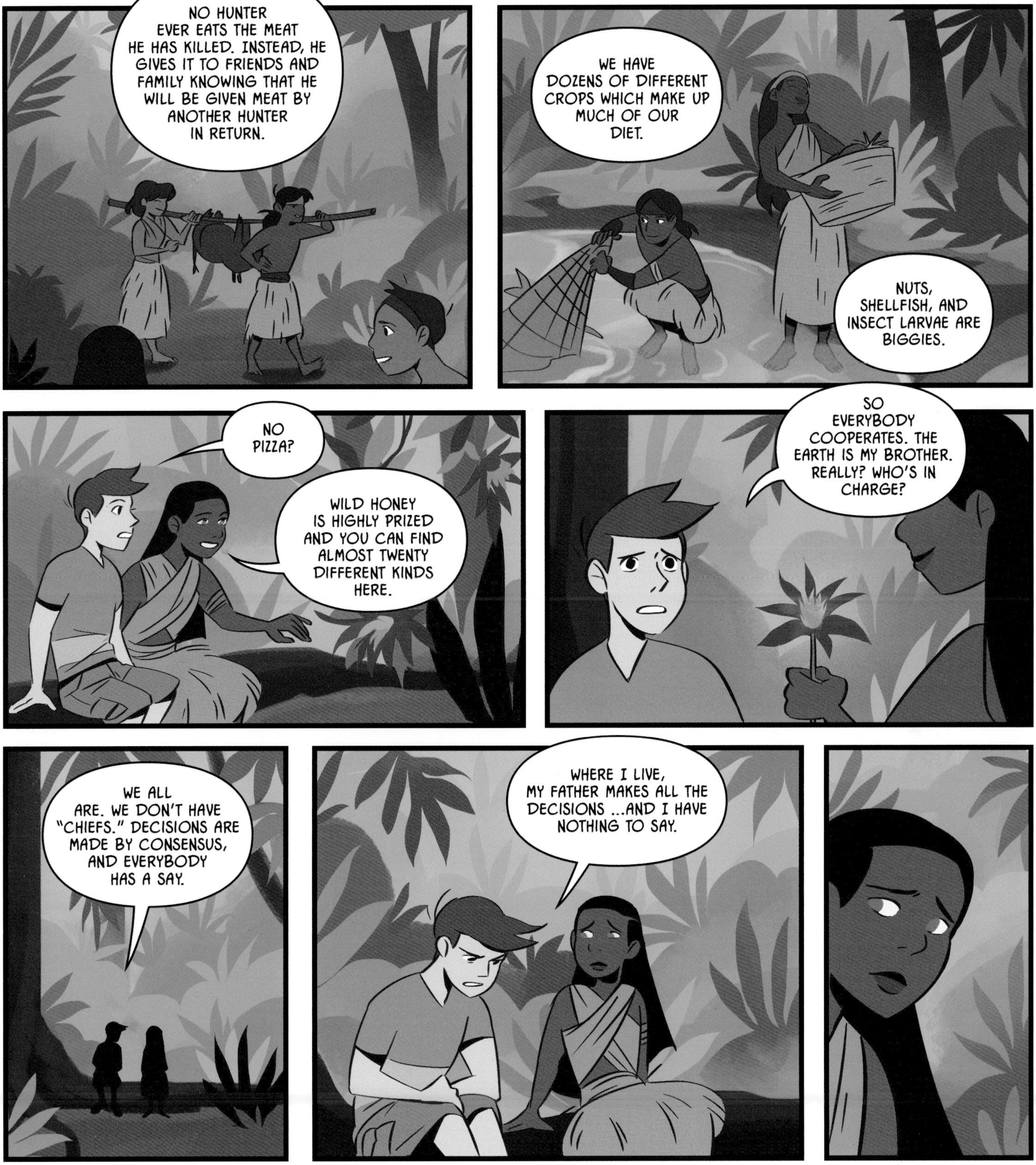
NO HUNTER EVER EATS THE MEAT HE HAS KILLED. INSTEAD, HE GIVES IT TO FRIENDS AND FAMILY KNOWING THAT HE WILL BE GIVEN MEAT BY ANOTHER HUNTER IN RETURN.
WE HAVE DOZENS OF DIFFERENT CROPS WHICH MAKE UP MUCH OF OUR DIET.
NUTS, SHELLFISH, AND INSECT LARVAE ARE BIGGIES.
NO PIZZA?
WILD HONEY IS HIGHLY PRIZED AND YOU CAN FIND ALMOST TWENTY DIFFERENT KINDS HERE.
SO EVERYBODY COOPERATES. THE EARTH IS MY BROTHER. REALLY? WHO'S IN CHARGE?
WE ALL ARE. WE DON'T HAVE "CHIEFS." DECISIONS ARE MADE BY CONSENSUS, AND EVERYBODY HAS A SAY.
WHERE I LIVE, MY FATHER MAKES ALL THE DECISIONS ...AND I HAVE NOTHING TO SAY.

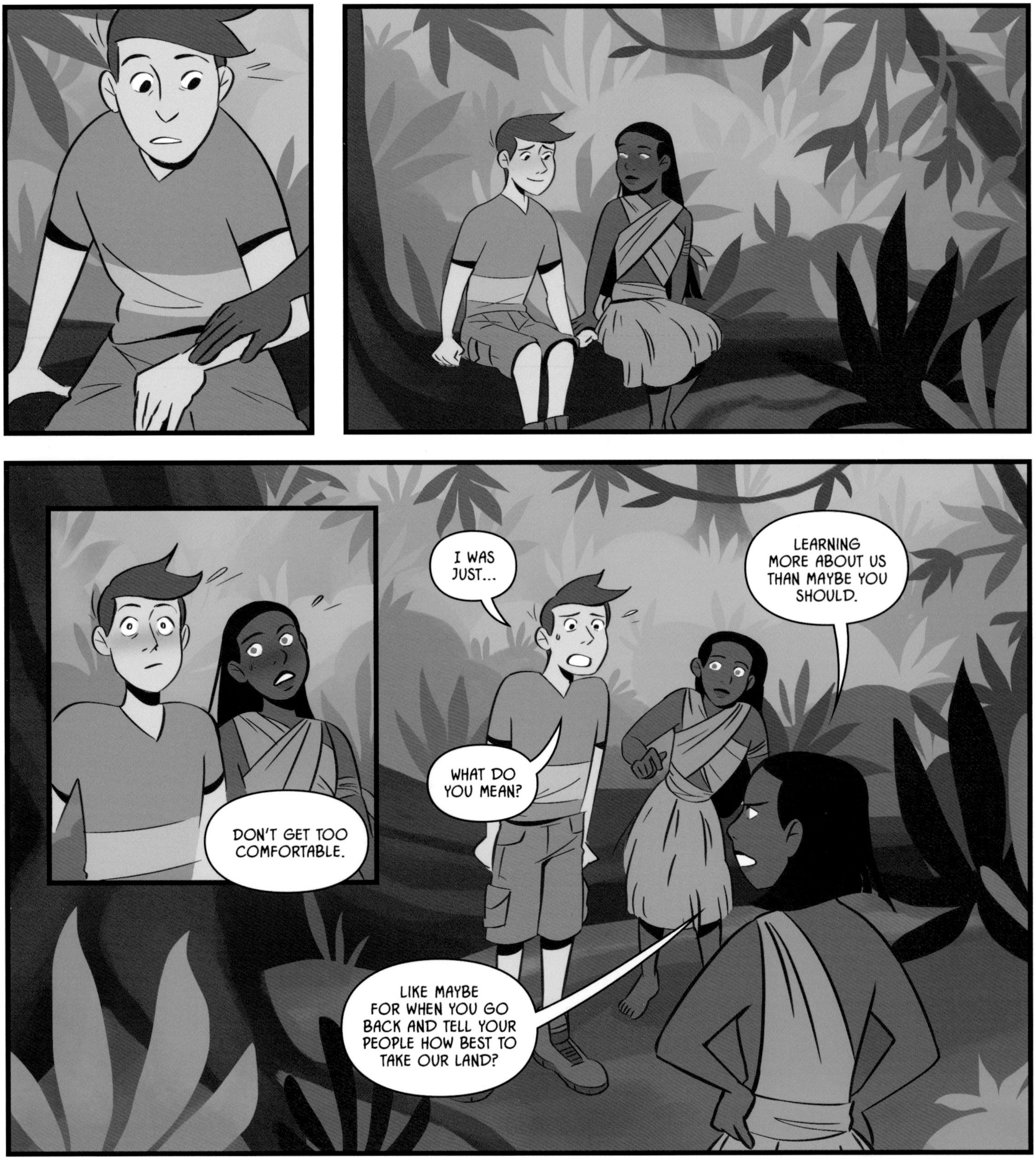
DON'T GET TOO COMFORTABLE.
I WAS JUST...
LEARNING MORE ABOUT US THAN MAYBE YOU SHOULD.
WHAT DO YOU MEAN?
LIKE MAYBE FOR WHEN YOU GO BACK AND TELL YOUR PEOPLE HOW BEST TO TAKE OUR LAND?

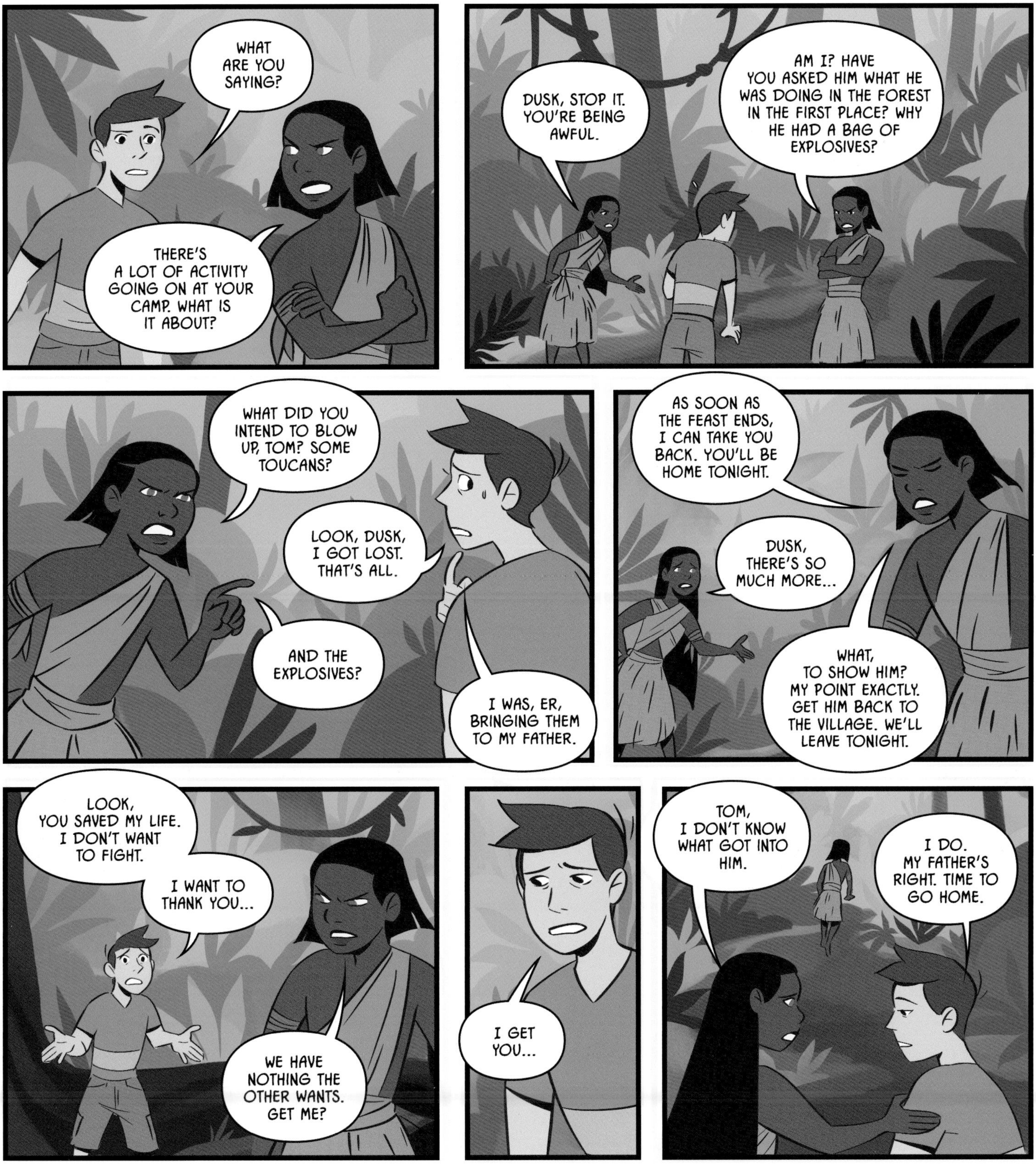
WHAT ARE YOU SAYING?
THERE'S A LOT OF ACTIVITY GOING ON AT YOUR CAMP. WHAT IS IT ABOUT?
DUSK, STOP IT. YOU'RE BEING AWFUL.
AM I? HAVE YOU ASKED HIM WHAT HE WAS DOING IN THE FOREST IN THE FIRST PLACE? WHY HE HAD A BAG OF EXPLOSIVES?
WHAT DID YOU INTEND TO BLOW UP, TOM? SOME TOUCANS?
LOOK, DUSK, I GOT LOST. THAT'S ALL.
AND THE EXPLOSIVES?
I WAS, ER, BRINGING THEM TO MY FATHER.
AS SOON AS THE FEAST ENDS, I CAN TAKE YOU BACK. YOU'LL BE HOME TONIGHT.
DUSK, THERE'S SO MUCH MORE...
WHAT, TO SHOW HIM? MY POINT EXACTLY. GET HIM BACK TO THE VILLAGE. WE'LL LEAVE TONIGHT.
LOOK, YOU SAVED MY LIFE. I DON'T WANT TO FIGHT.
I WANT TO THANK YOU...
WE HAVE NOTHING THE OTHER WANTS. GET ME?
I GET YOU...
TOM, I DON'T KNOW WHAT GOT INTO HIM.
I DO. MY FATHER'S RIGHT. TIME TO GO HOME.

CHAPTER 11

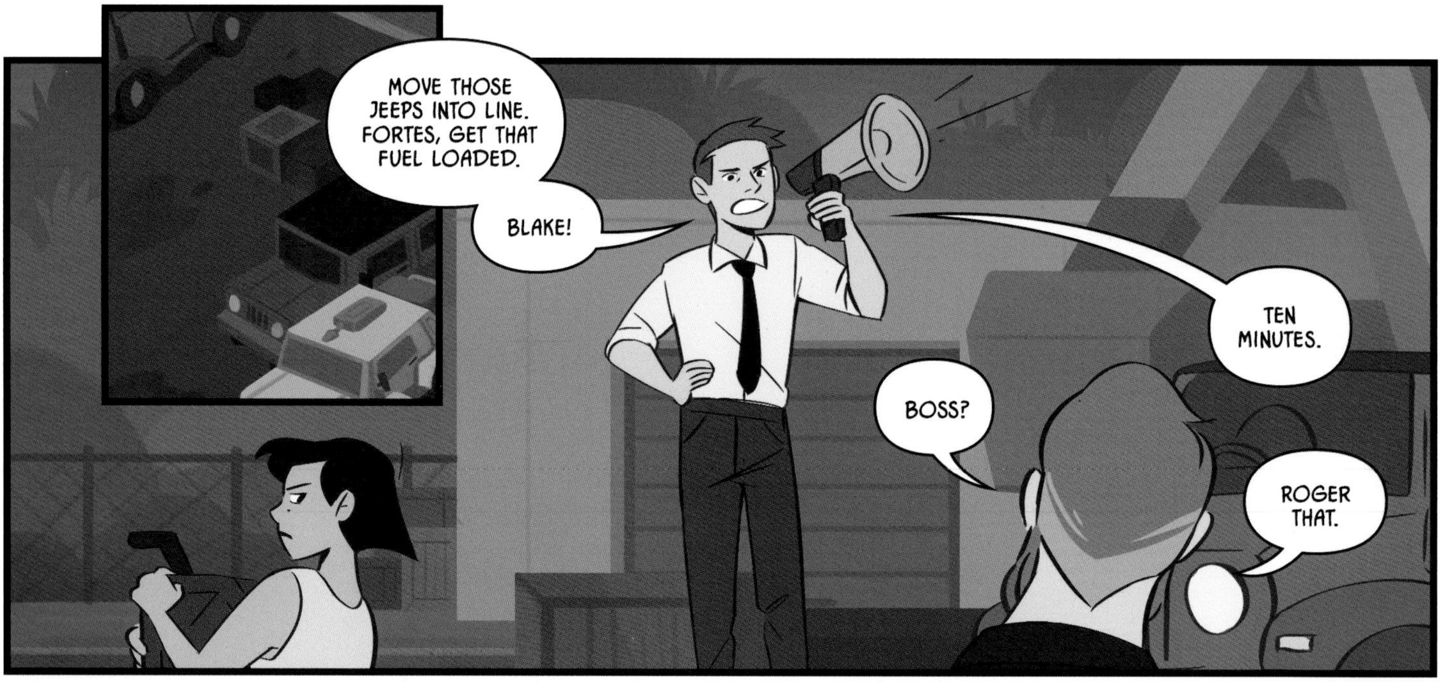
MOVE THOSE JEEPS INTO LINE. FORTES, GET THAT FUEL LOADED.
BLAKE!
BOSS?
TEN MINUTES.
ROGER THAT.

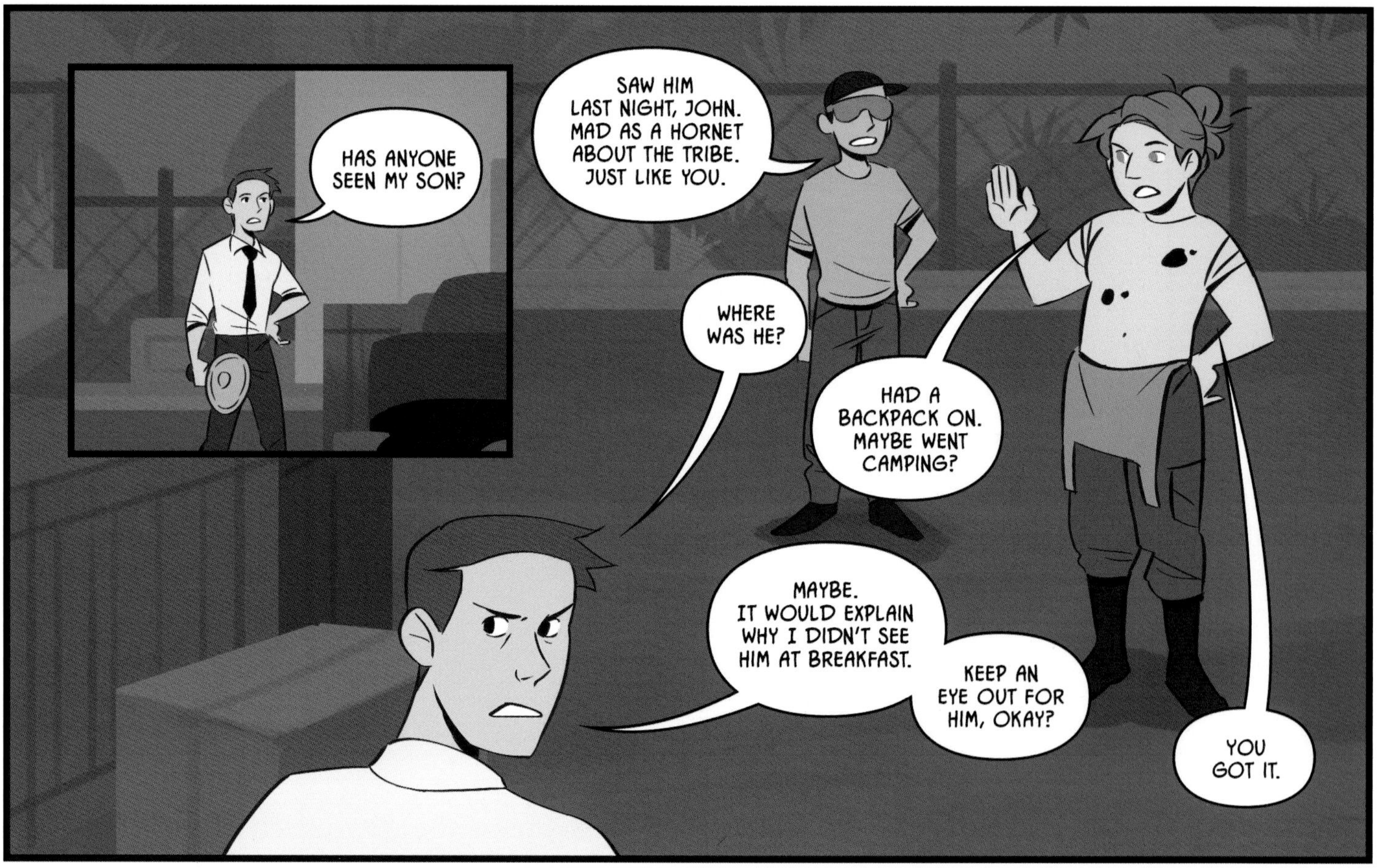
HAS ANYONE SEEN MY SON?
SAW HIM LAST NIGHT, JOHN. MAD AS A HORNET ABOUT THE TRIBE. JUST LIKE YOU.
WHERE WAS HE?
HAD A BACKPACK ON. MAYBE WENT CAMPING?
MAYBE. IT WOULD EXPLAIN WHY I DIDN'T SEE HIM AT BREAKFAST.
KEEP AN EYE OUT FOR HIM, OKAY?
YOU GOT IT.

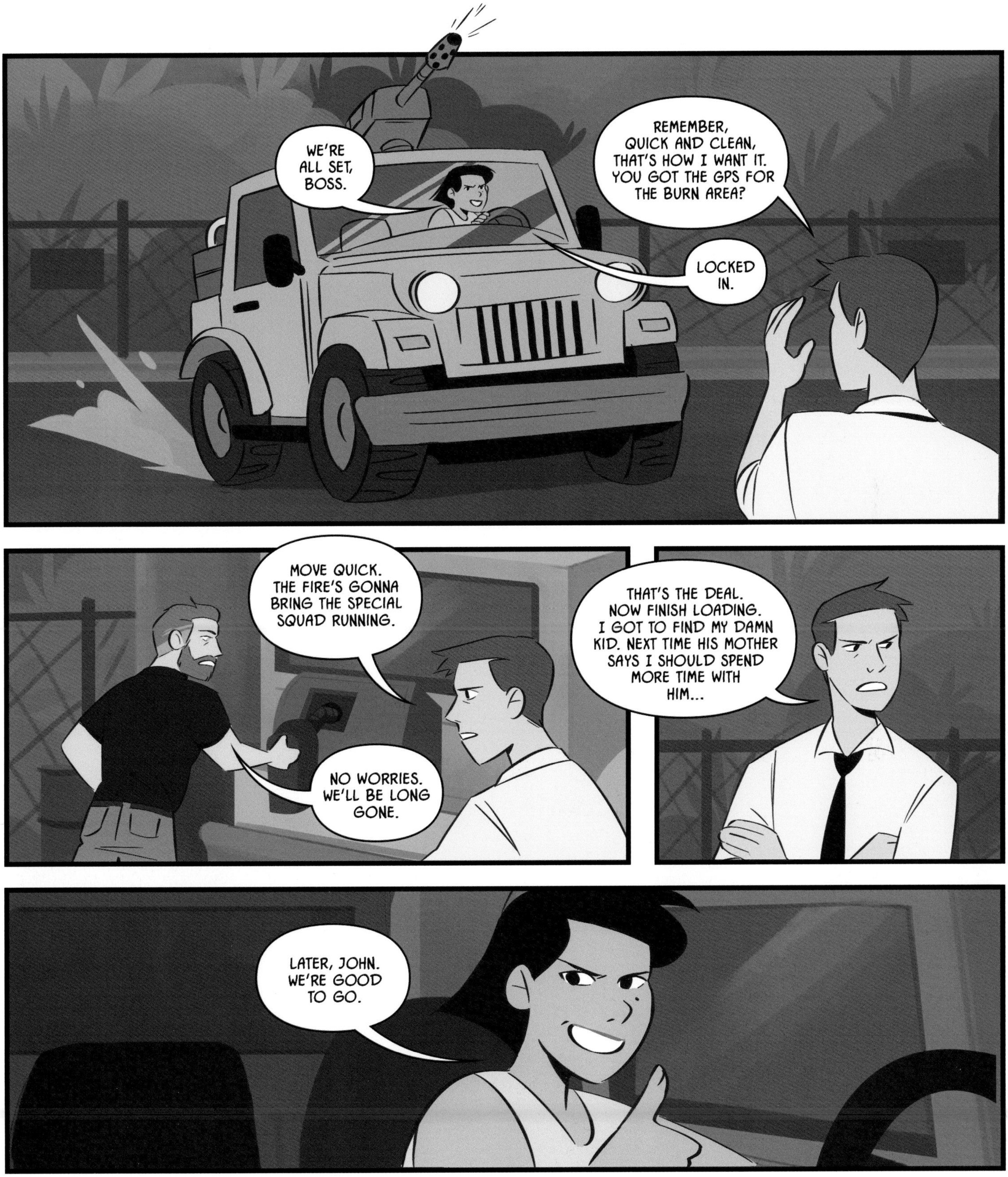
WE'RE ALL SET, BOSS.
REMEMBER, QUICK AND CLEAN, THAT'S HOW I WANT IT. YOU GOT THE GPS FOR THE BURN AREA?
LOCKED IN.
MOVE QUICK. THE FIRE'S GONNA BRING THE SPECIAL SQUAD RUNNING.
NO WORRIES. WE'LL BE LONG GONE.
THAT'S THE DEAL. NOW FINISH LOADING. I GOT TO FIND MY DAMN KID. NEXT TIME HIS MOTHER SAYS I SHOULD SPEND MORE TIME WITH HIM...
LATER, JOHN. WE'RE GOOD TO GO.

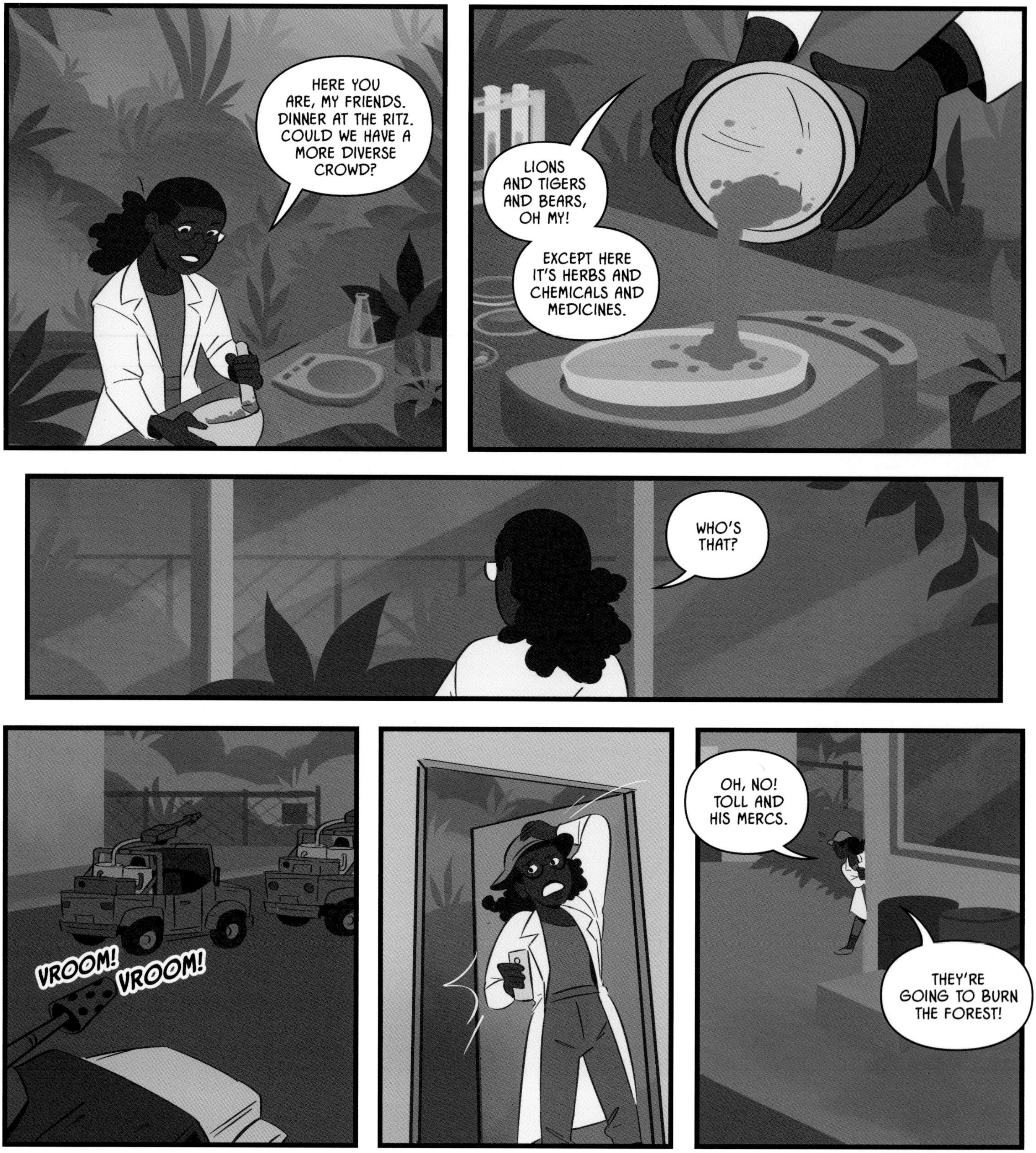

HERE YOU ARE, MY FRIENDS. DINNER AT THE RITZ. COULD WE HAVE A MORE DIVERSE CROWD?
LIONS AND TIGERS AND BEARS, OH MY!
EXCEPT HERE IT'S HERBS AND CHEMICALS AND MEDICINES.
WHO'S THAT?
VROOM! VROOM!
OH, NO! TOLL AND HIS MERCS.
THEY'RE GOING TO BURN THE FOREST!

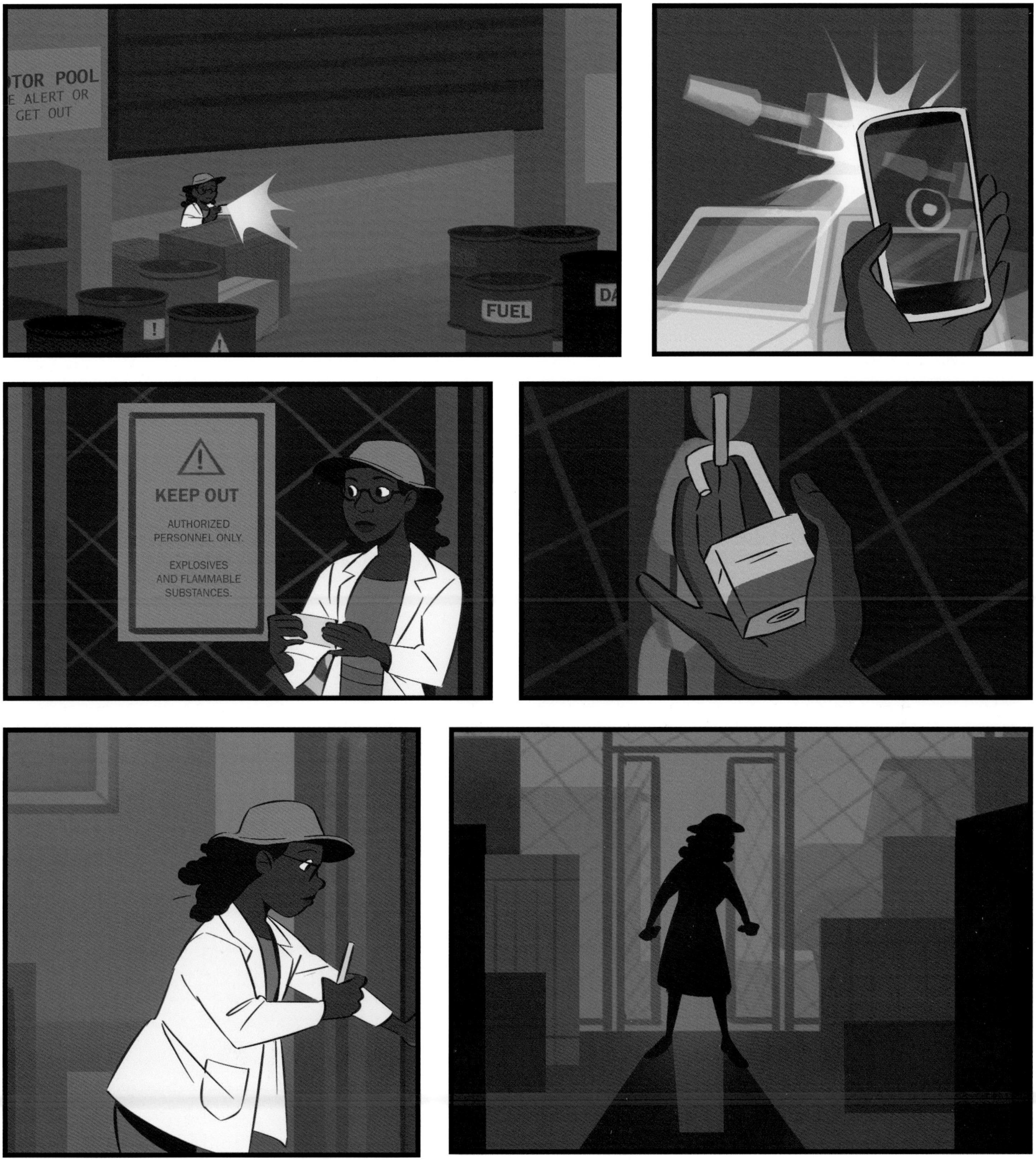

OTOR POOL
E ALERT OR
GET OUT
FUEL
DA
KEEP OUT
AUTHORIZED
PERSONNEL ONLY.
EXPLOSIVES
AND FLAMMABLE
SUBSTANCES.

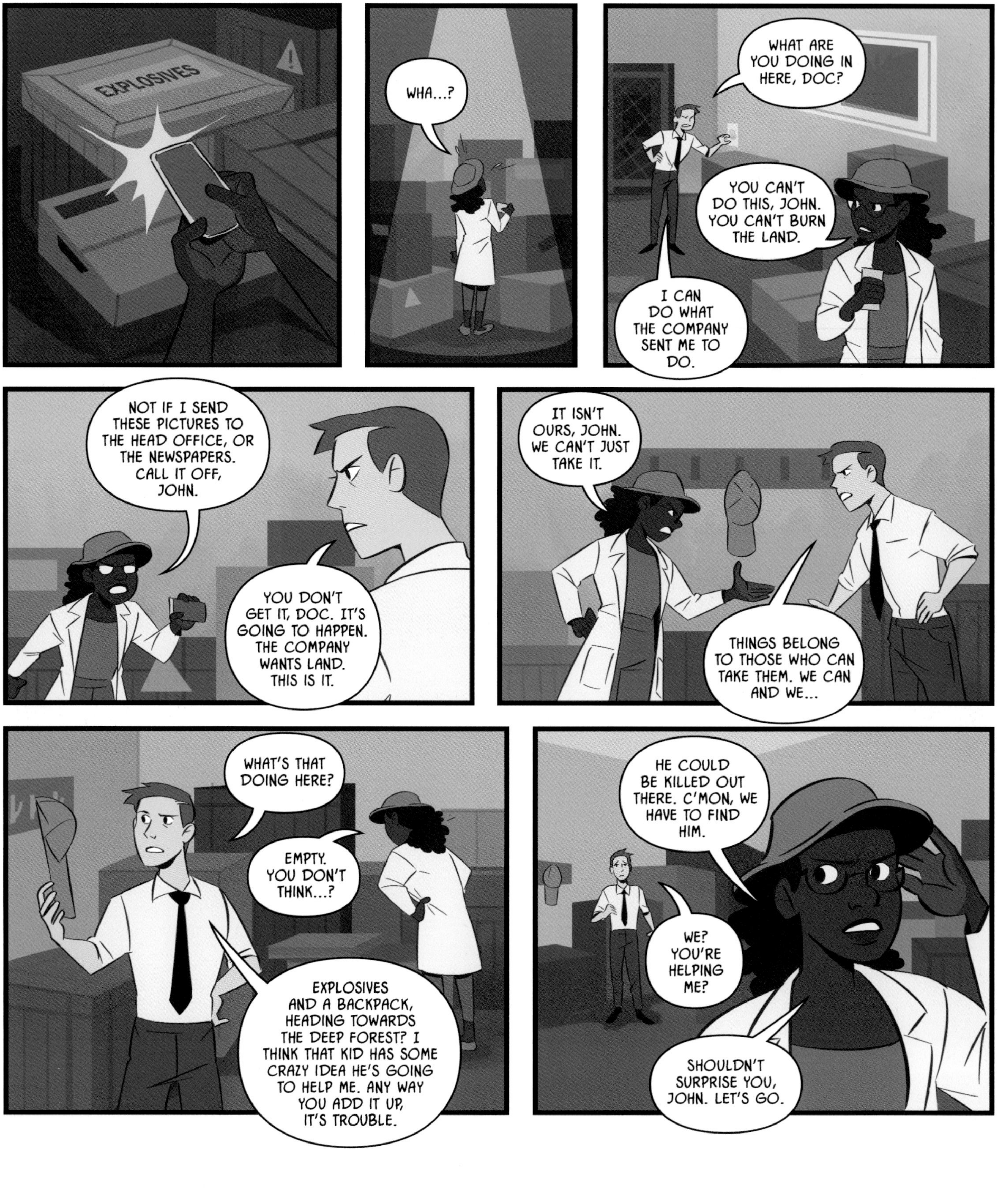
EXPLOSIVES
WHA...?
WHAT ARE YOU DOING IN HERE, DOC?
YOU CAN'T DO THIS, JOHN. YOU CAN'T BURN THE LAND.
I CAN DO WHAT THE COMPANY SENT ME TO DO.
NOT IF I SEND THESE PICTURES TO THE HEAD OFFICE, OR THE NEWSPAPERS. CALL IT OFF, JOHN.
YOU DON'T GET IT, DOC. IT'S GOING TO HAPPEN. THE COMPANY WANTS LAND. THIS IS IT.
IT ISN'T OURS, JOHN. WE CAN'T JUST TAKE IT.
THINGS BELONG TO THOSE WHO CAN TAKE THEM. WE CAN AND WE...
WHAT'S THAT DOING HERE?
EMPTY. YOU DON'T THINK...?
EXPLOSIVES AND A BACKPACK, HEADING TOWARDS THE DEEP FOREST? I THINK THAT KID HAS SOME CRAZY IDEA HE'S GOING TO HELP ME. ANY WAY YOU ADD IT UP, IT'S TROUBLE.
HE COULD BE KILLED OUT THERE. C'MON, WE HAVE TO FIND HIM.
WE? YOU'RE HELPING ME?
SHOULDN'T SURPRISE YOU, JOHN. LET'S GO.

CHAPTER 12

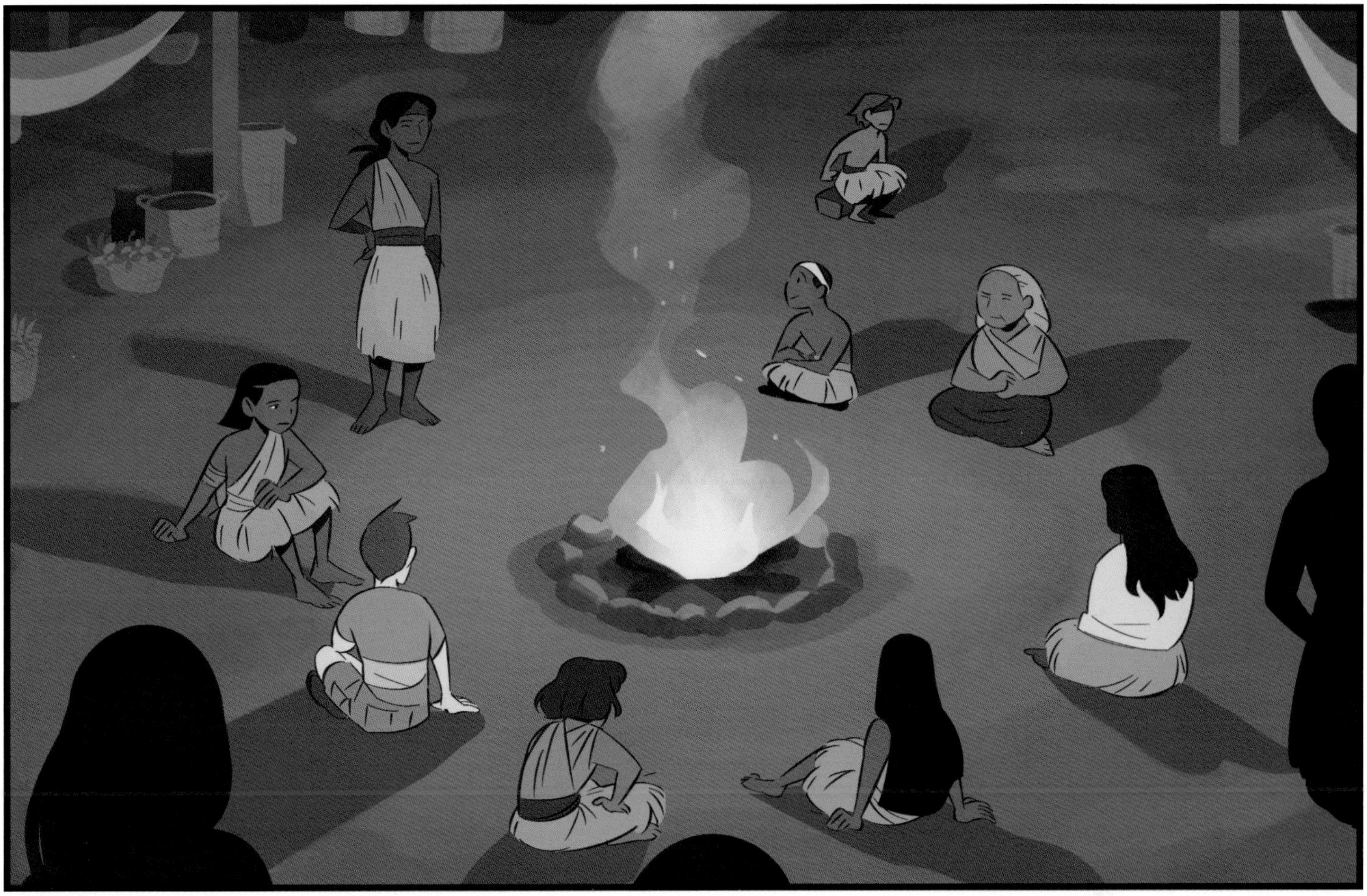

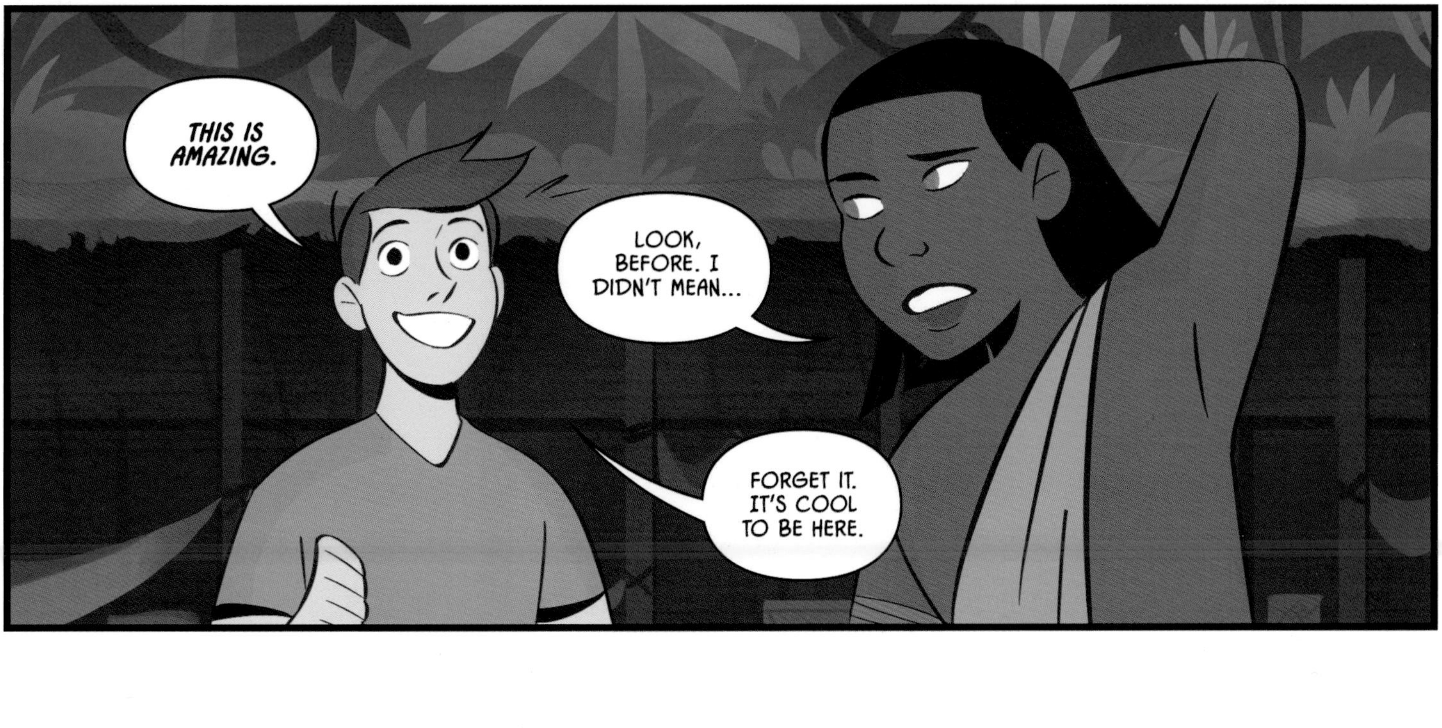

THIS IS AMAZING.
LOOK, BEFORE. I DIDN'T MEAN...
FORGET IT. IT'S COOL TO BE HERE.

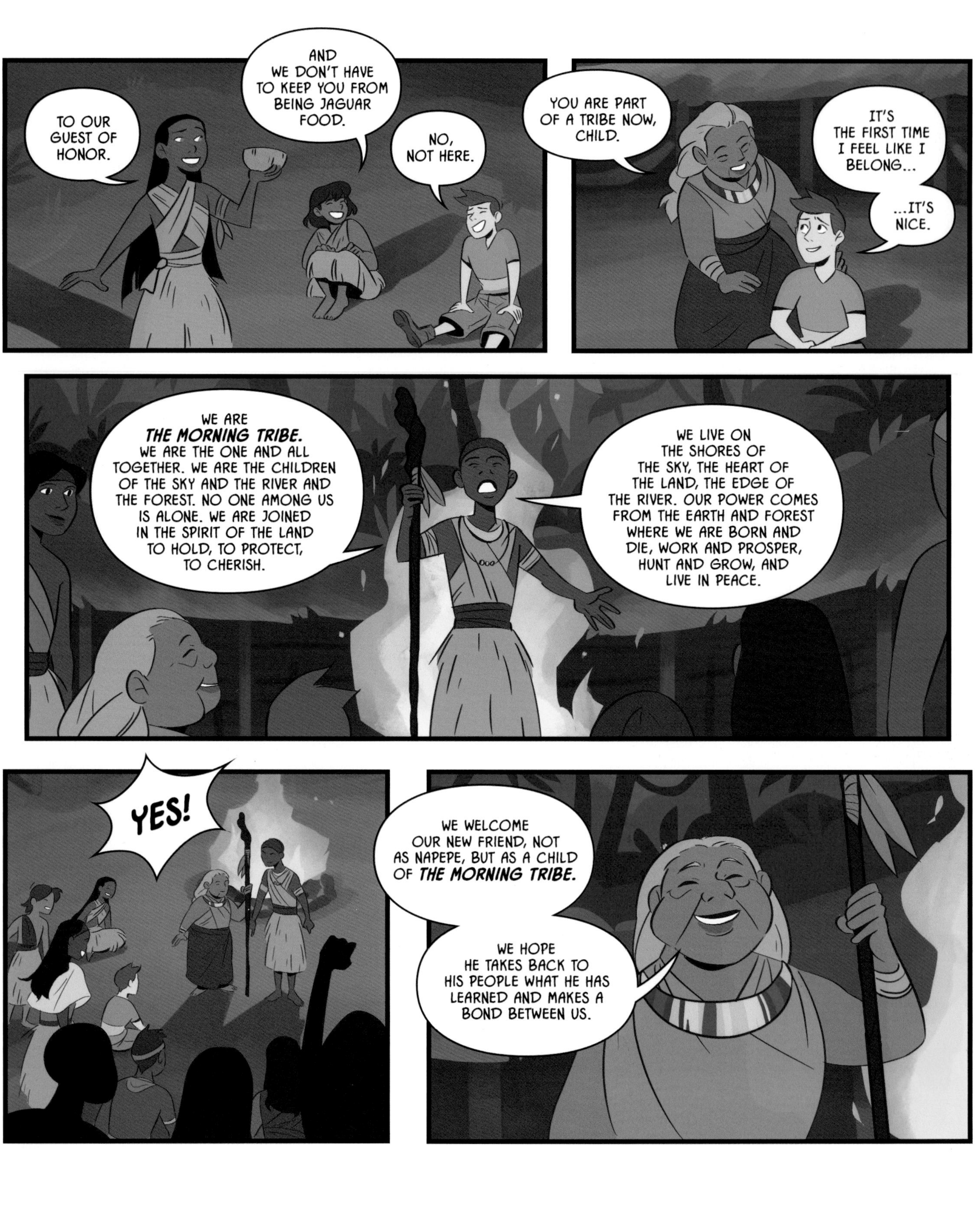
TO OUR GUEST OF HONOR.
AND WE DON'T HAVE TO KEEP YOU FROM BEING JAGUAR FOOD.
NO, NOT HERE.
YOU ARE PART OF A TRIBE NOW, CHILD.
IT'S THE FIRST TIME I FEEL LIKE I BELONG...
...IT'S NICE.
WE ARE **THE MORNING TRIBE.** WE ARE THE ONE AND ALL TOGETHER. WE ARE THE CHILDREN OF THE SKY AND THE RIVER AND THE FOREST. NO ONE AMONG US IS ALONE. WE ARE JOINED IN THE SPIRIT OF THE LAND TO HOLD, TO PROTECT, TO CHERISH.
WE LIVE ON THE SHORES OF THE SKY, THE HEART OF THE LAND, THE EDGE OF THE RIVER. OUR POWER COMES FROM THE EARTH AND FOREST WHERE WE ARE BORN AND DIE, WORK AND PROSPER, HUNT AND GROW, AND LIVE IN PEACE.
YES!
WE WELCOME OUR NEW FRIEND, NOT AS NAPEPE, BUT AS A CHILD OF **THE MORNING TRIBE.**
WE HOPE HE TAKES BACK TO HIS PEOPLE WHAT HE HAS LEARNED AND MAKES A BOND BETWEEN US.

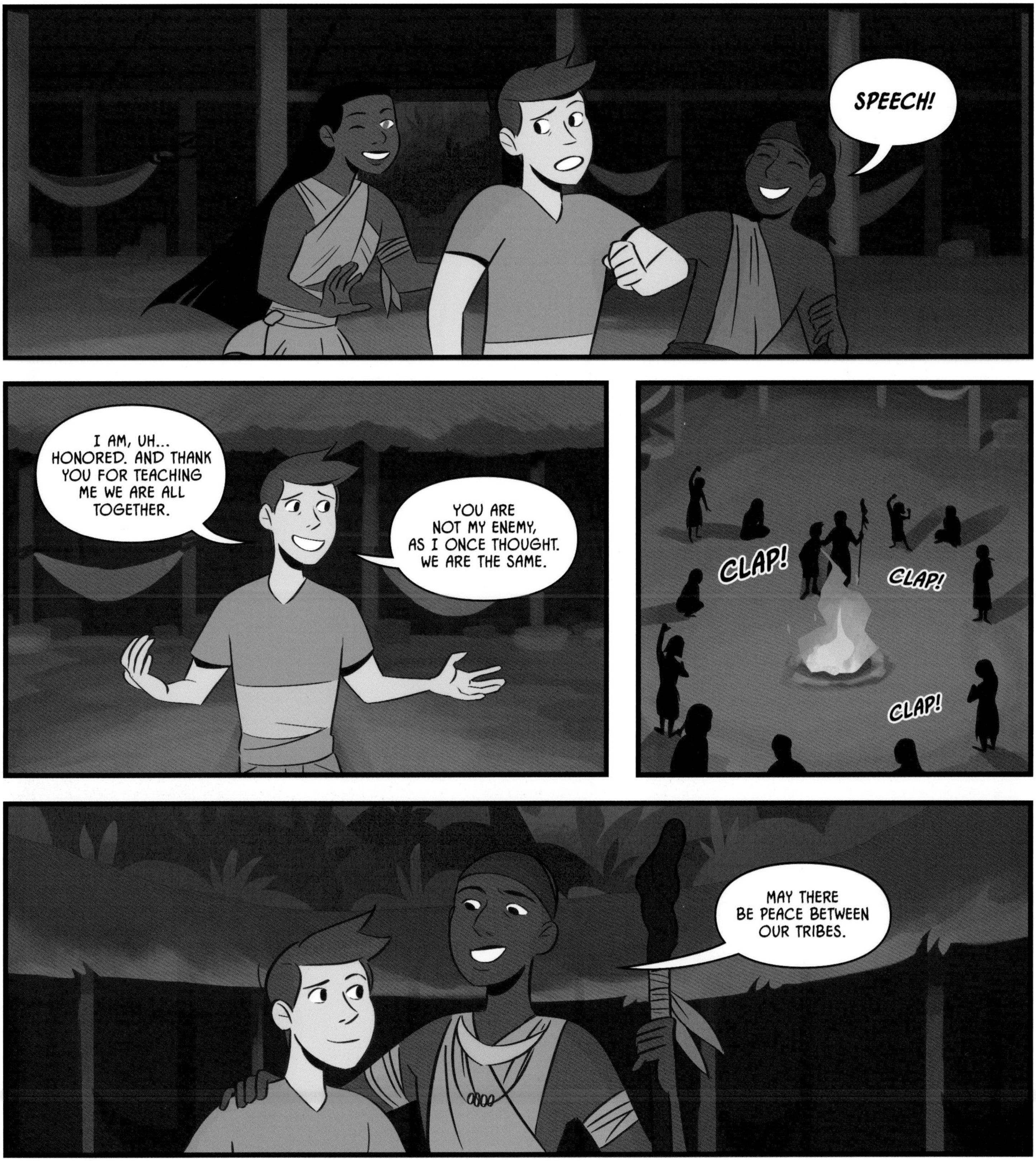
SPEECH!
I AM, UH... HONORED. AND THANK YOU FOR TEACHING ME WE ARE ALL TOGETHER.
YOU ARE NOT MY ENEMY, AS I ONCE THOUGHT. WE ARE THE SAME.
CLAP!
CLAP!
CLAP!
MAY THERE BE PEACE BETWEEN OUR TRIBES.

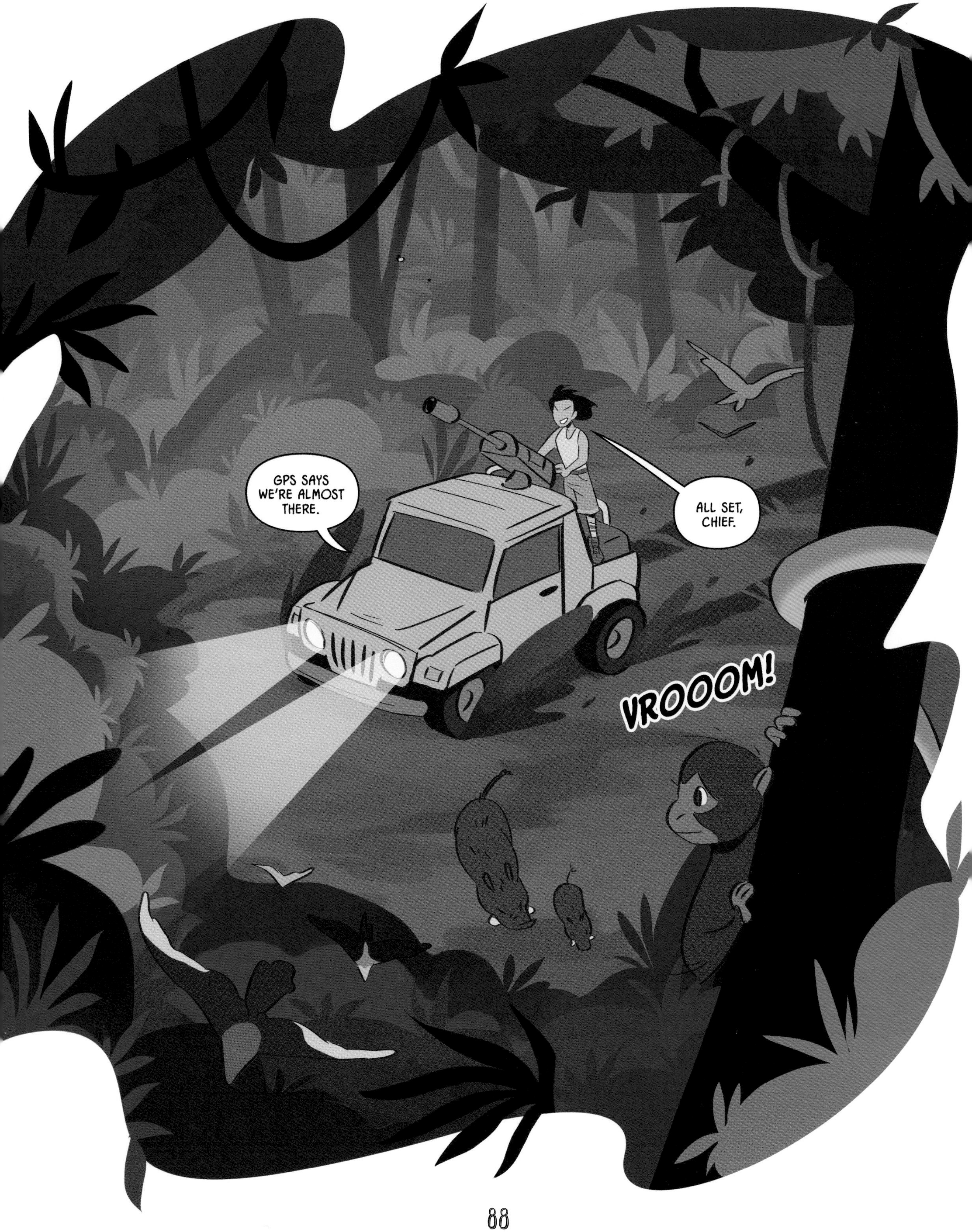
GPS SAYS WE'RE ALMOST THERE.
ALL SET, CHIEF.
VROOOM!

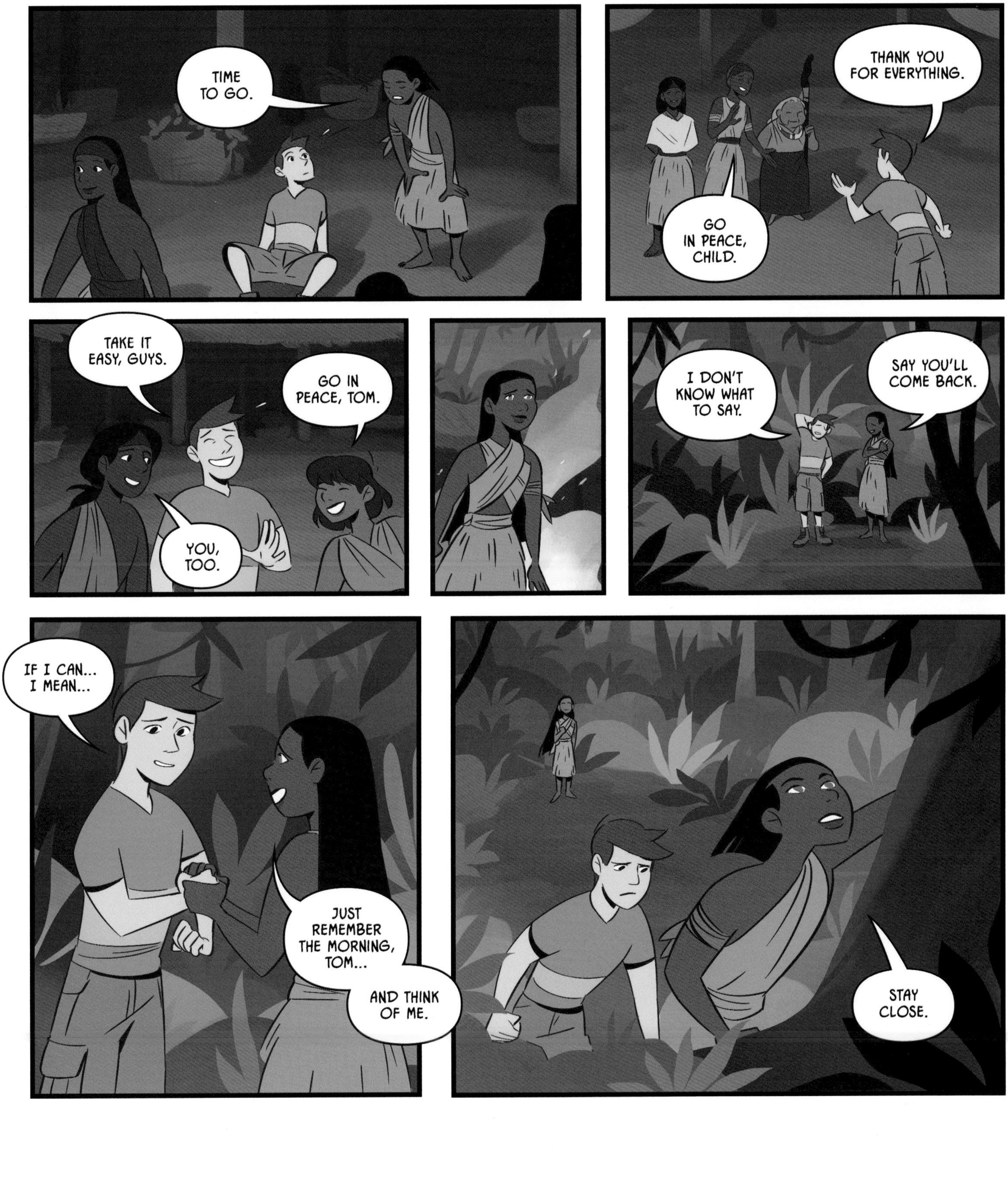
TIME TO GO.
THANK YOU FOR EVERYTHING.
GO IN PEACE, CHILD.
TAKE IT EASY, GUYS.
GO IN PEACE, TOM.
YOU, TOO.
I DON'T KNOW WHAT TO SAY.
SAY YOU'LL COME BACK.
IF I CAN... I MEAN...
JUST REMEMBER THE MORNING, TOM...
AND THINK OF ME.
STAY CLOSE.

CHAPTER 13

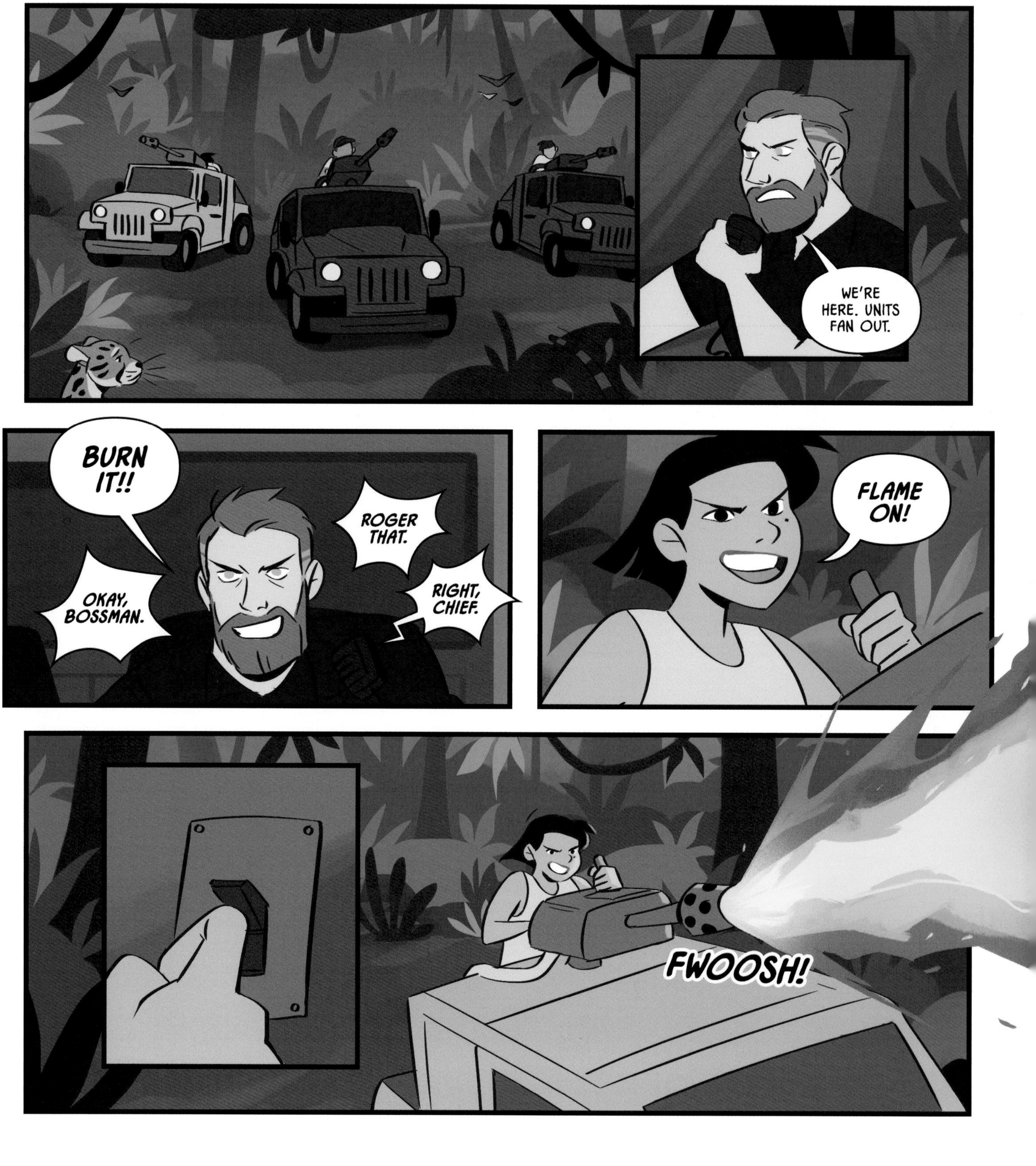
WE'RE HERE. UNITS FAN OUT.
BURN IT!!
ROGER THAT.
OKAY, BOSSMAN.
RIGHT, CHIEF.
FLAME ON!
FWOOSH!

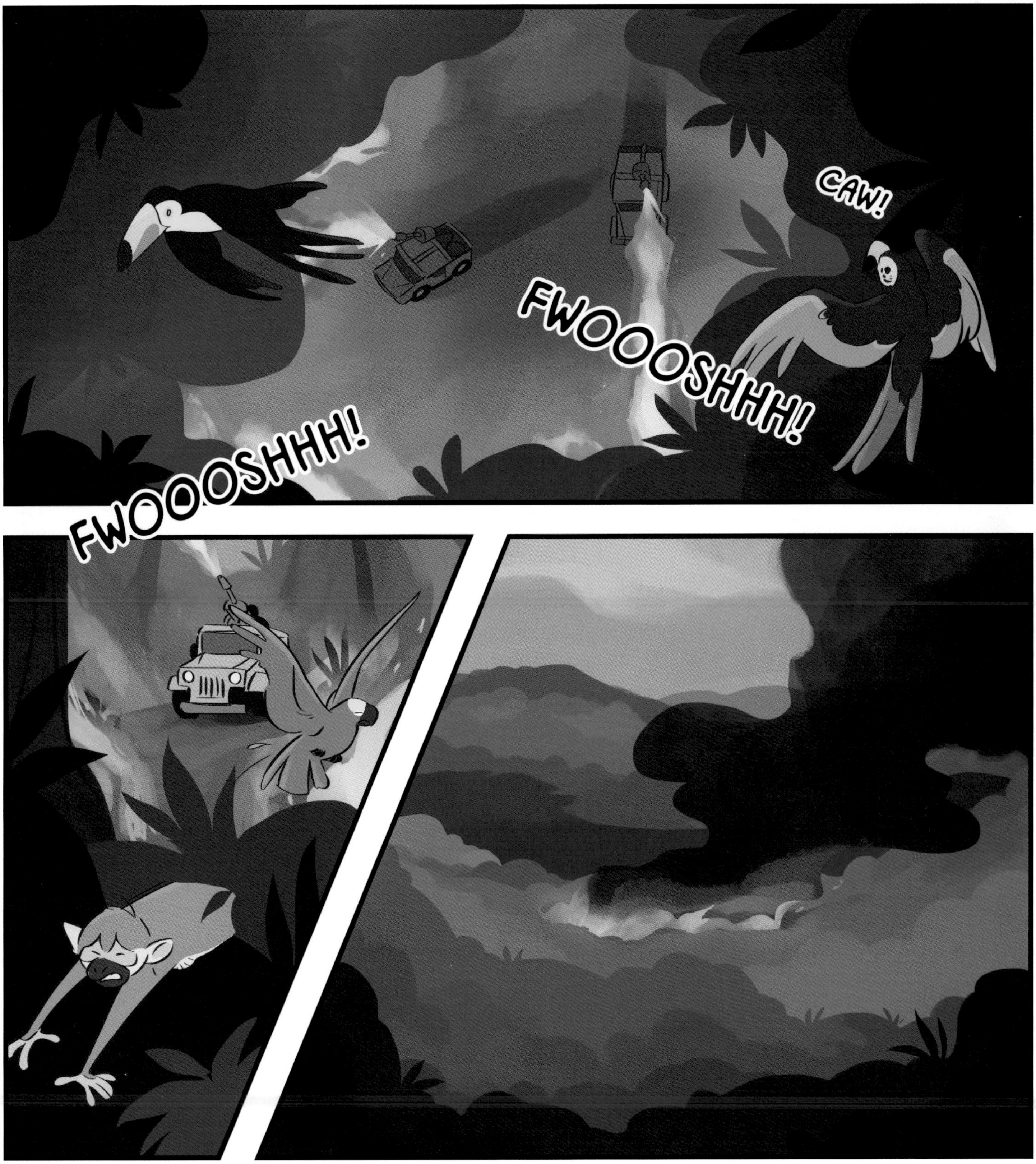
FWOOOSHHH!
CAW!
FWOOOSHHH!
FWOOOSHHH!

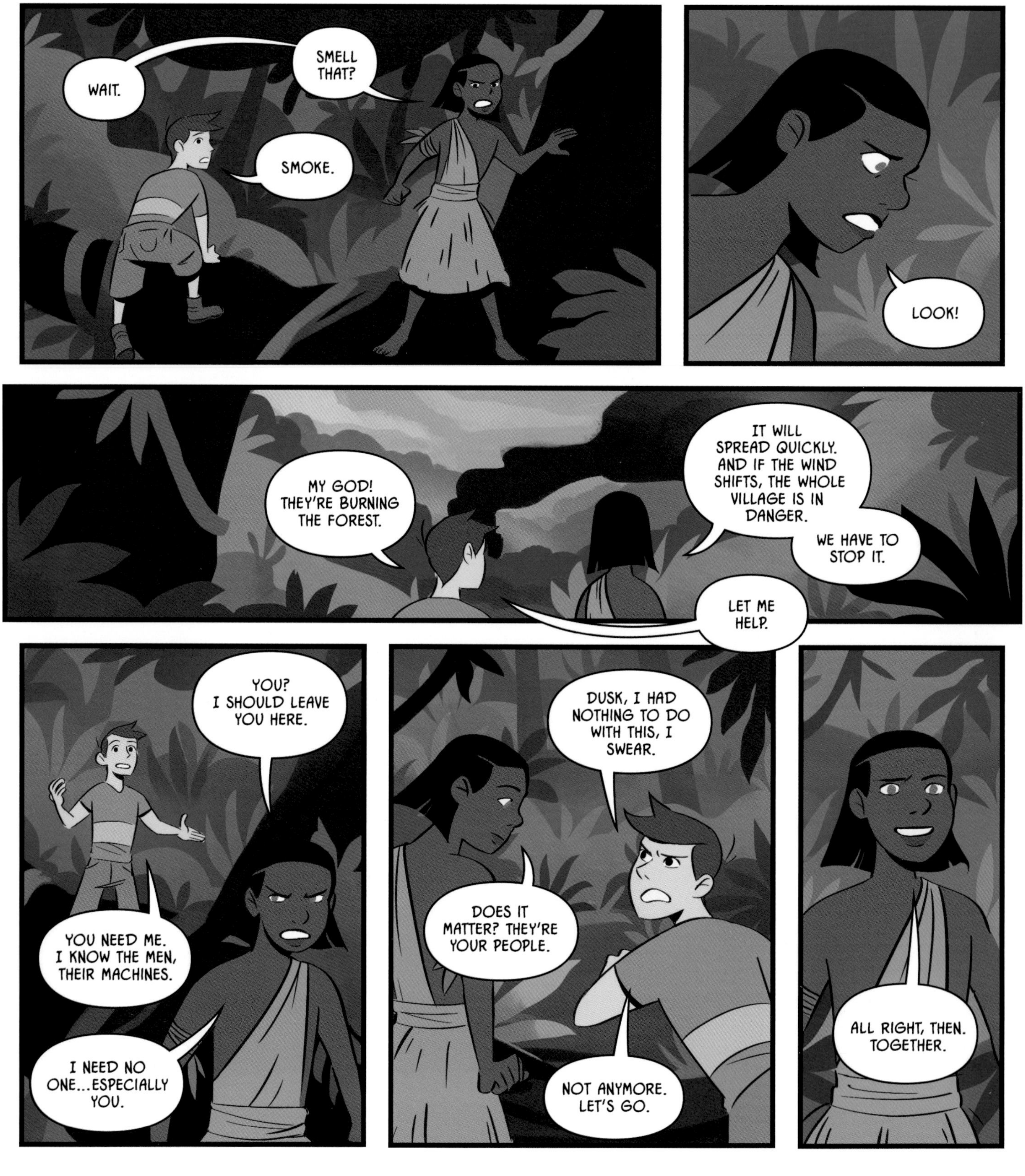
WAIT.
SMELL THAT?
SMOKE.
LOOK!
MY GOD! THEY'RE BURNING THE FOREST.
IT WILL SPREAD QUICKLY. AND IF THE WIND SHIFTS, THE WHOLE VILLAGE IS IN DANGER.
WE HAVE TO STOP IT.
LET ME HELP.
YOU? I SHOULD LEAVE YOU HERE.
YOU NEED ME. I KNOW THE MEN, THEIR MACHINES.
I NEED NO ONE...ESPECIALLY YOU.
DUSK, I HAD NOTHING TO DO WITH THIS, I SWEAR.
DOES IT MATTER? THEY'RE YOUR PEOPLE.
NOT ANYMORE. LET'S GO.
ALL RIGHT, THEN. TOGETHER.

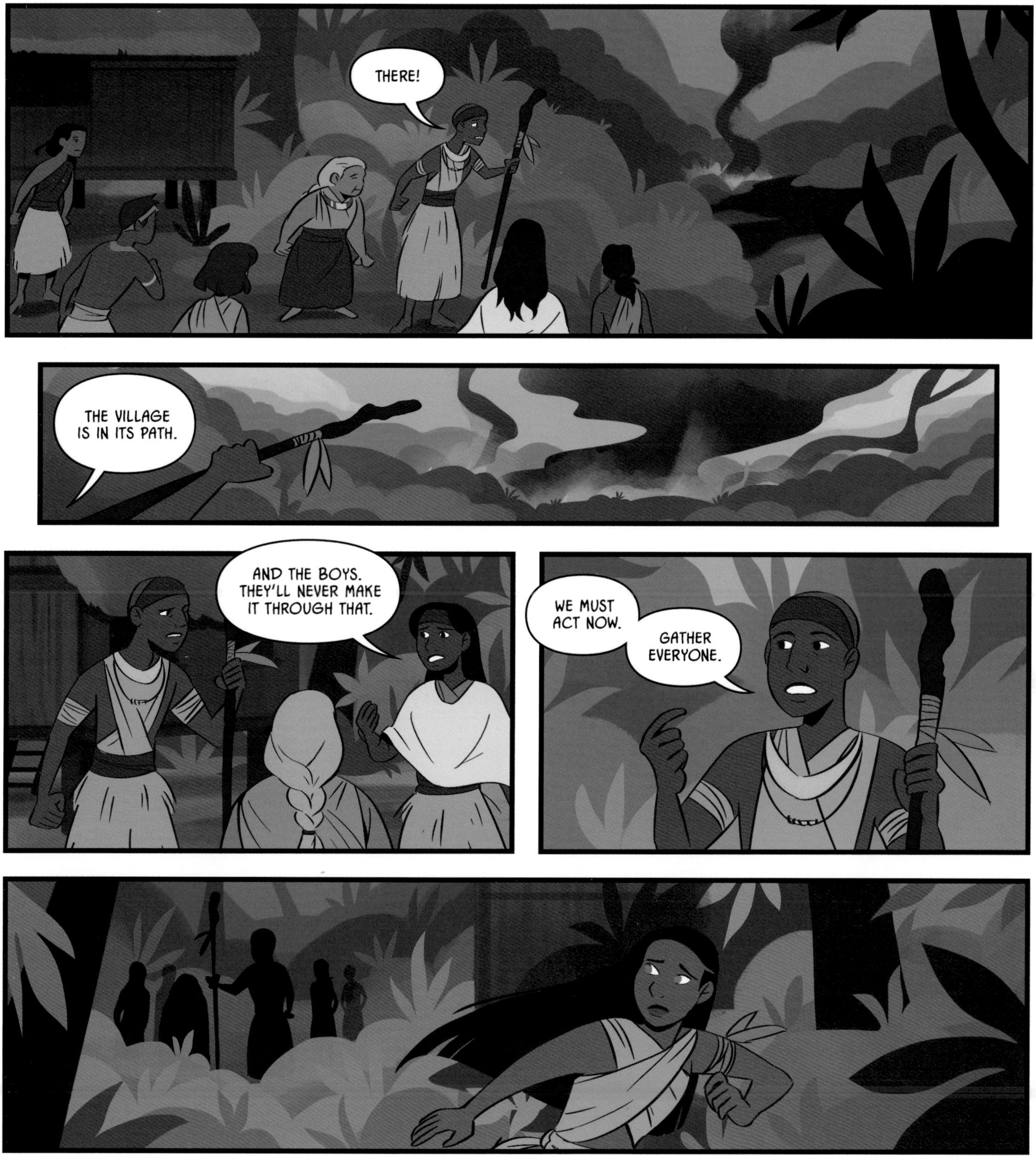
THERE!
THE VILLAGE IS IN ITS PATH.
AND THE BOYS. THEY'LL NEVER MAKE IT THROUGH THAT.
WE MUST ACT NOW.
GATHER EVERYONE.

CHAPTER 14

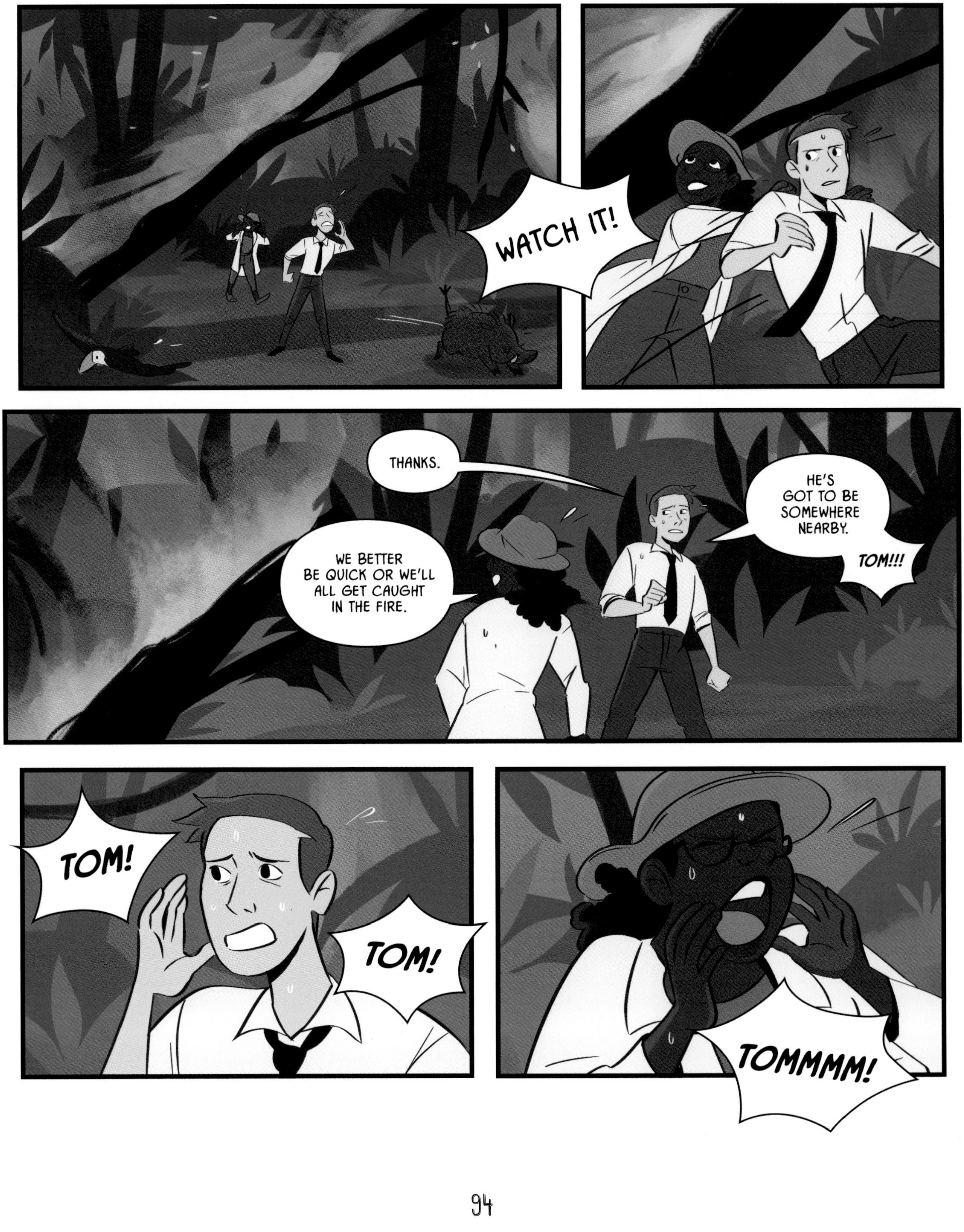
WATCH IT!
THANKS.
HE'S GOT TO BE SOMEWHERE NEARBY.
TOM!!!
WE BETTER BE QUICK OR WE'LL ALL GET CAUGHT IN THE FIRE.
TOM!
TOM!
TOMMMM!

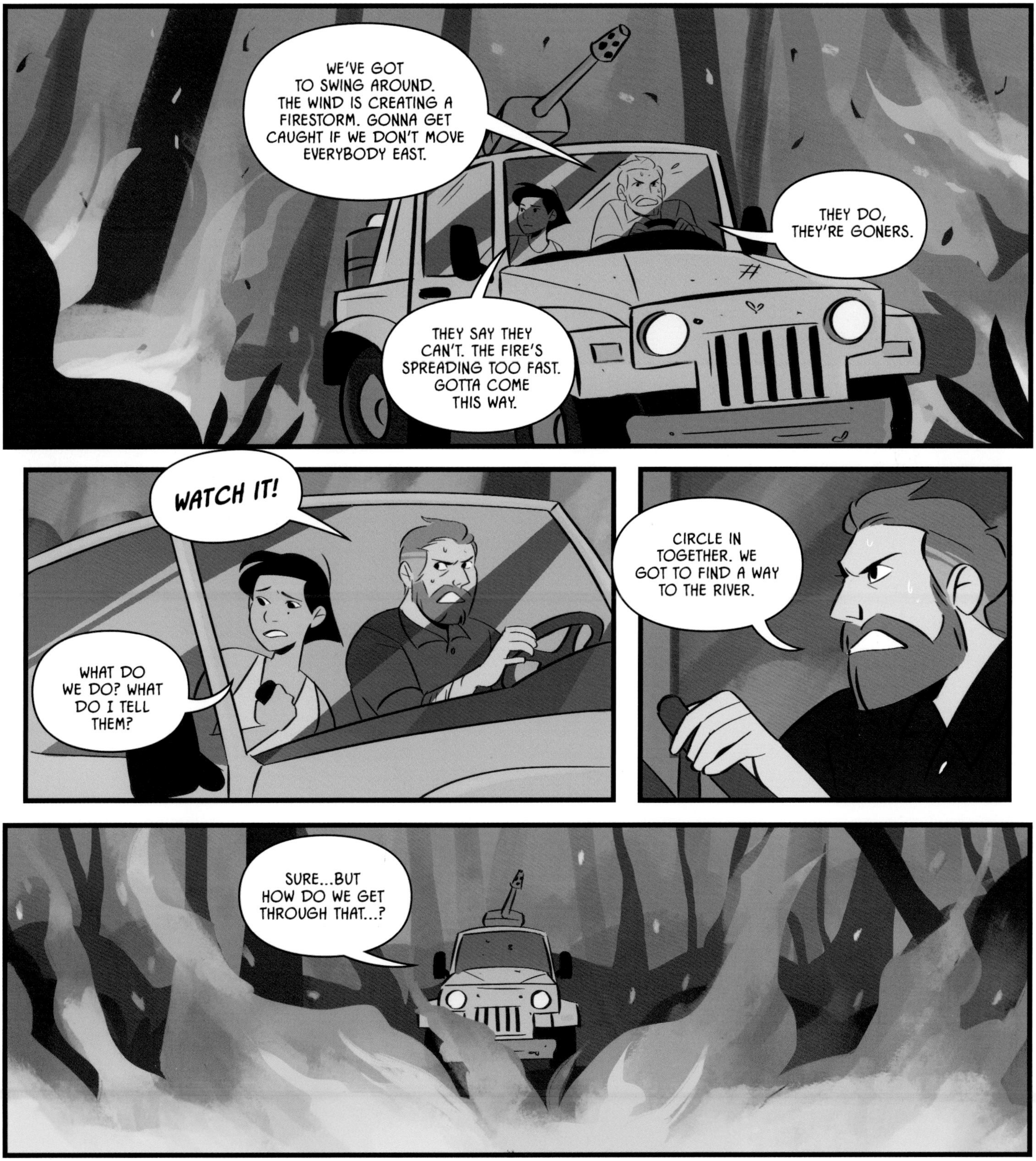
WE'VE GOT TO SWING AROUND. THE WIND IS CREATING A FIRESTORM. GONNA GET CAUGHT IF WE DON'T MOVE EVERYBODY EAST.
THEY SAY THEY CAN'T. THE FIRE'S SPREADING TOO FAST. GOTTA COME THIS WAY.
THEY DO, THEY'RE GONERS.
WATCH IT!
WHAT DO WE DO? WHAT DO I TELL THEM?
CIRCLE IN TOGETHER. WE GOT TO FIND A WAY TO THE RIVER.
SURE...BUT HOW DO WE GET THROUGH THAT...?

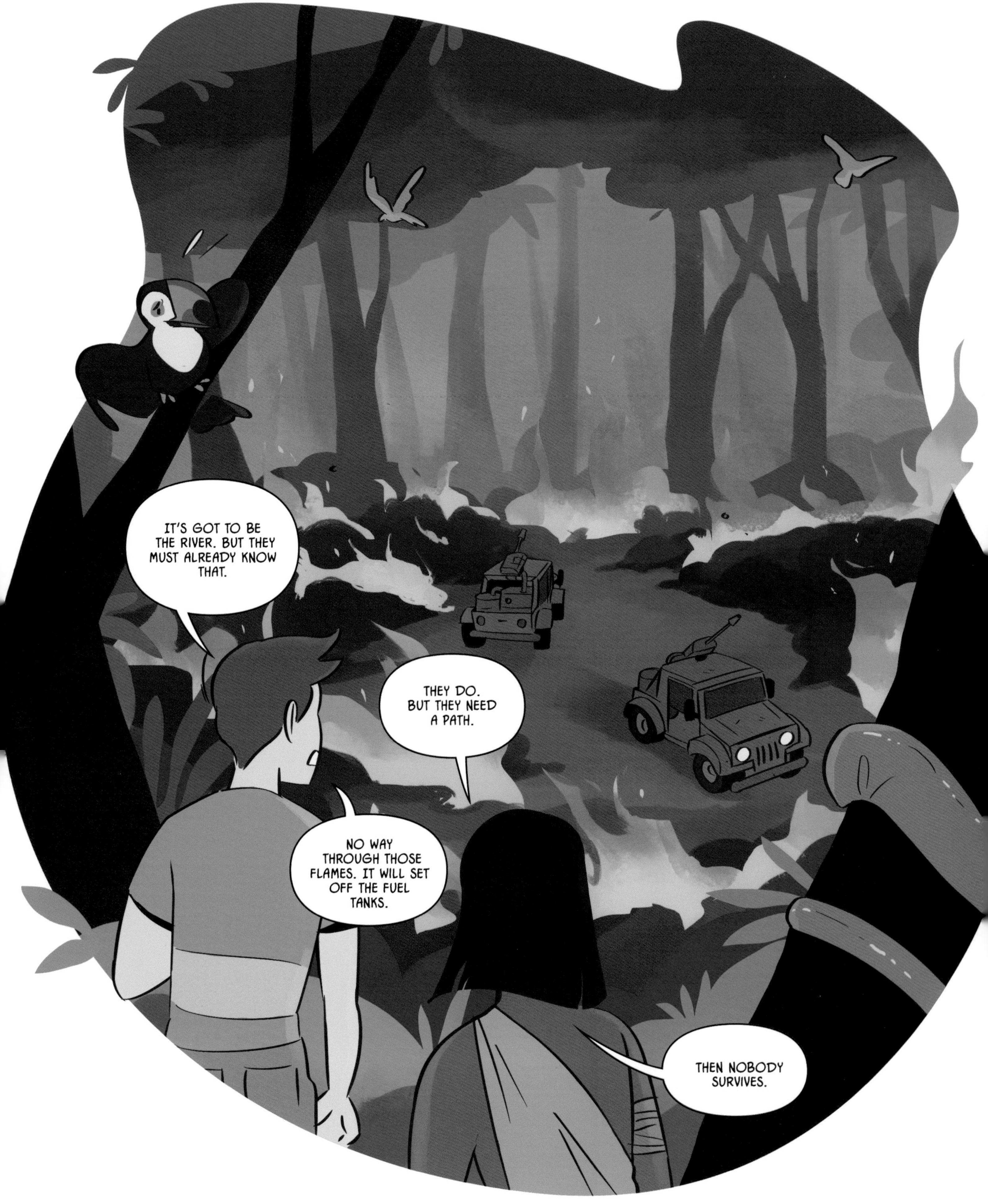
IT'S GOT TO BE THE RIVER. BUT THEY MUST ALREADY KNOW THAT.
THEY DO. BUT THEY NEED A PATH.
NO WAY THROUGH THOSE FLAMES. IT WILL SET OFF THE FUEL TANKS.
THEN NOBODY SURVIVES.

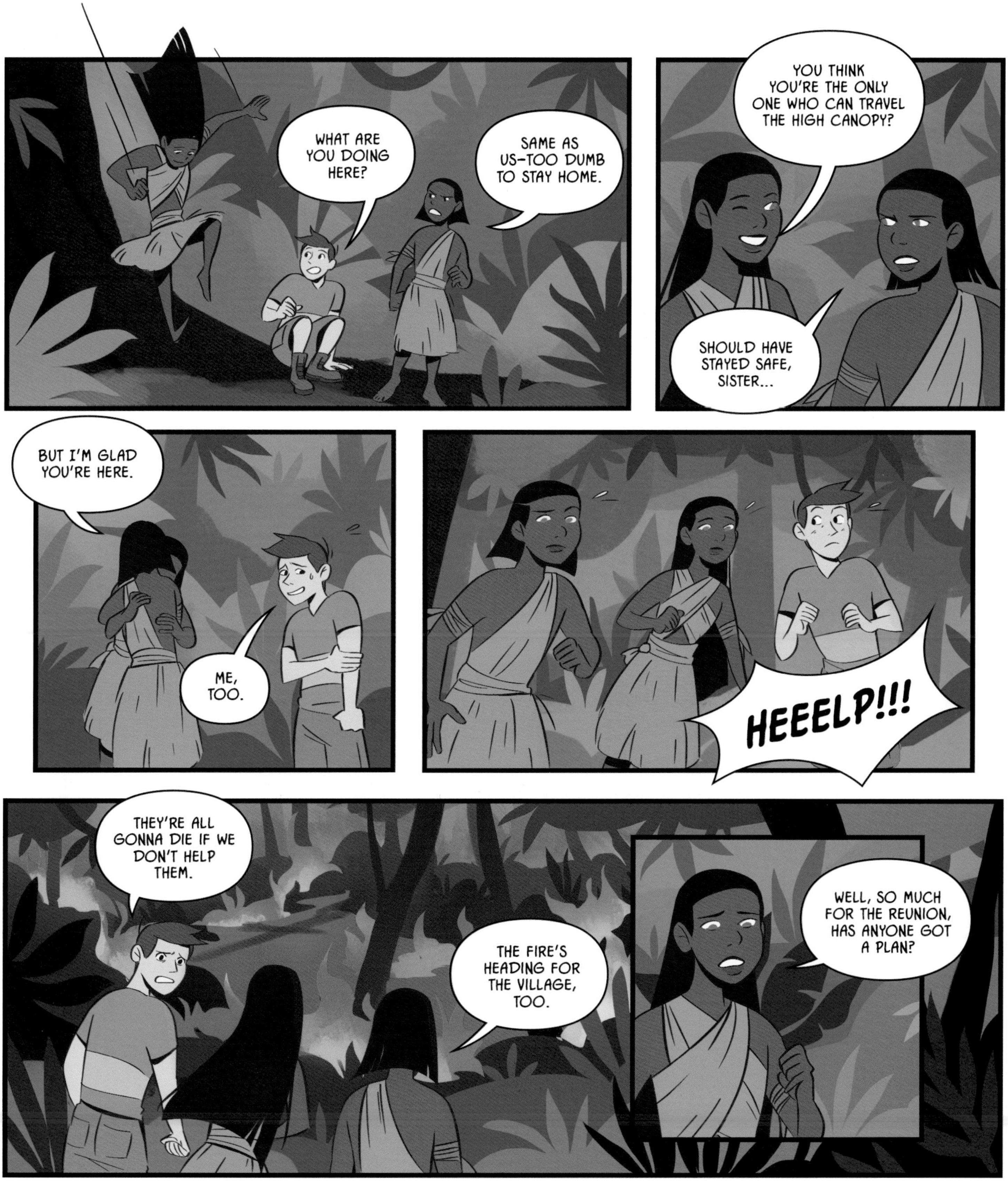

WHAT ARE YOU DOING HERE?
SAME AS US–TOO DUMB TO STAY HOME.
YOU THINK YOU'RE THE ONLY ONE WHO CAN TRAVEL THE HIGH CANOPY?
SHOULD HAVE STAYED SAFE, SISTER...
BUT I'M GLAD YOU'RE HERE.
ME, TOO.
HEEELP!!!
THEY'RE ALL GONNA DIE IF WE DON'T HELP THEM.
THE FIRE'S HEADING FOR THE VILLAGE, TOO.
WELL, SO MUCH FOR THE REUNION, HAS ANYONE GOT A PLAN?

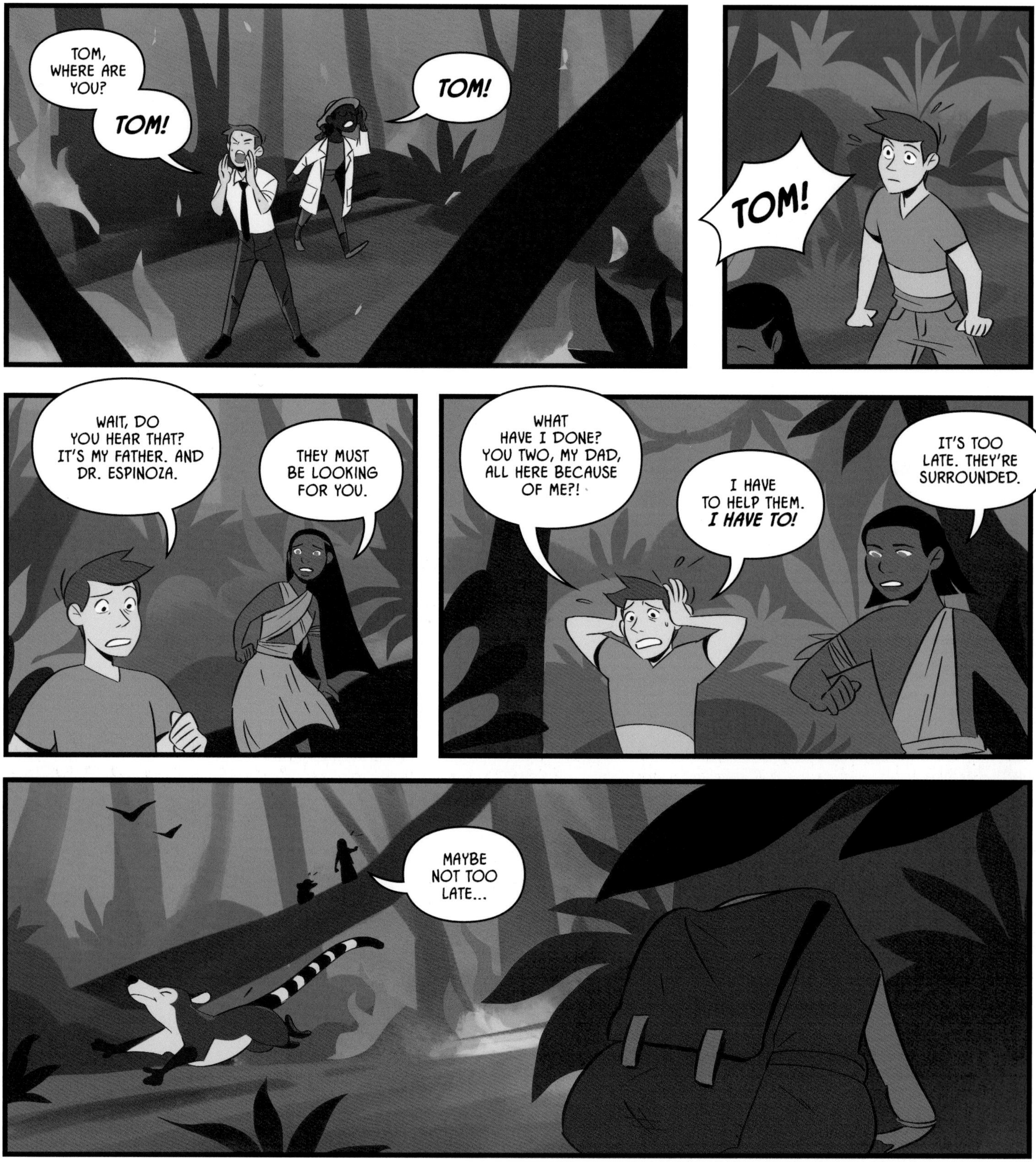
TOM, WHERE ARE YOU?
TOM!
TOM!
TOM!
WAIT, DO YOU HEAR THAT? IT'S MY FATHER. AND DR. ESPINOZA.
THEY MUST BE LOOKING FOR YOU.
WHAT HAVE I DONE? YOU TWO, MY DAD, ALL HERE BECAUSE OF ME?!
I HAVE TO HELP THEM. I HAVE TO!
IT'S TOO LATE. THEY'RE SURROUNDED.
MAYBE NOT TOO LATE...

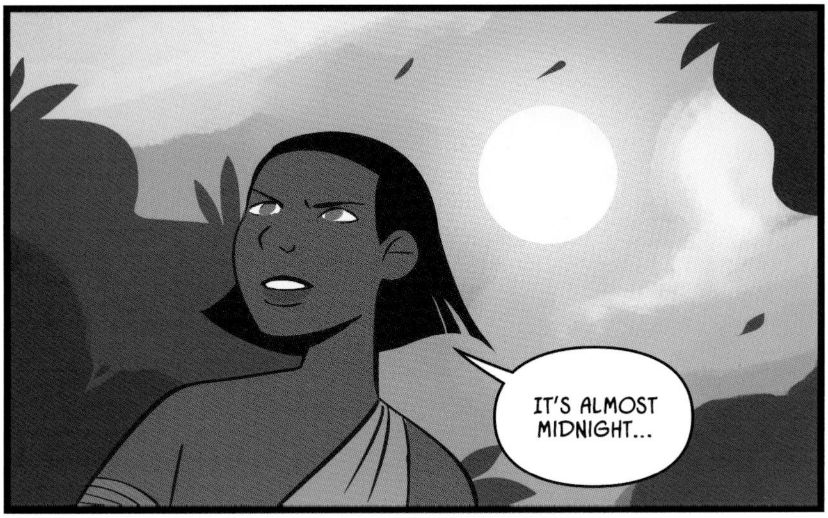
IT'S ALMOST MIDNIGHT...

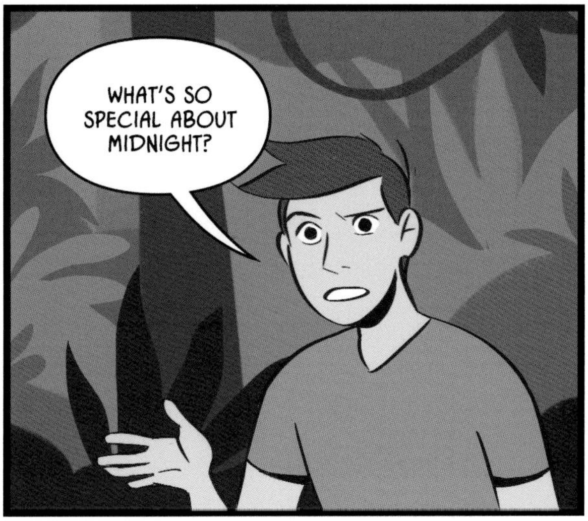
WHAT'S SO SPECIAL ABOUT MIDNIGHT?

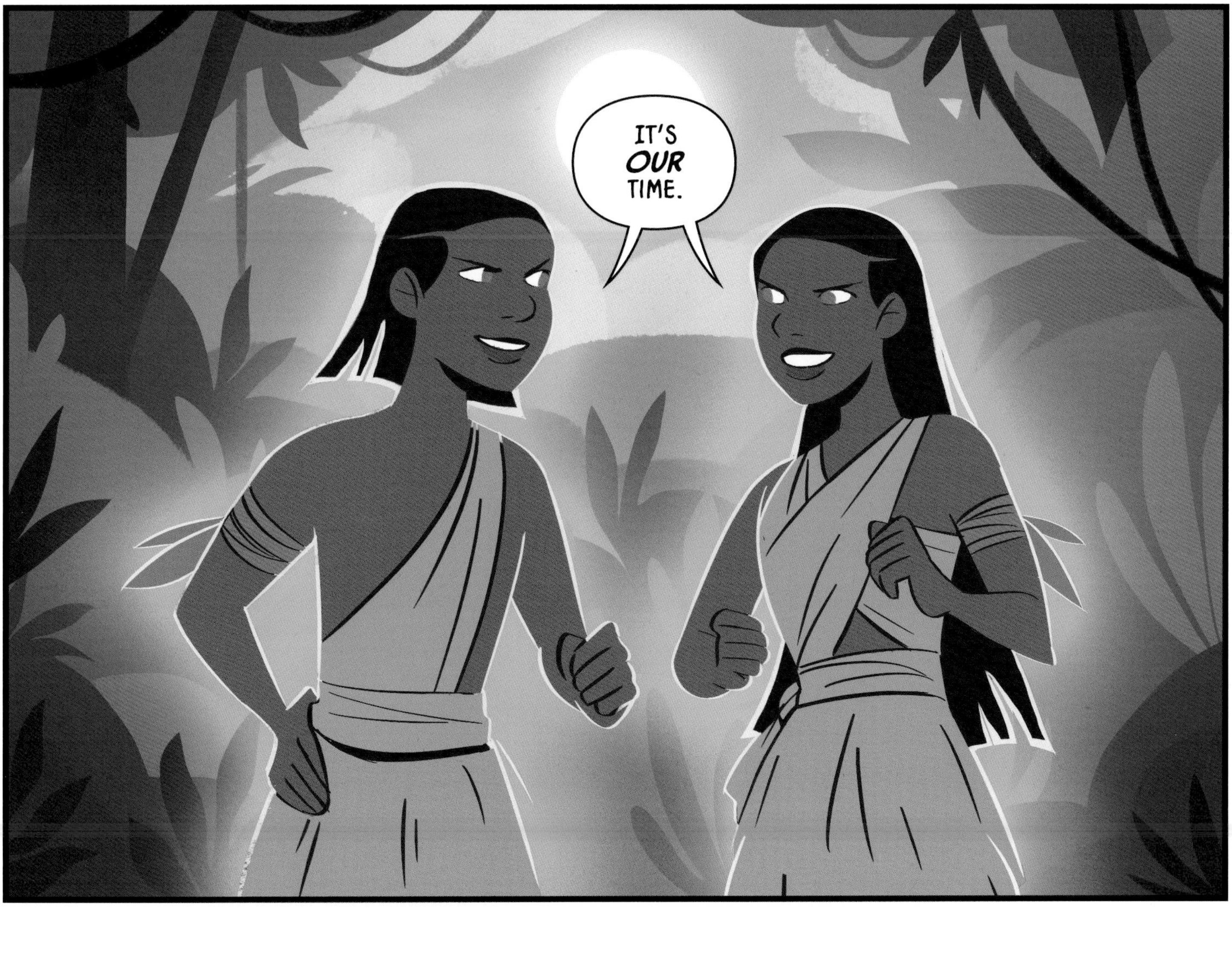
IT'S *OUR* TIME.

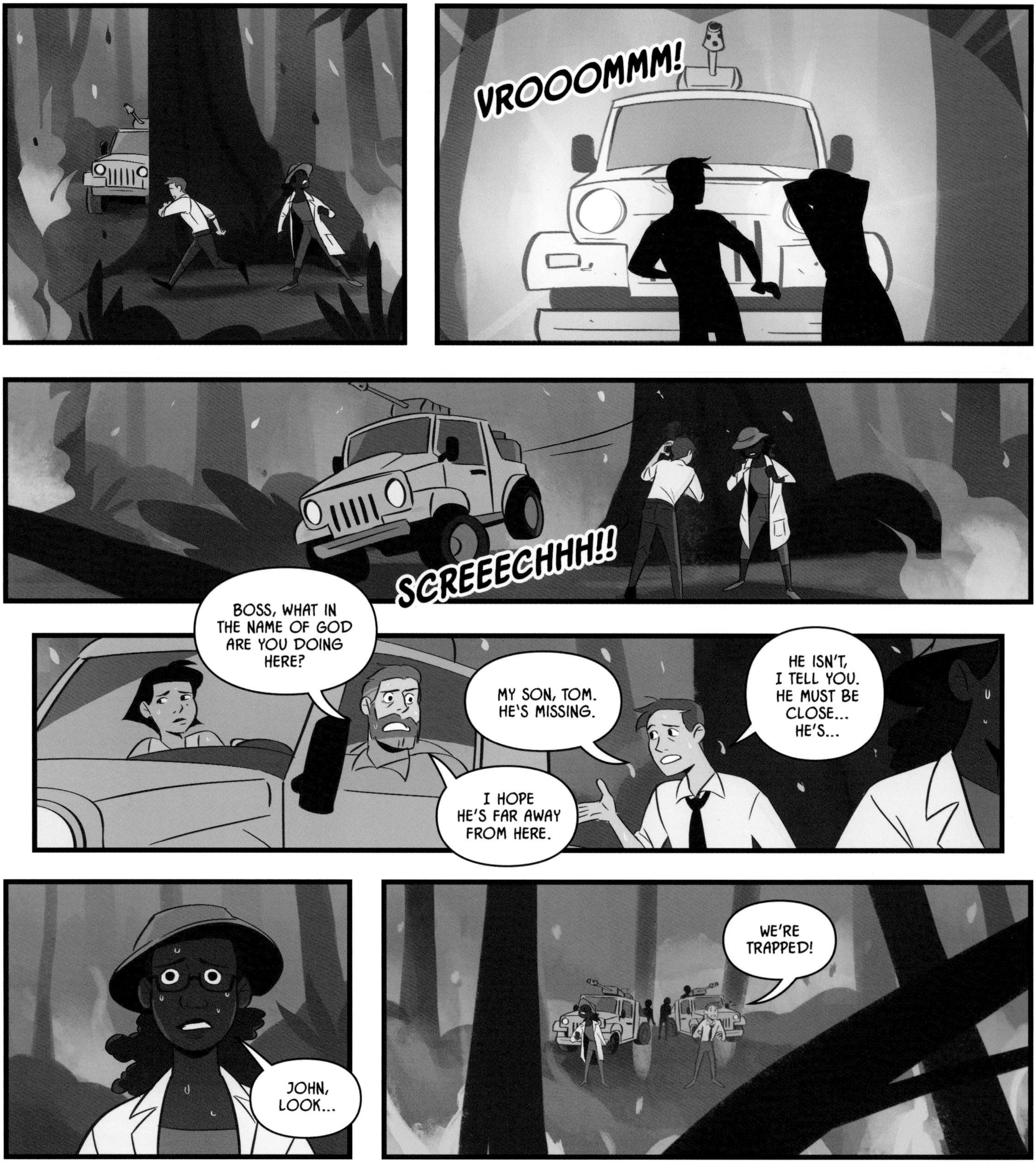
VROOOMMM!
SCREEECHHH!!
BOSS, WHAT IN THE NAME OF GOD ARE YOU DOING HERE?
MY SON, TOM. HE'S MISSING.
I HOPE HE'S FAR AWAY FROM HERE.
HE ISN'T, I TELL YOU. HE MUST BE CLOSE... HE'S...
JOHN, LOOK...
WE'RE TRAPPED!

CHAPTER 15

WE ARE WITH YOU...
WE ARE WITH YOU...
BA-BADUMP
DUM-BA-BADUMP
WE ARE WITH YOU...
WE ARE WITH YOU...

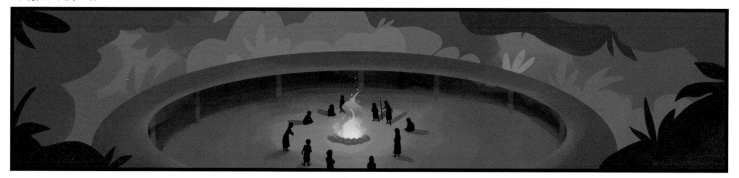

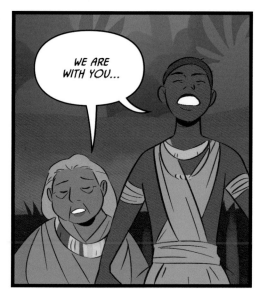

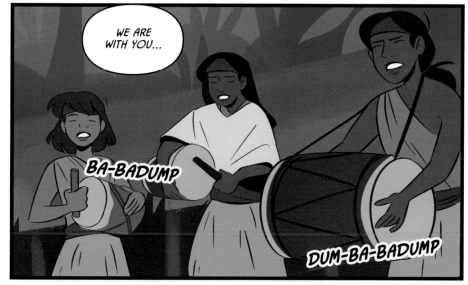

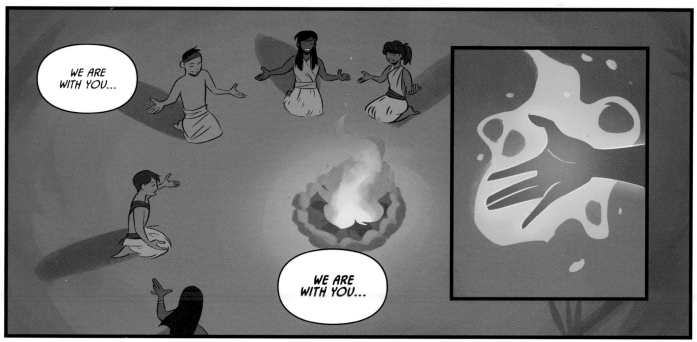

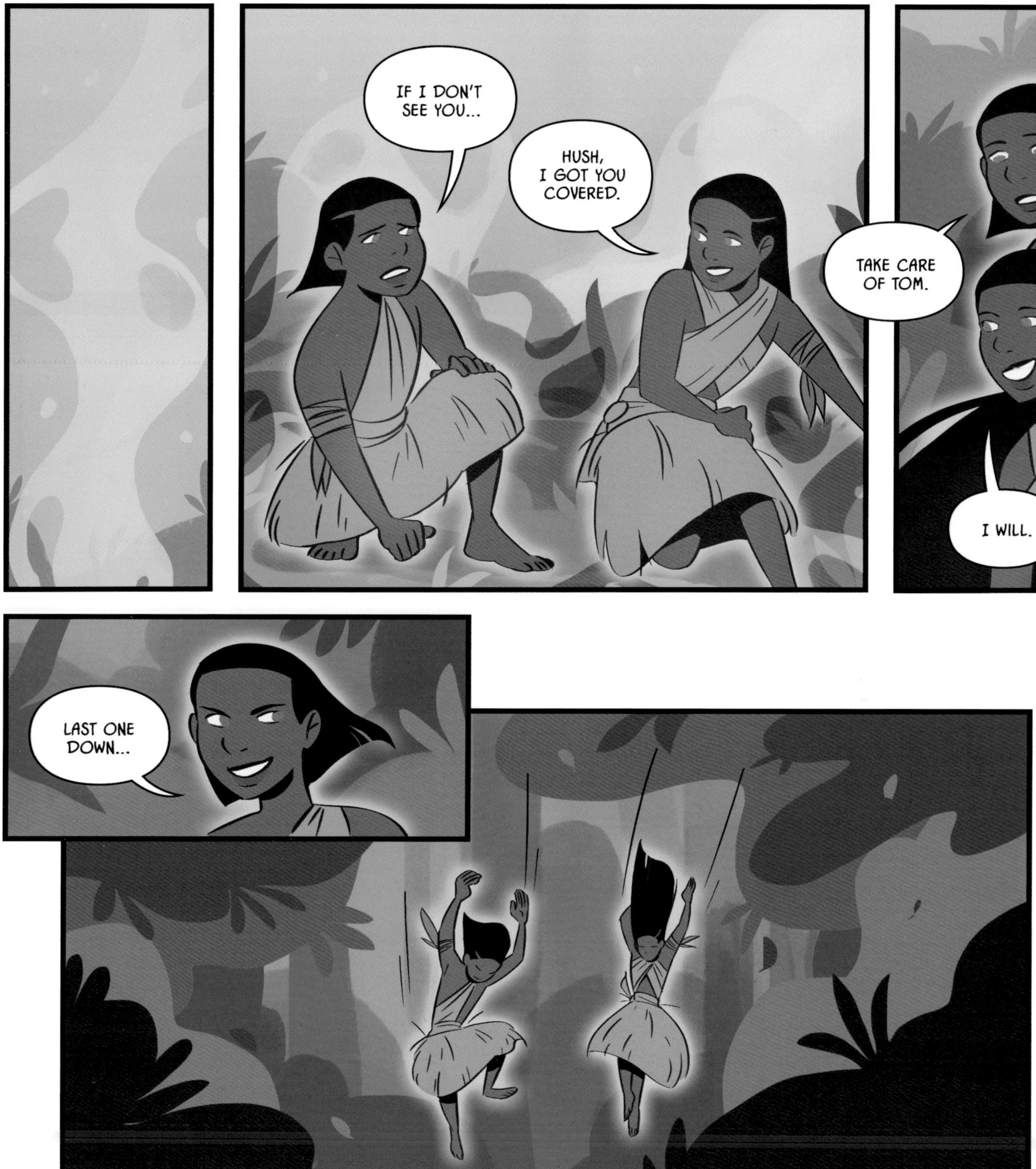
IF I DON'T SEE YOU...
HUSH, I GOT YOU COVERED.
TAKE CARE OF TOM.
I WILL.
LAST ONE DOWN...

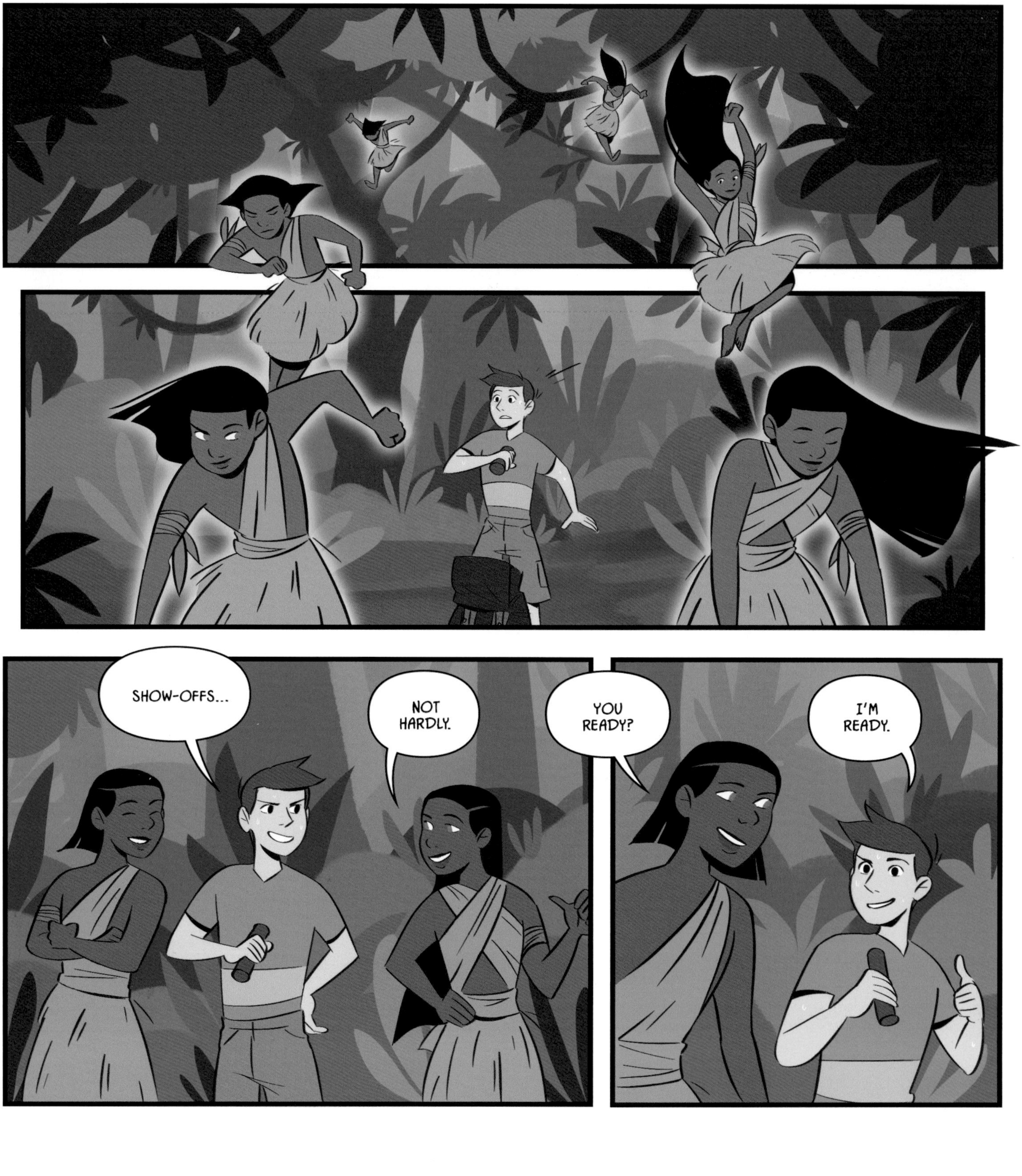
SHOW-OFFS...
NOT HARDLY.
YOU READY?
I'M READY.

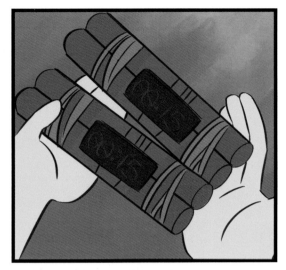

WE HAVE FIFTEEN SECONDS.

MOST WOULD HAVE RUN...

YOU'RE NOT SO BAD YOURSELF.

IF WE DON'T GET BACK...

I DON'T WANT TO HEAR THAT.

EVEN AT MIDNIGHT, WE CANNOT LAST LONG.

BE READY WHEN WE COME FOR YOU.

MY DAD... ME...

THANKS...

FORGET IT.

NOW!

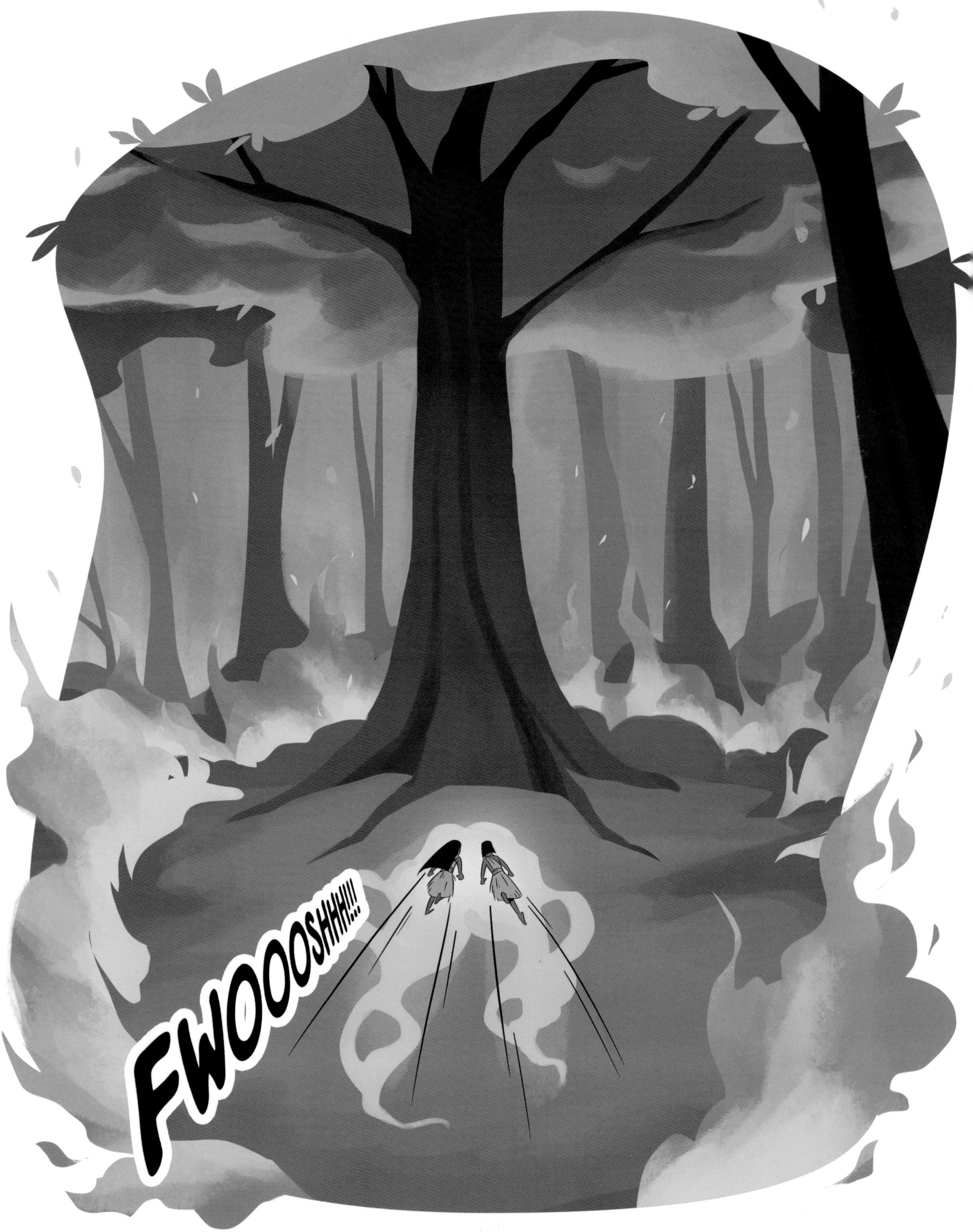
FWOOOSHHH!!!

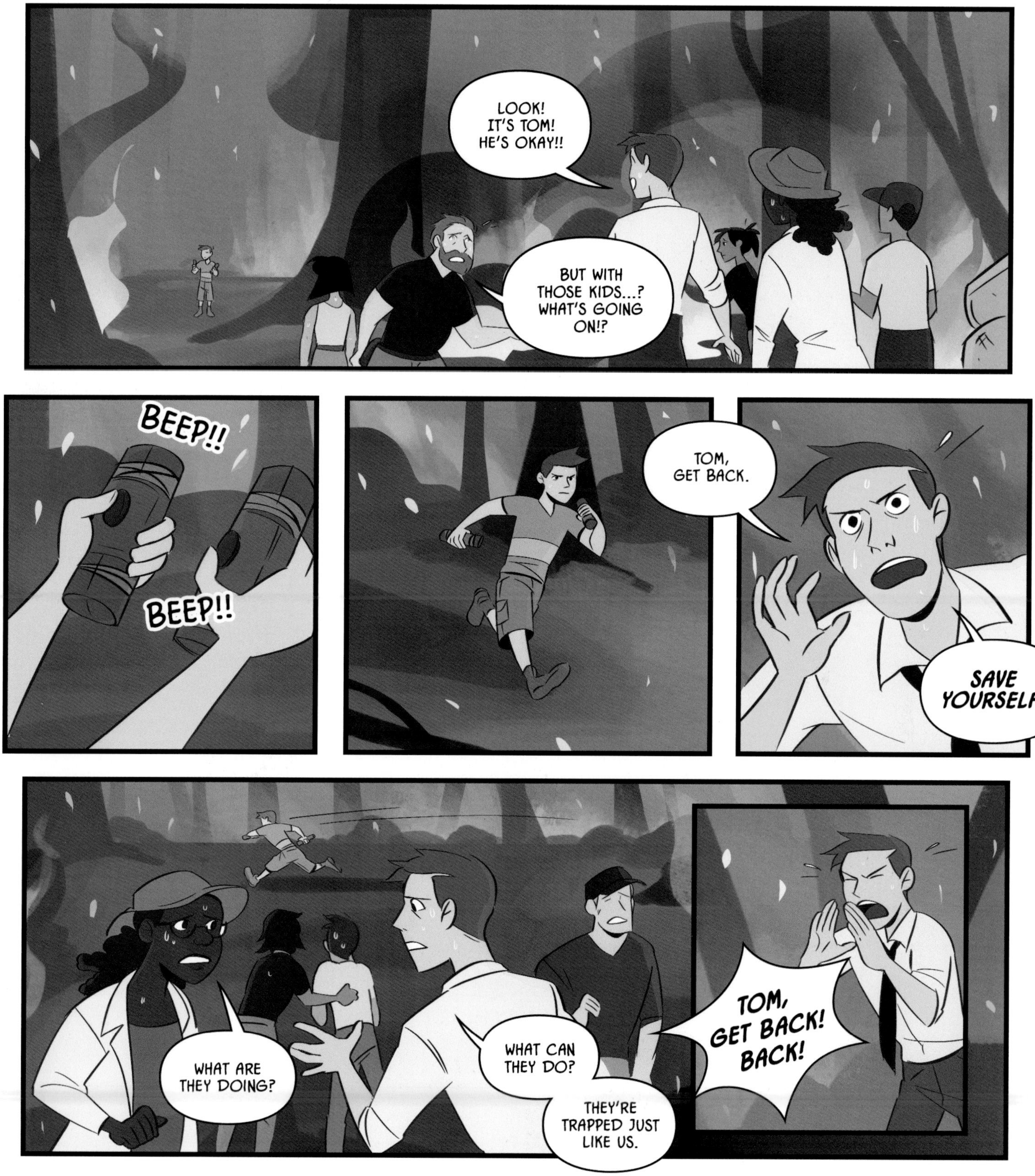
LOOK! IT'S TOM! HE'S OKAY!!
BUT WITH THOSE KIDS...? WHAT'S GOING ON!?
BEEP!!
BEEP!!
TOM, GET BACK.
SAVE YOURSELF!
WHAT ARE THEY DOING?
WHAT CAN THEY DO?
THEY'RE TRAPPED JUST LIKE US.
TOM, GET BACK! BACK!

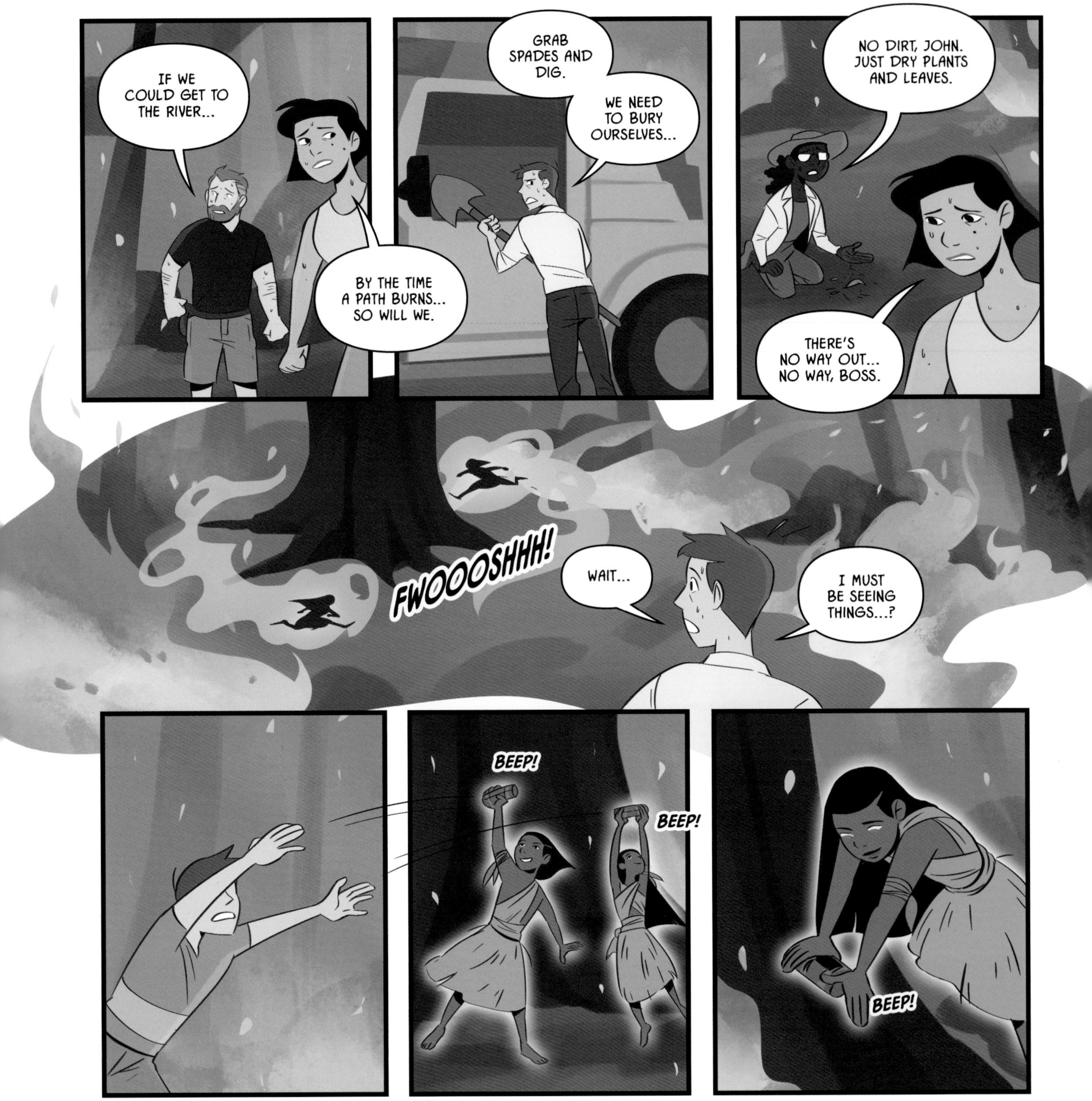
IF WE COULD GET TO THE RIVER...
BY THE TIME A PATH BURNS... SO WILL WE.
GRAB SPADES AND DIG.
WE NEED TO BURY OURSELVES...
NO DIRT, JOHN. JUST DRY PLANTS AND LEAVES.
THERE'S NO WAY OUT... NO WAY, BOSS.
FWOOOSHHH!
WAIT...
I MUST BE SEEING THINGS...?
BEEP!
BEEP!
BEEP!

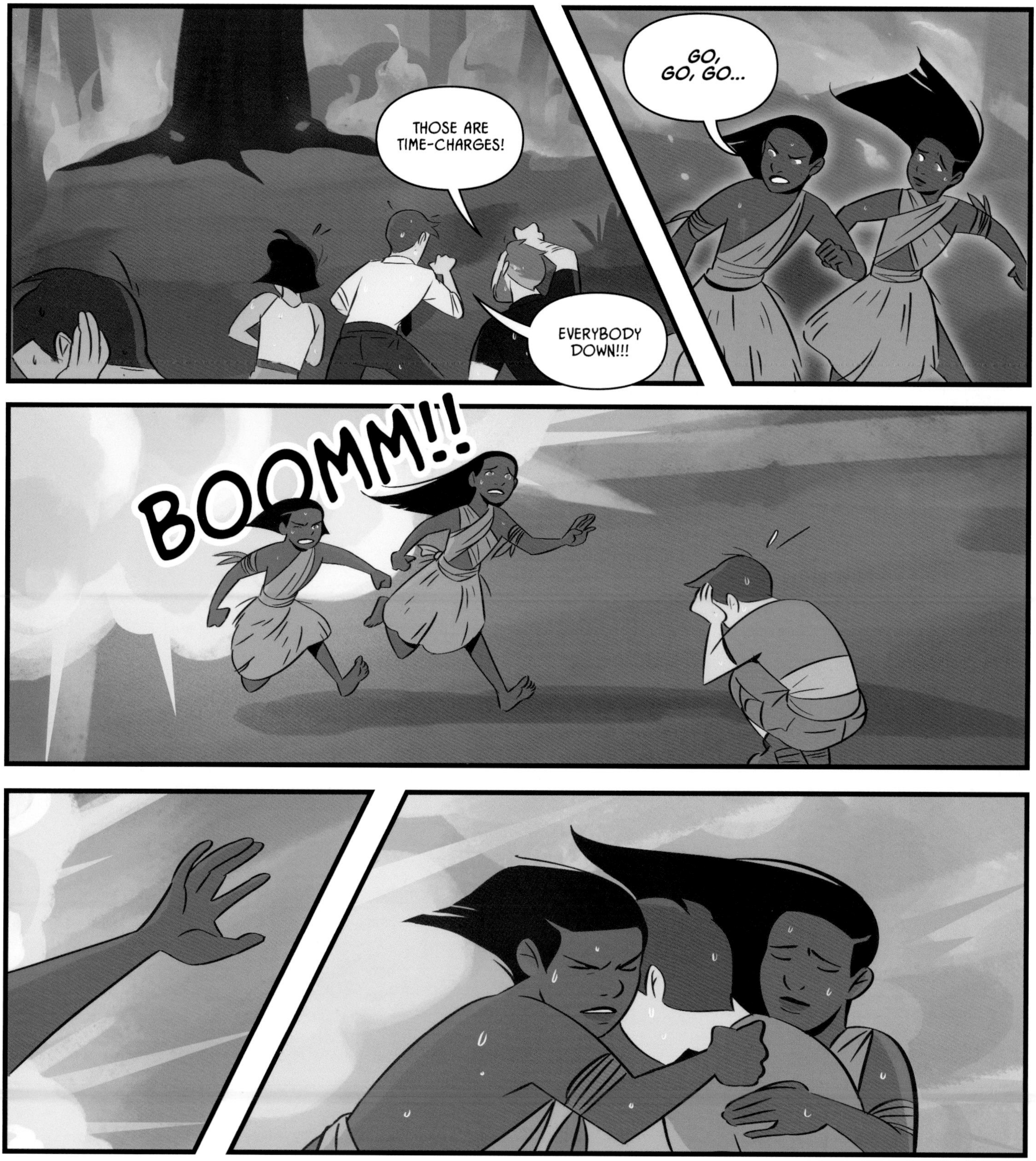
THOSE ARE TIME-CHARGES!
EVERYBODY DOWN!!!
GO, GO, GO...
BOOMM!!

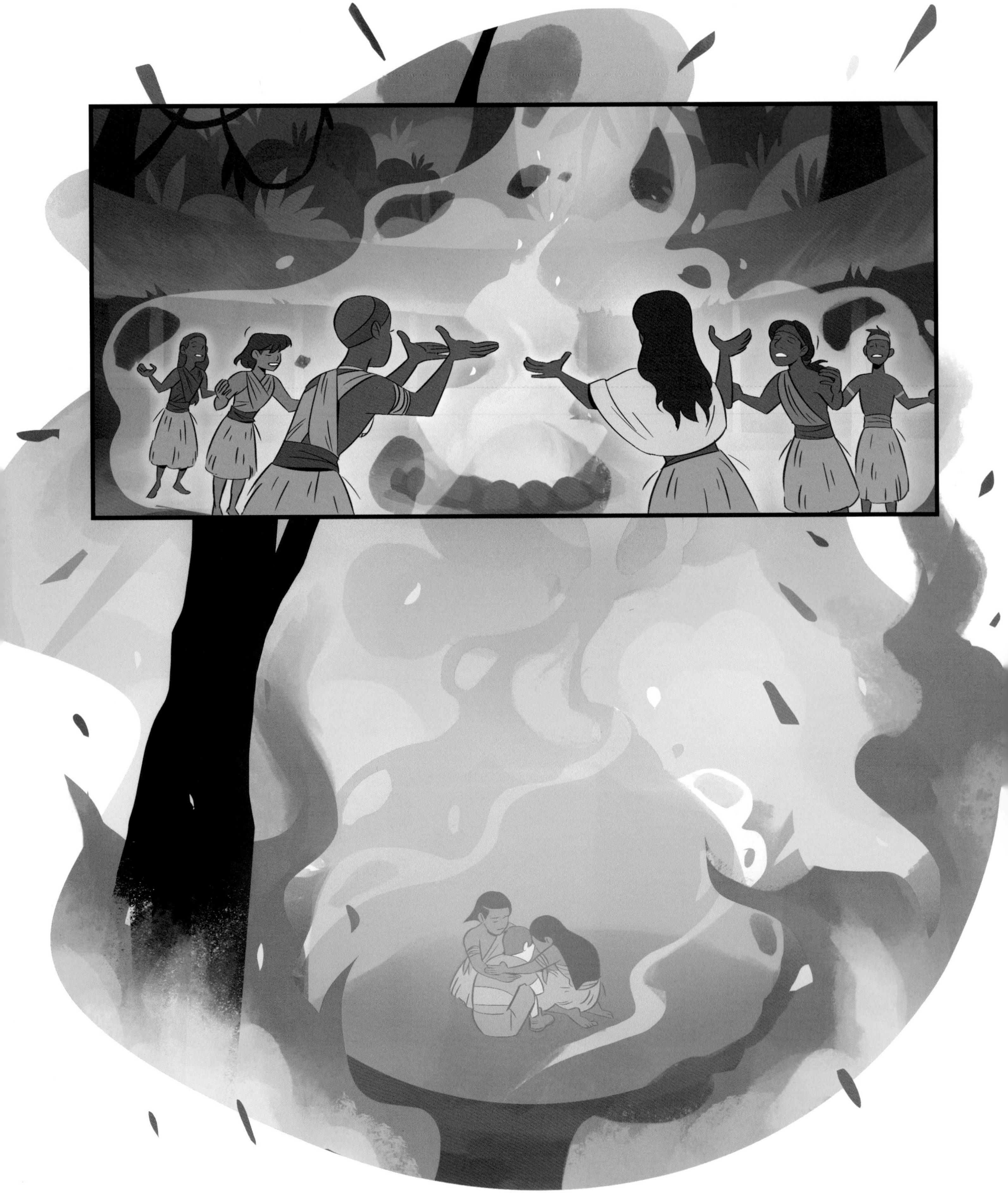

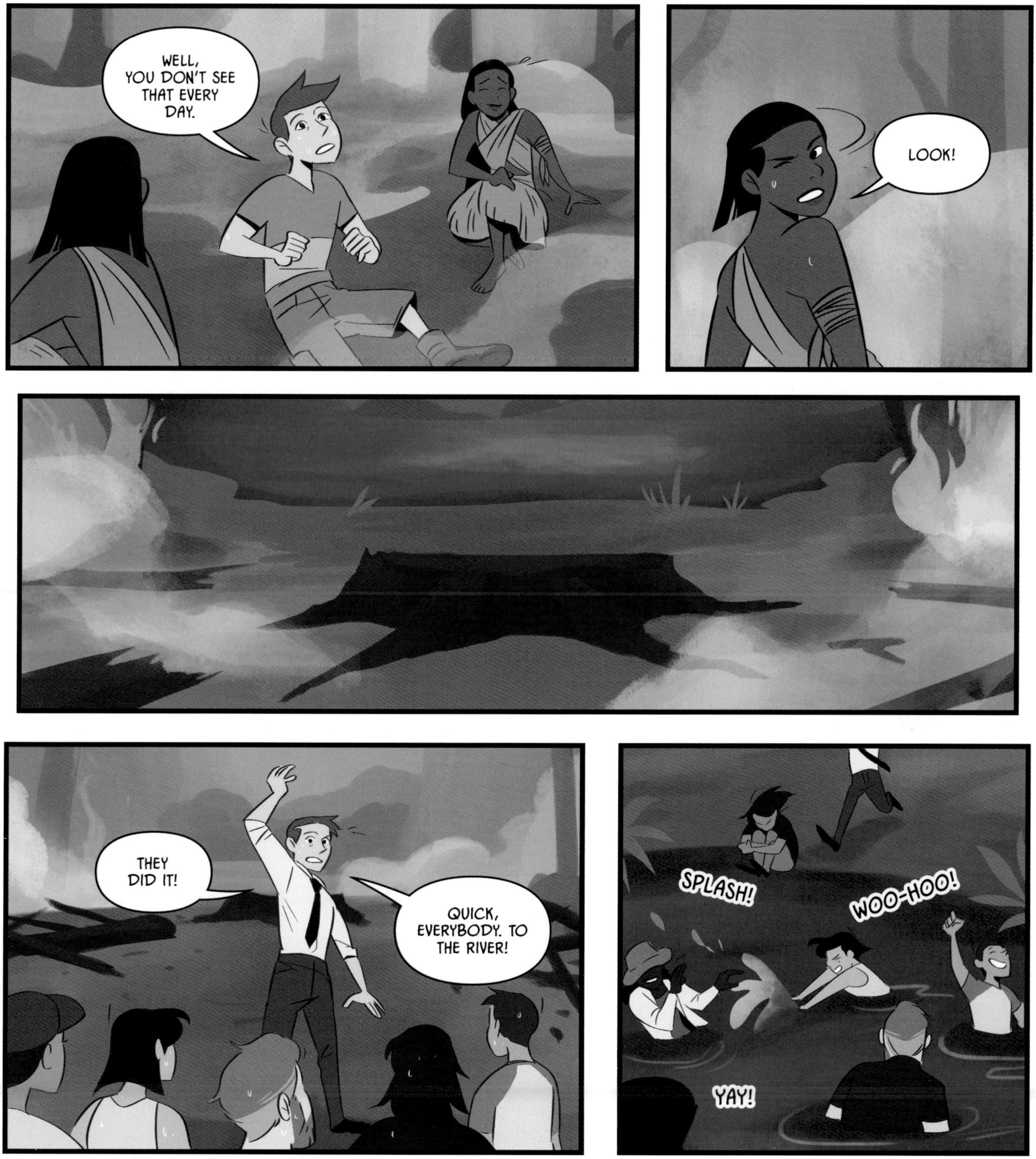
WELL, YOU DON'T SEE THAT EVERY DAY.
LOOK!
THEY DID IT!
QUICK, EVERYBODY. TO THE RIVER!
SPLASH!
WOO-HOO!
YAY!

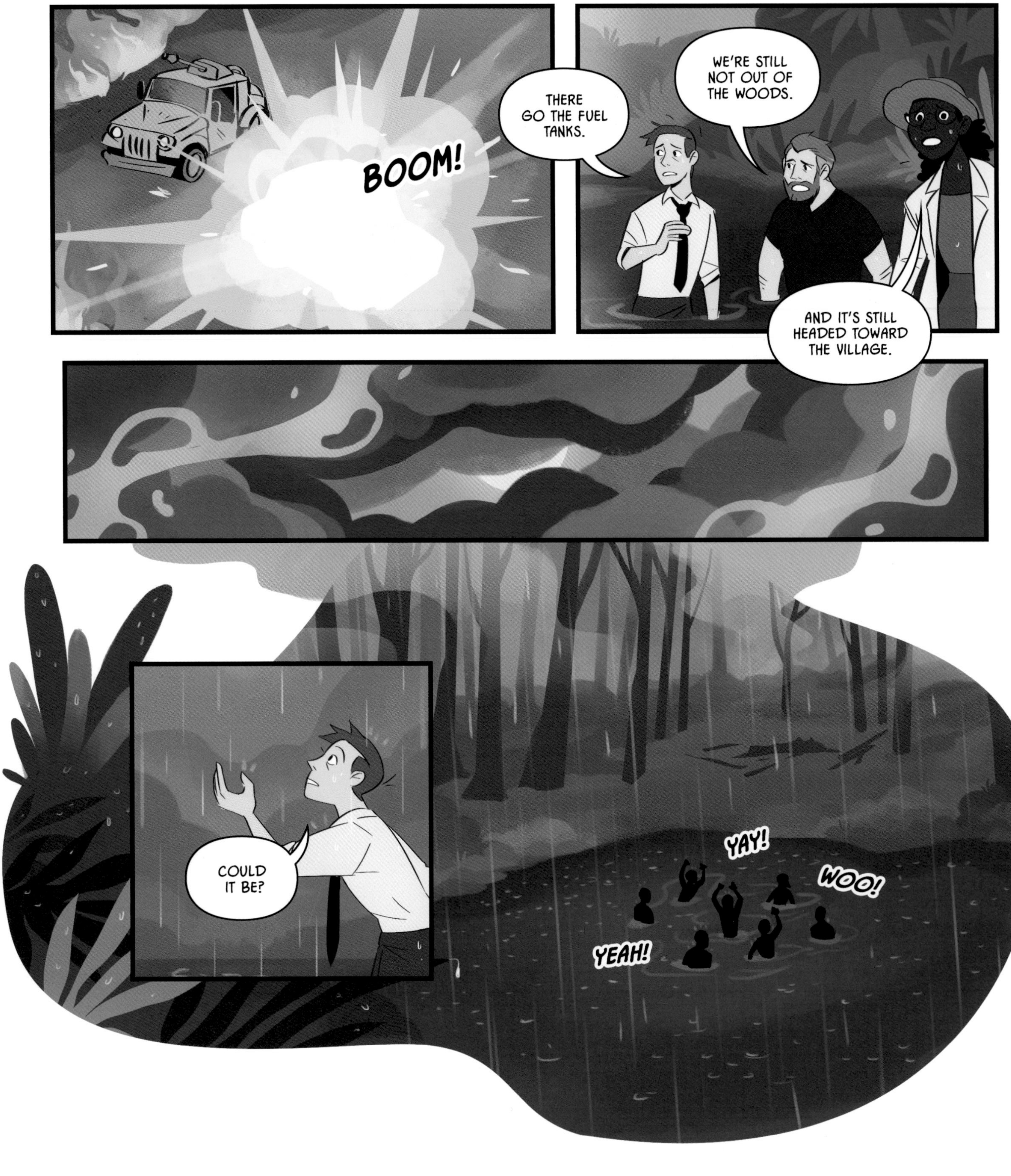
BOOM!
THERE GO THE FUEL TANKS.
WE'RE STILL NOT OUT OF THE WOODS.
AND IT'S STILL HEADED TOWARD THE VILLAGE.
COULD IT BE?
YAY!
WOO!
YEAH!

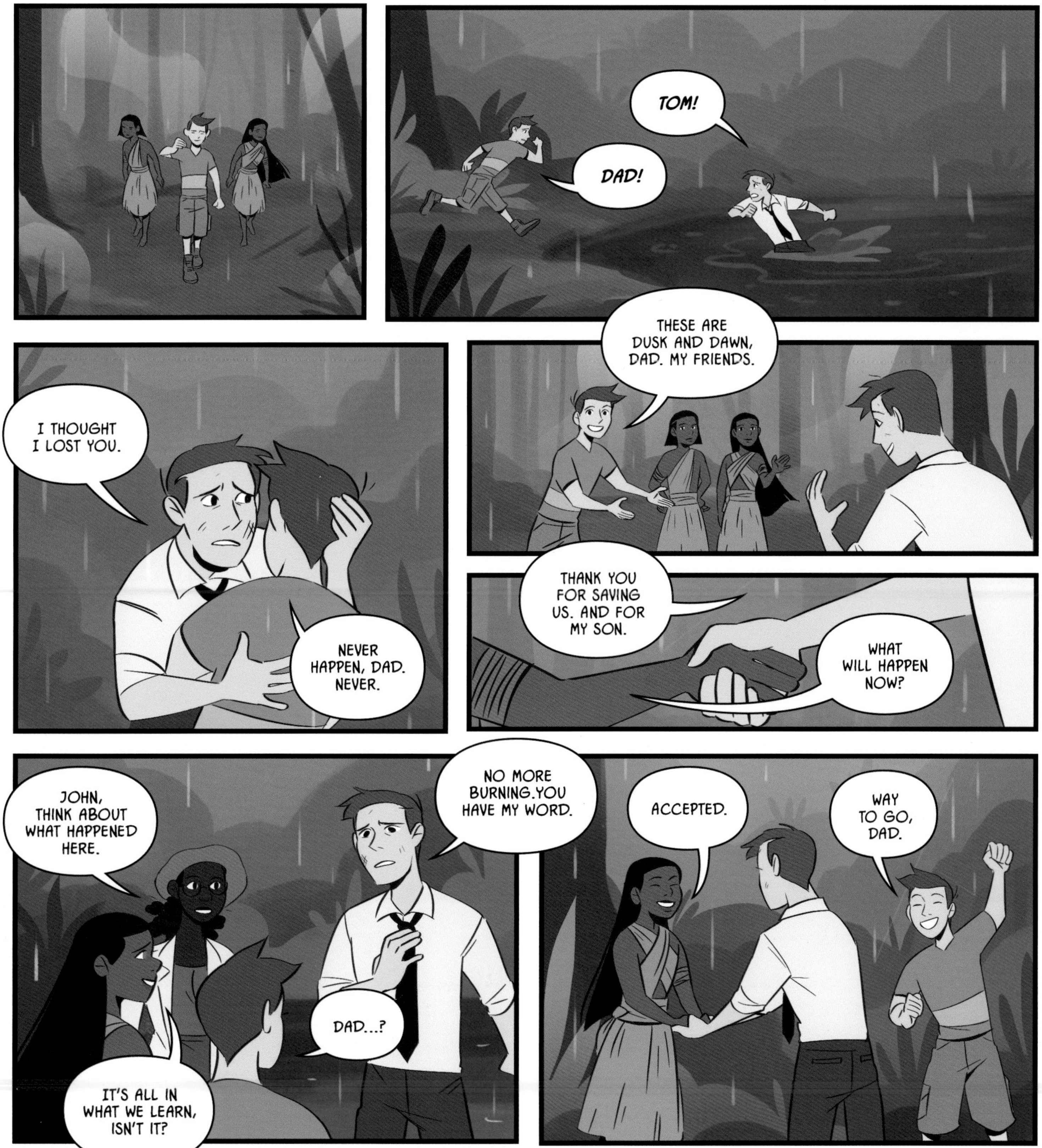
TOM!
DAD!
I THOUGHT I LOST YOU.
NEVER HAPPEN, DAD. NEVER.
THESE ARE DUSK AND DAWN, DAD. MY FRIENDS.
THANK YOU FOR SAVING US. AND FOR MY SON.
WHAT WILL HAPPEN NOW?
JOHN, THINK ABOUT WHAT HAPPENED HERE.
NO MORE BURNING.YOU HAVE MY WORD.
DAD...?
IT'S ALL IN WHAT WE LEARN, ISN'T IT?
ACCEPTED.
WAY TO GO, DAD.

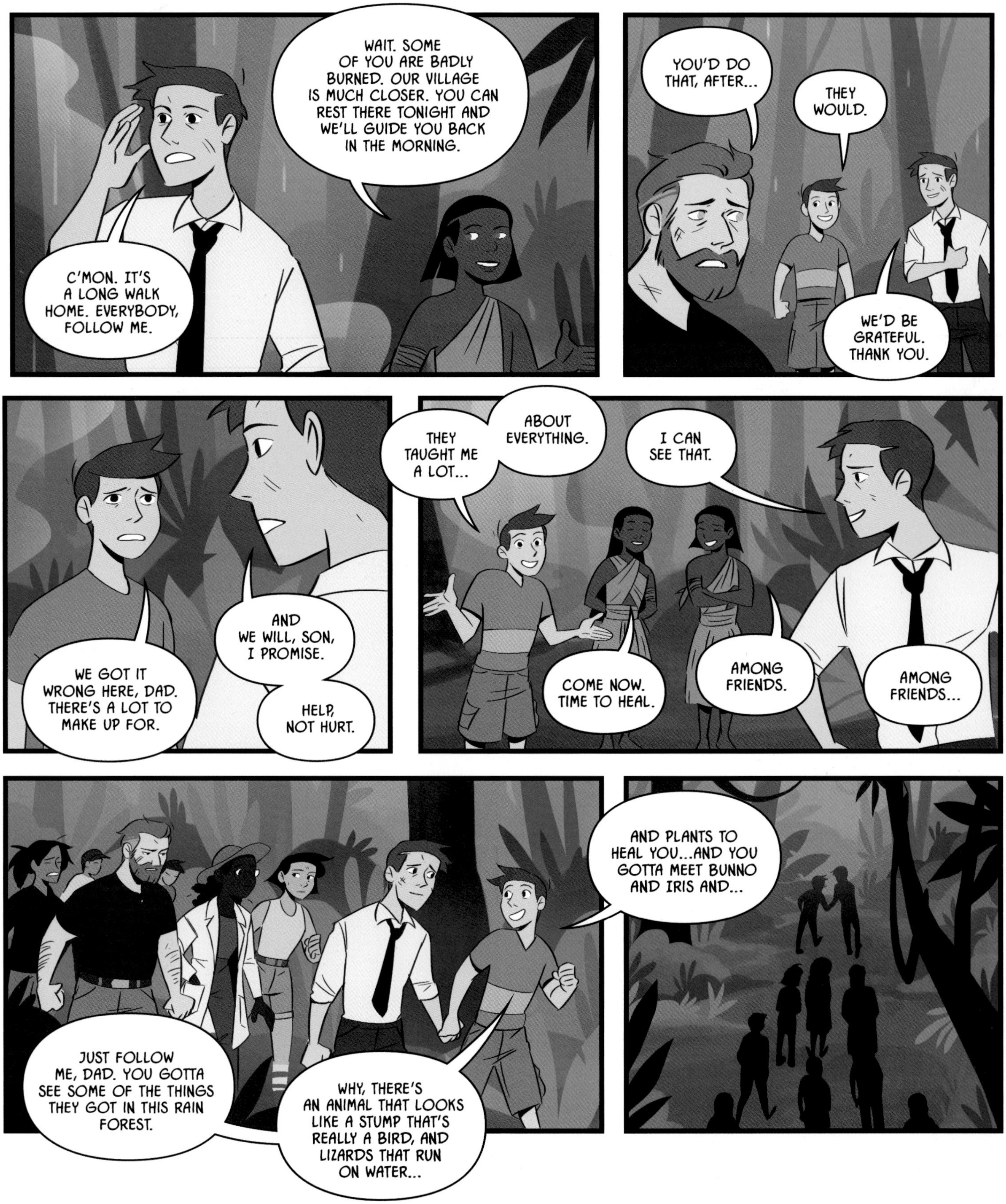
WAIT. SOME OF YOU ARE BADLY BURNED. OUR VILLAGE IS MUCH CLOSER. YOU CAN REST THERE TONIGHT AND WE'LL GUIDE YOU BACK IN THE MORNING.
C'MON. IT'S A LONG WALK HOME. EVERYBODY, FOLLOW ME.
YOU'D DO THAT, AFTER...
THEY WOULD.
WE'D BE GRATEFUL. THANK YOU.
WE GOT IT WRONG HERE, DAD. THERE'S A LOT TO MAKE UP FOR.
AND WE WILL, SON, I PROMISE.
HELP, NOT HURT.
THEY TAUGHT ME A LOT...
ABOUT EVERYTHING.
I CAN SEE THAT.
COME NOW. TIME TO HEAL.
AMONG FRIENDS.
AMONG FRIENDS...
JUST FOLLOW ME, DAD. YOU GOTTA SEE SOME OF THE THINGS THEY GOT IN THIS RAIN FOREST.
WHY, THERE'S AN ANIMAL THAT LOOKS LIKE A STUMP THAT'S REALLY A BIRD, AND LIZARDS THAT RUN ON WATER...
AND PLANTS TO HEAL YOU...AND YOU GOTTA MEET BUNNO AND IRIS AND...

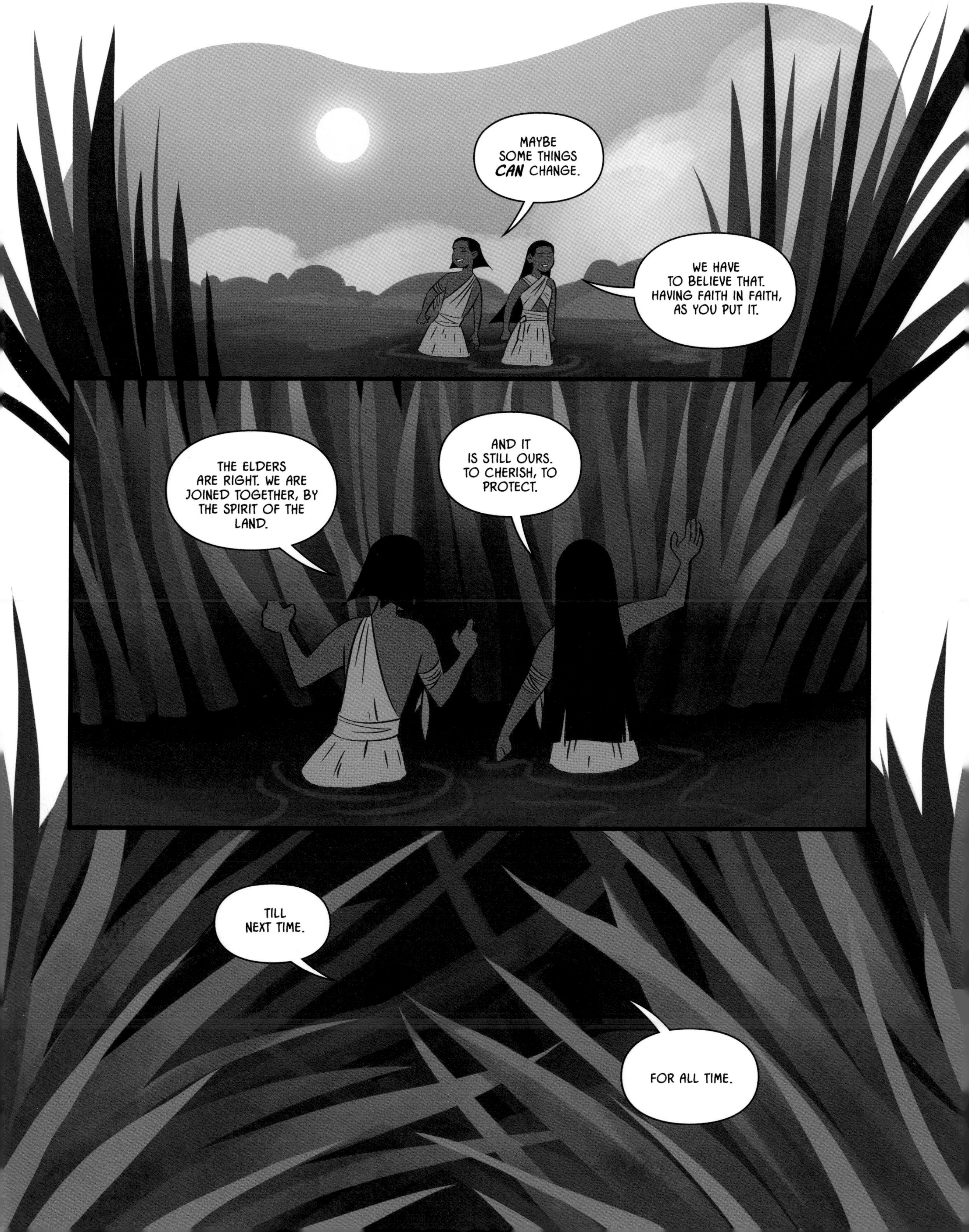
MAYBE SOME THINGS ***CAN*** CHANGE.
WE HAVE TO BELIEVE THAT. HAVING FAITH IN FAITH, AS YOU PUT IT.
THE ELDERS ARE RIGHT. WE ARE JOINED TOGETHER, BY THE SPIRIT OF THE LAND.
AND IT IS STILL OURS. TO CHERISH, TO PROTECT.
TILL NEXT TIME.
FOR ALL TIME.

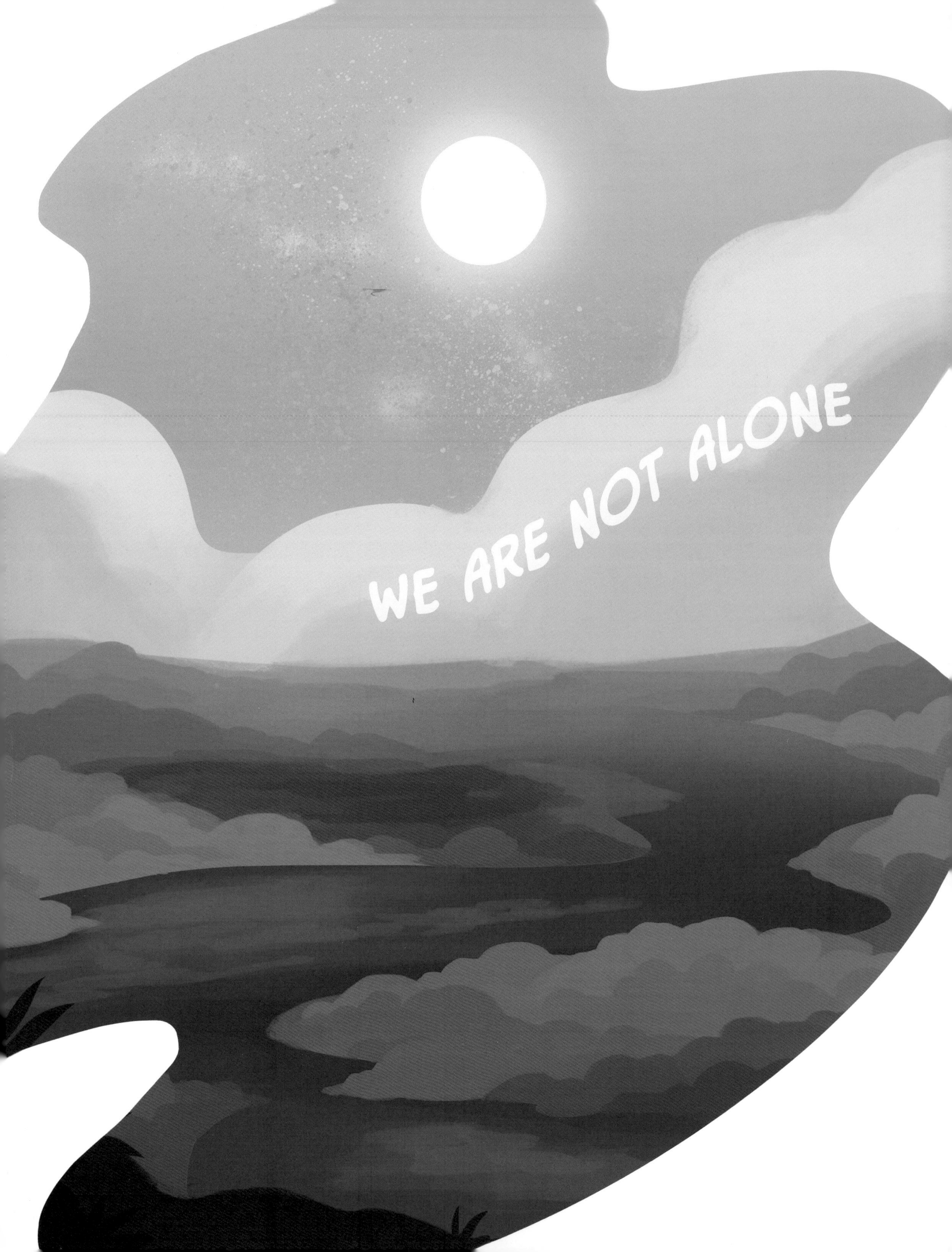
WE ARE NOT ALONE

ABOUT THE AUTHORS

Julian Lennon is a Grammy-nominated singer-songwriter, photographer, documentarian, philanthropist, and *New York Times* bestselling author of *Touch the Earth*. Born in Liverpool, England, Lennon is an observer of life in all its forms developing his personal expression through his artistic endeavors. In 2007, Lennon founded the global environmental and humanitarian organization The White Feather Foundation, whose key initiatives are education, health, conservation, and the protection of indigenous culture.

Bart Davis is an international bestselling author of novels and nonfiction books. His most recent is *Black and White: The Way I See It*, the biography of Richard Williams, father of tennis champions Venus and Serena Williams. He has also written two feature films and, with co-author Julian Lennon, the *New York Times* bestselling children's books *Touch the Earth, Heal the Earth*, and *Love the Earth*. Davis lives in New York City.

ABOUT THE ILLUSTRATORS

Alejandra "Ale" Green and Fanny Rodriguez are a pair of creatives from Mexico who love to create and illustrate stories. Ale is a freelance illustrator and comic artist that graduated with a degree in animation. Fanny is a freelance writer and illustrator with a degree in graphic design. Both have worked as artists for video games and now create their own comics, hoping to inspire others through their work. They are the authors of the graphic novel *Fantastic Tales of Nothing*.

ACKNOWLEDGMENTS

The authors gratefully acknowledge the essential contributions of:

Ale Green & Fanny Rodriguez, our artists, who brought the dream to life. We could not have asked for a more creative, dedicated, or talented team.

Nicole Frail, our Sky Pony editor, who worked tirelessly for the book, always keeping us in focus and always making it better. She is an authors' dream.

Stacey Parshall Jensen, our sensitivity reader/diversity editor/cultural consultant, who found that our "story will bring the young reader to a deeper understanding about Indigenous people" and "shows a reverence for life, a brotherly love and peace for everyone, even the enemy."

Mark Gottlieb, our agent at Trident Media Group, who brought us together.

Robert Gottlieb, who always looked to the White Feather.

Tony Lyons and Mark Gompertz, who never fail to believe and support.

Kathleen Schmidt, Skyhorse publicity director, whose drive lights our way.

Alexandra Davis, MPH . . . always generous with her knowledge.

Fernando Espinosa Chauvin . . . who made the rain forest come alive.

Nancy Lyon, who always listens.

Rebecca Warfield, Tassoula E. Kokkoris, Andrew Pothecary, and The Chicane Group, whose dedication to our mission always moved us forward.

The Amazon Conservation Team . . . partnering with Indigenous and other local communities to protect tropical forests and strengthen traditional culture.

Elder Bunna Lawrie and The Mirning Tribe . . . and all those fighting to secure the land and rights of Indigenous peoples worldwide.

Iris Bourgoyne, the Mirning Tribe Elder who first presented Julian with the sacred White Feather that began this remarkable journey. This book celebrates her memory.

JL/BD